M.R. REYNOLDS

THE
MOUNTAINS
OF THE NARE

Book Two of 'The Journeys of Michael Oakes'

novum premium

www.novum-publishing.co.uk

© 2020 novum publishing

ISBN 978-3-99064-979-4
Editing: Hugo Chandler, BA
Cover photos: Andrey Kiselev,
Ilya Podoprigorov | Dreamstime.com
Cover design, layout & typesetting:
novum publishing
Internal illustration: M.R. Reynolds

www.novum-publishing.co.uk

Contents

Drawn into Taleth

Since Michael Oakes was first drawn into Taleth, carrying the spirit of Mikael Dal Oaken, he has walked with the Powers, fought the Tsarg and ridden the fabled Piradi. He has heard the voice of the Corruptor and has conversed with the Wolves. He has found companionship, loyalty and love. He has learned much but he knows that there are still so many questions to answer, and Sorin, the Majann, for all his power, can answer very few. In his own world, he and David have a new travelling companion, Martha Spinetti, Netti for short. Events have conspired to force them to tell her their true situation, but Netti has taken it all in her stride. Michael has experienced the thrill of flying with the Valeen of the Antaldi, a rare offer of aid from the austere people of the Forest, but his journey to Tath Garnir, the King's city, has been brought to an abrupt and violent end. In his own world he had fled the noisy bar of the White Hart Hotel in Newport and has now woken lost and confused in a dark alley.

★★★

1

A Rare Woman

For a while he lay there, and he tried to calm himself after his fall. Here he appeared to be in a dark alley. In Taleth he would have landed somewhere just inside the city walls, but he had no idea what state he was in. The previous synchronicity suggested that he was there as he was here, winded, bruised, dishevelled and lost, but nothing more. Of course, he could not be sure until he switched back. He hoped that Fah Devin had made it safely to ground and that Sorin, presuming he survived the Garshegan, could halt the effects of the poison. He struggled to his feet and brushed himself down, trying to orientate himself. He had no idea how far he had walked; it had been Friday when he switched but there was little clue to what day or even time it was other than it was dark.

He heard traffic noise and he saw that the alley led out at one end to a road with streetlights. He made his way along, stumbling in the darkness, knocking over some bottles and falling once, against a pile of black bin bags, by the time he reached the road, his frustration at the darkness was such that he decided to make for the first friendly light that he could see and hang the consequences. What he saw on the other side of the street was a fish and chip shop, brightly lit, comfortably gaudy and, what was more, empty. He crossed the road and walked towards the open door. As he did so he caught sight of his reflection in the glass. He looked a complete mess, muddy stains criss-crossed his jeans and his shirt, his hair was dishevelled, and his hands bloodied. He contemplated retreat, but the woman inside the shop had seen him and she had come around from behind the counter; a look of concern on her face.

"Are you alright, love, have you been in an accident? Come in and sit down a minute." She was a small woman, but she had that natural tone of command that led people to accept proffered help without question. "You are in a mess and no mistake. Do you speak English? My Welsh is very ropey I'm afraid; I don't try hard enough with it I suppose. Here I'll get something for your hand." She left him sitting for only a moment before she returned with some antiseptic wipes and plasters.

Michael was glad that there was no-one else around. "Thank you, you're most kind."

"Ah, you do have a voice, good. How did you get into this state?" She asked as she cleaned his hands and knuckles,

"I'm afraid I got lost, I have a condition. I black out sometimes and if I'm not careful, I end up like this."

"Oh, you poor man, like petit mal, you mean. How unfortunate. Well, it's Saturday night so the hospital will not be a nice place to be, although it is still early. Are you staying in Newport?"

"Well, just outside, The White Hart Hotel, I think."

"There are several of those, I think, but we should be able to work out which." She had finished covering the two gashes on his knuckles with plasters. She now considered the next step. "Have you eaten? No? Right well it's early, as I said, I won't get much custom for at least an hour yet. There's always a gap between those who come in for their tea and the after-hours lot. Here, let me shut up for ten minutes while you have some haddock and chips on the house. I will have a look in the phone book and see which hotel you are in."

She reached up and flipped the Open sign to Closed as Michael began to protest. "No, no, it's no trouble really. Come on." She led Michael through to the back of the shop and sat him down at a table. She continued to question him as she piled a plate with chips and a portion of haddock. "Did you come down from the coast?"

"Yes, we stayed in Aberystwyth on Thursday."

"I like Aberystwyth, I have an aunt up there, by marriage, not that I am now, not since his lordship took off. But that will mean you either came down through Llandridnod Wells, through the beacons, or you took the coast road."

"We took the coast road. But we didn't join the motorway, we came across on the minor roads." Michael hadn't realised he was hungry, but the fish and chips were genuinely delicious. "This fish is excellent, sorry, I don't even know your name?"

"That's because I didn't tell you it's Dianne, and you?"

"Michael, this is really good."

"Best chip shop in the street." She laughed at her own joke. "So you didn't take the motorway." She sat down opposite him, she had an old Yellow Pages in her hands. "My son says that I should get a computer to look things up on, but I like the feel of paper personally."

Michael was able for the first time to look at her properly. Her hair was mainly hidden by a hairnet and a white cap, but what he could see was black. Her face was careworn, but still handsome, although her nose was a sharp thin one that gave her a rather severe countenance. She was slim but not thin and she gave off an air of confidence and control that probably stood her in good stead late at night. "Right, if you came in from Aberdare or Caerphilly then you would be on the north side so … ah, here we are. There's only one White Hart up that side, which makes it easy. I'll ring you a taxi, while you finish your supper."

While he was eating Michael realised that he had no way of paying, but when Dianne returned, she had anticipated this, and she produced a twenty-pound note from the till. "Here, this will get you home."

"I can't take that, although you're right I have no money on me. I will come over tomorrow and pay you back."

"There's no need, really, I rarely get the chance to play the Good Samaritan and maybe it will store up some reward for me if the Lord sees fit."

A car horn sounded outside. "That was quick, business must be slack. Here, I'll wrap the rest of that, and you can take it with you. The driver knows where he's going. Now you watch yourself, Michael, it's a big scary world out there and you need to take care."

"Thank you, you are a rare woman, Dianne."

"That's what I told his lordship, a rare woman, because I let him walk out. Most of the women round here would have broken both his legs for him. Off you go, I've got customers on the way."

So, armed with a twenty-pound note, a half-eaten haddock and the remaining chips Michael set off in the Taxi across Newport. The incongruity of his life made him smile as he continued to enjoy the fish, while the driver chatted away in the front. Not an hour ago, he had been high above the capital of Taleth, beset by storm and demon and now he was in the back of a rather dirty black cab, which was struggling through the Saturday night traffic in Newport.

After a rather stop-start fifteen minutes they arrived at the White Hart. Michael paid the driver and deposited what was left in a charity dog by the entrance. He put what was left of his free meal in the nearest bin and trying to appear more nonchalant than he felt, he walked up to the reception desk.

"Good evening, I …"

"They're in the bar, sir." The duty receptionist was a man, and by the look of him a rather surly one.

"I'm sorry?"

"Your friends, they're in the bar. They were out looking for you, now they're in the bar."

"Oh, I see." Michael was going to thank him, but since he had turned away, he decided not to bother. Instead he walked into the bar and he spotted David at the counter downing quite a large whisky. Netti was nowhere to be seen.

"Hello, David."

David spun round on hearing his name; his face was drawn and tired, he had obviously had little sleep. "Michael, where the hell have you been? Quickly grab those drinks and follow me. Netti is about to ring the police." Michael did as he was told and picked up the two large glasses of wine and followed David out of the bar and up the stairs. Their two rooms were at the top of the building and it took several flights to get there. As Michael reached him David was knocking on the door of Netti's room. "Netti, it's alright he's turned up. He's …"

The door flew open and Netti threw her phone onto the bed. "Thank God, Michael, we've been worried sick. We spent the whole day searching for you."

There was little he could say except. "Sorry, I went out for some air and I switched while I was walking. I've only been back for forty minutes or so."

David was concerned about whether Netti had instigated a full search or not, but Netti reassured him. "No, I was still on hold, fortunately. But I did ring the hospitals again, not that they keep records of calls necessarily."

"I suppose not, but Michael you look a mess. Have you eaten?"

"Yes, I have actually; a Good Samaritan by the name of Dianne gave me a fish and chip supper and the taxi fare to get back here."

"Well, there's a rare woman in this day and age." Netti was surprisingly calm about it all.

"That's just what I told her. Look, I'm really sorry, but I don't think that anyone is going to let anything really awful happen to me. I mean they all seem to have too much invested in me to let that happen."

David was extremely sceptical. "Are you saying that there are people who will not allow you come to harm because you are important?"

"Not people exactly, but certainly major players in the game that they are playing."

Netti took one of the wine glasses from Michael. "Okay, we've both had an awful fright and worn ourselves out all day looking for you, but that's done with, I have fuel in my hand now and I want to know what has been happening to you and don't go leaving bits out, I will be able to tell, we deserve all of it after today."

So, with Netti and David sitting sipping their wine, Michael sat on the bed and he began to recount the last few days in Taleth. He did leave out some things, his starlit encounter with Ayan, was not their affair; also the dream about Sorin and the two promises. All of that seemed too serious and sacred to be banded around a bedroom in a hotel. He also left out the house of the Mualb entirely, although he was not quite sure why, perhaps because he felt a personal attachment that was not necessary to share. Even without these there was enough to sate Netti's curiosity and she seemed fairly satisfied when he had reached the encounter with the Garshegan.

David was still concerned for Michael's safety. "But how can be sure that you have survived that fall?"

"I can't, David, not for certain, but I'm alive here and so it seems logical to assume that I am alive there."

"Logical, since when has any of this been logical. It has been one crisis after another and now we simply have to find somewhere where we can at least lock you in, even if you walk around and around the house in your trance or whatever it is." David was definitely in need of sleep. "The sooner we get to Street the better; I may buy some chains on the way to make sure that you stay in one place at a time."

Netti had clearly been weighing things up in her mind. "Now, now, David, calm down. I think I have a better solution. While the flat over the clinic is being refurbished, I am 'house-sitting' a really nice house in Glastonbury, on a semi-permanent basis. It is set back away from the main road; four big bedrooms and a study and a conservatory which opens onto a very private garden. It would serve us all very nicely. You could set your chain to a spike out in the garden and let Michael walk around that to his heart's content. It would save on carpet at the very least."

The notion of Michael chained to a stake endlessly walking round in circles obviously tickled David and he began to laugh, which caused the others to do the same. With the tension thus eased, Michael asked if he could have a shower before getting some proper sleep and David was now quite happy to let him. David and Netti returned to the bar to leave Michael to wash, so he stripped off his dirty clothes and he entered the bathroom. He knew that he would be disappointed; nothing now would match the exhilaration of washing in the house of the Mualb, but it was clean, serviceable and warm.

He took his time, letting the water cascade over his head and massage his shoulders. It was strange to think that his other self could be lying in the dirt somewhere close to the walls of Taleth, but perhaps he was being washed by the rain of the storm. He suddenly remembered how swiftly the storm had thrown itself against them; no natural weather could have appeared so quickly, perhaps closer to the mountains, but not out in the open plains. There was too much that made no sense about the attack. How had they known that there would be flyers? How had they known where they were? Were they so numerous that they could wait in ambush at every possible point on their journey, surely not? Was it his fault? Perhaps the Corruptor could always tell where he was. With that thought in his mind he dried himself, slipped into the bottom half of the pyjamas that David had given him, and lay down to try and sleep.

He found himself dreaming, before him was another mountain range and he seemed to be drifting down to it from above. The jagged peaks reached up like claws out of the snow which lay everywhere, frozen into great drifts. As he drew nearer, he became aware of a figure moving through the snow, a figure with the stature of Uxl of the Tarr, but as he finally came to rest upon the snow, he realised that this figure was not of earth. It was thinner, paler, fluid, like slowly drifting clouds moulded into shape and given limbs and a head. He surmised this to be a First One of Air, the Auwinn, long since thought to have faded from Taleth. The figure strode effortlessly through the deep snow, which seemed to part before it as it moved forward, and close behind it after it had passed. Its goal was a cave, the mouth of which sat beneath an overhang of rock and was thus protected from the snow. He followed now on foot as the Auwinn entered the cave.

They passed through several sets of great doors as they made their way into the mountain, each was differently decorated, but the detail of their decoration was blurred to his dreaming eyes. Finally, they reached an inner chamber, the walls carved and decorated with painted images. Around the edges were shelves and tables that obviously held objects of great value and import. Three other Auwinn stood around a great casket of green crystal. Upon the casket, a great wolf with pure white fur lay dying. She raised her head as they approached and howled painfully one last time before a shudder indicated the end. Michael sensed her spirit leaving her body and he knew in that moment that this was one of the Veyix, the Lost, and that her spirit was now condemned to wander just as Lonett must. The Auwinn bowed their heads and they began a long slow chant to honour the departed, but Michael's eyes were drawn inevitably to the casket. He began to have a terrible premonition that he would soon be standing there in the flesh and that meant that the casket contained one thing and one thing only. The Chiatt Crystal. The Doom of Taleth.

★★★

The next thing Michael knew was David shaking him awake.

"Come on, Michael, we need to make an early start." David was already dressed. "I'm going down to settle up and then we can set off. We'll pick up some breakfast on the way, that way we can miss some of the traffic. The weather's turned, sadly, it's been raining all night."

"Oh, okay, can we stop off to repay Dianne, the fish and chip shop Samaritan?"

"I suppose so, if you can find it."

"I think so, I'd like to try anyway."

"Alright, all the more reason for a swift exit this morning."

"Yes, sure, I'll be dressed when you get back."

Michael was as good as his word and with their few belongings gathered, the three of them made a dash across the car park in the now hammering rain and set off. Despite David's misgivings they found Dianne's shop without too much trouble, Michael mentally retracing the taxi journey, and he pushed thirty pounds through the letter box with a hastily written thank you note.

Driving became very difficult; the rain was so severe that the windscreen wipers hardly made any impact at all. David was finding it increasingly difficult, and he made the decision to stop for a while until it eased off. They found the first available road-side café and they decided to have something to eat while they waited for a pause in the onslaught.

The food was really quite good, and they settled down to eat while it continued to rain. David and Netti were in bet-ter moods today as they had had some sleep, but for some rea-son Michael became uneasy. Something was wrong, he didn't know quite what, but there was a nagging doubt growing in the back of his mind.

He voiced his misgivings to David, but he was unconcerned. "I can't see what's bothering you, Michael, it's probably just the stormy weather getting to you."

"Maybe, it is, but there is something, I'm sure of it, I just can't quite put my finger on it, that's all." He cast his eyes around the rest of the half-filled café; no-one seemed to be paying any atten-tion to them. It had that bleak impersonal look that places attain when no-one has any reason to invest real care in them. He had been in many such, airport lounges, hotel lobbies, doctor's waiting rooms; each cleaned and swept and serviced with soulless indif-ference, each as sad, crowded and lonely as the dayroom of a care home, where time passes despite the inertia of age. All of the others were doing what they had done, having a break from the terrible weather. All were eating or drinking, except two men who were paying their bill and talking to the woman behind the counter, nothing that was in anyway unusual. He tried to ignore his unease.

After a while the rain eased a little and David suggested that they continue their journey. As they settled into their seats in the van, Michael looked across the car park to where the two men, he had seen paying a while before, had also chosen to leave.

"Why did they wait so long before going to their car?"

David was more concerned with pulling out on to the wet road. "What do you mean, *'why did they wait so long'*?"

"Those two men in the blue car, the BMW." David was now on the road itself, "that left just after us."

"What about them?"

"Why did they wait so long after paying their bill, before they left?"

"Because they were waiting for this rain to ease off, just like we were. Why are you so concerned?"

Michael acknowledged in his head that David was probably right, and that it was nothing, a coincidence, but even so … "I just thought, I don't know, maybe they were watching us and that was why I felt uneasy."

Netti was equally sceptical. "I don't see how, Michael, we stopped at that café at random, we hadn't planned to, had we?"

"No, I know that … it was just … oh, forget it. You're right, they just left the same time as we did, that's all."

But for Michael it wasn't all and he couldn't forget it. He started to glance back every few minutes and each time they were still there. David stuck to his policy of keeping off the major roads and they were fairly empty. Michael tried not to look back deliberately thinking of other things, but he couldn't shake the sense that they were indeed being followed. For once, even Netti was quiet as they drove on, the insistent rhythm of the windscreen wipers and the drum of the rain, was a background to all their separate musings.

Suddenly David broke the relative calm. "You may have a point you know Michael; I have slowed down several times to give them a chance to overtake, most BMW drivers wouldn't be seen dead trundling along behind one of these, but each time they have slowed to match our pace. I'm going to make a few random turns when I can, and we'll see what they do."

For all her apparent desire for excitement, Netti, started to look very worried. "What if they turn too and they are tailing us? Who do you think they are?"

Michael tried to reassure her. "We'll think about that when we are certain that they are following shall we?"

David had spotted a crossroads up ahead. "Okay, we should go straight on here, but I'm going to go left, here goes."

He took the turn very deliberately and sedately, indicating well before he turned. Sure enough, the car behind turned left.

"Well, alright, it still could be coincidence, I'll try a few more."

David made a sequence of left and right turns, each time the blue BMW, matched their course. "That almost covers it, Michael, but I'm going to try a sharp turn in a minute without indicating, if they follow us, we will know for certain. Hold on tight." David threw the van into a sharp left turn and then accelerated away up the side road, he knew that he couldn't outrun a chasing car, but at least their pursuers would know that they've been rumbled.

Michael watched out of the back window and he saw their pursuers nearly overshoot the turning, but by braking hard they swung around in an arc that took them perilously close to the hedgerows. The speed, with which they caught up with the van, left Michael in no doubt at all that they were determined not to lose them. The way in which the driver was cursing also gave Michael the definite impression that they cared very little that they had been detected; in fact, it was more that he wanted Michael and the others to know they were not going to get away.

"Well, that confirms that they are tailing us, but who are they? They don't look like they're police, so any ideas Michael?"

"I don't know, I'm trying to think." Michael felt an anger building inside. He had remained oblivious to the problems in this world for much of their journey. Now he decided that he at least could take charge for once. "The one thing in our favour is that they don't actually seem to want to stop us, for now. How are we for fuel, David?"

"I filled her up yesterday; we should be well on our way to Bristol before I need to worry about it."

"Good, so well in amongst people. David, I think a change of tactics is in order, we head back to the main roads and then we will at least have other people around us should they, who-ever they are, decide to actually get physical."

Netti, who had been nervously quiet up until now, saw a chance to shake off some of her fear. "Absolutely, I think that's the right way to go. I think that we aim to join the motorway as soon as possible, at least then even the filling stations will be reasonably full."

"Yes, I agree with all of that and as strategies go, it is a good one, but it has a flaw that neither of you have spotted. Heading for the motorway would be fine if I knew where it was and where we are."

"You mean we're lost?"

"Exactly, and the rain is getting worse again."

Michael looked out of the window, David was right on both counts, the rain was much heavier than a few minutes ago, in fact it looked heavier than it had been when they set off, and the countryside, even if they could have seen it, was giving no hint as to where they were headed. He could hardly see the blue car behind them, but he knew that it was still there.

"David, just do your best to follow main roads, eventually we should hit somewhere that has some proper signposts, big enough to read at least. Can you remember how many turns you made?"

David racked his brains to remember. "Three, no, wait … four left, one of those was a fork rather than a turn, and two right and then the last one so five left in all."

"Okay, so, we were heading south-east at the start, and we have effectively turned left three times, so that means we're heading approximately north-west, does that sound right?"

"Yes, I see what you mean, heading back into the hills above Newport, that might account for the rain getting worse, we're heading back into it."

Netti had caught up with Michael's thinking. "So if we make another left turn, we will be heading down to the coast again and we can pick up the main road, is that what you're thinking?"

Michael had been thinking that, but he sensed that Netti needed to feel better about herself, she had been shaken by this new development. "Sort of but you got there before me."

She smiled. "My sense of direction isn't very good, but I can picture things in my head and clocks and compasses are easy when you do that." She reached over and squeezed David's arm. "Once we hit the motorway, I'll take over for a bit if you like."

David didn't turn, but he sounded grateful. "I won't say no to that if we can find a services to pull in at, we might even be able to find a big lorry that we can sneak out behind. You never know. Netti, write down their registration number, if we get a chance to give them the slip, then maybe I can find out who they are."

Michael was pleased that they both sounded positive. He turned his thoughts back to who these two might be, and how they had picked up their trail. They definitely didn't look like policeman, or none he had ever dealt with; they were certainly human, not Tsarg, he had a momentary vision of a Tsarg in full leather battle armour, hunched over the steering wheel snarling randomly at the traffic around it. No, Tsarg would have attacked in the café, wildly without pause, with fear only of their master's displeasure.

It was then that he remembered a shrill bird-screech of a voice. *'Don't you touch me! How dare you. I am of the blood and must not be assailed. I will not be ...'* the voice of the man in the hospital and at the reservoir, Mr Perkins; they had yet to solve the riddle of his presence. There was also the possibility that these two men were from the gang who had set up the scam at the art gallery. They would still be desperate to locate the curator and find out just how their comrades were blown to smithereens, and probably just as keen to discover why he wasn't. If their plan had been part of a large-scale operation then they might have contacts in all sorts of places and as Michael had wandered around Newport for twenty-one hours or so, he could easily have been spotted.

If he was right, they may well be hoping that he will lead them to the curator, possibly even to a few valuable paintings; anyone who was going to blow the gallery up would surely have removed a few selected works, which could be sold to private collectors. They rarely remembered their scruples when offered something special at a discount. That whole world of dealers and collectors and so-called critics disgusted him, and it angered him that he might be being drawn back into it all again.

He looked out at the rain, it hadn't eased, it seemed to be endless and the force with which it struck the ground gave the impression that it came from below as much as from above. David had made a left turn further back and so they should, in theory, be back onto better roads. The one they that they struggled along at present was narrow and hedge lined. The camber of the road was such that the rain was collecting at the side of the road and rushing down the curving incline that it had arrived at somewhat faster than they had. David took things slowly where the road was narrow although they had met no traffic coming the other way.

They did however pick up another vehicle in their modest convoy; a farmer in his Land Rover had slipped in behind them from a field and he was now in between them and their tail, who on this road would have no chance of overtaking. Michael started to hope that perhaps they might be able to shake them off after all, when suddenly David slammed on the brakes.

"Damn, the road's flooded ahead."

Michael was against the idea of stopping even with the farmer and his vehicle behind them. "How deep does it look? Can we make it through?"

"It's hard to tell, if I try and then get stuck, we really are in a mess. But I'm game to try it if you want me to."

Michael felt they had to keep moving if at all possible. "Try it, David, I'm sure that it's just surface water."

"Okay, here goes." He released the brake and they moved into the water. It was deeper than they had suspected, by at least eight or nine inches, but they were nearly through, when with a thud the left side front wheel caught in a hidden pothole and with a shudder, the engine stalled and died. "Blast we nearly made it. Now what?"

The solution was already squeezing past at the side of them. The farmer's Land Rover had no problem with the water and once past; he had jumped out and was signalling to them.

"Come on, Michael, I think he's getting a tow rope out."

As they clambered out into the flooded road, the farmer shouted over the noise of the rain. "Get this hooked up and we'll have you out in no time, man, once she's out I'd give it a few minutes mind, to let the water drain, before you fire her up. If your missus steers and you two give it a shove from the back it'll jump her out of the hole that wheel's in. I told the council about it months back, but they never take any notice."

Without trying to talk against the hammering rain they did as he suggested, and they hooked the tow rope to the towing bar at the front of the van. Then Michael and David waded back into the water to give the van a starting push. The water was cold, but they were both soaked to the skin in any case, a little more hardly made things worse. The farmer signalled and started his engine, Michael and David bent their backs and braced them against the rear of the van. Michael felt the initial shudder as the tow rope straightened and then two strong arms grabbed him from behind and he was thrown sideways into the flood. As he gasped for breath and he tried to regain his feet he was struck in the side and fell, this time backwards, losing his footing completely and crashing his head on the submerged tarmac of the road. The van had started to move and both Netti and the farmer were oblivious to the drama unfolding behind them.

Michael was dragged upright by one of his attackers and through blurred vision he saw David as he struggled with the other. He was losing his grip and when the man was free, he kicked David viciously in the stomach. As Michael was dragged to the blue car, he saw David staggering to his feet and Netti running down to the water, having finally become aware of what was happening.

Michael was thrown roughly face down into the back of the car. His arms were pulled back and he felt wire cuffs being snapped over his hands, finally a blanket was flung over him and a heavily accented voice barked. "Stay down, and no fucking noise, you hear!" The car was then slammed into reverse and Michael was thrown first right and then left as the driver spun the car around and roared back up the narrow road that now had the appearance of a small river. It was fortunate for Michael that the road was empty, unsecured as he was in the back of the car, at the speed they were travelling any collision would certainly have thrown Michael straight through the windscreen. But the weather had dissuaded all but the hardiest of drivers and these two now seemed to know where they were going, and they were determined to get there as fast as possible.

After about half an hour, the car made a sharp left and, from the vibrations, they appeared to be on a gravel access road. When they stopped, Michael heard the driver's door open and the barking voice shouted something that Michael couldn't make out, then as the back door of the car swung open he felt the tearing begin as he switched back to Taleth. As one darkness was exchanged for another, he wondered how they would react to being unable to interrogate him.

★★★

As he had expected he might, he found himself in darkness, or half-darkness. He lay on his back, hands bound underneath him, his clothes were damp, and he was cold. His eyes focused and he saw with a quick glance that he was in a small poorly constructed hut. The roof, and the walls were a mismatched patchwork of broken planks and sacking and the door was cracked and split. Near to the only light, which came from a space between broken planking, sat two men, who could easily have been part of the hut themselves, for their clothing bore the same hallmark of mismatched repairs. Their heads, their arms and their faces were bound in strips of cloth, partly Michael suspected to hide their appearance, but also as a makeshift protection against stray knives. They each had flagons of a strong liquor, the smell of which burned in Michael's nostrils like vinegar and they were engaged in the dual activity of playing dice and complaining.

"Ah, seven again, you have the dice on your side, Krakis, you son of a whore. Tomorrow I will steal us some different dice."

Krakis, laughed and gathered the handful of coins on the floor in front of him. "If anyone else had said that they would find themselves breathing through their neck, Duvan, but since you have met my mother and only speak the truth, I forgive you. Now let me take some more of your money."

Duvan took a long drink from the flagon, the fact that he needed to tip it at quite an angle suggested that they had been drinking for some time. "One more time, that is all, or else I will not be able to pay your sister what she charges these days."

Krakis took a drink in his turn and then he laughed again. "Now I know that you are poor at numbers, my friend, for you did not start out the evening with enough coin to afford my sister, even if she would consider accepting you as a client. She has risen in the world, Duvan."

"What she likes men who wash more often than I do?"

"Once would be a start, Duvan, or perhaps I could throw you in the river, back where we fished out this sack of meat, he was getting a good wash pressed up against the grating like that, looking for all the world like a corpse."

"He's about as much use as a corpse, no coin on him, nothing we could sell. I hope Frappo gets back soon and he has found someone to pay us for our trouble. He must have come from somewhere; he didn't just fall out of the sky."

Krakis drank again. "Maybe he did. They say in the south that there are desert storms that can whirl a man far into the air and deposit his body a day's ride away. Perhaps that storm that hit dropped him in the river. He could have come from anywhere."

"He hasn't come from just anywhere, Krakis, he is dressed Cluath style, and a Cluath rider at that."

"But we found no weapon on him, Duvan, nor any device to indicate family."

Michael stayed still, to avoid their attention, but he couldn't help flinching at that, his Nare axe must have fallen from his hand when he fell.

"Why are we sat guarding him anyway? He's not going anywhere, there hasn't been a sound out of him since we pulled him from the water. We could be out earning money somewhere."

"True enough, Duvan, true enough, but Frappo will pay us, he knows better than to expect us to do this out of friendship, and I regret that you are not earning, for when you have money in your purse, that you have gainfully stolen from someone else's purse, I am a happy man. Now show me your coin, you are in for one more round you said."

"Alright, one more, but then I'm off, they will be turfing out the taverns soon and that is when I do some of my best work."

"Oh, that you do, Duvan, you're are a master at relieving a drunk of his last few coins. Shall we say two gals a round, or are you feeling lucky?"

"Two is fine, Krakis, you swindler, you won't find me giving coin away."

Duvan reached into his belt and flung down two coins; a gal appeared to be a small coin, silver in colour. Krakis matched this with two coins of his own.

"Throw, my friend, you have the dice."

Duvan shook the small cup with the dice inside and slammed it down. "Five, ah, my luck changes at last, I'll stake you two more on higher, Krakis, what do you say?"

"Very well." He put down two more coins and Duvan did the same. Once more he shook the cup. Down it came.

"Nine, hah, my luck has started to change, perhaps I shall be shagging your sister after all, Krakis. I'll go four more on lower."

"Indeed, four it is."

Once more coins were added to the pile and Duvan began to shake the cup. It slammed down and Duvan laughed with glee. "Three, now I'm on a roll, four more on higher, Krakis, you are going to regret forcing me to play another round."

"I fear I may, Duvan, but only four more when you threw a three, surely it's worth more than that. Let's make it interesting how about ten? – or are you scared of losing it all again."

Duvan had taken another drink and this time he appeared to have drained the flagon. "Afraid? I am not afraid of anything, ten you say, let's say twenty, Krakis, you nyatt's arse. Twenty on higher!"

"Now you are talking like a real man, Duvan, not some scab from the sewer. But I want to give you a chance to afford my sister don't I, so how about we make it fifty?"

"Fifty? When I threw a three? Krakis you have had too much to drink, but I won't argue, you called the bet. Show me your coin."

Krakis put down a small purse. "That has fifty-three gals in it, Duvan. Put down yours and then throw."

"I will." He reached in his belt and pulled out a similar purse, tipping it up he counted out fifty of the small coins. Michael was watching Krakis, he had reached down behind the flagon and was tapping out a complex rhythm with his fingers in the dirt. Duvan added the last few coins to the pile and was unaware of Krakis tapping fingers.

"There, that matches yours and now I shall take the lot from you and watch you weep, Krakis."

He raised the cup and shook it. The tapping fingers moved faster as he shook the cup and then as he slammed down the cup they stopped. The cup was lifted and Duvan roared with anger. "Seven? Seven! Every time I stand to gain a tidy sum these bastard dice come up seven. You are a cheating durg, Krakis, I'm going to slice you up good for this." He staggered to his feet and fumbled for his knife.

Krakis laughed and he collected the money, he had obviously had far less to drink than his companion and the charm that he had worked was well beyond Duvan's understanding.

"Cheating, Duvan, you drunken bag of filth? How could I cheat, you rolled the dice each time? What do you think I am? Some sort of mage with powers over a pair of dice? That would be a fine charm to be able to work, now wouldn't it. Face it, Duvan; you are a born loser, which is why you work for Frappo, and so am I, which is why I work for him too."

Duvan had found his knife and he waved it in Krakis direction. "I don't know how you did it, but you did it. You are going to pay this time, Krakis, I want my money." He lunged forward, but Krakis was too quick, he slipped to the side and he kicked Duvan's legs from under him. He then stood with his foot on Duvan's arm so that his knife was pinned to the floor.

"Calm down, Duvan, Frappo will be back any time now and then he will either pay us or you can go off and find some other drunks to wrestle with. Either way you will be back in coin by the morning. Although sadly, my sister will be in the bed of some fine lord or other, so I would forget about that particular pleasure."

Duvan struggled for a moment and then he gave up. He was just getting to his feet when another man ducked through the broken door.

"I heard shouting, what has been going on?"

"Ah, Frappo, we were just talking about you, weren't we Duvan; wondering when you would return and how much we were going to get paid for this evening's work."

Frappo was a thin weasel of a man, with lank dark hair and a face that was as scared as Michael's own, though in his case, the wounds spanned the years and etched a permanent record of his career. His eyes were sharp, and they danced about above the snub of a nose he sported; it looked to Michael as if it may once have been longer. His clothes were less ragged and confused than his employees, but they were nonetheless shabby and old. His tunic may once have been green and it bore the hint of an emblem, but the colour and the design had faded. His legs were bound as the others, but all in the same material. At his waist, a thick belt held two wickedly curved knives and various keys hung in a bunch jangling harshly if he moved. Over everything else he wore a long black coat, long because it had been designed for a taller man, but this too had gashes and tears. The clothing, and the coat in particular, marked Frappo out as a man who knew that he had to scrap hard to make a living, but also that should you get in a scrap with him you'd better watch out.

"You'll get paid, Krakis, you know me I never expect something for nothing." His voice was thin, but as sharp as the stiletto, that he might be holding next to your ear. "But not tonight."

Duvan, who was brushing himself down, took a swaying step towards him. "What? Why won't you pay us? We could have been out earning, whereas …"

"You sat drinking slarag, that I provided remember, and if you lost money to Krakis at dice, then that is your affair, not mine. You'll get paid, Duvan, but not tonight."

Krakis too was a little frustrated by this turn of events. "Are we to assume that none of your contacts in the guard or at the court have any idea who this flotsam is, Frappo? How can that be? He certainly wasn't born here, he's a plainsman or I'm a cur-rack, so he must have come through the gates. Someone must have seen him. He has a memorable face, just as you do yourself, Frappo, and no one forgets you, however hard they might try."

"I'll forget your insults for now, Krakis, but one day I might remember them all together and then I'll slit your throat with pleasure."

"You may have to take your turn, Frappo, I have a habit of annoying people."

"You do indeed, but you are too good at what you do to be easily replaced, though no-one is entirely indispensable, Krakis."

"No, Frappo, no-one, not even you."

Frappo paused and he stared up at Krakis' grinning face. "That too I will ignore, but back to business, I gather that he hasn't shown any sign of life?"

Duvan sulkily turned towards where Michael lay. "None save a heartbeat." He kicked Michael's legs savagely to vent his anger and Michael had to concentrate to suppress a reaction. "We haven't touched him either, so any damage he had before we found him."

"Oh, I believe you, Duvan, but the situation is as before, he is dead to the world and we don't know who he is, so we can-not sell him back to his loved ones. But I do have a second op-tion; I always have other options, that is why I survive. There is a certain magic man, who thinks he is a mage, although I feel that he is deluding himself; he likes to do experiments … on people; living people, well living to start with obviously, and he pays pretty good money for strays who can't be traced. This sack of bones and flesh will suit him perfectly; there won't even be any screams to smother."

"Are you referring to the gentleman they call 'Old One Eye'? Oh, I know him, he's got about as much magic in him as a lump of durg fat, but he knows how to sew a wound nice and neat and his needles are mostly clean. I didn't know he liked to cut people, that's interesting, and he pays well?"

"He pays a fair price, Krakis, and asks no questions, neither. So, I reckon that we lug this one over to him while it's dark and get what we can."

"By we you mean us, I assume?"

"Naturally, Krakis, I am the broker, you are the hired help, and best you remember that."

"Oh, I remember, Frappo, I have a good memory." He turned to Duvan. "Come on, Duvan, stop sulking, it is a short drag up to Old One Eye's place and then you will still be ready for chucking out time at the Bandit's Head."

"Shut your mouth, Krakis, I'm sick of listening to you."

Frappo laughed as if he was slicing the air in the hut. "Krakis, it's a wonder you are still above ground. Now pick him up and let's get moving."

Since he had 'awoken' to the situation Michael had been trying to consider how he might escape, and he had come up with few options. He wondered if he might try falling and rolling away when they took him out of the hut, but he had no idea how the land lay, and he needed somewhere to roll into. He had considered telling them he had friends at the court and risk being taken there, but he had no way of knowing where Sorin and the others had got to, or whether Tuggid and Gath had reached the city yet. Now, it appeared as if he was being sold to an amateur anatomist of dubious standing and Michael expected little sympathy from him for his plight. His options were disappearing rapidly. He prepared himself to jump up and make a charge for the door and risk everything on the element of surprise. But then something happened that made them all pause.

In the centre of the hut a strange light had begun to glow. His captors stood transfixed as it began to grow in size and intensity, gradually forming itself into a vertical line, a thin column of piercing white fire. It began to vibrate like a taut string and then from it stepped a figure. Its body shone, and it seemed only semi-substantial, a figure of light and mist; Michael took it for a child at first, for its face was age-less and its body an-drogynous, though its eyes were entirely black. When it spoke, it did so haltingly as if the common speech of the Cluath was unfamiliar to it and in some way distasteful.

"Men … of Tath Garnir … my thanks … for keeping bound this criminal … dangerous he can be … dangerous above your mind's thought … to imagine it you could not … I a demon of his punishment … have been sent … his soul to claim … his body to the flames … will go in time. Rewarded for your … actions you shall be … take these and … be gone." With a gesture of its hand it caused coins of gold to appear and then fall to the dirt. The three men cast a quick glance at the money and then at the demon and then with much scrabbling and pushing they gath-ered what they could and made their escape.

The strange figure laughed, a laugh that Michael did not feel had any humour in it at all. It then turned its attention to him. "How easy it is … to buy the Cluath … it has ever been thus … I know you are … awake, Michael, and know I also … who and what you are … You seem determined … dangerous places you seek … but you will not … cannot be … allowed to die … im-portant you have become … perhaps always it has been so … even before … the mighty have felt … the echoes of your steps … be-hind the clouds … under rock and stone … in root and tree … and beneath the waves … they feel your feet upon the face … of Taleth … your every move disturbs the very threads … the strands that give … meaning and … shape. No, you shall not … die be-fore … the task is … complete … and then … none can tell … save One who knows … do not thank me … for this … event … I do what … must … be done … no more … although some would … say wrong it is." With another wave of its hand, Michael felt his bonds crumble to dust and then he saw the figure step back into the column of light, which then disappeared with a crack.

It was only when the figure had gone that he realised that it had addressed him as Michael.

★★★

2

Tath Garnir

Michael sat up and began to rub life back into his arms, partly because he needed to and partly to give himself time to think; to take in what had just happened. This being, whoever it was, seemed to know everything; more it seemed even than Sorin's secretive friend and certainly more than Michael himself. The words it had spoken confirmed some things but concealed much more. Who was it hinting at, *'behind the clouds … under rock and stone … in root and tree … and beneath the waves …'* Behind the clouds, the chamber of the First Promise, perhaps; under rock and stone, Corruption, maybe; in root and tree, Cerlinith and the other Powers, possibly; but beneath the waves, who was that meant to refer to? Michael had encountered none who referred to the sea, none who had even mentioned the waters. And just who was this strange being of light who could apparently travel anywhere at will. What had Sorin said about the walls being protected by ancient mage craft? Did that at least mean that the being was not sent by Corruption? Or maybe just that he was not a threat to the city?

He tried to gauge the time by the light, but it was difficult. The light coming in through the broken planks was not moonlight and he realised that it was from some form of lanterns. Maybe they lit them on the walls at night. Krakis had kept on talking about the drunks being turfed out of the taverns, when did that happen, he wondered, surely in the early hours. He decided to risk taking a look out through the broken door, without leaving the relative safety of the hut.

He found that he was gazing along a confusion of doors and crates, wood and sacking. It was a back alley. Huts and sheds and clutter lined the right side; to the left was the city wall itself.

High up, he saw as he had suspected a burning lantern casting a weak light into the alley. The sky behind was dark, but tinged at the edges with grey, the first hint of sunrise scratching at the darkness. Something with a tail scurried across from a drain cover and into one of the sheds; voices in the distance were calling orders along the wall.

Michael ducked back inside. It was maybe an hour before dawn, two at the most, he could afford to wait quietly here, Frappo and the others would be unlikely to return, and facing the city in daylight was a safer prospect than finding his way in the half darkness, especially when it was clear that there would be characters like Duvan and Krakis around. He was cold, and he had not yet dried out, which made things worse. He decided to search the hut to see if there was anything that he could use. After scrabbling round in the shadowy corners, he discovered some old sacking, dry but far from clean, Michael, ignored the dirt but he shook them well to disturb any crawling things that may have been hiding there. He then stripped off his damp clothes and wrapped the sacking around his shoulders and legs. With several layers in place he felt warmer and he settled down with his back against the wall opposite the ramshackle door to wait for the dawn.

He had not meant to fall asleep, but he woke with a start as he heard voices, close by. He jumped to his feet and clutched his makeshift blanket to himself, he tried to focus so as to catch the words in the air.

"Come on, Nargus, get a move on, he wants the stock down at the stall before the customers get there, not after they're gone."

"Shove it, Fahb, I'm going as fast as I can, you come and get some of these sacks if you think we are in such a hurry. Why does he store the stuff up here so close to the wall anyway?"

"Why do you think? Because it's cheap! Is that it? Good. Get up and we'll be off."

Michael looked out to see a cart trundle away from the end of the alley as the two men took their wares off to sell. His clothes were at least drier than last night. So, he shook the worst of the dirt off and he dressed himself. Stepping out he hoped that it wasn't too obvious that he had recently fallen into a river and then dried out on the floor of a hovel.

When he reached the end of the alley the street was already busy, despite the fact that it was still early in the morning. The buildings appeared to be mainly workshops and storerooms, with houses squeezed between them or built on top. Front shutters were being thrown up and fires being lit. He heard a few hammers being wielded here and there; the industrious life of the city was waking up. Overhead, seabirds called which reminded him that there was a river nearby with a culvert to take it under the wall, presumably where they had found him. He decided to make his way towards the centre of the city. He hoped that Sorin and the others had reached the court ahead of him, he really had little choice.

He turned right, away from the wall, and he began to try and find a way inwards. This far from the centre the streets were unplanned and chaotic, organic might be a kinder word. Space was at a premium and buildings had been extended or new ones built where ever there was room, often the upper storeys were larger than the ground floor, it reminded him of illustrations of Tudor London; some of the buildings were three floors and so he found it hard to keep heading for the white spires and the red towers of the King's court. After a while, the workshops had open fronts from which to ply their trade; many had covered yards to the side, with furnaces for smelting ores.

Michael noticed here and there, a Nare who sat cross-legged engraving metal or working on leather armour, but if they looked up, their sour expressions reminded him of what Gath had said, untrustworthy he had called them. Some looked away keeping their thoughts to themselves others openly stared at his scars and sneered. Many of the faces that turned to glance at him as he passed had their own scars and they appeared to wear expressions of stubborn defiance as a habitual mask. He passed one giant of a man, working a furnace, stripped to the waist, his back bore the distinctive scars of the lash. At the street corner a young woman stood, she didn't speak but looked up with an expression that to Michael was one of resignation and despair. Even this early she plied her trade; he shook his head and she looked away with a shrug. She had a living to make, there were other men.

He passed smithies with arrays of weapons and helmets; wood turners bent over spinning lathes. Most paid him little heed. In this part of the city a dishevelled stranger with a hideously scarred face hardly stood out. A few looked longer than was necessary, maybe they thought that they recognised someone, but he was left to wander on unhindered. The sounds grew as more people began work for the day; there were candle makers and glassblowers, potters and basket weavers. He saw looms for carpets and cloth; shuttles were already scudding backwards and forwards, nimble fingers tying in new threads and new colours. Foul fumes poured from a dyer's workshop, that appeared like a galleon as he turned a corner; recently died cloth flapped in the early breeze, waiting for young boys to clamber into the rigging and haul them in.

Further on, the acrid smells of hot iron and furnace gave way to the smell of blood and flesh. He had reached a whole street of butchers with huge carcases hanging from their ceilings. So far, he had seen no creature to match the mass of a cow bred for beef, but these headless bodies gutted and hanging on hooks were too big to be the smaller herd animals he had encountered. He could hear the dull thud as cleavers slammed into flesh, the crack as bones were snapped by the blows. He was struck by the similarity to the sound of axe or sword striking down a warrior but knew that in the end, flesh is flesh and whether it is sword or cleaver that slices it, the result is much the same.

And then fishmongers and fruit and vegetable shops all filled with such strange shapes and colours that he had never imagined possible. After that came the uproarious scents of the bakeries from which the blast of sweet heat from the ovens could be felt in the street. Flour hung in the air here and the smell of bread was so thick that it would have driven a hungry man insane. Finally, he reached one of the many market squares that were spread throughout the city, it was just about up and running for business, but not yet crowded with people. Stalls of fruit and cooked meats, pies and pastries, cakes and bread, ale and wine, herbs and spices, were spread out before him. Had he been inclined he could have spent the whole day browsing through the stalls.

He realised that here was the thriving life of a city like many in his world, but it was in Taleth and here were thousands of lives being lived, oblivious of him and his place in the two worlds. Not one of them caring about his troubles or his dilemma; but, unlike before, he no longer felt vulnerable and weak before this other reality, this colour and noise, this throng of people, he was here and the fact that that they ignored him meant he had somehow fitted in. When first his vision had cleared, and he had seen the light of Taleth it had appeared more real, more alive than his own sad and colourless world. Here that sensation was multiplied beyond constraint. This was life, visceral, violent in colour and sound, and so sharp that he could taste it on his tongue. He wanted nothing more than to melt into it, become one with the exotic fabric that was unfolding before him. Duty, love, responsibility even time itself seemed so unimportant before this panorama of a life that had not been his before, but now cast its seductive spell over him. He made his way through it in a dream forcing himself forward, recollecting, reconvening his senses on the other side, when with a deep sigh, he left the market square.

Beyond the market he reached wider streets and here there were cloth merchants and tailors, cobblers and he saw down a side passage, even a barbers' shop. It was here that he saw a reminder of the city's underbelly with which he had so recently become acquainted; Frappo would be one amongst many, he knew. A man came running past him, his face hidden by a scarf, his arms clutching a bulging sack, behind him two men with helmets and breastplates were in pursuit and gaining, it appeared. They carried short swords and nasty looking cudgels and looked in no mood to go easy on the thief. Since the streets were wider here, he risked moving to the centre of the street and craning up to see if he was still going in the right direction. He wasn't. He needed to veer left if he wasn't to simply continue on through the curving streets and find himself on the far side of the city.

He took the next left and he found it was a narrower street with shops with dark doorways, runes and sigils painted across the doors. Gazing in at one, he saw shelves of bottles and jars of strange and outlandish objects. These shops were surely those of the apothecaries and healers, alchemists and mystics. He decided that he wanted to be away from them as soon as possible. They might all be frauds, but one or two might sense that he was more than he seemed, as Danil and others had done.

Coming out of the end of the street he was able to see that he was now back on course, because here was a more open space. It appeared to be a square created to face a building on the Palace side of the square, a building unlike any Michael had so far encountered. It was built in stone with a wooden roof and it had three very large doors at the front, to allow access by steps in front of each. Carved pillars, covered with images of battle beneath stormy skies, stood on either side of the central door, which was decorated with an image of a female warrior bearing a huge sword. As he watched, it swung inwards. Red robed figures slowly processed out and stood in an arc facing outwards, below the steps. They were followed by a woman in a sky-blue robe, who stood on the top step and addressed the empty square.

"The new day begins, people of Tath Garnir, the Temple of Minead is open. The Lady has awoken; she runs now through your fields and swoops above you in the skies. Offer her your loyal service and boons you may receive in return. Blessed Minead hears all and has no favourites. She will listen to the Cluath if they will listen to her in their hearts." She then waited, arms aloft for a response which of course failed to come. After a silent two minutes, she lowered her arms and turned to walk back through the door, followed by her red robed acolytes. Michael got the feeling that this was a daily occurrence. He had met Minead and he did not feel that she was likely to listen to anyone, even Hantor. But it was obvious that religion did not figure high on the Cluath agenda, unlike the ritual bound Antaldi. He crossed the empty square, feeling, for the first time that morning, rather conspicuous. As he was nearing the other side, a strange procession began to make its way towards him. There was a long line of people, who at first sight seemed to be shambling in a strangely lethargic way, but as the distance closed between them Michael saw that they were chained together. His instant assumption was that he was looking at a line of slaves.

He was stunned; no-one had mentioned slavery, nor had he seen any evidence of it until now but considering human history, perhaps he should not have been surprised. The guards wore a livery similar to those who had passed him earlier in pursuit of the thief. Maybe these were prisoners. They had drawn level with him, their tattered garments and cast down faces suggested a long despair. These were slaves sure enough; the guards carried whips and the sour expressions of men suited to the meanest of behaviour. Some of those that passed him were hardly more than children. A woman towards the back of the line suddenly looked up and cried out to him,

"Help us! Please, I beg you, the Queen means to sell us, she …" her words were cut short by a whip and a snarl.

"Shut your mouth, woman, or I will shut it for you!"

The woman looked up again at Michael, blood and tears flowed together on her cheek, her face pleaded for a help that he could not give. The line moved on. As the end of the line moved away Michael looked after them and the last of the guardsmen, who seemed to bear himself with more genuine authority than the others, caught his eye,

"Forget it, master plainsman, these are debtors who must serve time as indentured servants to repay their debts. The Queen is the landlady to half the city, if truth be told, and as such she must appear business-like. Mercy is not good for business. Good day to you."

Michael turned and moved on, his mood had changed somewhat, he had lost the excitement that he had felt as he had made his way through the market. He reached the edge of the square and entered another wide street of merchants' shops, but also more and more private houses, some with entrances protected by a side door. Here and there were the odd jeweller's establishment and wine merchants. He also noticed open fronted shops that had no wares on sale, but men sat at tables armed with paper and stern expressions. *'Money lenders!'* Michael knew them from their look, and he was oddly disappointed by their presence, but as he had become so much more aware during his winding progress, here was a city, with everything that that implied. The streets were emptier here, perhaps the more affluent rose later, some of those who were about moved with a distinct air of not wishing to be noticed by too many souls. One such young man ducked down a side street and as Michael passed he saw money being exchanged for small packets. *'Well, that caps it all, dealers on the streets, I might as well be back in London.'*

As if to remind him that he was not, a shout made him turn and then he jumped out of the way. A troop of the King's Guard, mounted on what appeared to be thinner, lighter Trell than the ones that Tuggid and Gath rode, cantered down the street, heading Michael assumed for a barracks and stable somewhere further up towards the towers that marked Tath Garnir's heart. He didn't count them, but they took some time to pass and Michael realised what Sorin had hinted about regarding the size of the armies at the High King's disposal. Their mounts were not as sleek and graceful as the Piradi, but they certainly looked more suited to a cavalry charge than the working beast he had ridden.

He needed to swing right soon, so he crossed the road and walked on towards the next turning. His eyes still followed the retreating soldiery, so that when he turned the corner he collided with an old man and a young boy. Michael was the first to regain his feet and he reached out a hand to help the old man, who hissed curses at his young attendant. As his hand gripped that of the victim of his clumsiness, it was snatched away, and the old man turned his cursing upon Michael.

"Ah, you have the touch of death upon your hands, curse you, keep your ill-luck to yourself. Your skin crawls with filth, corruption and decay and may Hantor protect me from whatever the Powers have planned for you. Rikat, help me up. Where is the boy?"

Michael saw the bandage around his eyes, and he realised that the boy led him because he was blind, which made him feel even worse. He began to apologise.

"I'm sorry, it was my fault entirely."

"Of course, it was." The old man snapped back. "I don't pay this gutter-snipe to guide me into people, so it must have been your fault. Rikat knows what would happen if it was his fault, don't you, boy?"

The boy, Rikat, who was no more than eight years old, Michael was sure, had helped the old man to his feet by now and had placed the man's gnarled right hand upon his left shoulder. "Yes, Master Galeanid, I know, but as the man says it was his fault." Rikat turned his face towards Michael in an appeal for him to repeat what he had said.

Michael obliged, but the name had set a bell ringing in his head, was this Galeanid the Seer that Uxl had told them they must seek out. "Yes, certainly it was my fault as I was saying; my mind and my eyes were elsewhere. But is it right that you are Galeanid the Seer?"

The old man stopped grumbling and became very defensive. "What matters it to you if I am, not that I am confirming the fact, mind."

Michael had taken an instant dislike to this crotchety old man, but he needed to find Sorin and this old Seer might be able to help

"Well, Master Galeanid, if you should be him, I have travelled with Sorin the Majann to Tath Garnir and arrived just recently, one of our reasons for coming was to find you or Master Galeanid, of course, should you not be him."

Galeanid reaction to Sorin's name was an odd one, initially Michael saw him start as if Sorin was the last person he wanted to meet and then he tried to cover his response with words as of remembrance of an old friend. "Sorin? Well, well, well, so he still lives, I have not had word of him for many seasons. Where is he then, let me take his hand?"

"Ah, well, Master Galeanid, since you are quite obviously he, as fortune would have it, we have become separated and since I am unfamiliar with the city, I wondered if you might help me reach the King's court, which will undoubtedly be where Sorin presently is."

"Well, perhaps, we can do that for you. Travelling with him were you, just the two of you? That's a brave journey in these dangerous days." Galeanid was fishing for information and Michael was going to have to be careful to be polite but keep his conversation safe from mistakes.

"Yes, but we encountered little trouble other than the stormy weather."

Galeanid gave Rikat a nasty squeeze. "The western gate to the inner city, boy, and no detours." His tone changed back to one of friendly concern. "But surely, two men, one of them old, travelling without protection, some might consider that foolhardy."

Mikael's voice sounded a warning in Michael's mind. *'He assuredly does not know Master Sorin well, if he thinks he walks unprotected in the wild. He clearly has no knowledge of the great she-wolf, which suggests that he knows only his name and his reputation.'* It was a thought that Michael agreed with and was in keeping with his own reaction to the Seer. He thanked Mikael inwardly for it and then replied.

"I'm sure that wherever Master Sorin travels his reputation goes before him and that that is all that is needed for a safe journey."

Galeanid was not going to give up. As Rikat led them both down various side streets and along a passage beside a high wall he continued his questioning. "But, my friend you have not given me your name, you are a friend of Sorin, which is indeed enough for me to offer help, obviously; but a name would be nice, it would be a display of trust to a blind old man."

Michael felt that he had to give the Seer his name, since gaining admission to the King's court was the object and it would be impossible with a false name, but he kept his voice low. "I am Mikael Dal Oaken, son of Halkgar, who served the King whilst he lived, but there are some who may seek to do me harm should this name be bandied about."

The old Seer gave a nod of recognition that Michael was pretty sure was feigned. "Ah, yes, is that who you are. Yes, you are wise to keep it quiet then. Mm, that is a dangerous name."

Michael was going to question the old man as to why this was so when they emerged from the passage and he found that they stood at one of the two gates into the inner city. It was guarded by men similar to those who Michael had seen before and they looked decidedly unfriendly.

The old Seer put on his most pompous voice and he announced himself. "Master Galeanid Seer and Mage seeks entrance to the inner city."

"State your business, Master Galeanid, your name and your face are known to us."

"I seek to take this visitor to the city to the court where he claims he has been summoned."

Michael was going to object to these words by the old man, which were not exactly true, but he thought better of it.

"What is your name, stranger? Cluath you are, by dress a plainsman, but you bear no device."

Michael was about to name himself, but Galeanid beat him to it. "He is the son of Halkgar Dal Oaken, by given name Mikael. His father was a loyal servant to the King."

The guard took exception to Galeanid's lecturing tone, but since Galeanid could not be gainsaid he turned it against Michael.

"The name Halkgar Dal Oaken is known to me, old man, but since he is long dead it holds little sway here. We have no orders regarding a Mikael of that family, so although you and your guide may enter, he may not."

Galeanid seemed to be drawing great delight from Michael's discomfort at the guard's attitude. "Ah, well, yes, you must do what you see fit. I will attend upon the King and see what can be done ..."

Michael was finding the Seer more tiresome every minute. "Perhaps, if I had been allowed to speak for myself."

"No, Mikael, it always better to let someone of importance speak for you."

This was too much, had he not been interrupted, Michael may well have caused quite a scene, but as his irritation was about to boil over, a young man in fine clothes ran up behind the guards, and spoke quickly to them in hushed tones. The attitude of the guards changed in an instant.

"Forgive me my error, Mikael, son of Halkgar, it seems we had not been informed, you are expected of course. Manal here, will accompany you to your lodgings at the Palace. Once more, my apologies." He bowed.

Michael responded graciously. "It is of no matter; you were doing your duty as you saw it and I will mention as much when I speak to the High King. What is your name?"

"Guardsman Yathis, sir, and thank you."

Michael walked through the gate and Rikat was at the point of leading Galeanid through when Yathis stopped him.

The Seer was furious. "What are you doing? You have no reason to ..."

"Ah, well," Guardsman Yathis said. "Since you stated your business as delivering, Master Dal Oaken to the Palace and that is completed, you have no need of entry, Master Galeanid."

"What? How dare you! I am with Mikael and he has been summoned."

It occurred to Michael that Yathis actually disliked Galeanid nearly as much as he did. "Is that right, Mikael, son of Halkgar, is he with you?"

"No, Guardsman Yathis, he has served his purpose. I will have young Manal here to take me up to the palace and frankly his company will be much more pleasurable, certainly more fragrant."

"Indeed, Mikael. On your way, old man, and take your smell with you."

To the accompaniment of much cursing and bluster, the unfortunate Rikat led Galeanid away from the gate, receiving a kick in the process. Yathis and the other guards had a quiet laugh at their small victory. He turned to Michael. "He is an old fraud that Galeanid; always lording it over us normal folk and I know of nothing he has predicted coming true, save that eventually every boy he keeps will run off. I didn't know your father, Mikael, but my father fought alongside him several times and held him to be a noble and honest soul, and a good Captain, although rather dour of expression."

An image of the tall man with dark hair and sharp nose sprang into his mind, Halkgar, Mikael's father, sad and severe, stern, unable to love in the way a little boy craved.

"That he was, Yathis, his humour died perhaps with my mother."

"It is sometimes so, but I keep you from your business."

"Not at all, thank you again."

With that, he turned, and he began to follow Manal up the sloping paths of the inner city. Once a visitor was inside the inner wall, the opulence of Tath Garnir became immediately apparent. These were grand houses built in white stone, some decorated with carvings or painted tiles. Each had the distinctive sharply sloping roof of red stone that he had seen from the air; many had gardens and courtyards with fountains. The sounds here were of water and birdsong, many nests clung to the eaves of the houses, the occupants darting in and out in constant procession. The noise of the city below was a far-off thrum as of a distant hive of busy insects. At each intersection of streets, a member of the King's Guard stood, breastplate and helmet shining in the sun, the image of the White Hawk in flight, its talons clasping a bright sword, emblazoned on his chest. His tunic was sable and dark green, as was the standard of the King and he wore strong leather boots in the same colours. His helm was high, and it had on the left side a pair of curving hawk's wings in a shining white metal. Manal must have noticed Michael looking at it.

"The helm of the King's Guard is distinctive, is it not? The wings are made of Parilt, a metal which the Nare found deep in the mountains to the north. Only they were ever able to smelt the ore and put it to use. It has long since been mined out. The helms are passed on father to eldest son, they date back it is said to the founding of the city, but the veracity of that I couldn't swear to."

They had climbed steadily as they walked, and Michael wondered if the city was built upon a hill, he asked Manal about it.

"Of that I am not sure, there may be a small one under all of this somewhere, but the slope is mainly because the earliest cities here were destroyed by fire or assault and the later ones built upon the ruins of the last, each time expanding. Thus, over time, a hill has arisen. There are those who have tunnelled under the city and they say it is quite remarkable down there, but I have no wish to go crawling in the dark, personally."

The houses had now stopped, and they had come to the white towering spires of the palace itself. It was a vast building of halls and towers, with each lofty pinnacle connected to the others nearest to it by a series of rooms on the lower level and covered walkways and passages higher up. The towers appeared to have a multitude of balconies and vantage points as if their sole purpose was to provide views of the city. No two seemed to be alike, save in colour, and this gave the palace a rather eccentric appearance. The tallest tower was also the broadest, easily ninety metres across. It stood in the very centre and it rose high into the air. Michael tried to count the storeys and counted ten sets of windows; at the very pinnacle of its roof, a great standard blew in the wind, the sable and green of High King Leenal and the white feathered hawk of the Cluath. He wondered how long this palace had been in the making, perhaps each king in turn had added a tower or two, hence the variation in design. An architect would surely never have set out to create a building like this, certainly not a sane one.

Manal lead him through an archway and across a courtyard of trees heavy with scented blossom, then they entered a passageway and they began a circuitous route that Michael knew he would never be able to retrace. After several different passages and a few flights of stairs they reached one of the shorter towers, only five floors high, and Manal lead Michael up to the fifth floor where he knocked on a door.

The door was opened by a slim young man in a white gown, girded at the waist by a belt of gilded leather. He had long, blonde hair that was worn in a high ponytail and he was undoubtedly handsome of face with dark blue eyes and pale thin lips; but at present he had the look of a man who had drawn the short straw.

"Ah, Manal, you have located our guest, that is … good news, indeed it is. Would you be so kind as to inform Master Sorin that his friend has been found and is … safe." He plucked at his robe nervously as he spoke, casting quick glances at Michael. "Mikael Dal Oaken, son of Halkgar, your room is prepared, and … I, Sepho, have been given the … honour of serving you and … attending to your needs … while you are resident in the palace."

Manal bowed briefly to Michael and bade farewell and Michael entered the room. It was sumptuously furnished. Brightly coloured cushions and furs lay around on the floor, low tables held bowls of fruit and small cakes. There was a jug of water and one of wine. Scented oil burners hung in baskets from the ceiling and against one wall stood the most luxurious bed that Michael had ever seen. It reminded him of a scene from a film of the Arabian Nights that he and Mel had watched on late night television once, not long after they had married. Mel had said she had always wanted a bedroom like it; well this would be one that she would have loved. The sound of water being poured seemed to remind Sepho of something,

"Oh, Master Sorin suggested that you might enjoy a bath, so I took the liberty of having one prepared. I have also laid out a selection of garments that may suit you, while I have your own washed."

Michael's eyes lit up, a bath! Now that was a splendid idea. Sepho was standing by the door of an antechamber that was obviously a bathroom and he ushered out the two boys who had filled the bath. Michael stepped towards him to thank him and Sepho jumped back as if he had been stung. Sepho could not have looked more afraid of Michael if he had been holding a flaming sword in each hand. He decided to get to the bottom of it. He waited for the two boys to leave the room and then he turned to Sepho,

"You seem ill at ease, Sepho, is it something I have done? I am unused to the custom and practice of the court, so if I have offended you in any way …?"

Sepho almost squirmed with embarrassment and fear. "No, Son of Halkgar, it is nothing that you have done. It must be me; I simply do not wish to make you … angry."

Michael was bemused. "Make me angry? I am not sure what you mean."

Sepho if anything became even more agitated. "Er no, I didn't mean … angry, I meant I simply wanted to … I'm trying to do my best, honestly, I am, but they said …"

"They said what, Sepho? And who are they?"

Sepho suddenly sat down on the nearest pile of cushions. "I'm sorry, Son of Halkgar, I am obviously not meant to serve you, I can't …"

"Sepho, please, calm down." Michael had raised his voice more than he had meant to and the poor young man took one look at him and crumpled pressing his face into his hands and his hands into his knees.

Michael was a little angered by this odd behaviour, but he decided to try a different approach.

"Sepho, can we talk about this a little, what are you so scared of? Has someone told you something to make you scared?" He suddenly realised that perhaps someone at court had heard the prophecy and they knew who Michael was.

Sepho replied through his hands. "The others who came … we've been looking for you for two days … waiting, then your other companions, they told me all about you … your illness … that you mustn't get … angry… because when you do … you change …" his voice dropped to a terrified whisper, "into a Demon."

Michael would have laughed had the young man not been quite so scared. "They told you that did they … hold on, did you say two days?"

"Yes."

He had been in that hut for two days. He had taken it for just the night after the storm or had he fallen somewhere else and then walked into the river in his trance, he may never know. But that meant that the others Tuggid, Gath, Palvir and Dak had arrived too.

"The ones who told you this, Sepho, can you describe them for me."

"Yes, but I know their names, Son of Halkgar, Master Sorin was one and …"

"The others were a big man, from Darnak, called Gath and probably a Nare named Dakveen Halak. Am I right?"

"Yes, yes, they were most insistent that I be sent for and I was told how to behave. I am sorry."

"No, Sepho, I am sorry, very sorry that those three should abuse you in this fashion."

Sepho looked up. "What do you mean?"

"What I mean, Sepho, my good and gullible friend, you have had a trick played upon you. The three of them are notorious jokers, and no doubt they had been celebrating their meeting with a good deal of drinking."

"I believe they had, Son of Halkgar. There was some fuss later because they were rather noisy."

"That I can well believe. They have played you false, Sepho, I do have an illness and it is one about which you should be aware, but I do not change into a Demon when I get angry, in fact I very rarely get angry at all, particularly with people who have thoughtfully provided a hot bath for me." He reached out a hand and helped Sepho to stand. He was no longer nervous, but he was terribly embarrassed.

"Son of Halkgar …"

"Mikael, please."

"Mikael, what must you think of me. I have made a fool of myself in front of a guest of the King."

"No, Sepho, they have made a fool of you and I will be sure to make them apologise."

"Oh, no, Mikael, let us just forget it, please."

"If you wish. But I think none the worse of you for that."

"Thank you, Son of … Mikael. Should I attend to you while you bathe, or do you wish me to leave?"

"You can go … no, wait, would you mind sitting in here and talking to me while I take my bath, there is so much that I need to know about the court."

Sepho smiled warmly, he had recovered from his fright and the prospect of a good gossip appeared to please him greatly. "Very well, Mikael, there are towels beside the bath and I have added some tuva oil to the water, it is very relaxing, I find."

"Thank you, oh, before I get into the water, my illness; it is important that you know this."

"Yes, Mikael, I am paying close heed."

"Sometimes a kind of seizure comes upon me and I cannot speak or hear, but I will walk or move if someone leads me. It can last for a few hours or several days, and then it leaves me again and I am as you see me, until it returns. Master Sorin is trying to discover the reason for my infirmity and to find a cure."

Sepho nodded his head. "Ah, now I understand. Master Sorin, when he first arrived, asked questions of the Lady Frella. She is the one that attendants, such as myself, answer to."

"Before he had been drinking?"

"Yes, Mikael, and that is why I was chosen. My mother caught a strange disease when travelling in the south and in her later years she was deaf and dumb, and largely blind, I grew up as her eyes and her ears. We talked through her hands; I would write words on her palms."

Michael was struck by the matter of fact way in which Sepho spoke of such sadness. "How tragic, I am sorry."

"Thank you, Mikael, but that is in the past, but should your illness strike you, then you could have no better guide than myself."

"That is good to know, now when I am inserted into my bath, I want to know all about the High King and his court."

Michael went into the small anteroom and began to undress, two days in these wet clothes, that was not good, and it was a relief to peel them off again, as he had done in the hut. The bath was a sunken one of stone, small, but very comfortable, the stone was warm to the touch and suggested some form of under floor heating. The water smelt wonderful and the oil and the powders that Sepho had added had covered the surface of the bath with delicious bubbles, they did indeed tempt him to relax, but he was determined to be prepared for his meeting with the High King.

"Now Sepho, tell me all about the High King and his family and anyone else who warrants attention. I know names, but not the facts and I am sure one such as yourself will be able to give some of the real stories, rather than what the common folk are led to believe." He heard the young man almost purr with delight at this gentle flattery. Michael had guessed right, Sepho, despite the ease with which Gath, Sorin and Dak had fed him the Demon story, had a good eye and ear for the looks and glances, the little whispered asides that take up so much of the court's energy and time. The young man had poured two glasses of wine and stood at the half open door, cautiously handing one through to Michael. "It's alright come in, Sepho, find somewhere to perch and tell me some tales."

Sepho came in and sat on the sill of a small shuttered window that was at the foot of the bath. "Well, High King Leenal is still a powerful figure despite his age, he is in his sixty-fifth year, can you believe that, and he has been High King for over thirty years. Your father would have seen service in the early years of his reign I suppose, when you were a boy. That would make you …"

Michael laughed, even in Taleth, people seemed so coy about age. "I'm forty-four Sepho, although I probably look a lot older."

"No, not at all. You are still in your prime, Mikael." Sepho took a quick sip to hide his obvious lie. "King Leenal is taller than most and rarely laughs these days, he has become a very serious man not like he was in his youth, apparently he was quite the wild one; loved to ride and hunt and drink far too much. To look at him now you wouldn't believe it. He is still quite distinctive in appearance, although I suspect that he was never handsome. His eyes are small and piercingly blue, and his nose is crooked from falling face first from his mount, twice, the story goes. He leaves unnecessary speech to other people, preferring to listen when he can, although when he is roused to anger then he makes himself heard and others have to listen. The only person he really listens to, the only one he trusts I suspect, is Piat Kahord, his Majann, but I'll tell you more of him in a moment. If you ask me, and you did so I'll tell you, the King doesn't even trust his family anymore. Certainly, he hardly speaks to the Queen, and they rarely see each other outside of court sessions or banquets, it's a shame because I like her.

"Queen Finah was a great beauty in her youth and some of that is still there. She carries herself well and she still has beautiful blonde hair, but she looks weary now and her eyes have lost some of their sparkle. She is ten years younger than the king and there are still those who are prepared to flatter her and feed her vanity to gain favours. It works occasionally. She tolerates a few, but only for appearance sake. I think that they bore her now. She seems to prefer the company of Seers and mystics.

"She has a soft spot for the blind seer Galeanid, although most at court consider him an old fraud, but her big favourite at the moment is a woman who is just known as the Hooded Seer. I know very little about her, she comes and goes freely, but talks only to the Queen and no-one seems even to know what she looks like. Rumour has it that she is horribly disfigured, or that she has some disgusting disease. I heard one of the women in the kitchen insisting that she is actually a man, but I don't give that much credence. I have seen her walking in the palace, and she walks like a woman. Although so does Filius the bard, and he's a man, at least I think he is. He does sing very high some-times … Sorry, I'm getting side-tracked. Stop me if this is bor-ing you, Mikael."

Michael assured him that it was all fascinating. "Well, if you are sure. One of the things that the Queen is wearied by is the constant bickering between her children, which I'm afraid is often quite vicious and all very public. She had two children quite soon after her marriage to King Leenal. Princess Cassiell was born first and then she was followed fifteen months later by her brother Prince Hanallin and there has been little love between them even from the first. The Princess of course real-ised early on that even though there is no actual law that states a male heir supersedes a female, King Leenal was always going to name Prince Hanallin as his heir. Ever since they have been children, they have fought tooth and nail for their parent's af-fection and for the loyalty of the heads of the great families and the houses of the Cluath.

"There are some who even hint at Princess Cassiell plotting to take the throne by force when her father dies. She certainly has the support of some of the court and the Prince has a wick-ed temper that has made it easier for him to make enemies than friends. But there are still plenty who, out of loyalty to Leenal and to the line, would support Hanallin if it did come to a fight." Sepho paused for a moment and he looked out of the window. Michael could hear the call of sea birds as he had done earlier, and it reminded him that there was something to do with the water that he must talk to Sorin about, but at the moment he was too comfortable to worry about it. Sepho had sipped once more at his wine and he then turned back and continued.

"Hanallin considers himself to be handsome and strong, and a great warrior, when in fact this is not entirely true. He is a reasonable rider and he carries a sword with some skill, he can shoot well enough too, but as for handsome, well, he is fooling himself there. His eyes are far too close together and he has not the eyes of his father to compensate for his crooked nose, giv-en him by a woman so my friend told me, and sadly his hair, although a healthy black, sits lankly on his head like a sleeping gusha, but nowhere near as pleasing to the eye. He also has one shoulder that is slightly higher than the other, which does give him the appearance of perpetually leaning over to one side."

Sepho's description of the Prince left Michael expecting some hideous monster. "Would I be right in assuming that you have little love for the Prince yourself, Sepho."

"Oh, far be it for me to express an opinion, but if I was to give one, I would say that I would rather end my days on a nyatt farm than serve Hanallin as King, which is treasonous I know, but he's such an arrogant loudmouth."

"Not that you ever express an opinion, of course."

Sepho laughed quietly. "Sorry, Mikael, I am getting carried away with myself, but he treats his servants very shabbily and he had one of my friends whipped for no reason that I know, other than that his sister had won some argument or other."

"Do you favour the Princess's cause then?"

"Well, there you have the dilemma that faces all of us, Mikael. She is the elder, she has intelligence aplenty and the force of personality to rule certainly, and she is quite stunning to look at, although she is on the small side. Black hair like her father, eyes like her father too, good cheekbones and a good proportion between nose and mouth. The problem is that her veins run with pure poison and she is, quite possibly, totally insane. One moment she is calm and polite, speaking quietly and rationally with some Lord or other; the next she is spitting fire and bile and some poor soul is being carted off to be locked away and forgotten. She is not a woman to cross, Mikael, for that reason and because she has very powerful friends.

"You have to remember that the army that resides here in Tath Garnir, the High King's army, is only partly made up of men of Tath Garnir, the major part of it is made up of sections of men from each of the great houses. It was meant to stop the Lords and the most powerful families ever having big enough armies to fight against the other houses or even the High King, of course it didn't work, but then again, the Cluath would fight wars over dice if you let them. But it means that there are probably a large number of men in the army whose loyalty to the King is somewhat questionable; which is why the High King has always had a King's Guard. He knows someday he may need it."

"You speak honestly, Sepho, and I appreciate it. It will be most useful."

"I speak the truth as I see it, although it may come back to haunt me someday. Now two others you should know about, firstly Piat Kahord, the Majann. He has been the King's Majann for all his reign and he has tremendous influence over the King. Some say that he is the one who truly wields the power, but that will never be entirely true while the Queen lives. He is very powerful and brooks little opposition; they say that he is the greatest Majann of the age, but I feel somehow that is what he likes to think, whether it is true or not I do not know. He lost his left eye in an accident in his youth and wears a patch over the scar."

"Secondly, there is Grald Dal Hammett, the supreme commander of the Cluath armies, answerable only to Leenal himself. He has the visage of a man who has stood close to a fire once too often and he is undoubtedly the scariest man I have ever seen. His reputation for ferocity in battle and his ruthlessness in negotiation is formidable. He certainly terrifies me, and I make sure to stay out of his way. He must, I suppose, have been a boy once, but it is hard to picture. I think he was born fully grown as a man of fifty. The stories they tell of him could almost be true when you see him stomping along a corridor."

Michael was intrigued, he had heard the name from Greer or from one of the others, he couldn't recall who, something about the Frinakim never being accepted while Grald Dal Hammett was at the head of the army. In view of the office he held, Michael would surely meet him at some stage. "Stories? Such as?"

"Oh, some of them are most imaginative. That he never sleeps is the most common and probably true, but there are so many others. That he drank wyrm blood for a bet and it burned out his soul; that he once wrestled with four men at once and won, killing one of his opponents by mistake; that he once faced a giant Tsarg beast with no weapon and killed it by tearing off one of its arms and beating it to death with it. My favourite is that he is not really a man at all, but a statue brought to life by some magic of the King's Majann and that he cannot be killed. He will just return to the stone from which he was carved when Piat Kahord dies."

Michael had to smile at the obvious delight that Sepho took in retelling such wild notions, but he wondered about the truth of the man. "I suppose none of it matters if he is a good commander."

"Oh, they say that he is the best and that his men would charge into the belly of a great wyrm if he ordered them to, but he is not a man to cross."

"I heard that he refuses to trust, the Free Cluath Army, the Frinakim, why is that?" Michael wasn't sure whether Sepho would know the answer to that, but he felt it was worth a try. In fact, Sepho's reply was easily supplied.

"Well, whoever told you that is right, and the answer is simple. The so called Free Cluath Army are led by his brother Teldak Dal Hammett, although he calls himself just Teldak these days. He absented himself from the post which Grald had placed him in, to chase down a group of Tsarg, who had killed the woman who Teldak loved; a woman, what's more, who was the wife of another. To a man such as Grald there was much offence in that alone. As far as Grald was concerned Teldak was a traitor and he had brought shame on his family and to his name. He had lost all honour and broken every vow; Grald had his name hacked off the family carvings and now he refuses to even acknowledge that he once had a brother. I did hear that Teldak had requested a chance to meet with him and seek some way to reconcile their differences, but Grald refused to even see the messenger, calling the Free Cluath Army a *'misbegotten collection of criminals and drunkards, without discipline or leadership'* whom he would gladly see hanged to a man."

A voice that Michael recognised cut in from the outer room. "That, friend, would be difficult, not the least because many are women." It was Danil and he was none too pleased by Sepho's remarks. "And perhaps Grald Dal Hammett's energies would be better put to weeding out the tricksters and the thieves in the court rather than besmirching the name of some of the finest warriors that walk upon the soil of Taleth."

Sepho's initial reaction to Danil's words was jump up and in doing so drop his half-filled glass. He then, with a swift glance at Michael, dropped to the floor and was about to mop up the spillage when Danil's head appeared around the door.

"Ah, I see, Mikael has time to relax, while the rest of us are hard at work, and what's more he has hired an entertainer to keep him amused."

Sepho began to mumble apologies, but Michael cut in. "Don't worry, Sepho, he's just upset that I am being looked after … and possibly about what you said about the Frinakim."

Sepho endeavoured to stand up with some decorum but failed miserably. "I'm sorry, but I was just repeating what I have heard the commander say, I didn't say that I agreed with him."

Danil stepped into the small bathroom and was holding a towel out to Michael. "No, no, of course you don't. If I thought those words were your own you would already be dead, my friend. Come along, Mikael, we need you at our little meeting. Putting some clothes on would be a good idea I suspect." Michael could spot the amusement in Danil's words, but Sepho now wore a face of deep concern. While Danil waited and after Sepho had crept quietly out of the bathroom, Michael, stepped, albeit reluctantly, from his bath. He dried himself and then he went over to the bed where the fresh clothing that Sepho had selected was laid out.

The clothes were mostly of fine cloth with a silken feel to the touch, but more substantial. They were all in white or shades of green except a plainer pair of leather leggings, similar to the ones to which Michael had become accustomed. He felt that these were appropriate for the plainsman they took him for. As he picked these up, he saw out of the corner of his eye Sepho sigh and Danil nod approvingly. He put them on and then he slipped on a soft white shirt, which he tied with a green belt. He also put on the light boots that stood beside the bed. He was surprised at how well they fitted, but he supposed that Sorin had told Sepho his size and his height. Danil then stepped forward and Michael saw that he held one of the Frinakim riding cloaks.

"Sorin, felt that you should wear this, to make your allegiance quite clear to all."

"Will that not annoy General Dal Hammett?"

"Naturally, Mikael, which is why he sent for it."

"What is he up to?"

"Sorin? Oh, just about everything, I think. Now I have an errand to run, but I will meet you in the council chamber. The King has dismissed the Lords who had attended, but there is still much to discuss, we have sat through several hours of the Cluath bickering about territory and status and we have as yet been given no chance to speak. Oh, I almost forgot, you dropped this." Danil held out Michael's axe.

"What? How did you find that? It must have …" Danil was holding a finger to his lips and with his eyes he reminded Michael that they were not alone, "… fallen out of my pack when we rode to the city. Thank you, Danil, I really thought that I wouldn't see that again."

"Let us hope it is a while before you must use it again." Danil then turned to Sepho, which made him jump. "Master Sepho, accept my apologies for berating you, I would not seek you harm, despite my words. Please convey Mikael down to the council chamber where he is expected." He then walked briskly out of the door and away down the stairs.

Sepho stared after him. "I hope I did not offend him too much, Mikael, is he always this stern?"

"When it suits him to be, but he is as loyal as a friend could wish and quite deadly with his bow, his name is Danil Lebreven."

"I will endeavour to remember and to be careful what I say when he is present." He was obviously intrigued by Danil's appearance, but he wondered if he could ask without more offence. "His green eyes … and his hair … he's not …"

Michael interrupted to help him out. "He is half Antaldi on his mother's side and, yes, it would be best not to mention it."

"Ah, I see, I didn't mean to stare, but he has an unusual look … quite handsome in its own way."

"Yes, I suppose he is, but come I have a meeting to attend."

"Certainly, Mikael, please follow me."

★★★

3

In the Court of the High King

Sepho led him down the stairs and then partly retraced the route that Manal had taken; until they reached an open courtyard with a fountain and several trees with branches that appeared to twist themselves out from the marbled grey trunk with a determination never to grow straight; the effect was of dancers frozen in the midst of a wild, whirling and chaotic ballet. Their leaves were so pale as to be almost white and they hung like icicles along the snaking arms. On the other side of these trees was a doorway that opened onto a stairway, which led up to the second level of the central tower.

Once inside the tower, Michael saw that a corridor ran round the curving sides of the tower, with stairs up to the next level and stairs down. This level had many doors leading inwards to large rooms the purpose of which was not clear to him. Sepho had been quiet since they left his quarters and he wondered if protocol dictated that he assumed the role of silent servant outside the confines of his room. He was currently leading Michael to the stairs leading upward. It was the first of four flights he took them up.

When they had reached the next level, it became obvious that Michael's assessment of the tower had been inaccurate. The stairs proper ended at this level, but were replaced by a much narrower staircase, which he presumed led to the roof, and the windows continued upward, giving the impression of another four floors. The doors on this level were larger and grander and made it clear to anyone passing through that they were of little importance compared to what lay within. Sepho opened the doors and then he stepped out of the way, bowing respectfully to Michael as he walked into the council chamber.

The chamber itself was cavernous, a circle of towering pillars rose from the stone floor towards the distant ceiling, each one displaying intricately carved scenes of battles and heroic deeds; the walls were hung with richly coloured tapestries on similar themes. The chamber was lit by six great candelabra that hung from the ceiling, each bristling with huge candles. To Michael's left was a platform upon which stood an impressive throne of dark red wood. It's arched back was easily three metres high and bore, to Michael's educated eyes, rather unflattering depictions of Hantor and Minead. The throne was unoccupied. The High King sat at the head of a long table, with his Queen beside him. The table was set for a meal, but the fare was simple and seemed incongruous given the surroundings. There were cold meats, bread, cheeses and fruit, spread all the way along in front of the collected company. Michael noticed immediately, however, that no-one was eating.

Thanks to Sepho's tutoring, Michael was able to name all who sat along the sides of the table, even those who had their backs turned towards him and he realised how accurate some of the descriptions had been. To the King's right sat Piat Kahord, the one-eyed Majann, and then beside him Grald Dal Hammett, then came Princess Cassiell, with Sorin, Danil, and Dak. On the other side to the Queen's left was an empty chair, then next to that was Galeanid, Michael assumed that the empty chair was for the Hooded Seer. Beside Galeanid was a surly young man who had to be Prince Hanallin, then Vitta, without Sentielle, then Tuggid and Gath. There were many more chairs, but only one extra place had been set, beside Dak. It appeared that that was where Michael was to sit.

Michael was just about to walk further into the chamber when Sorin leapt into his mind. *"Michael, I am so glad you are safe, when you fell, we feared the worst and we searched for you without success. Danil found your pack with the straps broken, and the axe by a culvert, so we hoped that you had fallen into the water. It was only when you came back to Taleth that I realised you had gone, which was why I could not sense you. Our feigned lack of concern was to hide our worries and your importance. Be wary this is not the place for quick answers. Try to speak little even if questioned directly, I will help where I can. It is good to see you, by the way. Now walk to the head of the table and bow to the High King. I will introduce you."*

Michael did as Sorin told him and he walked around to the head of the table. The High King and the others had not at first noticed him enter, but now all heads were turned. He bowed and as he did so Sorin stood up. "Ah, may I present to you your Majesty, our missing companion, Mikael Dal Oaken."

High King Leenal looked him up and down. "Halkgar's son, eh, well though you look half the man your father was, you are welcome. Sit, Mikael Dal Oaken and join our table. Some of these you know and have travelled with I hear; others you will be unfamiliar with and so I will name them." He stood up, rather wearily Michael thought, and indicated each person as he spoke. "My Queen, Finah, you will know by name and status, as too my children Hanallin and Cassiell. My trusted Majann, Piat Kahord, you will know by reputation and history. As for General Dal Hammett, the whole of Taleth surely knows of him and his worth." He was about to sit down when an irritated cough from the Queen reminded him that he had not mentioned Galeanid. He looked at his wife, and then stood fully again with a sigh, "I think you will find, Finah, that Mikael and Galeanid are already acquainted, a fact that I know Galeanid told you when he arrived. He really must learn to whisper more quietly."

King Leenal sat and Michael turned and walked to his seat beside Dak. He had been greeted with nods of acknowledgement from all but Hanallin, who had ignored him completely, just as he reached his seat, Grald rose and greeted him more formally.

"I welcome you, Mikael, son of Halkgar, your father was a man I was proud to command and fight beside, we felt his loss when he fell, but his death was a good one and he is well remembered. Should you wish to join us, a place would be made for you."

Michael felt that an answer was required, he bowed and then he said, "To fight under your command would be an honour, General, but I fear my path lies elsewhere."

At this Galeanid snorted. "He has fine words, but no taste for a fight, perhaps."

Dak shifted beside Michael, but Sorin glared along the table and shook his head. "Oh, well, Master Galeanid, we are all well aware of your contribution to the mighty victories of the King's armies."

Galeanid snarled but was signalled to silence by the Queen. It was Piat Kahord who answered Sorin. "At least Galeanid has been here at the centre of things and not hiding in a cave, mixing salves and potions, Sorin. I am surprised that you were able to make the journey, considering your age."

Sorin appeared to nod sadly. "It is true, Piat, that I am old and that I have spent many years perfecting the skills of healing, rather than walking the corridors of the mighty, but not all of us are cut out for life at court. That takes a very particular type of person."

Piat Kahord either ignored or missed the irony in Sorin's words, but it angered Michael that he appeared to consider him a relic of a bygone age. "Ah, well, Sorin, Taleth moves on and maybe your journey has been a fruitless one, since there is little you can tell us that we do not already know."

Queen Finah was growing tired of this and her irritation began to show. "Leenal is it possible that we could get on with this council, I fail to see why we had to wait for Dal Oaken to join us, but now that he is here …"

The King interrupted her. "We waited, as you know, because Master Sorin and Master Vitta, insisted that Mikael has some importance in these events, though, as yet, exactly how is unclear, and I agreed to refrain from starting until he was present. But, as you say, he is now here, and we must put our minds to the matters before us. I will begin by setting out the situation as I see it and then …"

Leenal was interrupted by Hanallin, who spoke with little ceremony and even less courtesy. "Waiting for a Cluath from an ancient family is one thing, but why are the outsiders here? What need have we of advice from a half-breed or a Nare? I see nothing that requires mending?"

"I am surprised, brother dear, that you can see anything, since your eyes are still bleary with drink. You have as usual, excelled at the one thing you are truly skilled at, rudeness." Cassiell's voice was quiet and controlled, but Michael felt there was a vicious knife hiding in the shadows.

"My sight is fine, Cassiell, and I see beyond names and titles, something you do not. But I repeat, father, why need we the advice of those not of Cluath blood?"

King Leenal gave his son a glare. "You persist in your blinkered view of the world around you, Hanallin, something that must change, before you have any true power. It is not enough to see the world through a window in Tath Garnir."

"I didn't know you had raised your bed, brother, so that you could gaze out of the window from it."

"At least the bed I sleep in is my own, sister."

The King had had as much as he could take and, before Cassiell could counter this slur upon her character, his fist came down upon the table. "Enough! You will both be silent. Those present at my table are here because I have requested it and they are welcome, whatever their heritage. It becomes more obvious to me every day that none of us can be blamed for our parents or should be held responsible for our children." He paused to allow himself to calm down, and when he spoke again, he was back in control. "It had been clear for some time that the numbers of Tsarg upon our borders have grown, but they seemed confined to certain areas and we felt no threat. We still do not feel threatened here within our city, but there have been too many incursions and raids well within our borders, and since we cannot deploy our entire army to the task of chasing raiders, we must seek them out and tackle the problem at source."

Despite his father's warning, Hanallin was in no mood to be quiet. "So we lead out our army to solve a problem that has come nowhere near Tath Garnir, because a bunch of farmers and plainsman have not the guts to face up to a few bandits."

Cassiell was also quite ready to defy her father. "Are you worried that there would be no-one left to protect you, Hanallin, or more likely protect your wine stores?"

"You do not wish the army to leave, sister, for who would you play with if your soldiers left you?"

This time it was Sorin who spoke out. "These are serious matters that concern us, and it would help us all if your private quarrels were kept private, I believe that your father was speaking."

Hanallin was outraged. "How dare you …" but the King was grateful for Sorin's assistance.

"Thank you, Master Sorin, it is sad that my children appear not to hear my words, perhaps they will listen to you."

Michael looked across at Hanallin and saw the thunderous look in his eyes; Sorin was making no friends that was clear. Cassiell had hidden her thoughts and her face, but Michael saw a wry smile upon the face of Queen Finah.

King Leenal continued. "We must therefore decide how and where is the best place to flush out the enemy so that we can face it upon our own terms. That is your job Grald, but Master Majanns you must give us your news and your advice. We have heard prophecies aplenty from the Seers. Some are obviously nonsense, and some malicious in intent, but some may be truly seeded by the Powers into our dreams. My own dream that led me to send Tuggid Dal Tharl to seek out Master Sorin, I still do not understand, since Calix is a name from history and can have no relevance for us today save in inspiration. Master Vitta what can you say that will aid us?"

Vitta stood slowly and he bowed towards the King and the Queen. "My Lord Leenal, I am most honoured to be present at this council, but beyond what I have said in laying before you the words of the Seer and urging you to heed the words of Master Sorin, I can pledge no help without consulting the Triad as you know. This I would say, however, be not lulled by your apparent safety here in this mighty city, as in the past the

Triad have felt exactly that in Glianivere, distanced and protected as it is. Events are marching on and we must attempt to
keep apace of them."

"The city will never fall, while there is Cluath blood left to
defend it, Majanns may come and go, but Tath Garnir will prevail." Grald spoke with a tone that in a lesser man would have
seemed arrogance, but in him it was just a statement of fact.

King Leenal sighed. "Peace, Grald. As ever Antaldi reticence
may mean more delay. Master Piat, give us your thoughts."

Piat Kahord looked across at Sorin as he spoke with mock
deference. "My Lord, I would not speak before Master Sorin, let
us hear his wisdom first and then I will add my own unworthy
thoughts." Michael was reminded that Sorin had said that the
Cluath were prone to argument and petty squabbles. He disliked
Piat Kahord more and more, but he was also conscious that whenever the Majann cast a glance his way it caused him to feel uneasy.

Sorin got to his feet and Michael caught a hint of smoul-
dering anger in his eyes. "Very well, since your own Majann,
once again displays his predilection for insult rather than counsel, I will speak, and I speak as one who has faced the forces of
Corruption in the field, not tried to guess their numbers from
a distance. Khargahar has set his plans in motion, plans he has
been hatching over centuries. What we have seen so far of the
Tsarg gives us nothing, nothing to show us their true numbers.
He has released ancient terrors to wander free across the land
and he will have prepared many more terrible weapons waiting for his moment."

Leenal had listened with head down, but he looked up at
this. "Ancient terrors? We have had no such reports. How can
that be?"

Piat Kahord could not resist adding to the King's disbelief.
"He seeks to frighten us with supposition and rumour, my Lord."

It was Danil who half-rose this time, but Sorin signalled
him to remain still.

"You have had no such reports, your Majesty, because they
were dealt with before they reached your borders, one by the

Free Cluath Army, that your General treats with disdain and mockery, the other by Mikael here, he dispatched it with the axe he has at his belt, something he considers of minor importance, but I feel is worthy of mention, since some question his presence at this table." Michael could see that Grald Dal Hammett had barely controlled his anger at the mention of the Frinakim, but he also noticed that the others now looked at him with more interest, particularly the King's Majann.

"If that is true, it is a tale worth hearing, Sorin, but continue for now." King Leenal, had cast a quizzical look at Piat Kahord as if to seek some guidance, but the Majann was avoiding his gaze.

"He has used Garshegan, smoke demons, and shape-shifters, and other horrors that he has in readiness, he is indeed well pre-pared. He has also corrupted many that are not Tsarg but Cluath. We have seen incontrovertible proof that there are Cluath who have been seduced to his cause, who ride into battle under his banner and lead Tsarg against their own blood. Faradon and his son are only two among many, I fear."

Hanallin was on his feet, his voice raised in anger. "Where is your evidence? You can have no proof; you befoul the name of one such as Faradon at your peril, old man."

But Sorin was ready for him, his voice becoming dangerous. "It was the son of Faradon who so foully abused and murdered the Antaldi Seer, and there are seven of us who sit at this table with you who have met these traitors on the field surrounded by Tsarg and sporting the brand of the serpent. Do not speak of what you do not know, Hanallin, and I would be careful who I call friend if I was you."

The sheer power of Sorin's words forced the Prince back into his seat. His face was filled with loathing for the old Majann but Sorin ignored it. He resumed his usual cracked tone. "My apologies, your Majesties for raising my voice in that manner, but there are some things that must be heard and believed. But what is the Corruptor's strategy? What is he seeking? I will tell you." Sorin's voice now became less the old man and more the Majann that Michael had seen glimpses of. "Yes, I will tell you.

He seeks to incite you into doing just what you have in your heart; he wants you to follow your nature and fight. He desires nothing more than that the might of the Cluath, with or without help from the other races, marches to face him on the plain before the Castle of the Teeth, which no doubt he has caused to be rebuilt, and there he will spring his trap, just as he did before. I believe that he has an army, hidden underground waiting, an army so vast that we can hardly imagine it, countless numbers of Tsarg who will feed his hatred by destroying not only your warriors, but all of Cluath blood. Then Tath Garnir will fall, for there will be none to defend it and then too the other races will be swept away, whether they have chosen to fight or not."

There was a moment's silence as these stark words were digested. Queen Finah, looked up at Sorin. "And what would you have us do, Sorin of the Cave, what solution have you seen from your lofty position?"

Sorin ignored the insult. "If we can look to our defences, protect the lands of the five races, defend the river crossings, and ensure that no Tsarg can with impunity walk the plains and the forests, then his planning is for nothing. He must be forced to show his hand, be drawn out into open battle on our terms, for even if his agents have reopened his ancient fortress, he cannot leave the depths himself, his armies would have to face us without his strength, and we may then defeat them. As to the dreams and the prophecies, there are none who can say for certain what they mean, whatever they may tell you. Their meaning may become clear in time, but for now I counsel defence. Clear your lands of Tsarg, drive them out and ready yourself for Corruption's next move." Sorin sat down and waited for his words to take effect.

Leenal appeared about to speak, but Piat Kahord broke in with a disdainful laugh. "And this is your wisdom, old man, wait for this fictitious army to come to us? A vast army? Where is it hidden? Have you seen it? Oh, no, it's hidden isn't it, so we cannot see it. My Lord, we cannot see it because it does not exist. There are Tsarg, in great numbers, but not so great as the

Cluath army, who will need no help to destroy them, either from the timorous Antaldi or from some wild bunch of ill-led outcasts. We will beat the army of Corruption just as we did in the time of Kintell the betrayer."

Now it was Sorin's turn to rise again, his anger bursting from his mouth. "That battle was lost, as you know, Piat Kahord, until Calix sacrificed himself and drove back the waves of Tsarg, as no other could have done. You are more of a fool than Majann if you would fight that battle without the power that Calix wielded."

"No, Sorin, I am no fool, you have lived too long in your cave. Calix may be gone, but his powers are not, I am privy to the secrets of his power and should we face the need then once more we would win a mighty victory."

Michael half-expected Sorin to strike Piat Kahord down, but he became silent and he sat stony faced as the King's Majann glared from his one eye at any who would question his power.

"Yes, Sorin, Calix passed on his powers and they have now come down to me. So, go back to your salves and your potions, for we have no need of you."

Suddenly Danil spoke, not to the Majann, but to the High King. "King Leenal, wherever the battle is fought, surely any victory would be hollow and pointless unless the Corruptor himself is vanquished and that could only be accomplished by entering his lair in the depths and destroying him there."

This question was met with gasps from many around the table, it was as if he had spoken blasphemy. Cassiell laughed nervously and turned to face him. "What foolishness you speak, have you half a mind in your half-breed skull? The Corruptor cannot be killed, he is one of the Powers, twisted and terrible, but their equal and their kin. How would you have us assail him?"

Michael was shocked at their virulence towards Danil, but he knew that he had faced it all his life. Danil rose and bowed to the Princess. "My mind is intact, although I have not the lineage that is yours to boast of. Yet my question is still there to be answered. We cannot win this war with Corruption, if we do not fight Corruption itself."

Piat Kahord voice was full of contempt. "Your question is as pointless as your presence here; the Corruptor cannot be killed and therefore there is no point in fighting him. We must fight his agents and his army, though I suspect that Sorin has overstated this band of traitors that ride with the Tsarg; it is very hard to believe."

Grald Dal Hammett rose and he banged his fist onto his chest. "If traitors there are then I will hunt them out and their heads will decorate the walls of the city. I will issue warrants against Faradon and all his house if you give the word, my Lord, if this is true, his punishment will be swift and terrible."

Leenal nodded. "Traitors I can believe in, Grald, but hidden armies?"

Queen Finah had waited for a chance to be heard and the King's question gave her the opportunity. "They are, my husband, as Piat says, though it pains me to agree with him, figments of a mind long since lost in the mountains. We are Cluath and we fight our enemies, whoever they are. We are not daunted by ancient ghosts or tales of terror. This is not a time for faint hearts; we have no Antaldi blood in us. Let us face this threat and show all of Taleth our true metal. Leave the Corruptor to the justice of the One; let us take care of the rest."

Grald who had remained standing saluted Finah. "Spoken like a Queen, my Lady, I can lead an army against a threat I can see. A future threat, a hidden threat I cannot see, I cannot fight." Michael sat aghast that they failed to see the short sightedness of this attitude, but he remained silent, as he waited to see how Sorin would react.

The Queen's mistrust of the old Majann had become quite apparent. "What say you to that, Majann?"

"I still say caution is our friend, Finah, rashness now plays into the hands of our enemy, caution protects your people and gives us a chance. Caution brings our enemies to us; bravado delivers our armies into a bloody defeat."

Galeanid had obviously decided that the tide had gone so completely against Sorin that it was safe for him to throw out his own petty insults. "You urge caution because you are a coward like your friends, you are prepared to meddle in small things, but do not have the guts to face a real challenge."

Before Sorin could reply two people entered the chamber. One was a servant of the King; bowing low he spoke quickly in hushed tones. The King stood and he left with the servant without saying a word. In the doorway Michael saw a messenger still in cloak and boots; he had the look of one who had ridden hard and fast. The other newcomer was robed in black and purple, and had a face hidden by a cowl.

'*Surely*,' Michael thought, '*this must be the Hooded Seer, the one in whom the Queen has so much faith.*' She spoke in whispers to the Queen, but she did not take the seat that had been left for her. She looked around at those present until the hood faced Michael. Whereupon she spun towards Sorin and with a voice like a knife she lashed out at him.

"Think you to hide him from me, old man? Would you do the work of Corruption for him? You bring him here into our very heart, when you know what has been woven around him. Curse you, Sorin, for your arrogance, you will destroy us all."

These words had brought all to their feet, even Hanallin, but Sorin who remained seated flashed a warning to Michael. *'Say nothing, there is danger here, but let me face it.'* The Seer turned her attention to Michael himself, and he immediately knew what was coming, "Know you not who he is? Can you not see it in his face? You have heard the words of the prophecy and yet you heed them not, you let him live.

'*The Twice Dead comes, scorched by fire and claw.*
The touch of his hand shall call forth the Doom of Taleth.
He comes from beyond to redeem the outcast,
But Death stalks all who befriend him.
His coming will draw decay unto the Cluath,
Ghosts and demons he will bring amongst them.
To the wolves he must be sent,
To die and die again.
The touch of his hand shall call forth the Doom of Taleth.'

"To let him live is to bring the end of us all, it is the will of the One that he be suffered not to live."

Sorin had sat through her insults and through her repetition of the prophecy, but these last words drove him up out of his chair. "And what gives you the right to speak for the One? Are you privy to his thoughts that you so easily invoke his will? None but the One shall speak for the One, none but the One shall know the mind of the One."

Vitta too had been shaken by her revelation, but he was equally enraged by her words. "Your words bring shame upon us all, pray that the One is merciful in your heart. Presume not to know, few dare even to suspect. You should abase yourself in abject pleading for forgiveness, that your Sight be not taken from you." Vitta then turned upon his fellow Majann. "All this you knew? After learning of Enevien's prophecy, you still said nothing? Is this really *'the Decider, the Ender of Days'*? Why have you kept all this hidden, my friend?"

But Piat Kahord sensed only a further humiliation for Sorin in this. "It is as I suspected, this false warrior is the 'Twice-Dead' that the Seers have seen. I sensed as much when he arrived. We should do as she says and have him killed."

Sorin was beside himself with anger and he threw back his chair sending it crashing to the ground. "You are a fool, Piat Kahord, and your foolishness is only exceeded by your arrogance. You sensed nothing, or you would have spoken before now. You listen to the words of the prophecy and place a meaning there of your own making, because you have not the wit to uncover its true message. Vitta, you well know that all words are open to interpretation, but few there are who are not blinded by their own cleverness."

Queen Finah was incensed by Sorin's outburst. "While Leenal is not present I stand in his place, Sorin, and you stand perilously close to facing my judgement. The *'Twice-Dead'* will be kept under guard until we can make a proper decision as to his fate. You and your companions will …" but what she had in mind for them was left unsaid as King Leenal returned from the corridor with a face drained of blood, he held a hand up to silence all.

"Sorin, in some things you may be mistaken, but not in the matter of vile and loathsome treachery and I, for my part, apologise for my disbelief. All other concerns must wait, all voices now be silent." He paused to prepare himself, but when he spoke there was barely controlled emotion in his voice. "Lord Faradon has raised his standard against us and crossed the Ineth with a large force, curse him and all his kin, … what's more that force contains many legions of Tsarg. His true numbers are not yet known, but ride to meet him we must; he must not be allowed to cross the Heran. Grald we have much to do."

Queen Finah, though shaken by this news was determined to have her way. "Husband, we must at the very least imprison Dal Oaken, for he is dangerous."

Leenal, sighed for a moment. "Is that proven, just because of some ill begotten words? Yes, I heard your screeching from outside, Hooded One."

Piat Kahord wanted to press home his advantage over Sorin. "Whether it is or not, my Lord, he is dangerous and must be under lock and key, on this I am in agreement with the Queen."

"Under lock and key? He is still dangerous wherever he is." The Hooded Seer turned from one to another. "He should not be here, he should not be alive."

Leenal threw up his hands in desperation. "I have no time for this! War is upon us." He looked around at the faces of the Queen and his Majann, and conceded, as he still needed their support. "Very well, lock him up, but keep him alive until I return and then we can discuss his future."

Sorin started to protest, but the King waved him away. "Finah, I name you as Regent until I return, and should I do so perhaps you will think better of me. Hanallin you will come with me." His son gasped and opened his mouth to speak. "Yes, my son, it is finally time to earn yourself some glory in battle. Grald, Piat, Dal Thrarl, Dal Hurik come." The High King turned on his heels and marched away, his Majann beside him. Tuggid and Gath, who appeared to still be in shock cast a quick glance towards Michael as if to apologise, and then they followed Grald and the King with an ashen faced Hanallin trailing in their wake.

The Queen waited for her husband and her son to leave and then she spun around with a look of triumph on her face. "So, Sorin, you thought to come here and drag us all down into the mire of your plots and schemes. You accuse us of not having wit enough to understand the words of the prophecies, but we understand them very well. Of course, you knew of Faradon's despicable treachery, because you are in league with him." She paused for some sort of protest, but Sorin as he had done before silenced Dak, Danil and Michael with a look. "You sought to delay us all and give your friends enough time to gain an unassailable advantage in this war. But know you this, my husband may be an old fool, but his army is mighty and when the Cluath take up arms against an enemy, that enemy still quakes. You sought to bring this," and here she spat her words at Michael, "this cursed flesh into our city, into our very house, for your own twisted purposes, but we have foiled you, we have defeated you, Sorin. You are finished, go back to your mountains, your cave and fade away, old man; we will find a deep pit to throw your pet into. Leave Tath Garnir, take your half-breed and that filthy Nare with you and be thankful that we do not cast you into the depths where you belong."

When she had finished this tirade, she was flushed and breathless, her hands twisting together with the passion of the moment. Her daughter Cassiell was staring at her mother, seeing her in a brand-new light and thrilling to this release of spite. The Hooded Seer having set her Queen in motion was standing quietly a little way behind her. Galeanid, a leer upon his face, stood with one hand upon the back of a chair.

There was a moment's silence. The breeze from the open doors pushed at the great candelabra and they began to creak overhead. Michael's heart still pounded, his blood rushing in his ears. His emotions swirled around, shame, anger, terror, despair, all raging around inside him. He wanted to scream, but he fought to remain outwardly passive, surely this was not how things were meant to end.

Sorin after a deep breath and a shake of the head turned and picked his fallen chair from the floor. He then carefully pushed it under the table, before he turned to the Queen.

"If you truly believe that I would align myself with that traitor Faradon, that I would stand here as an agent of Corruption, then you are not just a fool you are mad. Your bile and hate have blinded you, and these so-called Seers you surround yourself with have fed lies and falsehoods into your ears. You berate me for my age, Dakveen for his race, and Danil for his parentage, all these I cast back at you, daughter of an ancient house, which now you shame with your vicious words. For all your understanding, you hear nothing and see nothing. If Mikael is the Ender of Days, think you that you can turn that aside by imprisoning him? If he is the one who will bring the Cluath to their Doom, think you that you can deny the path that is set with a lock and chain? He is a man, an honourable man, a brave man, who has courageously faced the forces of Corruption that sought his death. He is entwined in all of this, just as we are, and none can say how things will end, for all your Seers' whisperings and dreams. I will leave Tath Garnir, because my path takes me elsewhere. If you still persist in your decision to detain Mikael Dal Oaken, then so be it, but should harm befall him while he is in your care, then, although you be Leenal's Queen, I will pay back that harm a hundredfold and you will end your days in pain."

Sorin's words had been delivered slowly, but with such power that Finah stood motionless, her anger draining away leaving her pale and still. It was the Princess who struck back at the old Majann.

"You stupid old man. Do you think that we will let any of you leave after such a threat? You have no power; you are the bleached bones upon the sands of history, a sad relic to be crushed under foot. I will have the guards gut you and hang your entrails from the walls. You and your wretched companions will all regret your words …" but she tailed off as Sorin spun around and taking her by her shoulders forced her down into a chair.

"Save your breath, young woman, you have no comprehension of the forces at work around you. Your mother will realise soon that she has most foolishly made an enemy of me, who came here as a friend. You can have no idea what power resides within these 'bleached bones' or you would tremble with terror where you sit. Tath Garnir has become lazy and ignorant, choosing intrigue, bickering and lascivious pleasure over knowledge and wisdom. You think that Piat Kahord will save your father?" He released the now terrified girl. "Piat is deluded; but worse he fills the King's head with his lies."

"You are the liar, old man. Guards!" The Queen had recovered her voice.

"Well, we shall see. You will not attempt to detain me or my friends, Finah, and remember my words concerning Mikael." With that he nodded to Dak and Danil and they began to leave. Danil removed Michael's axe with a whisper. "This I will keep for you."

Six Guardsmen had entered the chamber and stood to bar Sorin's way, but Finah after a moment shook her head and pointed towards Michael.

"Take that one to a cell and watch him closely." Sorin leapt into his mind. *'Michael do not worry, we will return for you. These fools have backed themselves into a corner and I cannot help them, we must follow the path that is set and help the Nare that is now our course. Keep up your courage, I promise you your captivity will be short.'* He had no time to respond as he was roughly grabbed and marched from the chamber. As he was manhandled through the door he looked over his shoulder, where the Queen comforted her shaking daughter, while Galeanid laughed to himself; but the Hooded Seer had turned and she lifted her face towards him, her hand was raised to her lips and then to her heart. It struck Michael strangely; this was not a gesture of threat or warding, it was a gesture of friendship, he was sure. Confusion spread through him and the words of the spirit-wolf Lonett sprang into his mind. *"Be warned! Do not believe all you see in Tath Garnir, in the city of the High King …*

Trust not too easily. Look beyond seeing, sense beyond feeling; keep true intent hidden, true purpose concealed. The choices must be made." He was lost in all the chaos that had been unleashed.

He had had little chance to take in where he was being taken, other than that it was downwards, several flights of stairs and then a sloping corridor that now had no windows to let in natural light. The corridor became a tunnel and then they reached a circular chamber with doors of metal bearing large bolts. *'The dungeons,'* Michael thought, *'she really means to keep me here.'* One of the doors was opened and he was cast roughly into the darkness. As he fell, he felt the familiar ripping sensation as Taleth peeled away and he was back in the world of his birth.

★★★

'Hold and name yourself. You walk as if you are one of the herds, a 'bellower – antler-headed – grass-runner' and have the smell of skarl, but I name you not as such, for your true nature you attempt to hide. Name yourself and I will honour thee.'

'Wolf of the Dri, your senses are clear and quite correct. As skarl I walk, because I choose it to be so, but skarl I am not. I am Carun, bondmate of Cerlinith.'

'I give you welcome mighty one but would desire to know why you come wandering so close to the city of the Cluath.'

'I could ask you the same question, for you are of the Dri and not the Raell. Surely Tath Garnir is the concern of that pack and not your own?'

"You know very well, great Carun, that my duty lies with the Majann and one in particular. He at present has business in the city and so I hunt around the walls and await him.'

Carun laughed the snorting laugh of a skarl. *'Yes, I know, and I know your name, Sylvan of the Dri. But I am playful at heart and I enjoy the pretence of conversation. I will tell you why I am here, there is one who has been tasked, by means of dreams and visions, to undertake a certain duty, and I am here to ascertain what manner of success has been achieved. We cannot interfere directly, and so we must be subtle. Sadly, sometimes we are too obscure, and much is misinterpreted, but so is the way of things.'*

'That is indeed true, the Cluath hear what they want to hear and see what they want to see. I will not hinder you, Lord of Hoof and Claw, be swift and strong, bring honour to your herd.'

'Thank you, Sylvan of the Dri. Strength and honour to your pack, may your path run straight, and your companions be true.'

Sylvan stood for a while and watched as the huge skarl moved away into the trees. She had known who it was who had approached, and she knew that flattering him would lead him to tell her what he was up to. The Powers often forgot that the Avali were as old as they and, though they walked on four paws now, it was not always so.

Suddenly, she heard the crashing of a large beast racing for its life through the woods behind her and she spun around to face the sound, which was coming closer. She prepared herself to spring or leap from its path should it be the victim of a chase, but when the body fell heavily before her and rolled against a tree, she knew that she needed to do neither. There was no pursuer, nothing now moved, not even the twisted and bloodied remains that lay before her, death had taken it. To Sylvan's surprise and confusion the body was that of an enormous Tsarg. It had been ferociously savaged, torn by teeth and claws, cut so deeply around its chest and abdomen that it was amazing that it had been able to run at all, its face too had been almost shredded.

Sylvan looked at the wounds and considered what might have been able to inflict this much damage, these terrible wounds, and she knew in her heart that only wolves could have done this. But it could not have been a wolf alone, it must have been several together. She knew how to kill Tsarg and she had killed thousands in her many lives, but she also knew that wolves of the seven packs killed swiftly with no joy in the suffering of the victim in their jaws. This attack was cruel, vicious, dishonourable and slow, unworthy and un-wolf-like; she knew of none who would have done this.

And then she heard a sound. A sound moving away into the distance. A sound that chilled her blood and shocked her immortal spirit. It was the howling of wolves. Not the wolfsong of the packs, not the call to link minds, not even the lonely howl of the Lost. This was a mindless snarling, a hateful noisesome nerve-jangling cacophony of triumph, of despair, of murderous intent and of agonising pain. Sylvan now knew what had killed the Tsarg and racing away into the night, pounded out a warning with every stride.

★★★

4

Captive

Michael woke to the semi-dark of morning. He lay on his back, his hands bound underneath him, his clothes were damp, and he was cold. This was all too familiar, he half expected to hear the voices of Krakis and Duvan arguing over dice nearby. But all was silent except for the sound of water that dripped into a bucket somewhere close. As his eyes grew accustomed to the light, he saw that he was in a room with unplastered walls, the light coming from a double paned window above and behind him. The room was apparently undergoing repairs; there was what looked like a new joist that had been set to replace a timbered beam. The dripping water and the building work suggested a farmhouse that was halfway through renovation, or had been and was then abandoned, for the floor was littered with rubbish and newspapers, there was even a discarded pizza box in one corner. It occurred to him that this was a perfect place to hide a kidnap victim since no-one would come knocking and no-one would hear any suspicious sounds.

His legs were not bound, and he was just wondering if the door was locked when he heard a door open and then close, followed by voices, but not Krakis, Duvan or even Frappo, though their tone suggested that they had certain similarities.

"I've told you, this one will know where he is for sure."

"Jesus, you keep saying that, but he was caught in the explosion like the others, he nearly died."

"You think? If he was so badly injured how come he gets up and walks out of the hospital like he did. He was just laying low, giving us no reason to come after him and then, when he thinks we've all forgotten about it, he ups and leaves. They were all going through the motions, man. Giving it out that they're about to pull the plug and all of that was for our benefit."

A third voice joined in. "If you hadn't hit him so hard, we could have had something from him by now. Why'd you do that?"

The first voice was angry now. "For the last fucking time, I didn't hit him; he must have cracked his head when we shoved him in the car. Don't go blaming me. I wasn't the one who let that bald bastard Hounslow set us up and get Mikey and the others blown to bits."

"That wasn't Billy's fault and you know it. When we took on this job, we knew that Hounslow worked for Mr. Delgado, which is why we trusted him. Mr. Delgado has always been straight with us. But he is getting impatient, Gaz, he wants some return on his investment and at the moment the only one who is making anything out of this is Hounslow, 'cos he has the paintings and we need to know where he is."

"Alright, alright, I know that, and we will find him, because this one will tell us when he wakes up."

"If he wakes up, Gaz, if he wakes up. He's been out cold for nearly twenty-four hours now and we have got nowhere."

"We can wait. No-one has any idea where we are and with all this flooding on the roads the cops have got their hands full, so they won't bother searching very hard."

"They'll have the car registration though, 'cos they knew that we was behind them."

"Yeh, but what good will it do, the car will have been reported stolen by now anyway, so they can just keep looking. I ain't heard no helicopters, and that would be the only way they'd spot it."

"What about satellite cameras?"

"What? You watch too much fucking TV, Billy. Where would local Welsh filth get access to satellite cameras? This isn't NCIS, Billy."

"Not unless it stands for 'No-one Cares In Swansea', Billy boy."

The conversation had at least answered many of Michael's questions about the explosion at the gallery, and given the small balding figure a name, Hounslow. It triggered a memory, and a first name Jeffrey, Jeffrey Hounslow. He had seemed an innocuous, mild mannered man, of little significance; he knew his subject, but he was rather too intense, Michael hadn't taken to him, and in hindsight his judgement had been correct. He wondered where he was, and how many paintings he had taken with him. He really hoped that all of his had been destroyed, but since Hounslow obviously intended him to die in the explosion then taking his own hideous daubings would have made sense, their value would surely have been trebled by his demise.

The voices next door were becoming louder, and it had now become an argument.

"What's wrong with giving him a little slap to wake him up?"

"Because he might actually be damaged and then we will get nothing from him at all."

"Well, how long are we going to wait?"

"As long as it takes."

"What if we got a doctor to wake him up for us?"

"What with some drug or something?"

"Yeh, at least he'd know what he was doing."

"We can't bring a doctor here, Billy. He'd know where we was and …"

"I didn't say we let him go again after, we dump him when we dump the other one, the artist."

"He's got a point, Gaz, we can't wait forever. What if he's not going to wake up at all?"

"Of course, he's going to wake up, all he did was bang his fucking head, I keep telling you. We …"

Gaz was interrupted by the door opening and it sounded as if someone had run in,

"Gaz out front I heard voices! Sounds like there's loads of them."

"What? How did they find us?"

"I don't know, do I?"

"Well, get back out and take a look?"

"Billy, check the back, Charlie the side."

Michael heard a lot of running around and shouting, doors banging and chairs crashing to the floor, then Gaz could be heard over the others.

"Right, there's a good dozen of them and they're tooled up, but so are we."

The sound of smashing glass and then a burst of gunfire was followed by a pause, then a thump at the window behind Michael. He turned to try and see the window. He wondered why the police would still be trying to get in, when the kidnappers were obviously armed. What he saw answered his question. Whatever his captors were seeing, to him there were two snarling Tsarg, their jaws snapped at the glass, and their eyes were wide with terror.

More gunfire exploded from the other room; the frantic shouting broke out.

"They're still coming, Gaz!"

"Keep firing, Charlie."

"I'm not going down for killing coppers, Gaz"

"Give it here!" More gunfire.

"You killed them, Gaz! I'm getting out of here."

"Shut the fuck up! If they want to get shot that's their problem."

"Gaz, you shot two coppers, we'll go down for life for that."

"They've got to catch us first." Another burst of gunfire preceded the door of the room bursting open and a small wiry man in a black tracksuit diving through it. He held an automatic weapon of some kind. He took one look at the window and fired a long burst, shattering the glass. Michael saw the Tsarg snap out of existence; the man with the gun assumed that he had killed them all and had cleared the exit. His colleagues piled into the room behind him and saw an escape route. One of them pushed Gaz out of the way and started to climb through but he was confronted by two more snarling Tsarg. He fell back, and Gaz fired full into the face of the first Tsarg to come through the window. Again, the crack as it vanished, as did the Tsarg who had climbed through ignoring the broken glass.

"What the fuck?"

"Let's get out of here." All four men began a rush to try and make a break for it, when one more Tsarg appeared at the window. The largest of the men staggered back and fell against Gaz knocking the weapon from his hands; one of the others lashed out with a fist and fell forward as his blow removed the Tsarg from the room. His captors were now in a complete panic, they ran back out of the room, shoving each other out of the way except for Gaz who had started to follow, but then decided to leap through the now clear window frame.

Michael heard more muffled shouts and sirens followed by the screech of tyres; he tried to sit up, but he found his head spinning once more, as the half-repaired room tore away and became once more his damp cold and dark cell in the dungeons of King Leenal's palace.

★★★

He had no idea how long he had been lying there. He felt cold and stiff. He stretched his legs and rolled into a sitting position. Down in his cell there was little hint of the time of day, a filthy metal plate lay near him with the remains of a hunk of bread. He had been here long enough for food to have been thrown in and some hungry scurrying cellmate had devoured it. A day? Two days? He fought down a mixture of relief and anger at the way that he was thrown between worlds. He had accepted that it had been convenient to be unconscious while in captivity, but he knew in his heart that someone was controlling him, and he resented it. He had been told that he had choices to make but he could not even choose where he was and when he switched. The frustration would have driven him crazy had he not still felt that there was a reason for it all, a purpose, a truth, as Uxl had said, that somehow somewhere, someone would make sense of it all. He sought for something to settle his mind so that he wouldn't start to brood on the thoughts that swirled around in his mind.

He focused his eyes and tried to make out the details of the cell, it was larger than he had first thought, being a segment of the circle created by the curve of the tower. He could just make out the large regular blocks of the walls, the face of each furred with lichen and mould. A memory came to him from his school days of looking down a microscope at just such a stone. The strange unearthly shapes, a landscape of hollow hills, pale bark-less trees, delicate sails of emerald lace, bulbous protuberances of vibrant amethyst and amongst them bizarre crawling forms that existed in their own isolated world disconnected, separated from all, no sense of being observed, no knowledge of the eyes that bore down upon it.

He hadn't thought it then, but he did now; he had had the power to destroy that world, wipe away their existence with a sweep of his hand, or, should he have chosen to, to interfere, manipulate, nudge and poke, subtly direct the secluded existence, become in that moment a god. Was that how it was for the Powers? Was that the choice they faced? Destruction, manipulation or obey the rules and only observe in silence? Just then, the sound of a bolt being drawn back signalled the door being opened, as it swung out and the flickering light of a torch rushed in to fill the darkness. He saw that he had three visitors, who stood before a guard holding the flaming torch.

His visitors he recognised as Gath, Tuggid and Palvir, but now all were dressed for war. Michael noted as they stepped into his cell that they wore dark red tunics below their breastplates, which bore not the Malan Hawk of the High King, but a skarl before an ice-white tree, similar to the one he had seen in the courtyard above. It was Tuggid who spoke first.

"Mikael, three men of Darnak wish to bid you farewell. We ride out to face this traitor Faradon and his legions with strength in our hearts, but sadness also that you are not with us. I cannot claim to understand the words of the Seers, but Sorin saved my son Palvir here and I would trust him with my life, therefore I believe you to be guiltless and there is much shame in your imprisonment. But we cannot go against the High King, or his Queen, and thus we are helpless for now, but when we return it will be a different matter. Farewell." He reached down and he grasped Michael's hand warmly, as did Palvir, who muttered.

"I don't believe any of it Mikael."

Gath bent down and grasped him by the shoulders and looked him in the eyes. "I see no evil in you, Mikael Dal Oaken, only evil that has been laid upon you. We will right this wrong when time allows. Farewell."

Michael could not stand for the chain around his hands prevented it, but he was touched by their words. "I would have been proud to ride out with you, Men of Darnak, I have few friends that are truer in all of Taleth and I pray with all my heart that the Powers keep you safe. Be wary, there is much treachery still to be revealed. I do not think that Piat Kahord is the man the King thinks he is. Farewell."

Three fists thumped their chests in salute and then they were gone, and the door slammed back into place. Michael really did hope with all his heart that they would come through it all, he had grown very fond of them in their travels together and he realised that he could not think of anyone save David, and perhaps now Netti, that he would feel quite the same about back in the world he had just left. He had met many people and most of them were shallow and self-seeking. So many dinner parties, so many conversations filled with clever words that meant nothing. These men he had fought with, ridden with, laughed with, sung with. Their friendship was honest, loyal and so real that he could sense it in their handshake, see it in their eyes. He did not blame his so-called friends from his former life; the fault was his as much as theirs. He had never invested time in anyone except Mel and she … well, she was dead.

His thoughts were interrupted by the bolt once more scraping across the door, this time slowly as if the hand that moved it required quiet. The door swung open slowly and this time there was no guard, just a robed and hooded figure, who stepped inside and pulled the door shut. Without a word, the figure set the torch in a socket on the wall and bending down, signalled Michael to turn around, whereupon his chains were removed. As he turned back and rubbed the soreness from his wrists, he stood to thank his visitor, but his thanks died on his lips as he saw her in the light and realised who it was. It was the Hooded Seer.

"You? Have you come to do what the Queen would not?"

Her voice was no longer harsh, no longer cutting. "No, Mikael Dal Oaken, I have come to give explanation, for such you deserve and by explaining hope to gain your forgiveness. I ask you to listen and then decide whether you believe me or no, and as a sign of good faith I will open myself to you." She reached up and pushed her hood back from her head and Michael could not prevent a gasp escaping his lips. He had expected, due to Sepho's description, some sort of malformation, some repugnant scaring, some reason for the face to be hidden. But there was none, he was confronted not with ugliness or deformity, but with a beautiful woman, long dark hair, braided with ribbons that matched her robes, a pale face, near perfect in shape and form, the only abnormality were eyes which were entirely white and sightless.

"You are blind, I didn't know."

"No, none but the Queen herself have that knowledge, now that my mother is dead. Yes, I am blind, but my gift allows me to see in a way that is different to others. I need no stick to tap my way along the streets, I need no guide to walk me through this crowded city, like the false Seer Galeanid who sees as well as you, Mikael. His pretence is for the benefit of the Queen, who misguidedly believes that blindness somehow makes 'the Sight' purer. She is wrong in this. My 'Sight', my Gift, is strong and clear, but I do not see as you do. I am told that the world is filled with colour, which I cannot truly see, however, I see the heat upon your skin; I see the breath as it leaves your mouth and returns to the air. In summer, I see the columns of warm air that the flocks of Ballos use to rise so high, in winter I see the frost as it creeps through the air to settle on the trees. Oh, I am blind, but only to those who see little that stands before them."

Michael listened to her words and he felt the poetry in them; she saw a beauty in the world that was hers and hers alone. She spoke with a reverence that led him to feel that he must trust her even before she had truly explained herself.

"You listen now with a more friendly ear, Mikael, I am glad for your friendship is all that I desire, well … perhaps not all, but there are things I can never have, not in this life." He felt her white eyes upon him and there was a sadness in her words. "I have seen you in my dreams, Mikael Dal Oaken, and although I had never met you in the flesh I have long known you and known the true pain of duty above self."

She paused and cast her eyes down. Michael felt the emotion in her words, but he refused to let himself accept what she was saying. She raised her head and her cheeks were moist with tears. She fought to keep her voice steady. "I acted against you on the strictest of instructions from visions that I had received. Mikael, one of the Powers was adamant that you must not be allowed to ride out with the High King. That you must be delayed and imprisoned until the army had left. I was told to threaten your life. It scared me, what if the King had agreed, given orders for your execution; I could not have lived with your blood spilled by my hands. But I must follow the course I am given, or my Sight is nothing, my Gift is worthless. You must go to the mountains of the Nare, I know not why, but that is your path. I am glad that the King gave orders that you not be harmed, I truly am. Forgive me, Mikael, I feel so empty for betraying you like this, but my instructions were so precise. *'The Twice-Dead must remain in the city, he must not leave.'* Please, say that you understand." She stepped forward and she grasped his hands. Michael felt a deep warmth surging up his arms and filling his body.

His mind raced to the conclusion that he had resisted. *'This is passion, this is love, this is desire.'* How could he not believe her, or forgive her?

"I forgive you." He heard her sigh, a sound that strangely thrilled him in the silent dark, and then he saw a smile break across her pale lips. "And though I do not understand what game it is that the Powers are playing, I am willing to accept that some things are better left unquestioned. Yes, I forgive you, your reasons were honest and your intent pure."

"Thank you, Mikael, know that my true name I give to you, a name few have ever known, I am Siraal." She still held his arms, and as he looked down into her sightless eyes, she drew closer and whispered. "And this I steal for love's sake." Reaching up she kissed him lightly on the lips. "Live and be safe, Mikael, I will do all that I can." Then she was gone, closing the door and sliding back the bolt.

Michael realised that he was trembling. This outpouring by Siraal had taken him completely by surprise. Now he understood her gesture as he had been dragged away from the High King's chamber. She loved him, had loved him from the world of dreams and visions that she inhabited. Had he not felt the strength of her passion, he would not have believed it possible, but there was so much now to believe that would have seemed impossible before; that he was forced to imagine for a moment that perhaps he was still in his coma, and everything was one long journey of a mind lost in fantasy. No, that he would not contemplate, he had come too far, he had felt too much, felt with more intensity than ever in his life before. He tried to calm himself. He shut his eyes and tried to listen to the sounds outside his prison. Very little reached him, through the walls. He heard somewhere a drip, drip of water, the clang and clatter of a gate being shut, footsteps on the stones of a stairway, and then the braying of horns shattered the quiet before being joined by the strident beating of massed drums.

The ground thundered and shook as thousands of hooves began to pound and stamp upon the stones of Tath Garnir. The High King's army was moving, riding out to the war that Lord Faradon's treachery had set in motion. The horns continued to sound and the rumbling above ground fairly shook the stones around him. Michael realised that even though final proof of treachery had appeared to be a shock to the King and his commander, Grald had ensured that the army was prepared and ready to move. He tried to picture the scene that was being enacted above and then memories flooded into his mind, Mikael's memories, of watching lines of fluttering banners held high by proud warriors riding down upon a field of jade, drums and horns sounding, swords clashing against armour, a roar rising from a thousand throats. The might of the Cluath riding out to battle. Michael's heart began to pound, and he felt the rush of blood as Mikael yearned to be amongst it all. The sound and the memories faded away, the stones ceased to sympathise with the juddering of the streets above. He knew that the city would still be noisy and alive, but down here in the dark it seemed to him as if the world had been emptied of people and that he had been left behind.

Then unbidden a melody came into his head, a song that he hadn't heard since he was a child, no, he had never heard it. It was a song that Mikael's mother had sung to him as a young child. A voice began to sing, but no echo of a face accompanied it.

"Wait, my little one, wait,
For all your dreams, they are just beyond
The brow of yonder hill.
Wait, my little one, wait.

Hold, my little one, hold,
My heart will break if too soon you crest
The brow of yonder hill.
Hold, my little one, hold.

When you are grown,
Dreams you may chase,
Then all the world you'll see.
When you are grown,
Then join the race,
To find what you will be.

But, my little one, wait,
For I will have lost you when beyond
The brow of yonder hill
You rush to meet your fate."

It was a song to melt any heart, as if she had known even then that she would not live to see her son grow to be a man. Michael felt the tears as they fell and as he wiped them away, he found himself wondering how much of a father he would have been had Mel had a child. To be a father alone and to be everything to a son without it ever being enough. Such sadness he had felt in Mikael, to need so much and yet the love that he had found was stern and hidden.

The sound of the bolt being drawn back once more brought him out of the well of thoughts into which Mikael's childhood had drawn him. The door opened once more and once again the light of a torch flooded into the cell. This time his visitor was Sorin. He set the torch as Siraal had done and with a gesture to Michael to remain quiet, he checked outside the door and then pulled it closed.

"Well, that was easier than I had expected, the guards all appear to be in a deep sleep, not something that I would have expected. You would almost think that someone had drugged them, so as to leave you unguarded, and who might have done something like that, I wonder. Have you had any other visitors?"

"Yes, Tuggid and the others came to say goodbye."

"Ah, yes, I thought they might, but they wouldn't have needed to …"

"And the Hooded Seer."

"What? And left you alive?"

"Yes, in fact she was very friendly." Michael told Sorin what Siraal had said about her visions and about Galeanid, but he kept the rest to himself, it wasn't something Sorin needed to know, not yet at least.

"Now that is very intriguing, and she would certainly have the knowledge to dispose of your guards for a while. Well, so we have an unexpected ally, do we? It may be extremely useful, it may not, and Galeanid is a fraud, good that makes it easier. I still need to question him about the medallion that Uxl gave us." He paused for a moment, as if trying to remember something that he needed to say but couldn't quite locate in his head. "I'm sorry, I didn't come earlier, but I actually thought that you would be safer in here, at least while the King was still in the city. Now that he has gone, things may change of course, we have made an enemy of the Queen, I fear, which was not my intention, but unavoidable I suspect."

Michael then asked a question that had been in his mind throughout much of the ill-tempered meeting. "Does Piat Kahord have the powers he claims to have? Is he as powerful as Calix was?"

At first Sorin was silent, and then he laughed. "Piat Kahord is no fool. He either believes he has learned a power which he could never possess, or he is leading Leenal into a trap and will desert him at the last moment." He chuckled to himself again.

"I don't see that it is something to laugh at." Sorin didn't appear to be taking this very seriously. "If you are right, thousands of men are riding to their deaths."

"No, you are right, it is not in the least bit amusing, ignore me." He did appear to try, but there was still a hint of levity in his voice. "It is just that if people still sang the old songs and told the old stories they might learn from history and not repeat it. I will explain more about Piat Kahord when I return, I have a little errand to run … and by the sound of it the guards are waking up. I will be back very soon." With that Sorin slipped out of the door and replaced the bolt.

Michael was about to call after him and ask why he had to remain in the cell when the bolt was slid back for a third time, this time with some violence and a guard stood in the doorway, he had a bowl which he slid across the floor towards Michael. It contained a congealed mess which may once have been a stew of some kind. It was cold, grey and disgusting.

Michael's irritation at Sorin boiled over towards the guard. "I'm not eating that filth!"

The guard, who was still groggy from the sleeping draught that Siraal had administered, was initially taken aback. "You will eat it. We have orders to keep you alive and we always do as we're told, so you will eat it. Or I will come in there and make you eat it."

"And you think that you could do that do you?"

"I would take pleasure in it. The King wants you alive, for some reason, traitor, but that doesn't mean that we have to be nice to you." Michael's blood was up, and he decided that he was not going to take abuse without a fight,

"I am no traitor. I am a man of honour and that food is not fit for any man."

"The Queen has named you traitor so a traitor you are." The guard hadn't expected any trouble from him, after all he had been unconscious for nigh on two days. "Once you are past these doors, traitor," he was determined to hammer in the nails and fix the name, "you are in my hands. If I say you will eat it, you will eat it. And force it down your treacherous throat I will, if you keep on with your defiance."

"Then that is what you will have to do, for I will eat nothing willingly that comes from the hand of a man who names me traitor."

"So be it, traitor."

Michael knew that the guard was under the assumption that he was still chained and so he would have the advantage of surprise, he prepared himself to spring upwards and try and bring the guard down before he had a chance to defend himself, but he never got the chance. As his opponent stepped into the cell a figure appeared behind him and the guard was suddenly on the floor with Dak kneeling upon his back.

"It would appear, my friend that you know little of the finer arts of cooking."

"Get off me, you …"

"Now, now, don't interrupt, it isn't polite." He spun the guard over on to his back and then he held him down with one hand over his mouth. "You have offered a friend of mine food, that frankly isn't fit for a durg, but if it is fit to eat then I think it is up to you to set us an example. Mikael pass our friend his breakfast."

The guard struggled hard but Dak had him in a strong grip. Michael slid the plate across the floor and then he joined Dak in holding him down.

Dak had not realised that Michael was free of his chains. "Ah, Mikael, that makes things easier, did Sorin free your hands?"

"No, but I will explain later."

"Shall we feed this animal, Mikael, or do you think he has changed his mind about the contents of this bowl."

Dak released his hand allowing the guard a few moments of speech. "Get off me, you filthy Nare, I'll break your …" The hand was replaced.

"No, you won't, but I am willing to let you try once we have finished with this matter of sustenance. Is this bowl of slop fit to eat?" Again, the hand was removed.

"Let me up and I'll …" Once more the hand was clamped across his mouth.

"That is still the wrong answer. So, I'm afraid, since you were prepared to force this upon Mikael here, we will have to return the favour." He took the bowl and he raised it towards the guard's face. "I'll ask you only one more time, is this fit to eat."

This time the guard had got the message, when Dak released his hand he gulped for air and he appeared to have changed his mind. "No, you're right its slop. Don't make me eat it, I …"

"Ah, now we have the truth of the matter, good." He threw the plate into the corner of the cell. "Now, after all that mental exertion, I feel that you deserve a rest." He struck the guard a sharp blow on the side of the head and he slumped back to the floor. "There is never an excuse for ill-treating prisoners, Mikael. I could have sent our friend to sleep immediately, but he needed to learn an important lesson."

"It is good to see you Dak but is there any chance of an explanation. Sorin came and went but explained little."

"You want to know what is going on? You are asking the wrong person, Mikael, my friend. I have spent most of my time sitting around being told to be silent, even when insulted by those who should know better. Then when I suggest rescuing you Sorin turns around and says, *'No, why should we do that, he's better off where he is for the moment'.*" Dak's impersonation of Sorin's walk and his crackling voice made Michael laugh out loud, it was very accurate and extremely unflattering. "And then after a day of kicking our heels, he pipes up, *'Now I need to see Mikael.'* So in we sneak, only to find half the guards are drugged and the others are off to the war. Then to cap it all, off he suddenly disappears and says wait here and do nothing. Well, I had had enough of doing nothing and that meant someone was going to have to amuse me. So, when your guard woke up and I heard you shout I thought that sounds exactly what I need. But as to what is going on, I have no idea? And there is probably little point in asking him, for even if he knows he won't tell you, you of all people should know what he is like."

Sorin chose that precise moment to reappear through the cell door. "I have a suspicion, Dakveen, that you were complaining about me."

"Not at all, Sorin, I never complain."

Sorin gave him a hard stare, but then chuckled his dry laugh. "No, nor do you ever impersonate me for Mikael's amusement. Do I really walk like that? Never mind don't tell me, Danil is bringing our guest."

"Guest? Are we having a banquet?"

"I hope not, Mikael, the victuals in this part of the palace leave a lot to be desired."

"What about the other guards are they still drugged?"

"No, but Dak, here decided that they needed some more sleep."

"There were only three out there and this one, it wasn't difficult to persuade them."

"Who is Danil bringing down here?" Michael's question was answered by the arrival of Danil pushing a belligerent Galeanid before him.

"The Queen will have your head for this, you aberration, I will see to it that your death is slow and painful." Danil pushed him to his knees. "Where have you brought me? What are you going to do?" Danil suddenly drew his knife and, pulling up the Seer's head, held the blade to his throat.

"Now, you old fraud, before I slit you from ear to ear, tell me how you, a blind man, recognised me enough to pour forth abuse and insult upon me as we walked?"

The Seer squirmed away from the knife. "By your voice, I knew you by your voice."

"My voice?" Danil did not release the pressure and his answer was couched in tones of pure menace. "But I did not speak, Galeanid, not one word; you were the one doing all the talking. Now, you asked where you are. You tell me. Where are we? Where have I brought you?"

Galeanid breath came in short gasps and sweat sat upon his brow above the bandage that covered his eyes. "How can I tell you? I am blind, you know that."

"Me? I'm a half-wit half-breed, I know nothing. Tell me where we are. My hand is getting tired and when my hands are tired, they shake terribly."

Galeanid was failing to keep his mounting panic from creeping into his words. "I don't know … how could I know, I am blind I tell you!" The knife pushed harder and a few drops of blood squeezed their way along the blade. "Alright, alright, we're in the dungeons, down in the dungeons. I see well enough; the blindness is a lie." The blade slipped away from his neck, where the faintest red line was now visible. "You cut me! You actually cut me. You didn't have to do that." His head swung around to Sorin. "This half-breed cut me!"

"Here." Sorin reached forward and he ripped the bandage from his face. "Wipe your neck, I wouldn't have let him kill you, I have need of you. Mind you when you are no longer useful, I may not be able to control him. You know what half-breeds are like."

Galeanid stood up angrily and held the bandage to his neck. "He cut me."

"Yes, so you keep saying and if you are not co-operative, I may let him cut you again. He has many blades and they are all equal in sharpness to their fellows. So, tell me why the pretence of blindness, the bandage, the guide."

"Why should I tell you anything?"

Sorin kept his voice even, despite his irritation. "I thought that we had already made that clear, because we will kill you if you don't, but since you refuse, let me supply the answer to my own question. You have pretended to be blind because the Queen has a liking for blind seers, having convinced herself that their gift is purer if they cannot see; which is of course a ridiculous notion, but you saw it as a way to gain favour at the Queen's elbow. Have you any portion left of the Sight that was gifted to you? I hope so, for your sake, because unfortunately I need your assistance."

"Help you?" Galeanid laughed, but it was strained, and it lacked humour. "You need my help? So Piat Kahord was right you are a fading relic, no match for him, not now that he has learned the powers of the ancients. What do you want me to do?"

"Just one simple thing." He took out the stone medallion as he spoke. "Tell me the significance of this object. I was told that you would know, although I have my doubts." He held it out to Galeanid, who looked at it and then pushed it back to-wards Sorin.

"No, I won't help you. You will not harm me, for if you did Piat Kahord would seek you out and revenge me."

"Oh, I tire of this." Sorin was barely controlling his rising anger. "Listen, and listen well, you old fool. Know that I have spoken with Leenal, privately, while he sat regaled in his amour. I have told him what I will now tell you. Piat Kahord cannot possibly know the secret of Mage-fire as it is called by some, for of all the Majann of old few there were who were offered the knowledge to wield it. Calix accepted and he learned the skill, as did others who had come before him, but all of them died long before Kintell came to the throne. Nuall too had the skill, but he died when he was consumed by a great wyrm. Ukthor, refused it, preferring air and water to fire, and then she sailed out onto the seas with the Sylian searching for the lost isle of Kuathat, and never returned. So very few Majann have survived who could have had the knowledge, and Calix taught it to no one before he vanished amongst the Tsarg, for it was not a gift that he could bestow. The King will be prepared now for blundering failure, or heinous treachery, whichever it turns out to be. I know which I consider most likely."

"How can you know for certain that Calix didn't pass it on." His face was contorted, twisted with contempt. He spat his words back like venom. "I will do nothing to help you, you are a liar, just as the Queen said. I will do nothing for you, and you cannot make me."

"Enough!" Sorin's roar shook the door in its hinges. "Enough of you." He grabbed Galeanid by his upper arms and he thrust him against the wall of the cell. As he held him there his body began to glow with an inner light, which filled his whole being. It was if he burned with the white fire, it rippled under his skin, danced around his fingers, and flashed from his eyes. Just as it seemed about to consume him, he released it in a searing flood, not directly at Galeanid, but against the wall behind him, which under such violent attack began to blister and bubble, melting before the force of Sorin's power.

Slowly Sorin pushed the incredulous Seer into the molten rock and held him there as the fire began to recede. It took only a moment for Galeanid to realise the appalling position that he was in. He struggled for release and finding his voice, he began to scream in panic.

"No, please, no, I'll help you, please. Sorin, forgive me …"

The stones of the wall were cooling around him and began to squeeze the air from his lungs. His eyes bulged in terror as death approached and then Sorin pulled him forward letting him fall to the floor of the cell, where he lay gulping in air and shaking. The rock of the wall hissed and creaked as it cooled, in protest at the way that it had been used, the twisted shape of a man permanently carved into the face of the stones.

Michael's heart pounded, with shock, fear, exhilaration, dread and joy in equal measure. Now he understood at last. The light of the white fire had cleared his mind and answered his question. Calix did not pass on his secret and breath-taking powers for Calix did not die. He lived on with a new name. His true power hidden for centuries, but ready when the time came to be revealed once more. Now Michael understood the pain, and the agony when Gath had quoted from the 'Lay of Magellin', Sorin's words came back to him. *'And yet Magellin was far lovelier. Hers was a beauty to still the heart and becalm the soul. Hair like golden sunlight, held in purest crystal. Eyes as blue as a mountain pool beneath the noonday sun. Skin that shimmered like the palest winter moon. Had she but once named Calix as her love, so many things may have been different.'* No, Calix had not died, he stood before them now. Michael glanced across at Danil and knew that he too had made the same leap; he saw a look of fierce triumph in his green eyes. Here was a weapon against Corruption that he would remember and perhaps even fear.

Sorin did not look at the others, he kicked the sprawling shape of Galeanid, and he held out the stone medallion, his voice had returned to normal, but his tone was severe. "Now you will tell me what I need to know?"

Galeanid, still shook and with his breathing short and pained, he struggled up onto his knees. He took the round stone circle and he closed his hands over it. "Yes … wait … I need to …" then as his True Sight reasserted itself after a long sleep, his body stiffened, his eyes closed, and his voice became steady and firm. "Know you now that this is a key. The first key. The key to Ruok Vuall, the Place of the First Ones. They made it as a meeting place, a place of sharing, a place of safety. There they kept guarded all their most precious treasures; the first writing, the first sounds, the first waters, the first fire, and the first breath. They gathered them all and set a guard to keep them safe so that all would remember. They saw it as a sacred trust. Ruok Vuall was to be sealed and locked with this key, but one there was who had a desire to see the world once more, he felt that there was a truth in him to be found beyond the walls of Ruok Vuall. So, sealing the chamber, he left to seek his truth, intending to return to take his place amongst them. He took the key with him vowing to keep it safe. Now you hold it, Sorin,

Majann and healer, Uxl the Tarr bids you use it as you see fit." With a shudder Galeanid fell sideways and lay silent.

"So, his sight was true, his blindness false, can we trust his words?" Danil bent down and he retrieved the Key and handed it to Sorin.

"Oh, yes, I think we may, his sight was one of searching for understanding, not revealing the future, there would be little to gain from interfering with his vision. But I suspect that he will sleep for a while; he has not used his power for many a year, if my guess is right."

"In that case, I will chain both where Mikael lay, and let the guards deal with them when we are gone." Dak seemed to be ignoring the revelation that had occurred within the cell, but Michael could not.

"So, Sorin, are you going to tell us, or must we ask the question?"

"Ah, yes." Sorin seemed to gather his thoughts. "Yes, the small matter of Calix. Well, he did not die, he lived as you have guessed with a new name, not the one he uses now, he has had many names, Sorin is the last I suspect." He turned towards the door of the cell. "Do not ask me, how I survived, that is a tale I will not relive, nor how I have lived so long, that is not yours to know, yet, suffice it to say that I was Calix and know all that he knew, feel all that he felt, suffered all that he suffered, my memory is long, and I have woken to days beyond number. For me rest will come when all I have been tasked with is complete. Come, a long journey awaits, and I grow weary." He took a step through the door and stumbled, reaching out to grasp the door for support. Danil caught his arm and he helped to steady him. "Ah, my friend, none of you can know how much it takes to wield such power. I am so tired."

Michael and Dak both moved to help support him, but it was Dak who lifted Sorin onto his back., "Come, mighty Majann, be it Sorin or Calix, your name is not relevant, I will be honoured to carry you for a while, for I suspect haste is now required."

"Dakveen, I would normally consider this a most inappropriate position for a man of my standing to be in, but I really have not the energy to argue. Yes, haste is now required. We must leave the city in silence and secrecy. Vitta and Sentielle wait for us beyond the walls and then our journey truly starts, for we have a long way to go."

"You intend still then to take me to the mountains, to the lands of my people?" Michael was surprised by this, Dak and Sorin had obviously settled this matter when Michael was not present. He wondered if Dak knew that his people were dying. Sorin flashed a thought to him. *'I have persuaded Dak to return, but he does not yet know the true picture. We must break that to him gently. Leave it to me for the present.'*

"Yes, Dak, that is the way our path lies, as I have explained, and then beyond I feel. Uxl means me to go Ruok Vuall. That is why he has given me the key, there is a truth there that calls us." Michael caught a glance from Sorin, and he understood. *'Ah, yes,'* he thought, *'the Chiatt Crystal will be there, in the Place of the First Ones.'* His dreams of a chamber midst the ice-capped mountain peaks flashed back into his mind. Mikael had guessed it too. *'That is where the choice will be made, Michael, at Ruok Vuall.'* As they walked along the stone corridors beneath the palace, he felt their footsteps echoed with the hollow sound of a far-off bell ringing out for the bringer of Doom.

They walked on in silence for a while, down the darkened corridor, which to Michael's surprise sloped downwards. Danil then signalled a stop and he bent down to lift a metal grate that was set into the floor. He motioned Michael to follow him and then dropped through into the darkness. Michael did not like not knowing what there was below him, but he trusted Danil and he did as he had been told. The drop was short and ended in a splash; Danil pulled him to one side as Dak lowered Sorin down through the hole. There was a pause and then Dak followed, he held a short rope in his hand, with a gentle tug he pulled the grate shut behind them. He then once more lifted the sagging form of Sorin onto his back and they moved along the tunnel, feet splashing through the water.

Michael could see nothing of the walls, and he wondered if this was a drainage channel built by men or if it was a natural waterway carved by the water that ran past his feet. The water had not the smell of a drain but was fast moving so he could not be certain. Dak led the way, his Nare eyes being best suited to the task. No-one spoke, although Michael suspected none would have heard had they done so. The slope was not excessive, so their progress was not difficult, and Michael fell to wondering where they would come out. He knew that there were two rivers at least that flowed through Tath Garnir, after all he had fallen into one of them. Sorin had said that they were to meet Vitta outside the walls, but it was unlikely that this tunnel would rise beyond them. He was right, for after about half an hour's steady walking the noise of rushing water rose dramatically in volume and Dak called a halt.

He lowered Sorin to the ground and the cold of the water woke him with a start. "Ah, the river, I hear it, good. Thank you, Dak, I am in your debt."

"Indeed, I will remember." Dak laughed quietly as he lit a torch which Danil had taken from the wall. In its light Michael saw that they stood on a ledge and way below them was the river that passed below the city. It rushed with wild abandon below them and disappeared away into darkness. Stretched out across the water was a flimsy rope bridge that swayed back and forth in what Michael considered to be a most disconcerting manner.

"Sorin do you have the strength to make the crossing, or should we rest?"

"I will be fine, Danil, I am not fully recovered, but nor am I incapable."

Danil did not appear convinced. "Let me tie a safety line for you, my friend."

"Nonsense, there is no need. I am tired, but I will not fall."

Dak looked at him and shook his head. "Well, if you do you will not find me diving after you. I cannot swim."

"Thank you, Dak, that is most reassuring. If it makes you happier, we will rest for a moment, but we cannot know how long it will be before they discover that Mikael has gone, nor decide whether they will pursue us at all."

"I thought that the Queen would be anxious to keep me locked up?"

"Oh, I expect she is, but how much of her display of anger was real is hard to tell."

Danil took a rope from the pack that he carried. "Her anger was real, Sorin, she does not accept the truth of what is happening. She sees it only as another threat to her position, another disobedient Cluath Lord, who will be crushed. She has lived too long sheltered from the reality that faces the outer lands. She has never seen a Tsarg warband bearing down on a defenceless homestead, nor heard the screams of children put to the sword." The depth of Danil's anger was evident in his voice. "She believes the tales of Tsarg under Faradon's command to be a fabrication, lies to draw the King into battle. She listens to the meaningless riddles and dissembling from the Seers but not to the truth from honest men. There, now you will not fall." While he had been talking, he had knotted the rope and tied it around his waist and he now attached the other end to Sorin, who was going to protest, but then he decided that it was for the best.

"I am touched by your concern, Danil, and your assessment of Finah is quite possibly true. However, we must always consider the possibility of manipulation, by those that remain hidden by choice. She is susceptible to those with the power to bend others to their will." Danil had finished and he seemed satisfied with the line he had set between himself and the old man. "Happy now?"

"I will be happy when we are outside the walls, Sorin."

"Come on then."

★★★

5

'Jaws that slice'

Danil set out first and he worked his way across the swaying bridge. It was made up of two parallel ropes upon which you set your feet and two higher ropes that acted as handrails. Every so often the four ropes were connected with cross ropes, set to keep the others from swaying apart. Michael was sure that there should have been many more of these. Sorin started across after Danil had reached the first of these cross ropes. He moved slowly but he appeared confident. When they were halfway across, Danil called back for Dak to follow, and the Nare set his feet upon the rope. Whether it was his weight upon the rope or just coincidence was hard to tell, but at the same moment as Dak's foot moved along the rope, Sorin stumbled and fell. Danil must have sensed what was about to happen for he had instantly wrapped the higher rope around one arm and braced himself to take the strain. Sorin's fall was short and though he was stunned for a moment, he managed to swing himself upright and to hold the rope to keep himself in that position.

Dak began to move as swiftly as he could across to where Danil gripped the rope, "Mikael, stay off the bridge until we have him on the other side."

"Very well, if you are sure."

"I am, if you fall you have no rope to catch you."

Michael watched as Dak reached the straining Danil and then lay down upon the two lower ropes. He slipped his legs under and hooked them securely on both sides and then he took the weight of the rope that held Sorin. Danil was glad of the help and between them they pulled the Majann back up to the bridge. Danil and Dak then moved to the other side with Sorin sandwiched between them. Michael could not hear if they spoke, but he saw Sorin sit down upon the ground with some relief as Dak's arm waved him across. It was easier than he had expected, and he was making reasonable progress when, on looking down, something in the water caught his eye; a dark shape that had not been there before, moving from side to side in the current to keep itself stationary. He had seen fish do the same in a river, but this was far too big to be a fish, it was twice a man's length at least. Michael did not know what it might be, but he felt that being over the water was now not a good idea. He tried to move faster, but that made the rope swing uncomfortably, so he had to keep at his steady slow pace. He looked down and the shape appeared to have gone. It hadn't. It had let itself slip back a little to give itself room to build up speed. Michael barely had time to shout before a huge shape leapt out of the water in an arc as it aimed for the bridge, and what was on it.

What leapt from the water was certainly fish-like in shape, but it had rows of sharp teeth in its gaping mouth, it had four bulging eyes across its wide head and its skin was leathery and reptilian. It had powerful broad flippers and a horizontal tail, which allowed it to drive upstream and leap as it now did. Its first attack was misjudged because it fell short of the bridge, but Michael sensed that that would be followed by another more accurate attack. He was close enough to hear the others now, but still only halfway across.

Dak had untied Danil and he quickly sought to remove the rope from Sorin. "Mikael keep moving, I will get this rope to you, whatever that was will return."

"I know, I can see it under the water." It was dropping back for a second attack.

"Keep moving, Mikael, I will give it something else to think about." Danil was fitting an arrow to his bow as he spoke.

Michael decided that he would not look down or behind him; he focused on moving as swiftly as he could, but the bank got no closer it seemed. Suddenly he heard Dak shout. "There! It comes!" He still did not turn but he looked ahead at Danil who had released an arrow and was already fitting another. Then the bridge was struck violently downwards behind him, the monster had missed his attack, distracted by Danil, no doubt. Michael gripped the ropes for all he was worth, as the impact juddered along the bridge. He then heard a huge splash as the monster struck the water of the river. Would it attack again? How much had Danil hurt the beast? He saw Dak with the rope ahead of him,

"Here, grab this and be ready, I will pull you up should you fall."

Dak threw the rope to him and Michael looped it around his right arm as quickly as he could, not a moment too soon before the third attack came, and this time the leap took the creature high enough to land squarely upon the bridge, which sagged for a moment and then admitted defeat. Michael felt the first of the hand ropes snap and then he was knocked forward by the re-coil as the second rope too gave up the ghost. He flung his left arm across Dak's rope and gripped on, just in time to feel the walk ropes tear under the weight of the brute and the bridge disintegrate. He held on for all he was worth as he swung down and into the steeply sloping bank. The impact knocked the air from his body and stunned him, but his grip remained firm, he heard Dak shouting but could catch nothing of his words as they were lost amidst the choir of singing waters. He had not quite reached the swirling surface of the river in his downward plunge, but he could feel the spray around his ankles. He knew he needed to act, move upwards, but it took some moments to regain full control of his senses.

Looking up he saw Dak stepping away from the edge with the rope across his shoulders and he tried to bring his legs up against the earth and rock that faced him, to help propel him upwards. He hoped that the creature was unable to swim close enough to the bank to mount an attack, but he was mistaken. He had managed a few stumbling steps and moved perhaps a body length when jaws snapped below him, far too close below him for comfort. He tried to shout above the noise, but there was no need, Danil must have seen the need and was now help-ing Dak, because he began to move more quickly upwards and, despite another attempt by the vicious rows of teeth on display beneath him, he had soon crested the edge of the bank amidst the ruin of the bridge and was being pulled to safety. He sat for a while beside Sorin and tried to rub some feeling into his arm and calm his shattered nerves.

Sorin had not attempted to help, he was more drained than he had cared to admit, and he appeared to feel that Danil and Dak had the situation well in hand. "They're blind you know." He spoke with his eyes closed and his arms around his knees, "Their eyes are a relic from when they lived solely in the ocean. But they were hunted by the Sylian, so they swam up rivers such as this, or swam down out of their reach, to dwell in darkness. Now they hunt by smelling out their prey, I am told, and fear has a strong scent."

"But I wasn't scared until it attacked."

Sorin managed a laugh. "No, but I was."

Michael smiled, although Sorin could not see him. "What was it anyway?"

"Sloovili Saresh, the Sylian name them, it means 'Jaws that Slice' in the Cluath tongue, but they are usually referred to as Blind Slicers, by such as those who built the bridge. Smugglers and thieves mainly, who needed a hidden escape route from the city."

"The name suits it; those teeth were certainly vicious. Do they often get that big?"

"Oh, that was a young one."

"A young one?" Michael couldn't keep the note of disbelief from his voice.

"Oh, yes, I'm told that out in the deep ocean they can reach six or seven times that size, big enough to topple even the largest boats. Mind you, I have never sailed out onto the open seas myself, so I have no personal experience. It may all be sailors' tales, though having met that one I am more inclined to believe them."

"You didn't meet him, I did.

Sorin laughed again. "True enough, Mikael, but remember I now have every confidence that you will not die, and certainly not in the jaws of a big fish."

Dak and Danil had watched the Slicer's vain attempts to find its prey; it had finally given up thrashing around beneath them and then it disappeared downstream again.

"There would be good eating on that if you could land the beast."

Danil rewound the rope and stowed it away. "You would never catch it, my friend?"

"And why not? I am quite handy with a hook and line, or maybe a spear would be better."

"No, Dak, your skill is irrelevant; you would never catch it, because you would never find it. You were unafraid of it, so it would never appear."

Dak mulled this over. "That is easily solved. I would use Mikael as bait!"

"An excellent idea and if we used Sorin as well we could catch an even bigger one." Michael joined in with their laughter; none of them wanted to admit how near he had come to death, despite Sorin's confidence. It was Dak who remembered that the word haste had been used earlier.

"Now we must move on. Sorin this passage leads us where?"

Sorin stood up wearily. "It will lead us, I hope, out to the walls, close enough to the northern guard house to be near the drainage culvert that Vitta will have opened for us if he has concluded his other business. We have only then to distract the guards in some way and slip through."

The mention of the Antaldi Majann rang like an alarm in Michael's head. He had, as yet, failed to enquire after Fah Devin. He felt dreadful, how could he have been so remiss? Vitta was seated at the King's table in the palace, though Sentielle had not been present. Michael used this fact to rationalise his lapse of memory, but he knew this to be an excuse.

"Sorin, I forgot to ask you, how is Fah Devin?"

"Ah, yes, she will survive, but she needs time to recover, before she can fly again. She was distraught when you fell, she thought that she had killed you." This made Michael feel even worse, but he felt that he deserved it. "I assured her that you are capable of surviving most things, a point which you regularly prove."

"Where is she? Has she returned home?"

"No, Vitta has friends within the city who maintain a house for the Antaldi, she will be well cared for. You can ask him about her yourself when we are out of Tath Garnir."

Sorin did not once reproach him for his crass omission, but this last remark hit home. He was horrified at the prospect of returning to his old egocentric ways. He was determined that he would in some way at some time in the future make recompense.

The passage that led away from the bridge was little more than a roughly made tunnel, with, here and there, wooden supporting beams and props set to support the ceiling. The walls were jagged and the floor uneven, it was a sure sign that an unsolicited link had been made between the drainage tunnel and some point further on. He had once been shown down a 'smuggler's tunnel' in Cornwall which had a similar feel. There was little skill in the making, need had been the motivation, brute force had been the means. He wondered how Danil, who strode in front of him holding a torch to illuminate their way, had known of its existence.

"Is this way out of the city known to you, Danil? You found it with some ease."

"No, not known as such. Before I collected the reluctant Galeanid I scouted briefly down some of the passages that led away from the dungeons, where you were being held. I sensed that the one we took was useful and then I knew that an exit would present itself. My Gift, such as it is, is useful in that way, it gives me an impression of having been somewhere before, which actually means that I will be there soon."

"Did you know that we would be meeting a Blind Slicer then? You could have warned me."

Danil stopped and he turned for a moment towards him. "I did sense some danger, which is why I set the rope around Sorin, but I knew not what it would be. I am no Seer Mikael. My Gift is not prophetic; I just see more than others and I sense a little way ahead." He turned back and set off again, quickening his pace to catch up with Dak, who ignored the dark that he marched into, with sublime confidence. "It does mean that I rarely miss a target, for I aim where I know it is going to be, not where it is."

Dak had stopped. "If I had any skill with a bow I could shoot in the dark, Danil. Now, since you know where you are going to go, which way do we take?"

The tunnel had widened into a rectangular room, which had three passages leading from it, one they had come from and two in the opposite wall. Danil paused for a moment and he closed his eyes. For the briefest second Michael felt the room shiver as if stirred into life for a fraction of a second and then Danil's strange eyes opened and he spoke. "The left-hand leads to the surface, the air is fresher, and it rises quite sharply soon enough. But we will take the right-hand tunnel, though exactly where it leads to, I cannot tell."

"That is a strange answer and an even stranger choice, Danil, are you certain?"

Sorin patted Dak on the shoulder. "If Danil feels we follow the right-hand path then that is what we do. I learned long ago to trust him, even before he learned to trust himself."

Dak shrugged. "Very well, though the slope leads us further down, at least to start with."

The four of them set off in the same order, walking in the silence of their own thoughts through the tunnel which was much more skilfully made than the last. It had been properly constructed and the floor was even and smoothed by the passage of many feet. The downward gradient steepened still further, until Michael heard Dak calling back.

"We have reached a stairway, steep but secure. Do we continue?"

Sorin muttered to himself. "A stairway? Interesting. Continue, Dakveen of the Nare, but be wary, there are things that even your eyes cannot see."

"Continue it is then."

He started to descend with Danil following as before. Michael became increasingly uneasy as they progressed down the steps. He had walked some way uphill to get to the palace and it had taken quite a time to walk across the city. Since leaving the cells they had walked for a long time, so they must be far underground and well towards the city walls by now. Surely they would soon have to start gaining height; he was about to question Sorin about it when Sorin spoke.

"The walls have suddenly become quite interesting; I think we need some light." He lit a torch from his pack and raised it, then nodded to himself. "Mikael tell me what you can see."

Michael looked closely at the walls in the flickering light of the flame. They were covered with images, faded in places but still clearly paintings of animals. Initially they appeared to be random groups of animals. Some he recognised, there were certainly skarl amongst the other hoofed creatures. There were also fox-like shapes and many other small furred animals with ears and tails of various sizes. Curracks sat in groups amidst the trees, also larger monkeys or apes, and above them all, swooped and circled a huge variety of birds.

As he tried to make sense of the shapes he realised that they were not random groups at all; a story unfolded, certain individuals were painted larger than others and shown as moving from group to group and then moving together, almost as if each group had a 'spokes-animal' who represented their interests and had permission to speak for them. But where were they heading?

"It appears to be a story or a history of animal kind, perhaps."

"Yes, that was my feeling exactly. Have you noticed the wolves?"

He hadn't, but as he moved further on, he saw here and there, the shapes of wolves where each one stood head raised, calling one to another. Their presence appeared to be of little concern to the other animals, but their position on the walls seemed to create a pattern moving the watching eye on to the next image and then the next, as if guiding you down the stairway and creating a shield of protection around the visitor. But to what purpose? There was something else he had noticed,

"There are no people on any of these, who would have painted them?"

Sorin had certainly recovered some of his strength, Michael heard him chuckling quietly behind him. "They are old, older than many of the buildings above us. Painted in the early days of the city, when the Cluath still believed. This will not be the only such place, though they may have been forgotten and each would have been different. Remember when I told you that the Garshegan could not breach the walls. Well, that is due to the ancient places like this one."

"Yes, but what are they exactly."

"You might think of them as temples, places of worship, but it was more than that. They were chambers of supplication, places of acquiescence, submission, where the Seers and the prophets could remain in isolation, away from the noise of daily life and listen to the whisperings of the Powers, channel their power and explore their Gift. Each chamber was dedicated to one of the Powers, and even though they were not aware of it, the painters were also obviously under the guidance of the wolves."

"So, the Raell would have spoken to the early Seers when they were in the chamber? They bemoan the fact that the Cluath no longer listen."

Sorin reached up and placed a hand on his shoulder. "Yes, I had forgotten that you are privy to the thoughts of the wolves. Sometimes I wish I could tell all that I know to the ignorant and ill-informed Cluath, but I suspect that it would make no difference. They have lost the ability to listen and they live now by the strength and skill of their arms and they are swayed by the greed and lusts of their lords."

The steps of the stairway had begun to flatten, and they found that the passageway widened. After a short distance, the passage opened out, as they reached its end, where it led into a circular room maybe twenty paces across. The smooth walls here were undecorated and in fact the chamber was bare, except for a flat circle of stone placed at the centre. It too was smooth and unmarked save for the fact that the many feet that had stood upon it had left their mark, there were two distinct depressions slightly apart near the middle of the stone. Michael found himself wondering about the succession of Seers who had made the journey down here to await the voice of prophecy and how many times they must have held a fruitless vigil in this lonely place before returning to the city, their patience unrewarded. This prompted another thought that had nagged at him, the chamber appeared to have only one entrance and there was no way to progress any further.

The same thought had occurred to Dak. "So, Danil, you saw yourself coming down this passage, you didn't happen to see where you went next did you?"

"No, Dak, nor did I sense why it was that we should visit this place, but …"

Sorin interrupted and he held up both hands in acknowledgement of their situation. "As I have already said, Dak, Danil is rarely wrong and I trust his Gift. There is a reason for our presence here, even if we then trudge back the way we have come." He then turned to Michael. "Mikael, what are your thoughts on this? Have you any feelings to share?"

Sorin had asked the question without apparent guile, but Michael felt that he knew something that Michael didn't. Before he answered he cast his eyes around the chamber again. As he had first thought it was empty apart from the central stone. There was nothing to give a clue to the rituals that had occurred there, nor to whom it was dedicated. Then the images from the walls presented themselves to his mind; animal kind in all its splendour and the wolves moving in a pattern that … traced a name. He hadn't spotted it at first for of course the pattern had started from the end, but as he turned towards the end of the passage he could see that the wolves and animals together curled upwards into a large C. C for Carun the Lord of the beasts, he should have guessed from the start to whom the chamber was dedicated. He then knew what he had to do. Without saying a word, he walked forward. He removed his boots and he placed his bare feet upon the stone.

He did not hear the gasp from Dak as light flooded up around him, for the effect upon him had been immediate. The instant that his feet touched the surface of the stone he was no longer in the chamber he was amidst the great trees of the forest once more, and standing before him, was Carun himself.

"Welcome, Michael that is also Mikael, you stand in the ancient chamber of Garull, the Majann who conceived it and put the story of my children upon the face of the rock. I have led you to it so that we may talk and so that you may be safe." His voice rumbled and rolled amidst the trees shaking the branches, it was the bellowing of the stampeding herd, of the call to the rut, the voice of blood and bone, pulsating with the very heartbeat of life itself.

"I am honoured, great Carun, that you wished to speak with me again. May I know what concerns you?"

"You may in time, Michael that is also Mikael, but first I must remind you of the boundaries that govern my words. Remember I cannot be open and forthright in my speech. I must couch my words in some degree of mystery. That is as it has always been and so it must be still. You must listen well to hear what I must tell you. You were detained in the city at my request."

Michael was taken aback, why would Carun wish him to be threatened in this way?

"Yes, at my request, although I would not have suffered you to come to real harm. You are too important and must continue your journey. While the Cluath fight, your path lies elsewhere. More I cannot say, but Corruption sought to draw you close and resist him you must." So, he had been right to trust Siraal. He was glad that his feelings had led him right; her exquisite face with its sightless eyes came to his mind.

Carun had caught his thought. "Yes, Michael that is also Mikael, she is beautiful, beautiful and sad. But I led you to this place for another reason. You are once more betrayed; he that slept awoke, but did not initially inform his mistress, he plotted with the shadows to lie in wait for you. He has the Gift but has tainted it with greed and deceit. Thus, it was necessary for you to find another way out of the city. When you step from the stone you will have found it. I have not shown it to you, you have come to me in the chamber of Garull, and I have answered your request as I must do to all true believers."

"I thank you for granting an answer to my prayers, great Carun, and I will follow the path that is given to me."

Carun let forth a laugh that shook the roots of the trees. "I like you Man of Oak; you have a good soul. Good, follow the path that is given to you, yes, none can ask for more than that and now I feel the need to run. Step from the stone and you will return to the chamber. Farewell, Michael that is also Mikael, may your path run straight, and your companions be true."

"Farewell, Lord of Hoof and Claw, be swift and strong, bring honour to your herd."

Michael bowed and he stepped back off the stone. Around him the chamber was filled with light and Dak, Danil and Sorin stood shielding their eyes from the glare. The light came from the walls which glowed and shone with the power of the chamber. As the light began to fade around them, Michael saw that in one section of the walls there was a glowing circle that remained bright. He approached it carefully, not quite sure of what it signified, but he saw that just as the stone showed the wear of many feet, here was the pressure of many hands. He pressed his right hand within the circle and the wall moved under his hand with a quiet click and then the section of wall in front of him slid gracefully downwards to reveal steep stair that led upwards. He turned and gestured to the others.

"A friend has shown us the way forward. Come, quickly before it closes. I will explain as we climb."

The others did not argue, and they began to climb the stair, this time with Michael in the lead. He had no need of the torch for the steps glowed gently until they had passed and then darkened. As they made their way upwards, Michael explained about Carun's message.

Sorin was not altogether surprised "Galeanid is a fool, but his Gift is true as we know, it is sad that he uses it to further his own greed, doubtless he wishes to catch us and increase his standing with the Queen by turning us in."

Danil was practical about the whole matter. "Did your friend tell you where this comes out, Mikael?"

"No, but he implied that it would take us out of the city. Which is odd since the Seers would have been from within the city, why would they wish to leave."

"I think it is more to do with ritual, Mikael." Sorin was finding the steepness of the stairs to be tiring. "They may have believed that after a conversation with the Lord of the Forests, that they needed to go and give thanks amongst 'Carun's Children'. But we will see when we reach the top of this confounded stairway."

Michael had to agree with Sorin on that point. The steps rose steeply and seemed to go on forever, what's more the light that had assisted them had ceased and they were now back in torchlight. Michael lost track of time as he walked, and he found himself thinking about his encounter with Carun. He was not a naturally religious person and he had slipped into the weddings and funerals routine that most adults he knew adhered to. In fact, he had probably been to David's synagogue more often than his local church, what with one thing and another. His last encounter with religion had been Mel's funeral, his last encounter with religion in his own world that is. Here in Taleth he had met many of the Powers personally and he seemed to be on friendly, if not intimate terms, with them. He had not given it any degree of thought before, at home he would be considered either a madman or a Saint if he had reported conversations with 'gods'. It would depend upon whether he was believed or not.

Here his companions accepted it as perfectly normal for him to have had a conversation with Carun, although it was true to say that Dak had been silent since they left the chamber of Garull. He wondered if the ordinary people of Tath Garnir or the farmers and the Trell breeders of the plains would react in a similar fashion, Danil and Sorin were not exactly normal. He wondered also if he ever did return to a life after Taleth, to a life in England, would his attitude be different? He believed in the Powers because he had seen them, felt their strength and their energy. He had benefited from their gifts. Did this make him a believer? He doubted it; a true believer had faith and did not need proof. Perhaps he would get the chance to find out; he doubted that too, if he was being honest.

Suddenly, the stairs stopped and in front of him was a door of stone. There was no handle or hinge but there was as before an indentation made by the pressure of countless hands. He pressed against the stone and with a shudder the door responded, sliding downwards as the other had done and allowing moonlight to pervade the top of the stairway. The door led out onto a ledge which overlooked a small lake surrounded by trees. To Michael's left a few hundred yards away, the walls of the city rose in the darkness, the lanterns swinging in a breeze that came from the north and had a gentle chill to it. There was no way down from the ledge except to drop the short way to the water and swim to the bank. Michael had to laugh, Taleth seemed to delight in getting him wet on a fairly regular basis.

"It would seem that the Seers were content to take a cold bath after their encounter in the chamber below."

Sorin was not impressed. "It is nice to see that the powers have not lost their sense of humour. Well it looks as if we will have to swim for it."

Dak spoke for the first time since Michael had triggered the Seer's stone in the chamber. "You may all regularly converse with the Powers, you certainly all have more knowledge of them than I, but I come from a humbler background and if the mighty Carun feels that I should leap into a lake after entering his chamber, then I will not argue with him." He stepped to the edge. "After all it is not his fault that I cannot swim." He stepped off. For once it was Michael who reacted first, he leaped to his friend's help and he managed to secure his arms under Dak's as they both struggled to the surface. He then half swam half kicked his way towards the shore. He heard two splashes behind him as Sorin and Danil followed. Dak coughed once or twice and then he found his voice.

"Thank you, Mikael, I was hoping someone might help, but all this hobnobbing with the Powers is muddling my thinking rather. By the way, have you noticed that the water is both pleasantly warm and sweet to the taste?"

Dak was right, there had been no shock of cold when he had hit the water and Michael let the water fill his mouth for a moment and realised that it was not just sweet but delicious, tasting of summer berries with a hint of almonds.

"Sweet and fragrant, Dak, this must have been the Seer's reward for their patience and their sacrifice. Is this the point at which you decide that you should learn to swim?"

"Not quite, Mikael, but it would be at least pleasant to drown here."

They had reached the bank and Michael helped Dak out and then he clambered onto the bank himself, Sorin and Danil arrived shortly after.

Sorin shook himself dry. "Carun's little joke, tempered by the gift of Cerlinith. That water was almost good enough to drink, and you know my opinion on water in general."

"Yes, old friend." Danil stooped to fill a flask from the lake. "It does not have enough kick to it." He drank from the flask, "Now that is fascinating."

He handed the flask to Michael who accepted readily and took a drink. The water was cold and fresh, pleasant enough, but water pure and simple, the sweetness and the warmth had gone.

"So, the water is only warm and sweet when you enter it from the chamber side, take the water out of the lake and it returns to is normal condition."

Sorin shook his head, "They do like their little games, don't they. Now we are outside the city and away from the walls, but we need to meet up with Vitta. He will have been expecting us, but not here."

Just as he was speaking, they sensed movement in the trees and two wolves emerged, breathless and in haste. After bowing to Sorin they turned to Michael, he recognised one as Mishrell.

'Greetings, Michael that is also Mikael, Mishrell and Grinier of the Aurian bring warning and guidance. There is danger abroad for all that live and breathe. Be wary, move swiftly and wait not upon others to assist you. The Valeen Thinvere awaits Danil at Tal Neat, you must follow us to the east of here where mounts have been readied for you. Please inform your companions of this.'

Michael turned to Danil first. "They say that Thinvere awaits you at Tal Neat, why is that Danil?"

Danil lowered his head. "Because, Mikael, I must return to place myself at the mercy of the Triad. That was the price of assistance, they have promised to give me a hearing." He looked up, first at Michael and then at Sorin. "I will return if I can, I would go to face this journey with you, but my fate awaits me now as it has done since the day I was born. May your path be straight, and your choices be good ones." With that, he stooped and picking up his pack he took from it Michael's axe which he handed to him, then he sprang away into the darkness. Michael was stunned he had somehow assumed that Danil would always be there, just as David would be in his own world. He felt a sense of dread for his friend for he knew that the Antaldi Triad considered him an abomination. He feared that he would never see Danil again.

His voice shook as he turned to Sorin and continued. "We are provided with mounts, which they will lead us to. But there is danger abroad that threatens all of us, we must move with speed."

Sorin tuned to the two wolves. "Where is Sylvan? I have heard nothing for two days now, which is most unlike her."

Mishrel turned again to Michael. *'Tell Sorin Sylvan sends these words: 'A time is come that was not foreseen, for Corruption has become mighty and brings death to my brethren. I will come when and if I am able but look not for me.' Hurry, we must not stay here.'*

Michael repeated the words that Sylvan had sent and he saw Sorin's face pale, he suddenly looked old and grey. "So be it. It truly is the ending of all things if the Dri are filled with fear."

Michael remembered Sylvan's warning of earlier and he was filled with a desire to be far from this place. Without any more words, they followed the two wolves around the edge of the lake and moved through the trees that grew there. Michael's sense of dread did not lessen as they made their way deeper into the wood. They moved without speaking and Michael sensed the weight that was upon Sorin's shoulders. He was leaving his greatest friend to face an unknown terror by racing in the other direction. Duty was a cruel master and Sorin had served for so long, made so many sacrifices, and here he was doing so again. Michael felt ashamed of the despair and the anger he had felt when faced with the loss of Mel. His pain was nothing to the pain of this old man, who seemed to have lived for ever and suffered so much.

He cast a look at Dak, who strode a little to his left. He had lived his life in exile, wandering far from his home for a crime that he did not commit, *'the sins of the fathers'* as the saying goes, and now he had been persuaded to return though perhaps not fully aware of what would greet him and exactly what he was expected to do. Yet he strode with purpose, pragmatic as ever, the decisions taken not worried about. The path is set, and it is followed. He envied him his surety, his confidence that things would in some way always work out. He would need all of that when they reached the mountains. Michael suddenly realised that he had no idea how long it would take for them to get to the homeland of the Nare. His knowledge of Taleth's geography was minimal and he had heard only vague statements about the northern mountains, but nothing specific. He was determined to ask Sorin about it when the old man looked a little more like talking.

After fifteen minutes or so, they reached a place where the trees were thinner. The two wolves barked softly and then they disappeared into the forest. In the clearing, they found a young Antaldi standing with three Trell, not the heavy slow workers, but the same breed as the cavalry that Michael had seen riding in the city. They were readied for the journey and they appeared to be loaded with supplies. The young man turned to Sorin and bowed.

"Greetings, I am called Ulin Ruan, these animals have been fed watered and prepared as Vitta requested. He was warned in a dream to avoid the place you had set for a meeting and bids that you accept this aid and he apologises for not meeting you in person. He has returned to Glianivere to broach the subject of aid for the Cluath in the coming war."

Sorin bowed in thanks. "Thank him for me, Ulin Ruan. His aid is most welcome, although I would rather have my task than his, persuading the Triad to action will be a challenge."

"As you say, Master Sorin, although there are some of us who would see aid as the only logical step. Not all the Antaldi live with their head in the branches, smelling the breeze."

"Forgive me, Ulin Ruan, I meant no disrespect, but I have had a lifetime of refusal and indecision and my mind is unfairly prejudiced."

Ulin Ruan smiled and he bowed again. "No offence was taken, Master Sorin. That the leaders of my people are wise is undoubtedly true, but the fact that they need to see beyond the edges of the forest is also certain." He then turned and bowed to Michael. "I give you greetings, Mikael Dal Oaken, and two messages. Fah Devin would have you know that she is recovering and that she begs your forgiveness for allowing you to fall. She will await your return when you can explain how you managed to survive so that the way may be cleansed between you."

Michael was relieved that she bore him no ill-will. "I will return when I can and tell her she has my forgiveness although she does not need it. I chose to fall to try and save her. I pray the Powers will grant her a swift recovery."

"There is another message, from Sepho at the Palace. I will read it for I did not fully understand, so I made him write it down." He took a paper from a pocket and read. "'*Son of Halkgar, sorry Mikael, I am sorry that they put you in the dungeon. I don't believe you are dangerous; you didn't look dangerous in the bath. I hope what I told you didn't get you into trouble, sometimes I think that the whole family is crazy, and Seers are best ignored, if you ask me. They wouldn't allow me to see you, but I met Master Vitta and I asked if*" *he could return your clothes to you. I had them washed and repaired, a few seams were definitely looking stretched. You can keep the ones that you have, although they will probably not stand a long journey. I was honoured to have met you, yours Sepho.'* I hope that makes sense to you, Mikael."

Dak laughed and even Sorin had recovered enough to smile, Michael found that he was blushing. "Yes, that makes perfect sense, if you get an opportunity to thank him then do so."

"I will. May the Powers guide your beasts, and may your paths run true."

"Thank you, Ulin Ruan."

The Antaldi bowed again and then he was gone. They made ready to mount up. Dak was still laughing but mainly to himself. *"'You didn't look dangerous in the bath'* is there something you haven't told us, Mikael?"

"Enough of that, Dak, or I will give that Trell a slap and watch as you crash to the ground. Sepho was a very friendly and useful young man, I learned a lot about the King and his family from him, and it was good of him to send me my clothes. Stop laughing, or I will make that beast run under you."

"Very well, Mikael, as you know my legendary skills as a rider would indeed be stretched by a gallop, but at least now I know which end is which, and I can steer away from trees. Sepho as you say was a friendly young man and I am sure good at his job; however, he was just a touch gullible I'm sure that you will agree."

"Very probably, but you and Gath, and Master Sorin here, had him terrified that I might throw him out of the tower window if he did the wrong thing, which was slightly cruel."

Sorin was leading and he called back over his shoulder. "That is true it was but blame Gath he was the one pouring the drinks."

★★★

6

Beyond the City

In this mood, they set off as the first light of morning crept over the trees and signalled a new day. The terrain was not conducive to hard riding, so their pace was subsequently going to be moderate. Their journey initially took them along the side of a small river which ran through the forest. It was fast flowing and clear and Michael could see fish swimming against the current, waiting for the gnats and the flies that would skim across the water. This far from the mountains that spawned it there were few boulders to disturb it and so it sang the gentle song of pebbles and stones, rolling them, toying with them like gemstones. Once more he felt swayed by the life in Taleth; he would never have surveyed a scene like this in his world and drawn such pleasure from it. He knew this to be his fault; his jaded and purposeless existence had led him to ignore his own world, much like most of the people he met. He knew there were scenes of beauty and joy, warmth and energy in his own world too, but his senses had tuned them out for so long that he wondered if he would ever again be able to regain the power to look and really see what was in his own world that was beautiful. For him, beauty had died with Mel and love had died with her too.

These thoughts slid him down into that depressive spiral of self-loathing that he had managed to avoid for some time. He knew that he had to cleanse these thoughts from his mind, or he would wallow in them. He opened his mind to the breeze, to the singing of the river as she caressed her precious stones and to the humming of life as it woke around him. Mikael's thoughts came to him as he breathed deeply in the morning air.

'Will all this be there after the choice is made, Michael?'
'Who knows, Mikael, who knows?'

'There will come a point when decide you must.'

'Yes, I know, but that time is not yet upon me.' The words of the voice that he referred to as Mr Chambers came to him, when first the Chiatt Grain was discussed. *'Remember that there are always possibilities. Nothing is certain. You are from the outside. There is of you something that is not Taleth. Had you considered that this means that your thread in the Unfolding is your own to unravel?'*

'My choices and my decisions will be my own, Mikael, and I feel much more will be revealed before they are made.'

'What of after? Have you considered that?'

'No, not really, there is little point. What happens will happen and we can worry about it then.'

'Have you truly no wish to return to life as it was?'

'None, Mikael, your life had promise and a future, mine had long evenings of despair and self-hatred.'

'My future is gone, my friend, my promises broken. You may at least have a life after all of this.'

Michael knew this to be the likely outcome, but he had not thought beyond the choice, for him, if there was a future, then so be it. Another voice entered his thoughts, it was Grinier of the Aurian.

'Mikael, we have watched the start of your journey, but now we are summoned, aid must be given. Others will ward you, may your path run straight, and your companions be true.' Michael felt his voice leave his head, but it was replaced by another.

'Mikael, I am Zedak of the Veyix, that some call the Lost, I am not far off and I will ward you should the need arise. The Trillani await you further on, for your journey concerns them greatly. Much is at stake and you must not waver in your heart. You will find your own truth; of that I am certain. You are Uclan, as I have been and in this you will find strength. Fear not the future, grasp hold of the present, the past is behind us, but cares not. We will speak again.'

Michael realized that the two wolves had 'spoken' to him from some distance, which had not happened before. It concerned him that when he had opened his mind to the morning, he had broadcast his thoughts to the whole of Taleth. Another voice entered his mind, a very familiar one.

'Michael, that is also Mikael, do not wonder at hearing the words of the packs, they can project over great distances when there is need. Your own power is indeed growing, although not yet matching theirs. The longer you remain in Taleth the greater will be your ability to tune your thoughts to the warp and weft of this world. Do not falter, Michael, that is also Mikael, do not change your plans. Go to the land of the Nare for that is where your path lies. They have need of you, although they do not know it yet. Trust Sorin and trust your heart, you are becoming the man it was hoped you could be, Michael, that is also Mikael, worry not that all is not clear, your journey will teach you more than you can know."

And at last Michael was back with his own thoughts and his own voice in his head. He tried for a while to think of nothing, to clear his mind. They were all trying to help, he knew that, but for Michael making decisions had always been hard, he had tended to let others make them for him, even though he knew that this was weakness. Even in his relationship with Mel, she had made the choices, she had chosen to love him and then chosen to leave. He was surer now than ever that his journey back from death, through Taleth and beyond perhaps, was one of discovery for him. He had been given the chance to grow, become more than he was, take responsibility for what was happening and to make decisions for all of them, Danil, Ayan, Sorin, Dak, Siraal and the Wolves; he cannot know if he will make the right choice but at least it will be his to make, thanks to them.

They had reached a point in the river where the trees thinned, and the ground spread away in folds. In the far distance, the northern mountains rose steeply into the cloud. To the west, the rolling downs, fringed on the southern side by the continuation of the forest which they had passed through, lead eventually to the land of the Sylian and to the sea. North of that, lay the end of the range that held Fellas and gave birth to the Heran River that spread down to the plains of the Cluath. What lay beyond

the mountains Michael did not know, nor had he heard anything of the south, beyond what Havianik had told him, where
the Heran ran out to a wide slow delta of marsh and swamp.
Directly ahead, halfway between them and the mountains of the
Nare, two smaller ranges of mountains swung round to form a
wide elliptical valley between them. These mountains and the
valley between them lay shrouded in mist and cloud that ignored
the sun and resisted the wind. It was strange to watch as clouds
blown by the morning breeze drifted past others that appeared
tethered to the peaks beneath.

Michael had assumed that they would head directly for the
mountains in the north, taking them through these clouded
hills, but Sorin, who had stopped explained their next move.

"I think we now have to ride hard for at least two, maybe
three days. We must put distance between us and the forest's
edge, we can easily be tracked on these downs and we need to
reach the rougher terrain that lies to the east, which will give
us some shelter."

Dak was surprised by this. "You feel that the Queen may
send some pursuit?"

"She may, or there may be others that follow. To this end,
we will head north east at pace and only take short stops, to
rest our mounts."

"Ah, how delightful, Sorin, after that much riding I may
never walk again."

"I am aware of your dislike of the saddle, Dak, but need
drives us. It will be hard, but it is necessary I assure you. It will
take us perhaps six days to reach the Mountains of the Nare."

Michael had not realized how far away they were. His es-
timation of their height had therefore been also way off beam.
"Could we not shorten our journey, by heading straight ahead?"

Sorin shook his head. "No, Mikael, we cannot pass through
the ring of Drukann-Nadim, that marks the land of the Sha-ellev;
the Pha-Dishak it is called, the hidden valley and it is closed,
for reasons known only to the Sha-ellev themselves. None may
pass through and we must avoid it. We shall skirt it to the east

and that way we may remain hidden. It will certainly be safer than out on the open downs. The western route would be quicker, but far less safe."

Michael felt somehow that they should be making more of an effort to seek help from the Sha-ellev, but he bowed to Sorin's decision. They turned away from the river and took up a harder pace across the dark green of the downs. Michael had not ridden hard on the Trell and he immediately sensed the difference between these and the Piradi. Turic had flowed across the ground, making the process of riding a pleasure, these light Trell were quick, if not as swift as the Piradi, but they worked hard for it and that made riding them hard work. He needed his wits about him as they rode, even though the terrain was open and they met no greater problem than a series of water courses that spun a spidery web amongst the rise and fall of the land, when they stopped just before midday for a short rest near one of these, Michael found that he was very glad to be out of the saddle for a while, which he had never felt with Turic.

As he lay back on the grass, he considered the Trell as it stood beside him drinking from the stream. Undoubtedly, these 'horses' of the King's cavalry were fine beasts, but why did the Frinakim and no others have access to the Piradi.

"Why can only the Frinakim ride the Piradi and the King's men ride these lighter versions of the Trell?"

"I normally refuse to answer questions while I am lying down, Mikael, but since you ask and it is an interesting tale, if you pour me a drink from my flask and then refill the others while I talk, I will forgive you."

Michael obeyed and refilled all the flasks, while Dak sat rubbing life into his thighs.

"The Trell were bred first for workaday tasks and the naturally stronger breeds became highly prized for their strength and their endurance, where Gath and Tuggid are from, down in Darnak, there are few of these, and some of their work-beasts are enormous. But men wanted to ride quicker more responsive animals and they started to select smaller mares to breed and gradually, over hundreds of years, they produced the creatures that you see here. They are fast and strong and resilient, everything that a cavalry steed should be.

"As for the Piradi, the story goes that many hundreds of year ago a young Cluath man became lost in a storm in the lands beyond the Ineth River and as the weather worsened, he struggled through a mountain pass that he had never seen before, trying to find shelter. His Trell slipped and fell to her death, as they climbed through the rugged pass, and the man himself would have been dead too had it not been for a young boy riding a Trell-like creature that the man did not recognise. The boy helped the man up behind him onto the Piradi, for that was what it was. Imagine his amazement when she spoke to his mind and reassured him that he was safe, and then she carefully picked her way down the other side of the pass to the wild lands beyond.

"The man became ill, from his exposure to the storm, but the boy and his mother cared for him and he recovered. When he had regained his strength, he questioned them about the wonderful beast he had ridden, but the boy would not tell him. He said that she was a gift of the Powers and not to be discussed. This was not enough for the man and he began to secretly follow the boy during the morning to see where he went. Eventually, the boy unwittingly led him to the birthplace of the Piradi, a wide vale which lay beside the western ocean, a place where few Cluath had ever been. Thousands of Piradi ran free within this vale and they ran with joy in their hearts. At first the man merely sat in wonder at the sight of the Piradi, but greed entered his heart and he began to plan to capture them and make himself rich. But his avarice sang too loud and the Piradi were aware of him and they chased him from the vale. It was not in their nature to kill, but it may have been better if they had. He vowed to return and capture these fine beasts and use them for his own ends.

"The boy was overcome with remorse that he had led the man to their home, but the Piradi blamed him not. However, they did resolve to leave the vale and find a place of safety away from the Cluath and their greed. But the Powers were watching and Carun, who had made the Piradi, appeared to them and said that the Vale was their home and that they must not leave it, as the herd would be decimated by hunger, cold and disease should they leave. When the Piradi told Carun of their fears he agreed to place a confusion around their home so that none would ever find it, however long they searched. But he asked for a sacrifice in return. Should a man of pure heart come in Carun's name and request their aid then they should offer themselves as steeds to him and his kin, bonding themselves to their riders and serving with them until released back to the Vale.

"Carun was good as his word and none who searched ever found the Vale, and most never returned from their journey. The tale remained, but the searching died out. The story of wonder creatures who were swift, light-footed, could talk and lived in a mysterious vale by the sea became a legend much embellished by the story tellers, although even the telling of it died out, save in a few of the outlying homesteads. Teldak and Grald Dal Hammett both heard it, and when as children, they decided to seek out the Vale of the magic beasts, their father beat them both soundly for their childishness, this made them all the more determined and they ran away to hunt for it.

"Now great Carun knew in his heart that these two young boys were of great import for the future of Taleth and so he watched over their childish quest and when they stumbled upon the mountain pass and came upon a young female Piradi who had wandered from the Vale and gone lame, they wondered at her. Teldak bound her foot and he nursed her while Grald hunted for food for them both. When she could walk, she opened her mind to them and spoke, thanking them for their kindness. Teldak dared to ask if he could ride her and she replied. *'When all have abandoned you and hope is ending call my name and I will seek you out. But search no more for the Vale, for it is hidden.'* And then she whispered a name that only Teldak heard. She then left them, and they returned home where they received another beating from their father. Teldak never revealed the name to his brother and a barrier grew between them, which remained as they grew into men and rose in the High King's service.

"When Teldak left his post to avenge his love, Grald cut the final bond between them and he let it be known that none should speak with him nor give him even a mount with which to ride from the Taleth lands. Many were appalled at the harshness of his banishment and they offered to follow him into exile. He forbade them and he walked from his homelands until he could walk no more. Then he lay down in despair, waiting for death. The name of the Piradi came into his mind and without thinking, he spoke it into the wind and fell asleep. When he awoke, she was standing over him and let him ride her to the edges of the Vale. There he told her his tale and she listened, then in her mind, so we are led to believe, Carun reminded her of the bargain he had struck with the Piradi and so she and Teldak conceived of an army of riders who would protect the lands from the threat of the Tsarg. The rest you have experienced yourself. Teldak still rides her into battle, although she roams free until he has need of her."

Dak stretched. "That is a wondrous tale and well told too, it is the longest I have ever heard you speak, Master Sorin, without mentioning liquor of any kind."

Dak had made the mistake of standing too close to Sorin and he received a swift kick for his impertinence. "May I remind you, Dak, that old Trell kick the hardest, and since you mention it, yes, I will have a nip of the Viggan that you carry in your pack, thank you very much."

He stood up stiffly, as Dak handed him the flask with a laugh. "Just a small one, though, we have a long way to go."

"Indeed, we do." Sorin turned to Michael. "Did my tale satisfy you, Mikael? It is long, but it is a good tale nonetheless."

"It was excellent, and rarely have you been so forthcoming."

"Oh, is that the thanks, I get?" His voice broke into that familiar chuckle. "I had heard most of it before, but Greer told me the full story on our ride down from the bridge of Pliatt Heran. He may have embellished it a little, but it is mostly true.

Certainly, the Frinakim are the only ones who can ride the Piradi and when a warrior is accepted into their ranks, if there is no mount for him, a Piradi will arrive within a day or two without the need of asking. You are most privileged to have been granted a Piradi to ride Mikael."

"Yes, I felt most honoured, and with all due respect to these beasts here, I miss her terribly."

"What I miss, when I am riding," Dak said mournfully, "is the rocks and the good soil beneath my feet. I shall never get used to riding; I consider it unnatural and an affront to nature."

"Yes, Dak, well said," Sorin agreed, and then added gleefully. "Now mount up."

"When you cease being a Majann, Sorin, are you going to return to your natural role of torturer in chief?"

"Oh, that will be a job for my old age, Dak, when I finally get there."

With that, they set off once more and they rode until the light had gone from the sky. Sleep came easily to Michael when they had eaten and when in the last few hours of the night, Dak raised him to take his turn on watch, he felt quite refreshed. The night air was chilly, and he sat with his cloak wrapped tight around him. Little moved on the downs, the odd animal scuttled past in the darkness and something that resembled an owl, swooped and hooted occasionally. The sunrise when it came, spread a pale orange glow across the misty downs, waking flocks of birds, which rose to skim through the mists in a silent aerial ballet of their own devising.

They rose early and breakfasted in the saddle, Sorin was determined to cross the land as swiftly as he could, but he knew that he couldn't push the Trell too hard, so the second day's pace was slower than the first. The day started well but just as they set off after a short break at mid-morning the rain started, and it continued all the rest of that day. By the third day of their journey, they rode through the grey downpour at little more than a walk, with the only sound being the splash of the rain and the steady thud of hooves. Michael had even given up looking up to judge their position and he was quite surprised when Sorin signalled to turn to the left and he saw that they had indeed reached the rugged and broken land that marked the end of the Drukann-Nadim, the ring of mountains enclosing the Pha-Dishak. Sorin had obviously decided to seek out some sort of shelter from the relentless rain. Michael had seen rain like this many times before at home, with no wind to disturb it, it hammered down in rods, obscuring all, soaking all and driving even the good nature of Dakveen of the Nare deep into his boots.

Sorin appeared to have seen something and he dismounted. They did the same and led their Trell through the increasingly rocky ground towards a place where large boulders and slabs of rock had crashed from the face of the mountainside and created a shelter. It was large enough for them all to enter and tie their mounts at one side. It was mostly dry, although far from comfortable, but they were so glad to be out of the rain, that they would have slept on almost anything.

Sorin turned to Dak. "Do you think you can raise us a fire, my friend, I think we need to rest properly for a while and dry ourselves out."

"Well, I have tinder and stone, Master Majann, but what we use for fuel I cannot say. All I can see is rocks, and, much as I love rocks, they do not burn, although that is not quite true, for some burn if you grind them …"

"I am not in need of a lesson in rock lore, Dakveen, but I am in need of a fire."

Michael hunted around the back of their shelter and as luck would have it found just what they required. "Would a tree that has come down with the rocks and lain for some time drying out under them, be of any use do you think."

"Cerlinith be praised, oh, and all the others too, I don't want to offend anyone. Well done, Mikael."

It took some effort to break the tree out of its rock prison, but once removed, Dak made swift work of it and soon he had a good blaze going, which even the Trell turned towards for comfort. Dak also provided them with a hot drink which he prepared from herbs and water, even Sorin was impressed considering it had no 'kick' to it. They then changed into some drier clothes from their packs and they hung up all the sodden clothing on any rock that would hold it. It reminded Michael of a disastrous attempt at camping that they had all gone on when they were students, somewhere in the lakes, when the campsite had flooded, and they ended up in a farmer's barn wrapped in old blankets drinking warm cider from tin mugs, surrounded, like here, by dripping clothes. It cheered him to remember a time when he had been happy, and all the complications of love and betrayal had not yet tainted his world.

They found their voices as they warmed themselves and soon drinks were passed round, and stories were being told. It was a relief to them all not just to be dry, but not to feel that they were on view to the world as they had been when riding upon the downs. The warm fire and the drink and the mood led them all to sit dozing round the fire without thought of setting watch and so it was with a start that they woke to the presence of a great white wolf standing by the fire. It was Zedak. Michael stood up and he bowed hurriedly, but Zedak was already giving his message.

"Two messages I bring for you, Michael that is also Mikael, and one for Sorin. Know that the Queen has been persuaded to send riders out to bring you back, but that as yet they have not found your trail since they have no idea which direction you are heading in, nor even where you left the city. Know also that other riders are approaching, six mounts, but only three to ride them. I sense no danger in them. To Sorin say just this: the Dri are assailed, but despite his vow he must maintain his path, if at the last they need him they will send word. Farewell, my warding is over, the Trillani will bring word from now on. May your path run straight, and your companions be true."

Zedak was gone before Michael could even reply. The others had roused themselves and they stood as Michael turned towards them. "The Queen has seen fit to pursue us, but so far, her men have no trail to follow."

"Good, the scent will have been confused by the wolves, so even the best tracker will find little clue. Go on." Sorin had sensed that Zedak had been tense and in haste.

"There are riders approaching, three of them, but with six mounts. Zedak did not sense danger."

"Riders with extra mounts, that is interesting, and was there a message for me, Mikael."

"'*To Sorin say just this: the Dri are assailed, but despite his vow he must maintain his path, if at the last they need him they will send word*'."

Sorin once more paled in the light of the fire, but this time he was angry, and he let it show. "What new villainy has the Corruptor unleashed? He has been left too long to plot and scheme and now his strength is such that he can openly attack the packs. Oh, and how he hates the Dri, who have guided the hands of the Seers and the Prophets and have aided the Majann for years beyond counting." His voice rose to a roar that made the rocks tremble. "Do you hear me, Khargahar, Corruptor, in your pit in the fires below Fellas. I am speaking, Calix, remember me, who drove the filth you spawned back into the flames screaming in terror, who broke your armies on the rocks of your fortress. There is a reckoning that must be paid for all this and I will be part of it. They will not let me help them yet, but when they call, the world will shake beneath your feet and those that assail them shall burn."

The echoes of his voice rang around them, his tirade had drowned out the rain, and neither Michael, nor Dak, moved or spoke as Sorin stood eyes closed, drawing back the anger that had swept through him.

Silence fell, even the rain had stopped in the face of such an outpouring of emotion and into that silence a welcome and familiar figure stepped.

"It is a good many years since I have heard that anger, old friend. Such are the times that the righteous are raised to wrath and fury. Lead me to your foes I am once more ready to fight beside you."

Sorin's eyes snapped open. "Danil Lebreven, they let you live! Well now I know that miracles do happen. Praise be to Yvelle and Palleon that their people have seen sense at last." He strode forward to grasp his former pupil warmly by both hands. "I'm sorry that you heard my little rant just then, but I was moved to such anger by Zedak's news."

"I think the whole of Taleth heard your little rant, my friend, but what news moved you so?"

"The Dri are under attack, by what I cannot tell, but they will not let me aid them, they feel that I must accomplish my task. I pray to all the Powers that they can withstand this assault."

Danil's green eyes widened at this grave news. "The times are evil indeed if the packs are now in danger, but at least we have brought aid and assistance."

"We?"

"Yes, we, Sorin." He stepped out of the rock shelter and he returned with two Antaldi, one a tall young man with a serious expression and the other a stunningly beautiful young woman, with fierce green eyes and long white hair braided with black ribbons. Her manner exuded confidence to the point of challenge; she seemed to Michael to have a fiery Cluath heart beating in that perfect Antaldi frame. She carried something long and thin wrapped in a green cloth.

"My friends let me introduce my advocate with the Triad, my champion, and my kin although I knew it not, Suani, daughter of my mother's sister. It was she who saved my skin, although she did have some help." She bowed to them all in turn but did not speak. "And Mirell, a nephew of Vitta I believe." Mirell's bow was the merest nod of the head. "We have brought you mounts from the Frinakim," Michael's heart leapt with a sudden hope. "Yes, Mikael, Turic amongst them, Ayan had despatched them already, after having been woken by a strange dream. Mirell will return with the Trell to Glianivere, where they will be cared for."

Michael was about to greet his friend, his pleasure at seeing him as great as knowing that he would once more ride his beloved Turic, but now Suani spoke. Her voice matched her demeanour, there was strength and energy and yet it was a delightfully musical voice, that made you think of the breeze that shakes the blossom from the trees in the Spring.

"Greetings to you, fellow enemies of Corruption, your names are known to me, and for that I thank my cousin. It is an honour to meet you all." She bowed once more and then she turned to Sorin. "Master Sorin, to you I bring words and a gift from Vitta and all the Antaldi who would assist the Cluath in this war. The words are these: *'The Triad have been persuaded to assist Leenal and the Cluath, when you Sorin consider it right to do so, and they will prepare themselves accordingly. However, Blessed Yvelle and Palleon have gifted Vitta with a vision and will only sanction war if it is unavoidable.'* As for the gift, I have it here and Vitta bids you use it well."

With these words spoken she unwrapped that which she carried, and Michael saw that it was a wooden staff, at first, he thought that it had been carved but as Suani handed it to Sorin he saw that it was actually three different woods, woven in some way together in an intricate spiral.

"It is the Staff of Nuall, three branches from the most revered of our trees that grow at the very heart of the chamber of the Triad, three branches that grew together, binding themselves into one wand of power. It is one of our most sacred objects."

Sorin took it from Suani and for a moment Michael saw a great sadness in his eyes, but it was only fleeting and then he held the staff aloft. "Nuall's staff, I thought that it had perished with him. He was a mighty Majann, Suani, probably the greatest of all the Antaldi, he could sing the trees to bend and shape themselves, just as the First Ones could, and he could draw rain clouds into a clear sky or cast them out to sea with a word. He was also the most stubborn man who ever lived and, when his mind was set, it was set in stone and none could change it, not even me and I can be very persuasive."

It appeared that Danil's information concerning Sorin had left out a few details. "You met him, but …"

Danil muttered something about *'explaining later'* as she cast him a quizzical look.

Sorin hadn't noticed her surprise. "And with this he could project his thoughts halfway round the world. Or listen to the roots grow beneath his feet." He lowered the staff and he caressed its smooth surface following the winding of each of the branches. There was a deep rich brown, a vibrant silvery green and a pure white, to Michael's eyes it was one of the most beautiful things he had ever seen, and it seemed to shimmer and hum in the firelight. "I am honoured, Suani, very honoured to receive this gift, Vitta is a good man and his strength and his support will be needed in the days that are to come. But come both of you, sit down in our luxurious living quarters and warm yourselves, Dak will prepare you a drink, which is extremely good and contains nothing harmful that I know of, unlike most of the drinks that we Cluath consume."

For the first time Mirell spoke. "I will not stay, Master Sorin, but I thank you for the offer. I will convey your thanks to Master Vitta and he will await your thoughts." He bowed low and then he led the Trell out from the shelter and busied himself in removing their saddles and their packs and transferring them to the Piradi. Michael joined him, for he was anxious to see Turic. She stood patiently with the other Piradi and as he approached, she nuzzled her face against his neck,

"It is good to see you, Michael that is also Mikael, you are well, I sense that, but you have a few more scars it would appear."

"It is good to see you too, Turic, I have missed you and your companionship. Shall I see to your saddle and pack?"

"No, Mirell, will attend to that, return and listen to Danil's tale for I have caught some of their conversation, but not all, and I am intrigued as to how he survived."

"Very well, but if you need anything then tell me."

"I will, Michael that is also Mikael, I will."

He stroked her head once more and then after nodding to Mirell he returned to the fire. There had to be some considerable relocation of steaming clothes in order to make room for them all near to the fire, but eventually they were all seated and Dak prepared more of his warming brew.

"Now, Danil, since you are returned to us." Sorin spoke quietly as if he was determined not to think of things that he could not control. "Tell us how this feat was accomplished. The Triad do not have a reputation for leniency, nor for breaking their own laws."

Danil smiled, "There is much truth in that, and it was with a heavy heart that I flew towards Glianivere. It may to some have seemed a high price to pay for a small advantage, but I had seen myself in the air above the city and so I knew it was my path. The time had come to face my fate and if that was to be my ending then so be it, I prepared myself for death as we flew. On landing, I was met by Master Vitta, who welcomed me solemnly and thanked me for keeping my vow so readily. He took me to a place where I was to sleep, it was away from others and I felt like a condemned man. Unsurprisingly, I slept little and woke early. The birds midst the trees sang an animated chorus to the rising sun, even though she hid her face, perhaps suspecting what the day would bring. I was not allowed to walk amongst the trees, so I sat and ate the food that had been left for me. The Antaldi were at their morning observances and I felt more alone than I have ever done.

"After an hour or so Vitta returned, it seemed that since he had spoken with me before, that it was safe for him to speak to me. He told me that my fate would be decided by the Triad, but that I would be allowed to speak and plead my case. My 'trial' would take place on open ground away from the sacred grove, a place which would be defiled by my presence, so the decision would be made under the sky." Danil had heard Dak mutter at this. "Be not surprised, Dak, we are Uclan are we not and we should be prepared for all the cruelty that this entails." He paused and drank. "This is actually quite good; you must teach me the secret." He drank again and then he continued. "So I walked behind Vitta out into the grey morning, many faces turned away from me, many eyes cast down as I passed, but I defied them, I walked with my head held high, I was not ashamed for I was born of great love and great joy. I had Neemar's blessing and I knew that I now had blood and kin in the world.

"Three chairs had been set for the Triad, but as yet they were empty, Vitta stood to the right with Sentielle behind him, Kirielle the Seer stood on the left, other Valeen were present as were many austere and distinguished Antaldi. Behind me were gathered the rest of the Antaldi who dwell close to the Sacred Grove. We all stood in silence waiting on the arrival of the Triad. After what seemed an age they appeared, two men and a woman, robed in rich gowns of green and blue, crowned with woven leaves and walking with their staffs of office held aloft. They took their appointed places and Vitta stepped forward. He bowed to each of them in turn. Then he turned to me.

"*'Danil called Lebreven, son of Tuali, you have come here of your own free will and placed yourself at the mercy of the Triad. It is fitting that you know their names since they will pass judgement upon you. Know them then as Tarien, Vuar and Fah Nalisse. Tarien and Fah Nalisse have ruled us wisely for many years, Vuar was raised to her position on the sad and untimely death of Fah Risall.'* Each acknowledged their name with a nod of the head, but no words. Vitta then came close to me and said.

"*'You may now speak, Danil, and chose your words wisely for your life is forfeit unless you can persuade them.'*

"I looked at them, with their stern faces and their heads filled with rigid laws and I thought *'What words that could persuade them?'* For I knew that their minds were set against me. So, I looked at them and I looked around at the Antaldi and I spoke thus.

"*'I stand before you as a man who has lived his life in honour, doing what I can for the good of all. I have done no harm to any save those who live in Corruption's thrall and those I have pursued with all my energies and skill. I have broken no laws, transgressed against no edicts, foresworn no vow, what harm have I done that you should seek my death?'*

"I was met with silence and more silence.

"Eventually Tarien rose and spoke. *'Your life is forfeit because of what you are. How you have lived, what you have done is not our concern. You are an abomination to the very soul of the Antaldi and must not be suffered to live. Are there any who are not content with the judgement of the Triad?'*

"My heart was stilled by his words, but I had feared that this would be my fate and then I heard a voice behind me which said …"

Here Suani spoke for herself. "I am not content, Tarien, not at all content. How can a man who has committed no crime be guilty? He cannot be guilty for what he is; he had no say in that, made no choice in his parents, his birth. You speak of him as an object, a thing. You say that what he has done in his life, how he has lived does not concern you, but how can that be so. I have heard of his deeds, his bravery and his honour. You had him condemned before he ever set foot upon this ground and yet how is he guilty? What is he guilty of? The only wrongdoers here, the only criminals, are the Antaldi. We betrayed his father to his enemies, although he was not of our race, we drove our sister Tuali to madness and death. There are two sins of which we are guilty, but name me one that Danil Lebreven, robbed of race and blood and kin, has ever committed. If you can, then punish him for it, if not how can judgement be passed. I would gladly offer my life against his good character, if he transgresses in the future then punish me. I say again, he has committed no crime, how is he guilty."

Danil smiled at his cousin before he continued. "The power of her words moved every heart that listened around the fire, there was passion within her voice that thrilled the blood and tugged at the heart, here was a natural leader.

"Yes, Suani, spoke up for me, against her elders, against all who stood around and she too was met by silence. Then when Tarien had waited for Suani to become calm and he appeared ready to pronounce my doom, Vuar, the youngest of the three, rose from her seat.

"*'Hold, Tarien, we have not discussed what Suani has laid before us.'*

"Tarien did not even turn towards her. *'There is no need, her words change nothing, Vuar.'* For the first time, his words gave rise to some gasps within the Antaldi who stood in the clearing.

"Vuar did not give ground. *'I feel they do, Tarien, and no judgement can be given without the full agreement of us all.'*

"Now Tarien turned and all heard the irritation in his voice. *'You know the Law, Vuar, even you must see there is no need for discussion. You must steel your mind against the stirrings of your feminine heart.'*

"Again, there were gasps from some who were present, now Vuar was roused to anger. *'Are you saying that my mind is not clear, Tarien? Is clouded by the fact that I am a woman? Be careful what you imply, Tarien, all are listening.'*

"There were more gasps and whispered words. Tarien turned towards me, there was a fierce anger in his eyes and his voice trembled as he raised his staff and spoke. *'There is no further need for discussion, Danil that is called Lebreven, I pronounce your doom …'*

"Someone shouted. *'No'* from behind me and others joined the shout. Tarien was now beside himself with rage. *'What means this outrage? Be silent! We are the Triad and we are the Law …'*

"Vuar reached up and sought to lower Tarien's staff. *'And in this case, we are wrong, Tarien.'*

"Tarien pushed her aside and swung his staff in the air. *'No, the Law is the Law, he must not live to defile …'* It was as if he was about to strike me himself and then …"

Once more Suani took up the tale. "Then Kirielle the Seer raised her hands and Tarien's staff flew from his hands. Tarien himself fell to his knees as Kirielle, eyes rolling, body shaking, spoke with the voice of Blessed Yvelle within her.

"'*Oh, when did my people become the agents of Corruption, that they should pronounce doom upon His enemies? Your mind has become besmirched by His hatred, Tarien; your anger is not that of the righteous, but of the foul betrayer. My daughter Tuali was lost to us, but the fault was in us, let us make recompense and listen to her sister-daughter. The warrior Danil called Lebreven shall be under her good surety, should he break our laws both shall suffer the punishment. But for now, Tarien, calm your blood and clear your mind and you will see that your hatred was fed by the whispers of Corruption from afar. We blame you not; your faith in the Law has been our strength in the past. Let this live in my sanction and set your mind to the protection of the Antaldi now that the Cluath once more go to war. Danil called*

Lebreven go in peace from this place, Suani you have chosen well, your path now you must find."

Danil looked around the fire at his companions faces. "It was quite a sight to see the Triad discomfited by the Seer's words and then Vitta shaking my hand and others introducing themselves to me and wishing me well."

"And your face was a joy, sweet cousin, to see you realise that you had blood and kin and were not alone in the world."

Danil's smile became even broader. "That may be so, Suani, but I charge you not to tell too many that fact, for I will be robbed of my reputation as severe and unapproachable."

Suani smiled with him. "As you wish, Danil, but finish the story."

"Ah, yes, it was then after this great drama and the intercession of Blessed Yvelle, that into the glade walked the five Piradi. Sakia, my steed for many years, led the way with Turic. The Antaldi stared to see them come forward through the trees, unaccompanied as they were. Sakia explained that Ayan had been told within a dream that Mikael had need of the Piradi and when she rose, she found Turic waiting with Sakia and three others. We had no problem finding you, for Turic knew always where you were Mikael."

Sorin turned to Suani with a twinkle in his eye. "Would I had been there to see all of that, my dear." He turned to the others. "It would appear that for all their apparent pledge not to interfere in the affairs of the five races, the Powers have been throwing their respective weight about. Not that I don't approve, I do, in fact I think that it is long overdue. Did Tarien recover after his embarrassment?"

"He had not appeared again before we left, but I am sure that he will. He will accept the words of the Powers that his actions were not entirely his own, whether that is the case or not." Danil looked out into the gathering gloom. "Well, it would appear that the night will be dry, so we can make an early start in the morning. How many days riding are we from the mountains, Sorin?"

"It is hard to say, Danil, a day maybe two on flat ground, but the ground that we cross from here on is rugged and there are many rivers which have cut their way into the rock. We cannot ride swiftly, but we will at least be sure footed with the aid of the Piradi."

At that moment Mirell appeared and bade them farewell, when Sorin suggested waiting till dawn he shook his head.

"I need no light to see my way, Mater Sorin. We Antaldi all have gifts, some are prophetic, some more straightforward and to my mind more useful, I can see in the dark because I see the heat that all plants and animals throw out from their bodies. A simple skill, but as I say most useful. Farewell."

When he had gone and Suani had gone a short way off to make her evening observances, Michael was able to speak with Danil. "Well, Master Lebreven, how does it feel to have a family?"

Danil looked out in the direction that Suani had gone. "It is strange, Mikael, it will take some getting used to, I feel. I had considered, Greer and Ayan and perhaps Sorin as my family till now, but with that detachment that comes from knowing you are different. I am still different, I am still Danil Lebreven the same as before, but now I am called cousin, so should I feel a difference in myself?"

"No, Danil, no you should just enjoy the fact that someone else cares about you, someone else mentions you in their prayers. You are a lucky man, Danil."

"Yes, Mikael, I think perhaps I am, for a change."

When Suani returned they ate a supper of stewed vegetables that Suani had brought with her, they were plump and sweet and delicious. After that they arranged themselves so that the Piradi could come in near to the fire, which was a bit of a squeeze, but since one of them would be on watch there was just enough room. Michael volunteered for the first watch, he did not feel tired and he had become aware that he had been in Taleth for a good while. As before he did not want to sleep and wake back in Wales, now that Danil had returned and he was able to ride Turic once more.

7

The Sha-ellev

He sat on a rock outside the shelter, wrapped in his cloak and surveying the stars, when the drifting clouds allowed. He had been sitting there for some time when he heard Sorin moving behind him. He came and sat beside him.

"I will take over if you would like to sleep, Mikael. I know that it should be Dak who follows you, but my mind is too full to find rest easy."

Michael was about to ask what was on his mind when there was a shimmering in the air before them, Michael had seen it once before, it grew to form a vertical line, a thin column of white, glowing brightly in the darkness. It vibrated like a plucked string and from it stepped once more the strange insubstantial age-less androgynous figure with the black eyes. Michael re-alised that as the figure stepped into existence, that he had not told Sorin of his earlier encounter. Sorin however had stood up and he acknowledged the creature with a slight bow.

"Welcome, child of Takden, what brings you forth from Pha-Dishak, if indeed this is form in truth and not a sending of some kind."

"Greet … ings Calix, mightiest of … Majann, and you … Michael. You come so … close to land … that Sha-ellev home … give thanks for … and give us … no good grace … or warning is … this … polite?"

"The Sha-ellev have closed the Ring of Drukann-Nadim and they heed not the outside world. How could a warning be given? Is it polite to shut yourselves off from all that is around you?"

"Ah, Calix you … forget our weak … ness just as our … strength you impugn … He that was … cast down seeks always ... to know our ... gifts for in ... delusion He assumes ... freedom would be ... His if them He gained ... but He is ... mistaken ... it would avail ... him nought yet ... to this end ... Garshegan he sends ... to seek and ... con ... sume my kindred ... we do not end ... less violent death ... we meet and ... you must know that ... we know not the sight ... of the new."

"And so, for fear of the smoke demons of Corruption the Sha-ellev turn their back on Taleth and the other races?"

"Not quite Ca ... lix ... for I have served ... once already and ... will do what ... must be done ... though there are ... those of kindred ... hold me in contempt ... that help I ... he that comes from ... beyond ... for mighty one ... displeased may be ... but ... I tell you aid ... is sent unto ... the Dri ... Nemett also I have ... released from Drukann-Nadim ... for He has ... defiled Rhurash-Gahleth-Rhurash-Sheph-Semmett ... the Un ... folding ... of the One ... and this will not be."

"Aid for the Dri? That is news that gladdens my heart. Have you a name that I may thank you properly?"

"Name I have ... but speak it ... you could not ..." There was a pause as this was considered. "You may ... thank me as ... Uphik-Mresh-Ludim ... please me that ... would perhaps."

"Very well. Thank you, Uphik-Mresh-Ludim, aid for the Dri is sorely needed and they will not allow me to go myself."

There was a strange sound, like tiny bells ringing in the wind and Michael realised that the Sha-ellev was laughing. "Yes, please me ... it did ... Calix" The black eyes were turned to Michael. "Let them mock ... my choice ... move forward ... with bravery ... Michael for the ... darkness is coming ... remember ... behind the clouds ... under rock and stone ... in root and tree ... and beneath the waves ... they feel your feet upon the face ... of Taleth ... fare ... well." And then it was gone as before, disappearing through the thin line of light as before. They were left staring into the darkness.

"So that was one of the Sha-ellev."

"It was indeed." Sorin looked at him quizzically. "It said it had served once before, when …"

"Sorry, I forgot all about it till now. When Frappo held me captive after finding me in the river, it was Uphik-Mresh-Ludim who set me free?"

"Frappo? You'd better fill me in; you have mentioned none of this."

Michael related his encounter with Krakis, Duvan and Frappo and he explained how he had been released by the Sha-ellev.

"It referred to you as Michael, on both occasions?"

"Yes, can they read minds?"

"Who knows what they can do. Takden has always kept them separate and secret."

"What was all that about not knowing the sight of the new?"

"I think, and I am guessing to a large degree, I think that they do not die unless they are killed, and they do not have chil-dren, they *'know not the sight of the new'* if Sha-ellev die their race diminishes and they were never numerous. Thus, they fear that the Garshegan, who suck light and life from the world, could destroy their race utterly. If that is the case the barriers they have set upon Drukann-Nadim are necessary for their survival. But Uphik-Mresh-Ludim has risked a brief opening of the seal to allow some of the Nemett to leave, so they have responded in their own way to the problems of the rest of the world. Although Uphik-Mresh-Ludim seemed to have been on his own in help-ing you, he said that the others did not approve, and what he meant by *'behind the clouds … under rock and stone … in root and tree … and beneath the waves'* as yet I have no idea."

Michael had been thinking about what Uphik-Mresh-Ludim had said about Corruption seeking their gift and he had a sud-den flash of intuition that scared him half to death. "Sorin, I know why he wants the secrets of the Sha-ellev."

"To escape, I presume, this ability to step from the air is im-pressive, I give you that."

"Yes, but it is a logical extension of sending your thoughts, isn't it? If they have learned to do that in reality, move from one place to another by thinking, then the whole world is open to them. But Khargahar has already learned to send images of Tsarg into my world." Michael became increasingly agitated, for if he was right it was a truly terrifying thought. "With the secrets of the Sha-ellev, who is to say that those sendings could not be made real and worse could he not escape from Taleth entirely. Perhaps that is why I am here, he wants to use me to seek another world to dominate, it's too awful to contemplate ..."

"Calm yourself, Michael, you cannot know for sure that that is what he is doing or plans to do. And the Sha-ellev appear at the present to be capable of protecting their secrets, so he cannot accomplish such a plan, even if that was what he dreamed of doing."

Michael's fears were not assuaged by Sorin's words. And there was still the strange inconsistency of Mr Perkins in all of this. He knew that he was significant, but he had yet to find any explanation for his presence at the hospital and at the lake. The two of them sat back down, neither inclined to sleep, but as if by an unspoken agreement they remained silent and kept their thoughts to themselves. The darkness was complete around them, for clouds had cloaked the stars and no moonlight penetrated the grey. There were several hours before the dawn and little moved around them; all creatures seemed to fear either the threat of the Garshegan that may be hidden in the hills or they sensed the prohibition of the Sha-ellev.

Michael's thoughts still jangled with the fear that Corruption was playing with him, that all of the prophecies, the visions, were a smokescreen to hide his intention to escape this world. None of the beings forced through, none of the Tsarg, nor the serpent in the lake had been fully 'real', perhaps it was the same with Mr Perkins, but he had heard his bird like screech. *'Don't you touch me! How dare you. I am of the blood and must not be assailed.'* Had they actually touched him, or merely threatened? He had spoken, whereas the Tsarg had made no sound. Perhaps he was a sending of a person? That might have accounted for his ability to speak and Michael was worrying unnecessarily, he would have vanished just as the Tsarg did if he had been struck. But if he was a person who was he? Michael was lost in these thoughts when he realised that Sorin was speaking to him.

"I have told you very little of myself, Mikael, and perhaps it is time that I shared a little history. It may help you to understand the way I am sometimes."

"If you think it may help, then go ahead."

"My given name was not Sorin, as now you know, nor was it Calix, it was Tiok, you can laugh if you like. Sylvan still sometimes uses it to annoy me, although that was not what the villagers came to call me. Our village was in the mountains to the east of where I found you, we were nyatt farmers, scratching out a poor living with a breed of nyatt that gave good milk, but whose fleece was coarse and fetched barely enough to buy grain for our bread. None live there now, nor have done for many, many lives of men. My father Brakis and mother Varell had no other children and they had given up hope of a family, so when I was born, they were overjoyed. I was small, but reasonably healthy and for the first years of my life all was normal, until I had reached the age of two when I wandered off from the safety of the yard and I became lost amongst the roaming nyatt on the hillside. A storm was brewing, and the wind howled around me, becoming scared I sat behind a rock and I cried as any child would do.

My father and the men from the village searched frantically for me, but it was getting dark and I was small. Then I heard my father's voice calling and I was so relieved, I stood up and held my hands aloft to show him where I was. He couldn't see me and small as I was, I knew that he must, or I was lost. My voice wouldn't carry above the noise of the wind and I had become desperate, I wished with all my heart and strength for my father to see me and then from my outstretched hands came fire, white flames leaping into the sky. I screamed and fell into a faint. It was not just my father who had seen, all the villagers saw what I had done and now they named me anew, Crellack they called me, the fire demon from the tales old women told to scare the children.

"Crellack, I became to them all and none would come near me. I was shunned and ignored, it broke my mother's heart. I was not allowed to play with the other children or even tend the beasts as the others did. So, I took to sitting amongst the rocks high up the mountain, watching the birds swooping, listening to the sounds of the animals. One day I had just made myself very sick from tasting a new plant I had found. I had seen the nyatt eat it, so it seemed safe, how else would I know what it tasted like? As I was bending over, I saw a hollow in the ground that I had not come across before. In the bottom of the hollow were several stone jars, covered over as if they had been hidden ready to be recovered later. I assumed that they contained ale or liquor such as I had seen the men drinking, but when I removed the binding at the mouth of the jar, I saw that they were scrolls of parchment.

"Now I was by then five years old and I knew nothing of reading or writing for no-one in our village was skilled in that way, but I had witnessed a soldier once speak from a parchment such as this although I had not understood what he said. I took one of the scrolls out and I spread it on the ground before me. I did not know what I expected to see; pictures like the story tellers drew in the dirt perhaps, but to my amazement, what I saw made sense. Whether from some innate gift or by the will of the Powers at that moment I could read this scroll. My first reaction was to immediately put it back in the ground. I was already shunned, by my kin, this would surely make it worse, but then I realised that I did not have to tell them. I could keep these secrets and come up here to read them whenever I wanted to. It was getting late, so I marked the spot with stones that I would recognise, and I went home to my mother whose sad eyes were rarely free of tears.

"I fashioned a sacking bag from some spare cloth in our hut and I took it to the mountain to place the scrolls in so that I could carry them with me back to hide in the moss where I slept. Every day I poured over them, they were mainly histories of the early days of the Cluath, but some included herb lore and the names of animals and birds. I spent the whole of my time trying to identify the meagre flora and fauna that could be found on the mountain side, or learning the histories by heart, though to what purpose I knew not. I had made the decision to take out one at a time and learn that one before removing the next. There were some twenty jars in all and learning them took some time. Strange I would have seemed to a passing bird standing recounting the lineage of some long dead Cluath family to the listening rocks.

"I became eager for knowledge perhaps because I was starved of fellowship. I knew not how they would help me in my life, but it gave me something to focus my young mind on. I had not produced the flames from my hands again, or at least not when anyone was present. I used them very occasionally to light a fire when it was cold, but I found it hard to control and it scared me, if I am honest; remember how young I was! Well, whoever put those scrolls in the ground saved my life, for one day when winter was hard upon us, I had gone up to open and read the last of the jars, I was just six, and I sat in the hollow unrolling the last scroll.

"It was a history, but not of the Cluath, it was the history of the creation of the world, just as I told it to you, when you lay in my cave. I was astonished, I had never seen any beings but Cluath and then only my village folk and a few who travelled through. I knew nothing of the other races, or of the Power's. We had nothing but an old storyteller who came to the village sometimes, but I had to listen from behind the huts, so that none could see me, and I heard very little. I had learned much of the Cluath from the scrolls, but now this showed me that there was a world beyond the mountain and a world that held wonder and terror in equal measure, for I learned a new word, Tsarg. And I was to see them too that day, for unbeknown to us in our village, they had started raiding the settlements in the mountains. Likely as not, it was to clear them of Cluath. In those days the Grashkinark, the Castle of the Teeth had not yet been completed, but maybe it was just out of pure hatred for all life. On that day, as I sat pouring over the final scroll, I realised that I had not brought my sacking bag with me, so I replaced the scroll in the jar, and I stood up."

Michael knew that Sorin was about to recount the story of the attack on his village. His mind raced; would he mention a stranger who aided him? Had he really been there?

"I was too far away to hear the cries, but I saw the smoke and so I ran and as I got closer, I heard the screams and I saw the twisted blades and the snarling hideous faces. I ran towards my parent's hut, but I was knocked aside, and I fell unconscious, sliding down into the small brook beside the village. When I awoke the houses still smouldered, but none remained alive, not one man, woman, child or beast. All had been savagely killed. I had seen nyatt slaughtered, but that was done with kindness and the neck broken first, this filled me with revulsion, I ran back to the brook and I vomited, and then I sat shivering through the night. To be truthful, I do not know how I survived the night in the open, but when I awoke, I determined to do my best for the people of my birth village even though they had shunned me for my strange power. So, I gathered wood into the cen- tre of the village and then I began to try and move the bodies to make a pyre.

"It was then that I saw that a stranger had entered the re- mains of the village. He stood for a moment, horrified at the carnage around him and then he said …"

Michael did not know how, but he had been there, his dream- ing in some way had been 'real'. He finished Sorin's sentence for him, "… build up the pyre, I will see to the fallen."

Sorin stared at him in the sparse first light of the dawn. "It was you? I remember now your scarred face, but how?"

"I do not know, Sorin, our unnamed friend took me there in a dream, when I was ill from the venom and Sylvan told me not to tell you about it, I'm sorry."

"No, no, Mikael, do not be sorry. He must have had a good reason for taking you there, more than just to help me. Through all my years, long after Tiok was forgotten, I would think back to my first meeting with Sylvan, and the stranger who had helped me honour the dead. So, he was there too was he? Well, well, I didn't meet him till I had grown another two years, and Sylvan passed to a new cub. Then he appeared, and I began my proper training as a Majann, that was when I first met Nuall and Ukthor, and I found that Nuall too could cast the fire, though his was weak at first, whereas I had to learn to hold mine in check. So, it was you, and though I should have recognised you, I didn't, or perhaps that was why I persevered with your healing. Somewhere inside I had remembered. Well, though it is long overdue, Tiok thanks you, Mikael Dal Oaken, and he thanks Michael Oakes too."

Sorin stood and he bowed to him, which Michael found rather touching although it embarrassed him at the same time. "I only did what seemed right. But how could I have really been there?"

"Oh, he seems to be able to do whatever he wants, I mean you have met him in your world, although he said that was through you. He is a cunning one, and sometimes I don't think he even tells himself what he is up to, which doesn't make sense, but you of all people should see my point."

"But who is he, Sorin?"

"I have told you, if he wants to reveal a name to you then he will do so, it's not up to me. He may have several names; I always referred to him as Master, which seemed to work. Ukthor used to call him Filak, which is the name given to the old male nyatt who no longer breed, but guard the flocks, they have a distinctive long thin beard under their chins, and he sported a rather similar one. Ukthor always was a cheeky girl. It was always she who suggested the craziest and often most dangerous games to play, whereas Nuall was serious and solemn, but he was an Antaldi after all."

"Was Ukthor a Cluath then?"

"No, she was a Sylian, and beautiful, she knew it too and would delight in swimming naked in the rivers, leaving us red-faced and shaking on the banks. Well, it was very difficult. We were Majann in the making, sworn to celibacy and all of that, and she was determined to test us at every possible turn. When she came to full womanhood, she did stop doing that and always swam privately, which I thought was a shame." He began to chuckle to himself at the memory.

"Ayan is quite right, you are an old nyatt, Sorin."

"Yes, true, but one may look and dream, Mikael, and I am an old nyatt who has kept his vow for well over a thousand years which is a long, long time I can tell you."

A movement behind them made them turn, it was Danil. "Have you two sat on watch all night? Why did you not wake one of us?"

"We have had a good heart to heart, Danil Lebreven, and it has stirred memories in me that may take some time to subside." Sorin laughed again to himself.

"Well, so long as neither of you fall asleep and fall from your mounts, you can stay up talking all night and every night, if you so choose."

Michael saw the smile playing on Danil's lips. "You know very well, Danil, that the Piradi will not let us fall. Even if we fall asleep in the saddle."

"True, which is probably a good job. Now we should prepare to leave as we have some way to go yet and shelter such as this may be hard to find."

As the light strengthened, the companions breakfasted briefly and then they led the Piradi out of the shelter to finish making ready for the journey. Sorin and Dak were introduced to their mounts, Furaam and Metta, which startled Dak greatly, but he seemed pleased when he was mounted, and found that riding was at last a pleasurable experience. When Danil pointed out that he was the first Nare to be allowed to ride a Piradi he glowed with delight. Suani rode Korinne, she was full Antaldi and therefore taller than Danil, but not as tall as some and so she did not look out of place on her mount. Michael was looking forward to the journey now that he would be riding Turic and he greeted her as he lifted himself into the saddle.

"Well, Turic, we are setting off on the next part of our journey. Not into battle perhaps, but I suspect it will not be uneventful."

"That is true, Michael that is also Mikael. Are you going to stay with us all the way, or should I be ready in case you go wandering once more?"

"I have no wish to wander anywhere, but if I should …"

"If you should I know what to do. You shall not fall, and Furaam will inform Sorin."

Whether Turic had felt some premonition or not as they moved away from the rock shelter into the early morning mists, Michael felt the familiar tearing begin around him. He was not best pleased as Taleth vanished and he found himself sitting on a hard, wooden bench, facing a blank wall.

★★★

Never had it happened before that one of the packs had faced such an attack. Occasionally hunted by ignorant Cluath, without success, they had survived through the dark days of Corruption's rise and, with the exception of the Veyix, the passing of spirit from old one to cub had gone on for countless years in the six communities. But here was a being who was bent on their destruction; a tortured and twisted abomination that knew only pain and rage and sought their death along with its own. None but an Avali could have found its way through the mists and the warding that surrounded their ancient meeting place. But this atrocity that had been wolf, was still the tortured remains of the spirits of the servants of the One, and therefore had passed through the protection that had stood unbreached since the beginning. Here it now swayed within the circle of stones, screaming, snarling, howling, an impossible creature that stood twice the height of a man on four powerful legs with two heads that dripped poison from their slavering fangs, and, it was as if the beast had swallowed an entire pack, jaws and limbs, snapping and slashing, pressed and pushed from its body at every possible angle. It shimmered with a hideous sickly yellow light and at every breath a stench filled the sacred air.

It was not capable of coherent thought, but every circling pack member heard its confusion, its agony and its terrible desire.

'*Death! … Ending! … Rend and Tear! … Rip and Slash! … Fire and Flesh! … Kill us! … Kill us! … Kill all! … Ending! Destruction and Death!*'

Within the hearts of every Dri there mounted a rage at the extent of Corruption's hatred of life and the living, but also undoubtedly fear and a terrible emptiness at the sight of the eight dead wolves that already lay beneath their monstrous enemy. Their pack was diminished, their circle violated, and they could not fulfil their duty as they knew that to turn their backs upon this beast meant death.

Sylvan wept tears of fire in her heart for Karlynn, Friesse, Nilus, Tiriel, Uvan, Balior, Huinshi and Tulok whose spirits now were lost to wander in the wild until the end of time. But she watched and she circled as she searched for a way to bring down the beast. They could not risk the poison that it retched forth from every mouth that opened. That they had learned! Nor could they rip at the flesh that boiled and writhed, Karlynn had tried and she had choked as the contagion of its flesh spread within her. Perhaps the beast would burn if flames could be raised around it. The Mage-fire of Sorin would have consumed it, but they had told him to keep to his task, this was for the Dri to solve, but how would they resolve it?

To protect their minds from the anguished thoughts of the monster, the Dri had begun to chant the words of the vow that the Avali had breathed into the fresh new air of Taleth as the Unfolding began.

'*In honour of the One we become the Pack.*
In honour of the One we walk upon the earth.
In love of life we will serve.
In love of life we will ward.
In love of life we will guide.
In soul, we are the Avali, in name we are the Dri.'

Over and over they recited the words, voices inside each other's heads trying to find some comfort, some protection for the Pack, for themselves, for the future.

And then voices that they had not heard for some time joined their chanting, voices that they had not looked to hear.

'In honour of the One we become the Pack.
In honour of the One we walk upon the earth.
In love of life we will serve.
In love of life we will ward.
In love of life we will guide.
In soul, we are the Avali, in name we are the Nemett.'

Into the circle joining the prowling wolves came the Nemett, longer limbed than the Dri, purple and black of fur, but thinner and more angular of body. They spoke above the chanting to all who would listen.

'Brothers and Sisters of the Dri, we have come for we have heard your pain and your need. The Sha-ellev responded to our pleas to give assistance. We think that we may have a strategy that allows victory and gives you some vengeance over this outrage. It cannot be killed, but it may be contained. But to do this you must allow the Sha-ellev within the circle of your commune.'

Sylvan now spoke for the Dri. *'The Dri welcome the Nemett who have been absent so long. The circle of commune is defiled and so we need no longer protect it. If the Sha-ellev have some way of gaining victory over this creature then let them come, we would not lose another of our kin to this foulness.'* A chorus of agreement rang through the Pack.

'Then so be it, I Kuvarish of the Nemett summon the Sha-ellev to do as they have offered, in the name of the One and in the name of life.'

As the circling wolves watched, fifteen columns of white appeared within the circle that stretched, vibrated and increased in intensity, then from them stepped the Sha-ellev. They did not acknowledge the Dri, but they bowed to the Nemett and then they raised their hands above their heads and closed their black eyes. For a moment, they paused and the Dri ceased their chant. The only sound now was the snarling of the horror that faced them. Then a humming began as of giant insects, a vibration of the air, and the forty-nine stones of the circle began to vibrate and shiver in sympathy with the hum which grew in volume. One by one the stones were freed from the earth and they rose slowly into the air, swaying high above the heads of the Sha-ellev who now had raised their arms and the pitch of their humming. Then in one flowing motion they flung the stones forward slamming them into the ground around the creature, creating a new circle, trapping it. And as the volume continued to increase the stones angled themselves to close the top of the stone prison and seal the twisted beast within.

The Sha-ellev applauded their own skill and without a word to the wolves they stepped back though their pillars of light and vanished. The Dri looked upon the stone chamber that had been created to enclose the monster and at the devastation of their ancient circle of commune. But Sylvan knew that thanks were in order. She turned to the members of the Nemett.

'Skilled have the Sha-ellev become that they can move such stones with their thought and travel without moving. We are grateful for your assistance, Kuvarish.'

'Skilled indeed they have become, but with it they have become insular and perhaps uncaring, for they remain unmoved by the plight of Taleth, they helped because they took pleasure in the challenge, not because they were touched by your plight. Assistance one of them has given to the Twice-Dead, but it is at odds with its kin, we fear. However, we accept the thanks on their behalf Sylvan and we mourn for your loss. We urged their help because we saw the need. That being would attempt to consume us all in time, and although the Nemett have been long lived we have not had cubs for many, many years, the Pha-Dishak may maintain the Sha-ellev in perpetuity, but for us it has left us barren and sterile. Should any of the Nemett meet death the Pack will be diminished as yours has been.'

'This is sad news, Kuvarish, but your Pack is not diminished yet?'

'No, though many feel the onset of age, Sylvan, and fear it will be. The weakness of the Sha-ellev, their arrogance and their near immortality we have kept in check, but we are concerned that should we diminish, the Sha-ellev would be tempted to try to rule the other races, for such has their power increased. They would not do so for evil ends, but out of boredom and wilfulness. It is our duty to pass this on, though it pains me to speak ill of them.'

'No, you do right to bring us your concerns. Will this creature remain trapped?'

'Yes, unless Corruption himself comes to free him, the stones are sealed. It will not die, but it will not escape, and we will set guard over it, for we cannot now return to the Pha-Dishak, it is once again closed.'

Sylvan was stunned, the Sha-ellev would close the ring of Drukann-Nadim even to their own. *'They will keep you out?'*

'Every opening lessens the protection; they will not risk another, for any creature.'

'This in itself is reprehensible, but you have aided us, and we would not abandon any to unnecessary wandering.' She cast her thoughts out to all. *'What say you, shall these Nemett who aided us in our plight, become a part of the commune of the Dri until they can re-join their pack.'* A chorus of agreement went up from the assembled Dri. *'Then welcome, Kuvarish and you others, our Pack was diminished by the onslaught of Corruption's weapon, but now it is enhanced by your presence.'*

'We thank you, Sylvan, and we shall honour the Dri as we would our own Pack, in the name of the One and all the Powers.'

★★★

Michael was unsure as to where he was. He looked around and decided that it must be a waiting room of some sort, bare and soulless. A hospital perhaps? He could hear voices coming from another room, one of them was David's. Since he had been left there they were obviously coming back, so he sat quietly seething to himself and wishing he could control this apparently haphazard switching between worlds. If he had someone he could rage against it might help, but no-one claimed responsibility. He had tried to influence it to his cost, and he knew that he just had to let it happen. There might be some sort of method in it somewhere, but he had failed to find it.

A door opened and Netti and a young female police officer entered. *'Ah, a police station.'* Netti realised that he had returned, but she signalled with her expression to keep silent. With exaggerated care, she began to lead Michael out towards the waiting van, Michael could hear David thanking the Sergeant for his help in getting his brother back and then he joined them, and they made a great fuss of helping Michael into the back seat of Stanley and then they boarded themselves and took the van out on to the road.

David drove carefully, but with as much speed as he could risk. He wanted to be as far away from the police as quickly as possible. "Well, I am glad that is over. It's good to have you back, Michael, in both respects."

"Yes, thanks for whatever you've had to do. I don't seem safe in either world do I. How did I get to the police station? Last I knew Tsarg were attacking the place where I was being held. My captors thought that it was the police."

Netti was desperate to tell the story, her head bobbed from side to side in anticipation. "David, you just drive, and I will fill Michael in and then he can tell us who they really were?"

"I can try, but I'm not sure that I know for certain. How long was I gone for?"

"Since you were kidnapped, just forty-eight hours. You see once we realised what had happened and I helped David out of the water the car had gone, but of course I had already written down its number and make and model, when we realised that they were following us. Since we had no choice but to involve the local police, we made up false names and addresses and claimed that you were David's brother and that you normally lived in a sheltered community, but we had taken you on holiday."

"And they believed that?"

"Well, yes, because people do, don't they? We said that we had no idea why anyone would want to kidnap you since we had nothing to give them in ransom, they accepted that. I mean, if we were rich would we be driving Stanley? No, of course not. So, they concentrated on finding the car, rather than any description of you. They were quite ready to keep it to themselves, since they get very little excitement. *'Most of the time, it's lost sheep and vandals, so not very interesting, a good manhunt does us all the power of good.'* And I know my Welsh accent has not improved very much."

"No, it hasn't, but no matter, carry on."

"It turned out that they had several sightings of the car, driving too fast apparently, and then a surveyor turned up early for an appointment to look at the site before the repairs got started on the house proper and he realised that someone was using the house, so he rang the police. When they arrived, they were furious because it appeared that your captors were in a gun battle, well one of the kidnappers had a gun, anyway, and they were fighting with members of a neighbouring police force. But when they rushed in to assist there were no officers to be seen only the kidnappers, who were babbling about being attacked by vanishing people dressed as the filth. The detective inspector put it down to drugs; according to the sergeant he puts everything down to drugs. They decided that the attackers had been another gang disguised as police, probably foreign, who had run off when the local boyos turned up.

"The inspector was thrilled that they had found you without recourse to assistance from any larger agency, they have to contact them after forty-eight hours usually and he even had the station mechanic give Stanley a once over. They do want to speak to us all later just to complete the paperwork, but they were happy to wait till you were well enough and since all the addresses were false, they will have a job contacting us. I know that we haven't told them the truth, but the worst that they can charge us with would be giving false information, we weren't wasting police time, because you had been kidnapped."

Netti's story had as usual been rattled off at high speed, but it made sense. The Tsarg would have vanished when touched or shot at and Michael knew that they had done nothing much that was actually wrong, but he wondered how long this could go on without them coming up against someone who required a proper explanation. "It sounds as if you did a good job, under difficult circumstances. As to who they were, they worked for a character called Mr Delgado, which is probably not his name of course, and it was to do with the art gallery as we thought. They are still looking for Jeffrey Hounslow, the curator who went missing after the explosion. They think that he has the paintings and by now they assume a lot of money. He appears to have double crossed Mr Delgado which may not turn out to be a good idea, but they were sure that I would know where he is, which I don't of course."

David asked the obvious question. "How did they find us?"

"I'm not sure but possibly someone spotted me when I was wandering around, I have no way of knowing where I went or who saw me. I think it was just bad luck, they didn't seem organised enough to have contacts everywhere. Unless of course …" He had just had a horrible thought, if Mr Delgado was Mr Perkins or someone similar the whole thing could have been engineered to create Michael as he was now, the Twice-Dead, Twice-Born whichever way you wanted to look at it. Was Khargahar's reach so long that he could manipulate our world to that extent? Could such circumstances ever have occurred merely by chance? He was thrown back into the whirlpool of self-doubt that had gripped him before. Who really was behind all of this?

Netti was intrigued. "Yes? Some flash of insight, Michael?"

"No, not really, just more questions and more doubts to deal with."

"Well, tell all, we need a catch up on what has happened in Taleth."

"Yes, I suppose you do, we've had little time to talk for a while. And a lot has happened." Michael spent the next two hours recounting the events starting from the crossing of the bridge at Piat Heran, though he left out a good deal, partly because it was too personal, and partly because it required more explanation than he could give. As it was his tale was constantly interrupted by Netti probing, as ever, for new nuggets of information. She was like a human vacuum cleaner with one of those long thin nozzles that lets nothing escape. He was not going to tell her of the two very different kisses in the dark, particularly because he did not as yet want to think about them himself.

The rest of their journey for once was uneventful, other than the normal traffic and losing their way because Netti misread the map, and they arrived in Glastonbury as evening was beginning to bring in grey clouds across from the west. The house that Netti was looking after was up behind the Abbey and it was spacious and elegant. There was a good size garden, which had several trees and enough other greenery to make it quite private. There were four bedrooms, one with an en-suite, a large bathroom and downstairs there was a big lounge that led on to the garden, a dining room, kitchen and study.

"It belongs to a family who moved to Australia but didn't want to sell. I was really lucky, it's bigger than I need now that I have the clinic, but to start with I saw patients here. And early on I took in a few lodgers, but once money started to come in, I didn't need to anymore, as they haven't changed the rent since I moved in, I think that they're just happy it's being lived in. Come on let's make some supper, no I've a better idea I'll order in a Thai curry, there's a place just round the corner that is quite wonderful, and they know how I like things."

While Martha Spinetti ran around reclaiming her home and playing the hostess, Michael walked into the garden. It was dark now, but there was light from the windows that glowed along the paths that ran down both sides of the central lawn, so he could easily find his way. One of the larger trees, a big willow, had a seat that enclosed the trunk and he sat for a while with his back to the rough bark watching, listening and breathing in the smells of the garden. Taleth had taught him to do this; he would never have done it before. He had brushed against a rosemary bush as he walked down the path and the strong scent clung to his clothes. Bats had started to swoop around the eaves of the house as they chased insects too small for Michael to see. Somewhere in the distance he could hear the chatter of people as they walked along the road, and somewhere someone played the piano, haltingly, slowing up on the harder passages and then stopping and trying them again. He liked the atmosphere of the house and despite his anger at the moment of his return he felt at least that he would be able to rest here for a while. In the grand scheme of things, some coincidences were good, meeting Martha Spinetti was one. He heard footsteps and saw David approaching with two glasses of wine.

"The food is on its way, I let Netti order, but I found this rather nice Côtes du Rhône in her kitchen, I'm not sure it goes with a Thai curry, but it tastes good. Here."

"Thanks, I will not refuse." Michael accepted the wine and David was right it was good. He felt rather guilty feeling good about the world after all that had happened in both of his lives, but he couldn't help it, perhaps for once he will sleep without dreaming, or travelling, just go to bed and wake up after being asleep. It would make a nice change.

Netti was quite right about the food, it was excellent and after they had cleared up and finished the wine, Michael left the two of them happily arguing about some new shirts that David insisted he certainly didn't need to buy, and he went up to the room that Netti had allocated to him. It overlooked the garden and so Michael undressed in the dark and he left the curtains open, so that he could see the drifting clouds. The mattress was firm, much firmer than he would have ever bought himself before, but now he had become used to sleeping on the ground and the firmness was quite welcome. He had nearly opted to sleep in his clothes, but he had no riding cloak to wrap around himself and so he resisted, he did open the window, though, so that he could feel the air moving around him. As he lay on the bed he tried to picture the landscape he had left, and he fell asleep with the growing shadow of the mountains in his mind.

★★★

Once again, he found dreams took him. He walked in a wooded vale with a bright moon lighting the way. Beside him walked a pale thin boy, with jet-black hair. There was an air of terrible sadness about him and he paced slowly looking to neither left nor right. After having walked in silence for a while they came to a shelter made from branches and moss. It stood as if the grass beneath it had spawned a tent to give a home to a tired wanderer. Before it a small fire smouldered, and hanging above it was a pot, which steamed gently. As they approached an old man stepped from the shelter and he greeted them.

"So, Terann, you found a friend in your wandering."

"Yes, Master, he was in the woods, I have not asked his name."

The old man stretched, he was thin and aged beyond telling, but he was a head and shoulders taller than Michael, and although his eyes were watery from age they were still a piercing green,

"No matter, names are unimportant here. Come sit, the soup is still warm."

The three of them sat around the small fire and the old man, whose hands were frail, thin and almost transparent, spooned some of the soup into three bowls. Michael accepted it without speaking, and they sat in silence for a while, sipping at the weak broth, that had a fragrance that Michael thought he recognised. It reminded him of the Anlithian, the Moonflower, the rare and powerful plant that could recall spirits of the near dead. Strange that they would make soup from it.

The old man looked up at him and he answered as if his thoughts had been spoken aloud. "Ah, yes, in normal circumstances, making soup from the wondrous Moonflower would be sacrilegious, but this is not a normal place, not normal circumstances. We sup from this each day and we await the time when all grief is ended. The spirit is a strange thing, it can pass in a moment, into the compass of the One, or it can, if it has given itself reason, remain bound to Taleth, rock and soil, and never leave. Foolish we are with our oaths; they should never be made without thought. We both swore oaths and they have kept us here for they can never be fulfilled, so, foresworn, we are bound in Spirit."

The boy, Terann, began to sob quietly and the Old Man moved to comfort him. "Terann, there is nothing gained each day from your weeping, we must accept this long wait, it will end one day."

"But, Master Nuall, I am not strong like you."

Suddenly the names meant something to Michael, Nuall the Antaldi Majann; his was the staff that Sorin now carried, and Terann Dal Farak the orphaned boy who had been given the dagger of Magellin for safe keeping.

"What were the oaths that bound you, Master Nuall, if I may ask such a question?"

"You may, for it will change little. I was brash and foolish, and I listened not to wiser heads than mine. I went to defeat a great wyrm, the last great wyrm or so we thought. Suumik the Terror of the southern deserts, and I took with me the treasure of the Antaldi, my staff, the binding of three trees, powerful and beauteous. In anger, I left my good friend, who had warned me against my quest and against taking the staff, for should I fall it would be lost. He offered to guard it for me, but I stupidly thought that he just wanted it for himself. I swore an oath that he would never hold it, save when I was dead, and the Ender of Days walked upon the face of the earth. In my arrogance, I ignored his warnings and I fell into Suumik's trap, he was old, but young still spawned, he was not the last, I faced four great wyrms and I died for nothing. The staff I assume was also lost." He shook his head. "For young Terann here, it is simpler, he had been entrusted with an object of beauty, a present given in love, but rejected out of duty, he swore …"

Terann spoke his own folly. "I swore that my spirit would not rest until I had found Master Calix and returned the dagger to him. But Master Calix was lost, and I ran from the battle, ran and ran until I could run no more and I crawled into a cart that headed for the Heran River. I had caught a fever and I was ill, so when we reached the Fort by the bridge, I thought to hide in the cellars till I was well again. But … they found me, and I lost the dagger and now he will never have it and I must wait …" His sobbing began anew.

Michael was stunned. This was no dream; he had been sent to give them a message across the worlds. He felt emotion rising in him. Terann had waited so long for this, he tried to keep his voice steady. "I know not how I come here, for me this is a dream, but I have news for both of you. I am Mikael Dal Oaken, named in prophecy by Seers as the Twice-Dead, the Ender of Days, I found the dagger of Magellin in the cellars beneath Pliatt Heran and I returned it to Calix the Majann, and I have seen him holding aloft the staff of Nuall, retrieved by the Antaldi and gifted to Calix in this time of peril. I feel that someone has sent me here to tell you this and perhaps bring you peace."

Nuall rose to his full height. "Calix has my staff, it is not gone from the world, of this you are certain?" Michael nodded. "That is good, that is very good. Then I must speak with him. Is he still as cantankerous as ever, friend Mikael? Never mind, I thank you, on behalf of us both." He turned to Terann. "Come boy, your sadness is over, Calix has seen the dagger again and though he cannot touch it, it is his once more. He was not lost in the fire and darkness."

Terann stood and he took Nuall's hand. "But Master where should I go?"

Nuall looked at Michael. "You must truly be a messenger of the Power's my friend, take Terann with you back through the vale and help him on his way."

Michael did not know where he was supposed to go, but he felt that someone would show him. He took Terann's hand and they turned and walked back the way he had come. It was getting lighter, but Michael realised that it was not the sun rising it was Terann who was beginning to glow and almost imperceptibly change into a being of light. Although it would have been shocking in life, here in the dreamscape it was right. They stopped walking and Terann, now brilliant and shining turned

and smiling he bowed to him and then he was gone. As the
dream faded Michael was sure that he heard a deep voice whisper. *"My thanks, Michael that is also Mikael, it was a task I could
not undertake, but it is well done."*

★★★

8

Julia

He woke feeling refreshed and positive about both worlds for once. They had finally made it to somewhere he hoped that they could remain for a while and he had unequivocally been able to be a positive agent for good, which left him with a warm feeling. He felt better about himself and less torn with doubt, at least that had been clear. He tried not to question how it fitted together or how it was achieved and just allow the good feeling to continue.

The weather was fine, and he sat enjoying his coffee. He watched as a squirrel ran mischievously round the garden poking its nose into the bushes and then scuttled away whenever a bird hopped down onto the grass. He had not looked at the time, having risen when the sun woke him and showered. When David came down and pointed out that it was still only eight, he was surprised.

"Sorry, did I wake everyone? I have got out of the habit of watching clocks."

David gazed at him suspiciously. "You look and sound in a good mood? Is there something I should know?"

Michael smiled, it was hard to explain, as most things were. "Just a dream which was more life affirming than usual, that's all. Did you sleep well?"

"Yes, when I got to bed. We stayed up rather later than we had planned. You know the way you get going when you talk about things, and Netti got me talking about all sorts of things, including my family, which, as you know, gives a lot of scope for discussion, and so another bottle of wine was opened, and it became a late night."

"Nothing wrong with that David, there's nothing urgent to do today apart from a bit of shopping, which if you give me some cash, I can do if you like."

David looked reluctant. "Well, I would, but …"

"You're worried that I'll switch and end up wandering around Glastonbury with milk, eggs and bread in a bag, well, okay, but you have to admit I wouldn't stand out, the place is packed full of the strange and unnecessary of life, so I will fit right in."

David laughed. "Fair enough. That coffee smells good, is there any left?"

"No, but I'm up for another, I'll make some fresh."

"Okay, look, don't worry about the shopping, we can do that later, but I'll give you some cash anyway, so you can go for a wander if you want. Just …"

"Just don't get lost, I know I will try my best, honest."

He ground some more coffee and set the machine in motion. The smell was wonderful, and David had found some frozen baguettes, which were the half-baked variety, so that when Netti entered the kitchen there was warm bread, coffee and jam waiting on the large central breakfast bar.

"Well, I like having guests like you boys." She laughed. "Do you do cleaning and ironing too?"

"Not sure what those words mean, David's a whizz with an iron though. We used to leave stuff in his pile at college and he'd quite often iron it before he realised it wasn't his."

"Yes, I remember that. But I'm afraid that when I was in chambers, we had a chap who did it all for us. Got to look smart in the Law you know."

"Oh, well, I'll take breakfast for a start anyway. Have we any plans for today."

David shook his head. "Not really, I thought, that maybe we could just be tourists today, I haven't seen the town; but there's no rush, we were up rather late."

Netti smiled broadly. "Yes, sorry about that, I get rather chatty when I've had a drink, even more chatty than usual, that is. Still now I know almost everything about your family. I must say there are some therapists I know, who would love a crack at your relations."

It was Michael's turn to laugh. "Maybe so, but there would be casualties, mostly among the therapists, I suspect."

They sat drinking the coffee and sampling several jams that had been sitting in Netti's cupboard. They were mostly good, apart from the marrow jam that had been bought at a local craft shop and was roundly declared as the worst jam ever created, by all three of them.

David and Netti decided to sit in the garden for a while, but Michael wanted to go for a walk and so he set off along the road and walked around the wall that enclosed the Abbey grounds. It was a while since he had been here, but he expected little to have changed. He turned from Chilkwell Street into Silver Street and he followed it around to the High Street. Once there, he wandered in and out of the shops, with all their wonderful names, 'Gothic Image', 'The Goddess and The Green Man', 'Pandora', 'The Rainbow's End Café', 'The Psychic Piglet', 'The Speaking Tree'. It did occur to him that he was, perhaps, in the one place in the world where his story, should he have told it, would at least not seem out of place. Whether it would be believed he was less sure about. Being open minded was different to truly believing; a sceptic requires positive proof, but a 'free thinker' is often harder to persuade, because they allow you to believe what you want, but they don't feel any need to believe it themselves. He had met them in the past and there were one or two who accepted everything, but actually believed nothing.

In one of the book shops he found two of his own books in the art section. They sported a suitably studious image of himself on the inside sleeve, and he was amazed to see himself as he looked then, with more flesh and no scars. At least no-one would recognise him, that was certain. He flicked through one and was surprised that though there was much of it that he could hardly recall now, it wasn't bad. It was on the Italian Artists of the Renaissance and was full of beautiful images and 'stunning' insights that obviously at one time in his life he had seen fit to put down for others' edification. A helpful assistant came over.

"Ah, yes, a very fine collection of essays on the Renaissance in Italy, sir, we sell quite a few of Mr Oakes' book, it's such a shame that he died."

Michael was shocked and he must have shown it in his face. "He died; I didn't know that."

"Oh, yes, he was in an explosion at a gallery in Manchester, he died later in hospital."

Michael almost didn't say anything, but somehow, he felt affronted. "I thought he had just lapsed into a coma but was still alive."

"I don't think so. I think we had a release from Galliard Press about six months ago. I may be wrong, of course." Perhaps Michael should have a word with his agent after all.

"I think you will find, Miss, that they were premature in sending that out and that Mr Oakes although unlikely to write again for a while, is still with us."

The assistant was becoming uncertain both of her information and of this customer. "Oh, I see, er … did you know him, sir?"

Michael opted for something that was not actually a lie. "I was at University at the same time as he was. We had mutual friends, that sort of thing, I really suspect I would have heard had he died. I knew about the accident. He was about to have a one man show of his paintings I believe."

"That is interesting, sir, I didn't know that he painted as well."

There was another, older woman at the till and she had decided that the young woman needed support. "Can I be of assistance, Margret?"

"Well, this gentleman was looking at one of Michael Oakes' books on Art."

"Yes, they're really good; I have that one at home, a signed copy, no less."

"He seems to think that Mr Oakes is still with us and I was under the impression that we had been told he had passed away."

"You know, I think you're right we had a release from the publishers didn't we."

Michael began to wish that he hadn't started this, but now that he was involved he wanted to see where it would lead. "I really think they are mistaken, but …"

"No, no, it has piqued my interest, sir. Let me get them on the phone."

The older woman disappeared for a good ten minutes. Margret had gone to serve other customers and Michael himself was about to give up waiting when she returned.

"Well, sir, it would appear that you are right. The release was premature, and they have since retracted it and apparently he has come out of his coma, but his whereabouts are now not known, having left the hospital under strange circumstances with his legal representative."

Michael was relieved that he wasn't dead after all and that in that case the company would still be paying royalties. "I'm glad to hear it, thank you for clearing that up. I will take this, if I may, I have a friend who will appreciate it."

"Thank you, sir, and it was no trouble, to tell you the truth it was quite entertaining, particularly their embarrassment when they had to admit their mistake. Would you like me to wrap it for you?"

"Thank you, yes." Michael couldn't remember how much he earned for each copy, it wasn't much, but at least it proved that he still existed, even though it showed him as he was, not who he was now.

He left the shop clutching this memento of his former self, feeling that this had been one of the stranger moments in his life, which was saying something, considering everything that he had been through. However, it didn't affect his mood and he continued his wander down the High Street. There were more shops with great names as he turned the corner into Market Place, 'Cat and Cauldron' and 'Man, Myth and Magik' caught his eye in particular, the latter possibly promising more than perhaps it could deliver. Further around in amongst the other side roads and eateries, he spotted in the window of one shop a walking stick with a wolf's head handle. He would never in his former life have known whether the carving was accurate or not, but now he had met a good few wolves, five of the seven packs in fact, and this carving was definitely of a wolf of the

Dri; a large grey, strong and serious, powerful and solemn. The forehead and the eyes were just right and had Sylvan been standing there in the shop you would have said it was carved from life. Although he had no need of a stick to assist his walking he felt that he had to buy it.

Initially, he felt very subconscious with the stick in his hand, but the wood felt warm to the touch and it nestled nicely into his hand, so it was not long before he was wondering why he had not bought a walking stick before now. He decided to find somewhere to sit for a while and he found a small café, ordering coffee, water and a goat's cheese and chutney sandwich, he sat in a window seat and watched the world go by. He hadn't really been hungry, but the sandwich when it came was very good and the coffee was a full flavoured Italian blend and thus worth savouring.

As he watched the people who passed the window, he realised that it was less than a week since his walk through the shops and markets of Tath Garnir. He began to wonder if people in Tath Garnir ever just browsed, wandered without a conscious purpose. He hadn't seen anyone who he would have described as a casual visitor, a tourist; it was an odd concept. Society had to develop to a point where there was time for leisure and relaxation; he couldn't imagine Sorin or the others ever going to places just to see them, just to be there. Time was too precious.

There had been a time when people only travelled for trade, for war or for pilgrimage. Even exploration had been for similar reasons, striving to become richer, and stronger. Even climbing a mountain to be closer to the gods wasn't exactly tourism. In Taleth they seemed to still be at that stage. Journeys had a purpose, a direction. He may well have been the first person to wander the streets of Tath Garnir with no express reason other than because they were there, and that he was passing through. Glastonbury High Street and Market Place had that same feel, people being there because of where it was, being tourists, and he watched them, fascinated by the different groups and the dynamics of each. He imagined their relationships and their conversations. Did that make him a people tourist?

Suddenly he realised that someone was talking to him. He looked up; it was an elderly woman, who seemed to think that she knew him.

"What have you done to your face, Peter? Have you been in an accident? No-one told me."

"I'm sorry … do I know you? I'm not Peter, my name's …"

The woman sat down on the chair opposite with her hand-bag placed upon her knees. She was small and thin, noticeable even under the thick coat with its tight defensive rows of buttons. She peered at him and then she continued. "Goodness, you're so thin. That girl not's feeding you, that's what it is. She never did know how to produce good food, you need fattening up, Peter, you really do. Thin as a rake you are."

"I'm really sorry; I think you have me muddled up with someone else …"

"And you didn't come and see me, on my birthday, you didn't come. I waited, but you didn't come."

Michael wasn't sure where she had come from or whether she was with anyone, he hadn't even seen her enter the café. Her eyes were intense, and he noticed that her lips moved even when she wasn't speaking. He tried again. "My name is Michael, it isn't …" but it was no good. She was quite determined that he was this Peter, whoever he was. The waitress who had served him came over and he was about to explain what had happened, but then he caught a change in the old woman's face. The intensity fled and it was replaced by a sad frightened look that stung him. Her eyes began to flick around for something to focus on that held no fear. He suddenly felt terribly sorry for her.

"Would you like to order something for your mother, sir?"

"Oh, she's not …" he couldn't do it. She looked so vulnerable, "er … yes, a pot of tea and a couple of small cakes I think."

"Very good, sir."

The old lady looked out of the window for a moment and then, feeling safe now, she began again. "Did you remember to get that watering can I wanted? The one with the long neck, I hope so, because it's so difficult to water the hanging baskets with the one I've got. I have to stand on a chair to do it and I'm not supposed to do that, because standing on chairs can be dangerous. Mr. Hodgkins fell off a chair when he was dusting, and he had to go to hospital. Dorothy told me that at church, I think, but she hasn't been around to see me for a while so I don't know how he is now. She used to play tennis with me and your father, you know, her partner was … was … oh, you remember, the tall chap, with the silly little moustache and a Morris Traveller, which smelt, because he let the dog sit on the seats, you know, Peter … what was his name, come on, you must remember … you must …"

Michael didn't know what to say to her, but he could sense her rising panic. "Come on, Peter, help me out, tall, thin, he taught violin at the school, oh, what was his name … I can't … remember …" and then he realised she was crying, great big tears that rolled down her cheeks.

"It's alright it doesn't matter …"

"But it does, I can't remember, and I should and …"

Then two things happened simultaneously, the waitress arrived with the pot of tea and cakes and a woman in a smart navy trouser suit appeared through the door of the café.

"Mother, there you are! I turned my back for a second and … I'm terribly sorry …"

The waitress, as if this happened every day, turned around quietly and went off to get another cup. Michael stood up and he reached for a chair to allow the woman to sit beside her mother.

"It's alright honestly, here."

"Thank you. Now, Mother, dry your eyes and I'll pour."

"I'm alright, Julia, don't fuss. Peter can pour the tea." Then instantly with an accusation, she turned on her daughter. "Where did you go? I was waiting for ages and then the bus didn't come so when I saw Peter …"

"I didn't go anywhere, Mother, and we weren't waiting for the bus, we were in the bookshop, and this isn't Peter …"

The waitress arrived with the second cup and Michael found himself pouring tea for these two complete strangers as if he had known them all his life.

"Not too much milk, Peter, and half a spoon of sugar. Thank you."

"No sugar for me, er ..." The woman, Julia, looked up at Michael. She was probably in her early forties, but she wore it very well and apart from the tiredness and the stress that hovered at the corner of her eyes, he found himself noticing that she was still an attractive woman. He was also momentarily caught by the realisation that he had seen that face before, or at least one very like it,

"It's Michael, Michael Oakes."

"Hello, Michael. Julia, Julia Sharpe, sorry about this." She accepted the tea, and she risked a smile, a smile that, amidst the stress and the race of daily life, lit up her face like a sunset flashing its final throws of the day across the countryside. "She does this a lot I'm afraid. I have to watch her like a hawk; I could do with reins like the children have." Her mother was happily picking at a fairy cake. "She thinks you're Peter, my brother. He died ten years ago, in a boating accident, she's never really accepted it."

"I'm sorry."

"Oh, don't be too sorry, he was a monster. Spoiled by my parents, he bullied his wife and frittered away dad's business. He was always her favourite, though, and she fixates on him constantly." She sipped the tea and watched her mother for a moment. Michael saw an errant lock of hair fall across her cheek and be whisked away with long elegant fingers. "What was she upset about?"

"She couldn't remember someone's name, Dorothy's tennis partner, if that makes any sense."

"Oh, that would have been Harold, the violin teacher, that Dorothy was engaged to on and off for about twenty years, eventually he got fed up and moved to Scotland, I think."

Her mother without eating any of the cakes had converted them into a pile of crumbs. "Harold that was it, good backhand, but weak serve. Dorothy was engaged to him, but never did get married, they used to go for weekends to Cornwall together when Dorothy was in the mood; that was what she always said, *'I'm in the mood, Gloria, I think I'll get Harold to take me to Cornwall.'* I mean everyone likes Cornwall, don't they?"

Julia looked at Michael and a laugh erupted from her, a musical laugh of understanding without a hint of judgement in it. It drew Michael into laughing too, he realised almost with a jolt that he was enjoying her company. "Dorothy died a few years back and the funeral was attended by a good number of elderly single men, so I suspect that Dorothy was often in the mood, but not always with Harold. Still good for her, I say." She laughed again, quietly as if to herself.

Michael smiled back. "Sounds as though she made the most of life, which is more than a lot of people manage." The nagging thought that he had met this woman before continued. "Sorry if this sounds silly, but have we met before?"

"No, I don't think so. I think I would have remembered." She smiled, "I know what you mean, about Dorothy, though, I never get the time to find a Harold and swan off to Cornwall, not since Dad died. I have my hands full, what with work and Mum to look after."

"What do you do?" His eyes followed the curve of her neck as she sipped her tea again, before replying.

"I'm a Translator, French, German and Italian. Well I was, I still do a bit, but I have to rely on written translations mostly now, so that I can work from home. I used to do the live stuff, conferences, business meetings and the like, which was more stimulating, but I take what I can get. What about you?"

Michael was in the mood for honesty. "I was a writer, Art History, Critiques and articles in the press, and I painted a bit too. But I don't do that anymore. I'm in what you might call a transitional phase."

"That sounds horribly serious. Art History did you say? What did you say your name was?

"Michael Oakes."

"Yes, I thought it rang a bell. I translated one of your books, for Galliard. It was on Italian Artists of the Renaissance, if my memory serves." Michael began to feel that this was too much of a coincidence; he picked up the book and he unwrapped it.

"You mean this one?"

"Yes, that's the one … what a coincidence. Why do you have a copy of your own book?"

"I was going to give it to someone. I found it in one of the bookshops, just by chance."

Julia's mother saw the book and she reached out for it. "That's a very lovely painting, Masaccio isn't it?" She pulled the book towards her.

Michael was surprised that she recognised the painting on the front cover. "Yes, it's the 'Madonna and Child with angels', it's in the National Gallery."

"Mother leave that it isn't yours, and your hands are covered in crumbs …"

"No, its fine honestly, she can have it if she would like it. Most people know nothing of Masaccio, did she study art?"

"No, but her and Dad used to like going around galleries. If it's in the National Gallery she'll have seen it many times. We lived in London and that was their idea of a fun day out. Let me pay you for it."

"No, no, she can have it as a gift; I can always get another can't I."

"But I thought that you were going to give it to someone."

"Well, yes, but only because I bought it. I hadn't really intended to do that." Michael explained to her about being told that he was dead.

"I knew there was something about your name, yes, I remember the explosion, it was all over the news for a while and then of course it was forgotten, like everything else. So how long were you in hospital, then?"

"Six months and they were about to turn off my life support when I revived."

"Well, I'm glad they didn't turn you off." Her tone was genuine, and it warmed him to hear it from a stranger. Michael thought about the 'friends' he had had, most of them Mel's really, none of them had come to visit him in the hospital. In fact hardly any had spoken to him since she died. None of them would have cared if he had been turned off, but this woman did or at least appeared to.

"Thank you."

"And thanks for being nice to my mother. Some people can get quite cross. They don't understand, she can't help it. She just forgets where she is and then sort of wakes up and is in a different place, it's hard to explain."

"No, I understand perfectly," *'more than you know'*, he thought.

Julia's mother held the book up to show her. "Look, Julia, Peter bought me this book with such lovely pictures in it."

"Yes, Mother, it's lovely. Look, are you sure I can't pay you for the book … or for the tea? Or perhaps a fee for watching Mother?"

"No, no, if it makes her happy, then that's good. Would …" It was a long time since he had done this. "Would you like to do this again?"

Julia was caught rather by surprise, but she rallied quickly, and her blue grey eyes shone. "With or without Mother?"

Michael had to laugh. "Either, I don't mind."

Julia smiled, she looked at him and Michael felt the look pass under the scars and search out something in his face. "You know I would like that. Are you staying in Glastonbury or just visiting?"

"Staying for a while, with friends, I'm still in recovery."

"Do you have a mobile number?"

Michael realised of course that he didn't know the land line number or even know the house number of where he was staying. "No, not since the accident."

"No problem, here, this is my business card, give me a ring tomorrow and we'll arrange something."

"Okay."

She stood up to go. "Come on, Mother, we're going."

"Oh, is Peter coming."

"No, Mother, he has a plane to catch."

"Yes, I thought so. Can we have salmon for dinner?"

"If you like, Mother, we'll get some on the way home." Julia turned and she reached out a hand. "Thank you, Michael; you really have been very kind."

"Not at all, it's been a pleasure." He shook her hand warmly and he saw her smile spread to her eyes. "I'll give you a call."

"Yes, do that and next time I'll pay for the cakes." Her mother had started through the door without her and she turned and pursued, calling a goodbye over her shoulder. Michael sat down again, feeling both very strange and very normal. It was the most normal thing in the world to meet someone and find their company pleasurable and then express a desire to see them again, but it also felt strange for him to be doing that. He had not looked at another woman since he met Mel. People often say that, but for him it had been true, there was just no-one else, she had captivated him from the beginning; and this was happening in his own world, not in the raw emotion that flowed through Taleth, amidst the terror and the beauty that accompanied the constant threat of death; it was in a small café, in real time. He did not let himself speculate as to the next meeting. He had to contend with the possibility that his 'condition' might preclude even that level of normality.

Still it had been pleasant, and he was grateful for that, even though the coincidences involved still gave him some pause. Finding his books on the shelf was perfectly reasonable, it was a good bookshop and the books had been well received, by the sort of people who buy that sort of book. Meeting the translator of his book, or rather her mother, was also perfectly possible. After all, translators could live anywhere and so he could have met one of them at any time. But he hadn't, he had met her here and now, with the book on the table beside him. He looked down at the table and he saw that there was a set of keys, car keys by the look of them; Julia must have put them down. He got up quickly and looked along the road in both directions, but he couldn't see her. So, he went back in and after paying the bill, he asked if they had a phone that he could use, and he explained why. They agreed when he handed over some money to pay for the call. He was shown through to the back of the café where there was a small office. He dialled and let it ring, after a while a voice answered, a male voice.

"Hello?"

"Hello, I was trying to contact Julia Sharpe; ... this is the number on her business card. Who is this please?"

"Miss Sharpe? Ah, yes, this must be her phone then. It was on the table and I heard it ring. Who shall I say called?"

Michael had felt an instant twinge of recognition, but had ignored it, but as the voice had continued, he knew who it was, and all his rationalising of coincidence fell away, and he stood once more on the abyss of confusion and doubt. The voice on the phone was Mr. Chambers.

"You know, damn well who it is, why can't I have just a day when things are normal."

"I'm sorry, I don't follow, who shall I say called."

"It's Michael, but you know that don't you, what are you doing here?"

There was a pause. "Michael? I'll leave a note for Miss Sharpe."

The phone was cut off. "Wait, I want to know what's going on." But it was dead. He fumed inside against everything and everyone and putting the phone down he left the shop and stood in the street leaning on his walking stick; he wanted to scream. Was it because he had stopped focusing on Taleth, on his task, his truth, he hadn't forgotten for a moment, he was just enjoying another person's company, and his lonely and tired soul had leapt at a chance of a moment without responsibility, without someone looking over his shoulder? But there had been, hadn't there, Mr. Chambers, was here too.

"Michael? Michael, are you alright?" It was Julia, she had come back, but she was on her own. He looked up, and he almost shouted. *'No, no. I am not alright, and I never will be.'* But he held it inside and tried to smile.

"I'm fine. I just needed a moment's pause, that's all. You left your keys."

"I know, I must have put them down on the table."

Michael handed them over. "Where's your mother?"

"Oh, I met one of my neighbours at the car park; she has her safe in the back of her car. Can I give you a lift somewhere or are you in town?"

"Oh, just up behind the abbey, not far. I rang you from the café."

"Did you? I didn't hear my phone, perhaps mother was talking, hang on." She retrieved her phone from the pocket of her jacket. "No, no missed calls. Perhaps you rang the wrong number. Let me see that card I gave you." He took it out and he gave it her, he knew that he hadn't got it wrong. "Ah, stupid of me, that's one of my old ones, I changed my phone contract and so the number's different. Sorry, that number's been defunct for months." She took out a pen and wrote the new number on the back of the card. "I'm sorry, but thanks for trying. And thanks for the book, Mother was proudly showing Georgie and explaining that Peter flew in specially to give it to her."

Michael's confusion had not lessened, in fact it had increased, for now there had been no reason for the deception, it was just cruel. "Never mind, I could have signed it for you, but I didn't think."

"Well, there's plenty of time for that, Michael, you're going to ring me remember. Bye." She kissed him gently on the cheek and then she turned with a wave to walk back up the street. Michael's heart leapt while his mind railed against the life that he couldn't have, and he gripped his walking stick to prevent himself from shaking his fists at the sky. He must walk; walk anywhere, away from eyes and faces and doubts and fears and all the craziness. It seemed to hit him all in that moment, why was this happening to him? What had he done that had singled him out? Was it all the anger and jealousy, the twisting knife that had sliced through him after Mel left him, or the silent passion with which he hated the world after she died? Or even all the bitterness because his mother left him still blaming him for his brother's death? Her favourite, her Peter, she had called him Peter when she was dying … Oh, and then the penny dropped. Once more he was the butt of the world's cruel jesting, Julia's mother had thought that he was a Peter too. Everyone saw him as someone else. In Taleth he was Mikael, not Michael, it was Mikael that Ayan loved, it was Mikael that Siraal loved in her dreaming. No-one even saw him as himself and here this stranger, called him Peter. He wanted to run from all of them, let them suffer the results of their own madness. Why did he have to help? Why did he have to do anything? He closed his eyes on the world and he went to step from the pavement. He was stopped by a hand on his arm and a voice behind him.

"Michael? We wondered where you had got to."

It was Netti and David. They were smiling, and he wanted desperately not to think about anything at that moment, so he smiled back. "Oh, hi, having a wander around the town?"

"Yes, playing tourist. Who was that woman? An old friend?"

"What? No, we've only just met. She left her keys in the café."

David gave him a sideways look. "She seemed very friendly."

"I was kind to her mother." Now Netti had given him a strange look.

"Look …" He explained what had happened, but he left out the voice on the phone, he would deal with that himself, somehow. "So, she was very grateful."

"Yes, I could tell, so are you going to phone her?" Netti almost dared him to say no, so that she could scold him.

"Of course, I am, she seemed very nice and I promised to sign the book."

"Yes, the book. Interesting. Who were you going to give it to before you gave it away?"

"Well, I was actually intending giving it to you, but I shall …"

Netti feigned shock at his behaviour. "So you bought a present for me and then gave it to the mother of some woman you had only just me, well, I'm really hurt."

David laughed. "No, you're not, you're thinking what I am, that it is a stroke of genius. He couldn't give her a present, too soon, too obvious, but give her mother a present and then he comes over as gallant and compassionate and so unselfish."

Michael needed this friendly teasing from the two people who actually did seem to care, it drew him back from the brink and his anger subsided completely. "Go on, have your fun, Julia is an educated woman with good taste, that's all."

"In everything except men. Alright, only joking ..." David had received a gentle poke from Netti for that remark. "We're walking up to the Tor; do you fancy coming?"

"Yes, alright, I can properly try my walking stick out."

Netti was genuinely impressed. "Now that is very nice, and somehow very suitable."

"Yes, I thought so too."

They set off together along the road and up the hill. It was a long time since Michael had walked up to the Tor, but he remembered the way quite well. The first time Mel and he had done it, it had been a roasting hot day and they had both bought ridiculous sun hats. It seemed a lifetime ago now, several lifetimes in fact. He went back to watching people again as they walked. Some children were being taken to the Rural History Museum. They all had matching back packs, in bright colours. As they passed he heard them chatting, they were French, by the sound of it, speaking rapidly and giggling as they scuttled along after their teacher, like a group of naughty mice.

As they passed the Chalice Well gardens, they heard singing; a group of women in white, circling around a very large lady with a drum. They all had wreaths of flowers in their hair and their song was enthusiastic if not tuneful. Michael caught snatches of the words, it was a song of thanks to the goddess, the Mother with so many names, Isis, Demeter, Hecate. He could have given them a new one, Cerlinith, but they would have scoffed at him. He was a man, why would a goddess commune with him. Of that he wasn't sure, but of her power he was living proof. But their belief was real for them and if it gave them comfort, hope and pleasure, then he for one wouldn't dream of judging them, though he might have suggested some music lessons.

They turned up the road that led to the path on to the Tor itself. The bushes leaned over them and he smelt in the hedge-rows, amongst the elder and the bramble, the heady scent of the local fox, pungent and powerful, filled with messages for a nose clever enough to interpret. He had walked as a wolf and he had seen the forest as animals do, witnessed the scent trails, the map of the world, coloured by smell. He imagined that here it was the same, except there were no wolves, but even without them, the fox, badger and the vole, must perceive the landscape in the same spectacular display of odours and colour. Thinking of Taleth again forced him to acknowledge that he might switch again, and he needed to be ready. He also realised that if he switched, he might not be able to ring Julia and that was suddenly very important to him. He decided to ring and explain why he might not ring as he had promised to do.

"David have you got your phone with you?"

"Yes, why?"

"Can I just make a quick call?"

"Of course, here. Something important?"

"Well, it might be. I'll explain later."

"Okay, you and your walking stick can catch us up."

Michael waited until they were out of earshot and he rang Julia's number, he was dreading the possibility of Mr Chambers answering again, but thankfully it was Julia's voice at the end of the phone.

"Hello?"

"Julia, its Michael. I borrowed a phone."

"Oh, is it tomorrow already?" She didn't sound displeased and he was grateful for that.

"No, sorry, but I need to tell you something important."

"Oh, I see. Is it that you don't like Cornwall?"

"What? Yes, Cornwall's fine, not that I've been for a while."

"No, nor have I." There was a pause; Michael felt he had missed something. "Sorry, Michael, same old family joke."

"Oh. Look, if I don't ring, I need you to know why."

"But you're ringing now."

"Yes, but I might not tomorrow, because I might not be able to."

"Oh, right. Go on then."

Michael wondered how much he could say. "Since I came out of the coma, I sometimes lapse, and I can be unconscious for an hour or two or sometimes days."

There was another pause. "And you're worried that you won't be able to ring me or that you won't get there even if we arrange to meet up."

"Yes, sorry."

"Don't be sorry, Michael, that's really sweet of you, because it means that you really do want to see me, even if we have to wait."

This time Michael paused. "Yes, that's just it, I do. Sorry, I'm not doing this very well, am I?"

"You are doing fine, Michael, I will wait for your call, but if you don't ring for a few days, I'll ring this number and your friend will answer even if you can't. How's that?"

"That sounds very sensible, I will explain to David. That's whose phone I borrowed."

"Good, then that's all fine, so long as you like Cornwall we're in business. Ring when you can, bye."

"I will, bye." He felt like a mumbling schoolboy again and he had probably sounded like one, on the other hand Julia had sounded confident and in control. *'What was it about Cornwall?'* There had been something about it before, but he had been too busy studying her face. He would have to remember to ask her later. He looked up and saw that David and Netti were not far ahead, so he pursued them through the gate and across the field.

The air had grown chill as if rain was coming and he looked up for dark clouds, but there were none to be seen. Wispy strands of white stretched across the blue as if drips of white paint had been unsuccessfully wiped away. There was the merest hint of a breeze, but nothing to even tug gently at his shirt or hair. Very few people were about and those that were moved in small groups spaced out around the hill, it was as if there was a conspiracy of not quite silence, but reverential quiet, that had descended upon the countryside. Here was the same lack of sound that echoes around a Cathedral when the visitors obey the natural law of imposing spaces. *'Thou shalt keep silent in the face of grandeur and spectacle and sheer size'*. The early church reasoned that man could not understand the immensity of God, so it gave him a 'bigness' that he could understand, and it made the buildings enormous. Michael knew that the response of cowering peasantry everywhere has become a memory which we find hard to shake, he had seen even hardened atheists whisper in Cathedrals.

This outdoor Cathedral was today at least receiving the same respect and Michael was pleased, it gave him the peace to revel in the walk. David and Netti had obviously chosen to walk directly to the top, rather than take the longer winding labyrinth path. His wolf's head felt firm and strong in his hand and he soon caught them up as they followed the sloping path. He gave David his phone back.

"Thanks, David."

"All sorted out?"

"Yes. It's just that I had said I would ring Julia, the woman you saw leaving, sometime tomorrow, but if I switch, I might not be able to."

"What did you tell her?"

"Just that since the accident I sometimes relapse and can be out of circulation for a while."

"Did she accept that?"

"Yes, she was fine, very understanding, but she might ring to ask how I am. So, I thought I'd explain and …"

David smiled. "You need say no more, I think it's a good sign. We all need company," He turned to look after Netti who had continued on up the path. "Sometimes it's the best form of therapy, come on."

He followed. The sun was lower in the sky now and so the shadows had lengthened and what strands of cloud there were had dissipated to leave a single thin layer. The view was much as he remembered it, as he suspected little had changed, the Tor rising out of the neat fields and orchards, edged with an oval of trees, the Somerset countryside rippling away from it. It wasn't hard to imagine it as an island upon which the dying Arthur sought a peaceful end, even when you knew that none of the stories have any verifiable basis. It still held a rare quality of mystery that was in no way diminished by all the eccentricity and pseudo-science that appeared to surround the town these days.

They had reached the stepped section now and Michael was delighted to see that the top was empty of people. He knew that it wouldn't last, but it gave them a moment to themselves. David and Netti wandered round to the marker stone in front of the tower and Michael stood with his back to the cold stone gazing out towards the south. Suddenly there was someone standing beside him, a man hooded like a monk.

He took Michael's arm and said, "Michael, walk with me a little, I feel I must explain." It was Mr. Chambers.

★★★

9

The Staff of Nuall

Michael's anger boiled up in him again. "What are you doing here? Get off me! Why did you have that phone? You're just playing with me; I wish that you'd all just leave me alone."

"Michael be calm, we must speak together, or at least you must listen."

"I don't want to be calm; I want to know what's going on. I need to have some answers. I …" Michael felt the air around him grow very cold, and his voice died in his throat. There was a mist enveloping the Tor, a thick fog that rose from the ground to shroud them and to deaden all sound.

"Now, Michael, you will listen. I am not playing with you, nor is anyone else. There is no game, it is all deadly serious, but I cannot give you the answers that you seek, for I am not the one who has them. I do not know who does have them, but I do know that what I have done, I am still doing, and what my Sisters and Brothers are doing, is to keep you safe, to keep you free, to keep you as you are, the Uclan, the outsider, that which is not Taleth. You must remain so, or your decisions will not be your own, and I am certain that above all that must be so.

"But I have been watching you, and I have something that I can share with you, it will be hard to hear, but you must hear it. Recently you performed a task, not for me for another, it was well done, two are at peace who were not so, but it made you feel content, at ease, comfortable. That cannot be, Michael, I am sorry. Since the betrayals that were visited upon you, by friend, spouse, colleague, kin, you have been angry, angry because you knew that you had been betrayed. Mikael was equally betrayed, but he knew not till after, his anger is there burning, and raging within you, but yours was there before you fell into the fire, before you 'died'. It is this anger, this fury at the world, at your wife, your friend, your mother and at yourself, that sustained you. It is this anger that helped bring you back; it is this anger that now helps keep you alive. And it is this anger that protects you even from him, from our brother that you call the Corruptor, I am certain of it. He sees your ire as a means to trap you, but he is wrong. You are vulnerable when your anger fades, when you are content then you have no protection, no defence. It is the storm inside that will save you Michael. And I am sorry, it was cruel to use the phone as a weapon, but you were off guard and you cannot allow that to happen.

"I see from your eyes that you need one answer I can give. Julia Sharpe is not part of any plan that I am aware of. She is as she seems and is no threat in herself. I will not interfere again, but approach all things with caution, Michael, and above all do not forget that you have been betrayed. Do not let your anger fade, Michael, it is your life blood, your protection. From this moment onwards, it will become more perilous, more deadly, for if he realises that you cannot be trapped, cannot be controlled, he may then decide that you must be destroyed."

And then he was gone moving away with the fog that clung to the hillside where he walked, masking his footsteps from the watching world. Michael heard David's voice calling, he shouted back but he heard his voice echo strangely in the remnants of the mist, then David's voice faded but the echoes of his own voice hung in the air with the fog. Another voice, hushing him, a figure walking out of the fog hand raised for silence. It was Danil.

"Mikael, be silent for all our sakes." He was leading Sakia, his Piradi, and Michael realised that he stood holding the reins of Turic, his own mount. Around them a thick mist shrouded the rocky hillside.

'Michael that is also Mikael, you have returned. It is good to sense your mind free from sleep.'

'It is good to be back, Turic, and my thanks for warding me during our ride. What is happening?'

'A large contingent of Tsarg are moving past us. We could not tell if they were following us, but we sought to evade them. When it was obvious that there was no place to hide, we prepared for a desperate battle, but then a fog rose from the ground and hid us from their view. We believe it to be the work of the Sha-ellev, for we stand on the foothills of the Pha-Dishak, but we have no proof. Danil wishes us to follow.'

Danil was indeed signalling to follow him and so the four of them walked silently a little way to their right, picking their feet carefully over the rough shale that made up much of the ground. After five minutes or so they reached the others who stood perfectly still as they listened to the sounds of running feet, snarls and orders barked in the harsh tongue of the agents of Corruption. Suddenly a chant began, a marching song of the Tsarg, for soldiers are soldiers, whatever army they are part of. It chilled Michael's blood for he had heard it before.

'Tsarg u-kankar ta ven!
Tsarg na ki gnartish rakk!
Tsarg u-kankar na Khargahar!
Khargahar ta gakken rakk!'

It was a chant of hate, a chant of fear, an oath of loyalty sworn in terror and in pain. Michael looked at the faces around him. Sorin, eyes closed, searched the mist for the end of the column. Dak head bowed thoughtful and resigned. Danil's eyes blazed with anger and his hands were clenched in readiness. Suani head held high defiant, but tense and trembling, Michael realised that she may never have faced death as the others had, never stood before the might of the Corruptors hate and smelt the fetid breath upon their tongues, but he saw in her eyes a fierce determination, a strength, that he knew would give her courage.

"Tsarg na ki gnartish rakk!
Tsarg u-kankar na Khargahar"

Michael knew what it meant; he had heard the words in the Cluath. *'Tsarg for drink whiteskin blood! Tsarg will kill for Khargahar!'* He like Danil was filled with anger and the desire to be rid of this stain upon the face of Taleth, and he now knew, for Mr Chambers had told him; that he must use his anger, his rage against the world, channel it as a weapon against the shadows and the darkness that threatened him in both worlds. The sound of the feet and the rasping of the voices began to fade and finally silence fell. No-one stirred, no-one moved so much as a muscle until the fog drifted back up the mountainside and left them in the darkness just before morning. Sorin opened his eyes and without looking at the others or giving them permission to move he raised his hands to the mist that lingered higher up the slope.

"We thank the Sha-ellev for their aid in giving us protection from the lengthening arm of Corruption." No reply came; silence folded itself back to nestle amongst the rocks. Sorin turned to the others. "It always pays to give thanks, even if there is no-one listening." He looked up at Michael. "Ah, I see you have returned to us, I was beginning to get worried. You have been gone for nearly two days."

"Two days." He tried not to show his surprise. "I suppose I should be hungry then."

"Well, we were able to get you to accept small amounts of water and some soup, enough to ease our concerns. Oh, by the way, Danil's cousin here is undoubtedly the most persistent and inquisitive person I have ever met, and I have met a good many people, so after a day of constant questions, I eventually gave in and I have told her and Dak the truth."

Michael felt that he should be shocked, but he wasn't he was relieved. He considered Dak to be a friend and he had felt that he was being deceived. As for Suani, she was Antaldi and had probably sensed that there was something more than she was being told.

"I hope you are not offended Mikael, but it seemed the right thing to do."

"No, not at all, in fact I am very much happier with them knowing, but I would ask that I remain Mikael in case others are listening."

"Oh, certainly that must be the case, thank you for being so … understanding."

"No, really it's better this way." Michael felt Sorin leap into his mind. *'She really was driving me to distraction, Michael, now she can address her endless questions to you instead. Is there anything I need to know since last we spoke?'* Michael told him briefly of his conversation with Mr Chambers. *'Ah, those are his thoughts on the matter, well, it may be so indeed. We must be doubly on our guard then, for the Corruptor may well need to show his hand more clearly. I have spoken more with Dak, so you may speak openly with him about why we must come here.'*

'Why has the journey taken so long, Sorin, if we are still riding around the Pha-Dishak? I thought that we had reached that before I … left.'

'We had, and we are now but two days from the borders of the land of the Nare, but we have had to cling to the foothills of the Pha-Dishak to avoid riding on the open downs and it has been slow going, as I knew it would be; made slower by the constant movement of the Tsarg and a certain party member who was asleep.'

'Sorry, you know I am not in control of that, I wish I was.'

'I jest, my friend, some of my sense of humour has returned, but not all, I have yet to hear from Sylvan.'

Michael felt the pain and distress that were behind his words and knew that he would have been constantly searching for the thoughts of the great She-Wolf.

'Have you thought about using Nuall's staff to find her?'

'I have thought about it but have not done it, Michael. I will admit to being scared, no, not scared, concerned. If I, unused to its full power, open my mind to search, who knows who else I may alert to my presence. Nuall is dead and only two others could have the strength to use it, and Ukthor is gone. It would be like lighting a beacon and saying, 'Here is Calix, come and get me' in letters as high as the mountains. So, I have not used it. Am I wrong?'

Michael wondered what to tell him, Nuall had said that he must speak with him. *'I think you may be. I have spoken with the spirit of Nuall.'*

"What? How? When?"

Sorin had been taken completely off guard by this and he had spoken out loud.

"Who are you talking too, Master Sorin? None of us have spoken." Suani couldn't quite understand Danil's amusement.

Sorin ignored her and he turned to Michael. "You spoke with him? Tell me quickly."

Michael explained about his dream and all could see how moved Sorin was by the meeting with Terann and Nuall. "Poor misguided child and he escaped the battle only to meet death in that cellar, at least now he has found some peace. But Nuall did not leave, you say, and he wished to speak with me?"

"Yes, his exact words were, *'Calix has my Staff, it is not gone from the world, of this you are certain? That is good, that is very good. Then I must speak with him. Is he still as cantankerous as ever?'*"

"Now, I know that you speak the truth; me cantankerous, huh!" He turned to the others. "If you would give me leave, my friends, I would attempt to speak with Nuall and then we must be on our way."

Suani bowed to Sorin. "I will pray to blessed Yvelle and Palleon that you are successful, and she moved away a little and knelt down, her eyes closed."

"Thank you, Suani. The rest of you be ready to scrape me off the mountainside, should it all go horribly wrong."

Sorin removed the Staff from the saddle of his Piradi mount and he carefully unwrapped it. In the pale morning light, it glowed and shimmered as if it had a life of its own. He placed one end upon the ground, and he gripped the staff with both hands. He then slowly closed his eyes and he began to concentrate. Michael felt the surge as the old Majann let his power flow into the winding wood of the Staff. The air around Sorin hummed and sparked and then it began to coalesce into the figure that Michael recognised as Nuall the Antaldi

Majann. When he had taken on his full form the spirit of Nuall spoke.

"Well met, old friend, it has been a long time."

Sorin's eyes opened, but his body remained tense from concentration. "You could say that, so you have been hanging around waiting all this time."

"Yes, and no thanks to you. I kept dropping hints to the Seers and those of the Triad with the gift, but you changed your name didn't you. So even if I had said straight out, 'Find the Staff and give the Staff to Calix' they would have done nothing."

"Yes, well I did that for lots of reasons, Calix did die in the Battle before the Teeth, well, to all intents and purposes he did, but I was roundly told that my task was not complete and since, you had got yourself fried and Ukthor went sailing, I was the only one left."

"She did go. Oh, well, she had always said that she would, but if she was dead, I think I would have seen her, even in passing. I saw a lot of others passing, but I don't remember her, unless she was avoiding me. Was she still angry with me?"

"No, she forgave you, but you listened to neither of us, Nuall, and we were right."

"I know that now, Calix, but … never mind."

"So, you think that she might not be lost."

"Ah, no, I only said I didn't think that she was actually dead, lost she may be, considering where she went. But listen, I have two thoughts to share with you, I had them a long time ago and I have kept them ready for when I could eventually pass them on. Firstly, that which was done to seal the prison may not have been done in anger; it may have been done in love. For though there was defiance, he only cast him down, he was not destroyed. And secondly, remember there is always balance, warp and weft, light and dark, hate and love."

There was silence for a moment, and then Sorin spoke. "And I am supposed to understand all that, Nuall, am I? A bit more detail might help …"

"There are rules, Calix, you know that. We all swore to abide by them, in life and in death."

"I know, I know, but it is so aggravating sometimes."

"Try using that legendary wisdom, Calix, old friend, oh, and don't break my Staff, it's …" He vanished as Sorin withdrew his power.

"… valuable, I know, old friend."

Danil held out the wrapping and Sorin laid the Staff in it. "Did you gain from that, my friend?"

"Well, I know that I can use it, so that's a start, but as to his message … I will have to give it some thought. Come on, we should be on our way."

They mounted up and they began the last stage of their journey to the mountains. The sun had risen, but the air was still chilled. Winter held sway here and the mist still clung to the outcrops of rock that thrust angrily from the Pha-Dishak. The terrain here was not conducive to riding swiftly, harsh white stone forced itself through the earth all around them, which meant that they followed a twisting, winding path, never a straight line. Here and there, the sparse grass had tried to grow upon the rock, but always failed leaving dead brown clumps, clinging in defiance to whatever crevice had originally given hope of survival. Some of these stones had been shaped by wind and rain into monstrous sculptures and as they rode Michael's imagination peopled the landscape with hobbling crones or fat old men and in one case a Valeen with broken wings. He could see why Sorin had predicted another two days riding, even though the mountains towered above them. They were riding three times the distance in the route they had to take, a straight path would have taken them there in a day.

Michael rode behind Dak with Danil following him. As yet, he had not had a chance to speak to him properly since his return and Dak had been unusually quiet.

"How does it feel to finally be returning home, Dak?"

Dak turned in the saddle and then returned his gaze forward. "It is my homeland, Mikael, but whether it is my home is hard to say. We shall see."

"It has been hard not revealing to you the plight of your people, my friend."

"Yes, but Sorin had his reasons, I am sure. I just hope that there is something that we can do to end this curse." He lapsed back into silence.

"What was the nature of your ancestor's crime? The punishment was so severe; I cannot imagine what he could have done."

Initially Dak said nothing, but then Sorin dropped back and asked Danil to lead for a while. "I'm afraid that it is time to answer that question, my friend. There is no reason other than the secrets your ancestor sought that would require you to return, and the Trillani were insistent that return you must."

Dak looked across at Sorin and he sighed. "I would attempt to deny your questioning and your logic, but you may have been taking lessons from Suani and I have no wish to be bombarded for the whole day, so I will answer." He paused for a moment to look up to the towering mountains that rose ahead of them like a tidal wave, frozen as it reached its peak.

"It has its roots in the beliefs and culture of my race. We believe that Ragarad created everything within the rock and soil upon which we live; therefore, we believe that everything that is dug up or hewn from the rock is sacred and subject to detailed rules. That which is retrieved becomes Ragarad's blessed gifts to us, they can be melted, shaped, moulded, cut and beaten, but they must remain pure. Jewels can be set into the handle of an axe, silver inlaid in the blade, but that is an association, a partnership, a marriage. To seek truly to combine the individual elements, to break the purity of a substance is to the Nare as horrific as that joining, the Nakuatak, that Mikael slew in the forest, when we first met.

"My great grandfather, Bakund, began to believe that this was a misguided view and he began to experiment in secret. He discovered that by grinding certain rocks together he gained a powder that became a liquid as he watched. What was more that liquid could consume other substances, dissolve other rock as if it were dust. He found to his cost that it also burned skin. He hid his knowledge from everyone, even family to begin with, so that no-one could be accused of assisting him, and he was by all accounts quite terrified himself of what he might create. He wrote a letter to his son, that he kept upon his person at all times, a letter to be read after his death, a letter that was in the end to seal his fate,

'I fear the consequences of what I do and tremble as my hand raises the mallet or the pestle, but I know deep in my heart that I must do it. My mind races through the wondrous things I may discover and the horrors that I might unleash. What if I find a powder that like the first eats rock, but also eats metal and anything else it touches? Would it eat its way through the very ground I stand on? Where would it stop? Who knows what power I might release, for surely it took power to create the blessed rocks at the beginning of time? My mind is in a whirl, my son, but my destiny is clear.'

"He found other combinations, one which burst into flames and burned with a brilliant white light, others that released noxious fumes. He was certain that there would be a positive use for his discoveries, particularly when he found that one mixture appeared at first inert, but when he made it into a paste it cooled and healed the burns upon his skin. But he was betrayed, by a neighbour, jealous of his standing with the Elders, who were appalled when he admitted what he had been doing. He tried to explain to show the Elders that his intent had been for the good, but they found his letter and his own fears, his own words condemned him. He had blasphemed against Ragarad and the sacred Law and what was worse, they assumed that as he had written to his son, that his family knew of his work and so they were all to be punished, despite his protestations that they had not known, that they were innocent. The family were cast out in the middle of a deep winter and some died upon that first trek into the wilderness, others continued the journey. I was but a child and I remember little other than the snow and the wind, and the bitter, bitter cold.

"One by one my family were scattered, faded and died and that left only myself and my brother and my father sick and ill. We had made ourselves a home to the south of Tath Garnir, although my brother and I still travelled much, finding work where we could. One day my father called me to him, and he handed me a leather-bound book, it was filled with notes in a thin scrawling handwriting, notes that made no sense to me, for they were in no language that I could understand. My father looked me in the eye, and I knew in that moment that he was dying.

'Dakveen, my loyal and obedient son, as you are the elder you will now be head of our dwindling House. It is my duty to pass this book onto you. Do not try and make sense of it for it is the blasphemous ramblings of Bakund and it is the reason why we are wanderers and outcasts. Do not destroy it for it is a reminder of our shame, if you die as the last of our line let it be returned to the rock with you and so our House and our misery will be ended.'

"He told me what he knew of Bakund's trial and our journey into the wilderness and then he died. I have kept this book always and I have sometimes taken it out and tried to read it, but the words are just jumbles of letters and I can make nothing of it. In my travels I have seen much invention and discovery amongst the other races. It would appear that the Nare are the only ones who made curiosity punishable by banishment."

Sorin had been quiet and very thoughtful during Dak's tale, when he spoke it was as if his mind turned a multitude of things over and over, but he could reach no conclusion. "I had presumed as much from what your father said when I met him many years ago. Bakund's work was, in a way, similar to my own with plants, herbs and fungi, I would hate to think of the numbers of men who would have died had I not been able to carry out my experiments. You yourself Dak would certainly have died from the wound you inflicted upon yourself to remove the Witherer's touch. But my craft can only go so far, and I have had many, many years to work at it. I cannot hope to cure a whole nation."

"In my world, what your ancestor was doing would have been called Chemistry and many learned men have devoted their lives to the study of it."

"And it is not performed in secret or prohibited?"

"No, though many generations of school children may wish that it had been." Michael had to laugh at Dak's incredulous expression.

"It is a craft taught to your children?"

"And has this study always led to positive and useful outcomes?"

"No, Dak, sadly, many great discoveries have cured disease and saved lives." He saw no point in being dishonest. "But just as often men of learning have discovered exactly the horrors that Bakund feared. Men have unlocked a power that could destroy the world."

"And no-one tried to stop them?"

"Well, many have tried ever since to make their leaders bury the knowledge, but something once learned is not easily unlearned. But for all that, the good that they have done cannot be questioned, millions of lives saved from disease, farmers helped to grow more and more food, suffering alleviated for those in pain. Men have felt, like Bakund, that the risks are worth taking and any demons unleashed must be faced and contained."

Dak mused on what he had said. "It may be that in Bakund's notes there is something that may help cure the plague that ravages my people, but whether the Elders will welcome me and allow us to try and help is another thing altogether."

"That will be the question, Dakveen of the Nare, and it may take a good deal of persuasion from us both. I feel that I need a refresher course in how not to annoy the Nare Elders. Will you ride up front with me and help me? I am a little rusty on some aspects of lineage and hierarchy, which I suspect will bore the others to death."

Dak laughed gleefully. "Oh, my friend, I think it may well bore us and our poor mounts to death too, but if you wish, ride on."

The order, thus changed, it left Michael, Suani and Danil riding close together while the droning tones of Dak reciting ancestral lines in his own tongue drifted back upon the breeze. Suani was indeed very beautiful and her voice was pleasant to listen to, but Michael quickly saw what Sorin had meant about her questioning. Danil was of no help, he simply rode behind, laughing occasionally as Suani probed Michael with question after question about the 'other world'. He tried to be circumspect in his answers, but she was very persistent.

"So, there are many different races in your world too?"

"Well, to your eyes you would probably see them as many different types of the same race, since we all resemble the Cluath to a large degree, although skin tones are different and to some extent height and stature."

"And there is no magic of any kind, no Majann?"

"Again, no and yes, there is much that you might see as magical. We can communicate over very long distances, but we use devices to do so. I suppose science is our magic in a way. But there are none who truly have gifts such as the Powers bestow upon Seers or on the Valeen."

For a moment, she went quiet. "Do people hate children such as Danil? Do they hate those who are different?"

"Most people don't, but there are some who reject the intermingling of races, just as here, wars have been fought over such reasoning. But most ordinary people happily see people as people; at least I hope they do."

"Are the women beautiful in your world?"

Michael heard Danil laughing. He knew he was getting himself into dangerous waters here. "Yes, Suani, many of them are very beautiful, just as in Taleth."

"Are you married Mikael?"

Michael paused. He had been told to remember his anger, very well he would remember. "I was married, married to a woman of such beauty that it would still your heart to look at her."

"You were married? What happened?"

"She betrayed me, with someone I thought of as a good friend and then they both died."

"Oh, I am sorry, that is very sad." There was a pause, but it was not a very long one, her sympathy was genuine, but brief, her inquisitiveness was by far stronger and it could not be contained. "Tell me some more about the trees are they very different to here?"

And so, the ride went on, Michael did not really mind, but it did leave him tired when they eventually stopped. They rested in a hollow, which gave very little shelter, so even though the night air threatened to be cold, Sorin forbade a fire and he insisted upon watches being an hour on and then a new pair of eyes. He was about to take the first watch himself when two pairs of eyes appeared over the edge of the hollow. It was two wolves, black of fur and thin of limb, they came forward and they bowed to Sorin, but then they looked at Michael and once more he was drawn in and heard their words and understood.

'Greetings, Michael that is also Mikael, we are Kuvarish and Ushkoriv of the Nemett, although now we run with the Dri. We have news and offer aid and warding.'

Michael answered out loud, so that the others could hear. "Welcome Kuvarish and Ushkoriv of the Nemett, we thank you for your offer of aid and warding. What is your news?"

'For Sorin, from Sylvan of the Dri – I will join you soon, the pack is safe, thanks to the intervention of the Nemett and the Sha-ellev, but eight of our Brothers and Sisters died and are lost, Karlynn among them, it appears that I lead the Dri now and I must attend to the dead.'

Michael was horrified, eight dead. It was almost impossible to accept. Sylvan had known there was danger, but surely even she would not have believed … He relayed the message and Sorin nodded and sighed deeply. "Eight dead, for this alone he must be made to pay if nothing else. Is there no longer a threat?"

'No, the threat is contained, for now.'

"They say it is contained … for now." Sorin nodded but his face was grim, and anger burned in his eyes.

'For you Michael that is also Mikael, we say – Fear not the darkness, for now is the time for strength. We will warn you if your pursuit is close, farewell."

"Thank you Kuvarish and Ushkoriv of the Nemett, we thank you for your news though it is hard to hear. Strength and honour to the pack, may the hunting be good, and your path ever run true."

The two wolves bowed their heads briefly and then they were gone, their black fur allowing them to melt into the darkness in an instant. Sorin turned without speaking and he settled himself to take the first watch. The others sensing his need for quiet thought kept their voices low. Danil enquired with his eyes and Michael felt that he should know.

"The Dri, Sylvan's pack, were attacked and eight are dead."

"Corruption has grown bold indeed, Mikael, this is grave news indeed."

He moved away and lay down, but Michael noticed that he laid his dagger beside his head.

Suani moved close to Michael and her eyes shone with admiration. "I had no idea you were gifted Mikael. Can you speak with all beasts?"

"No, I have no gift as you would perceive it, Suani, I can speak with the wolves of Taleth because they allow me to. They are not like other beasts."

"Yes, my cousin has told me of this, but I do not fully comprehend what makes them special, I …"

Michael suspected that if he let it this conversation would run on into the night and he needed rest, so politely he interrupted. "Can we continue this in the morning, Suani, then I will gladly tell you what little I have learned about them."

"I am sorry." Suani smiled, "My desire for knowledge is I am afraid unrelenting and sometimes I forget myself." She turned away to take her place next to Danil, while Michael wrapped himself against the gathering night and tried to find a comfortable spot sleep. He lay listening to the wind as it played around the rocks, and in the distance, he heard wolf song, all the packs had felt the loss of the Dri. The sound was unlike any he had heard before, there was such sadness in it that it made him ache in sympathy. Here was emptiness and desolation; here was an unending loneliness. Eight spirits wandered like Lonett, unable to fade, unable to live and unable to truly die. He fell asleep with the grief of the wolves in his ears.

★★★

Once more a dream began. He stood within a circle of pillars, the open sky above his head. Around him shimmering and glowing were thousands of figures, the Sha-ellev. Pointing and laughing, speaking their own tongue in shrill rapid bursts of syllables that meant nothing to him. He was cold and he realised that he was naked. He turned to seek a way out, but the circle was complete. He tried to push his way through, but this made things worse and the laughter grew. They reached out to poke long fingers at him, becoming bolder one of them pulled down Michael's head and began to pull at his hair. He slipped and he fell to the floor. There was more laughter and applause. Then a hooded figure appeared beside him and wrapped him in a cloak not unlike his own. He then turned upon the crowded Sha-ellev, who howled in protest at his interference. The voice, which Michael, recognised spoke loudly and with anger.

"People of Takden, you of the Sha-ellev, what right have you to mock and abuse this man? Have you no shame? Answer me, what excuse have you?"

One of the Sha-ellev stepped from the throng and he held up his hands for silence. "In the Pha-Dishak … the Sha-ellev do … as they please … we wished to … see this man for … ourselves … but by what … right do you … oh master of … the shadows … by what right … do you defile … our home … permission was granted … not to you … to pass … the ring of … Drukann-Nadim … you are not … welcome here."

"The Sha-ellev have grown arrogant indeed if they would deny me or my kind entrance and I come only to retrieve, Michael that is also Mikael, and end this nonsense. I defile nothing"

The Sha-ellev howled and they shouted louder than ever and then they went silent as another figure strode into their midst. A woman, tall and hard of face, with long crimson hair, and skin like alabaster.

"Brother, your presence here is outrageous."

"Sister, your children's treatment of this man was the outrage."

"This is their home and you have no right …"

"I have every right, Takden, and you know full well how badly your children have behaved. They have become powerful under your guidance, perhaps too powerful, but have seem to have gained little wisdom from it."

"Do not seek to lecture me; you know nothing of my love for my children. You hide yourself away and teach tricks to the favoured few, I give my children real magic."

"And break all your vows, Sister, the rules were made for a purpose and you know full well what that was and why we must adhere to it."

Takden turned her back angrily. "I told you not to lecture me. One has given aid, therefore we all have given aid, although I would have had it otherwise. When the Nemett begged me and my children agreed, I allowed aid for the Dri, but it will not happen again. Now take the outling fool and begone and look for no-more assistance from the Sha-ellev."

"I will go, Takden, and I will take him with me, but be warned for though you shut your people, your children, away from the reach of the Corruptor, and leave the other races to face this struggle. Should they fail, should Corruption be victorious, Drukann-Nadim will be no defence and the Sha-ellev will also fall."

"Leave here, Brother, before I change my mind."

Michael found that they were no longer in the chamber of the Sha-ellev, but he had felt no motion or sensation, they were just somewhere else. He looked around and he was surprised to find that it was Sorin's cave. He sat upon the bed and he looked up at the robed figure in front of him.

"I don't understand. The Sha-ellev have helped me, helped all of us. Why would they then do that to me?"

"I cannot tell you, because I do not know. Takden has sealed them off from all the other races and cultivates them, feeds them ideas, gives them new powers, but she is wrong to do so. She has not given them understanding or wisdom. They are like children, naughty, but very powerful, children. They are not evil, not in any sense, but they have become uncaring and devoid of feeling. And although I dislike speaking ill of my brethren, Takden appears to be following her own secret path."

Michael looked around the cave. It was just as he had first seen it when the bandages had been removed from his eyes. "Why have you brought me here?"

"I didn't Michael, you did."

"What? I don't have the power to do that."

"No, not by yourself, but it was you, nevertheless. I simply removed us from the Pha-Dishak and sought a place where you would feel safe, you selected Sorin's cave. Much of what has happened to you, Michael, has happened through you, although you have had no control over it. I suspected some time ago that you are the link that allows my brother, whom you call Khargahar, to push images of Tsarg through into your world, although I could be mistaken. That I can appear in your world I will explain when I feel it is necessary."

"But are you truly there or is it all just inside my head?"

"Oh, I am there when I need to be and, yes, it is real for the most part. How else would I have saved your life? But it is complex and difficult to explain to one who, with all due respect, is not my equal. Some things I can do, because I can do them. Could a bird explain how it flies?"

"So, are we actually in Sorin's cave or not?"

The figure laughed and he threw back his hood allowing Michael to see him for the first time in Taleth. His face was old and lined with care, but his eyes, his wolf eyes, sparkled with life. He looked different to how Mr Chambers had appeared, longer and thinner in a way.

"Yes, and no, Michael. We are here in his cave because our eyes see the objects around us, but in reality, it is just an image drawn from your head and you are in what you call a dream. Where I am is unimportant. But I have decided to tell you a few things, because I feel that it is important that you have faith in the people around you. My name is Uvarin and, when my Brothers and Sisters worked to create the new races, I walked amongst the First Ones. I helped them to learn the songs of all things so that they could shape the world to suit themselves. It was because the First Ones were careful and slow that my

Brothers and Sisters tired of them, but to me they were a wonder. Their world was a timeless one and so they tired not of the world. They could sing the waters of a river to take a new course and their song would last long enough for the waters to cut their way through the rock and bed themselves deep. They could sing the trees to take new shapes and their song would last long enough to watch it happen. They are neither dull nor slow-witted as the Cluath seem to think and yet, so few remain.

"Thus, it was when the new races were given life, I did not stand with one race alone, but amongst all the races I scattered gifts, gifts of healing, prophecy, divination, telepathy, and others were gifted with skills which they would have to discover within themselves. When those who had received the gifts were ready, I helped them explore their gifts. If they had enough tenacity and perseverance, I continued to teach them, to guide them to seek out their true strength. For the aid of all the races in Taleth I created the Majann and the Seers. Each new generation sees several born to each race, save the Sha-ellev, since Takden would not give permission, but none are forced to follow the path and in these sad days few do, wasting their gifts to gain coin or favour. Of all the children I have tutored throughout the long history of Taleth there were none more adept than Calix, Nuall and Ukthor, each very different, each very special, would they could have fought together, then truly the war would have been won. But Nuall fell in a pointless quest and Ukthor is lost."

Michael was happy at last to have a name to put to the voice and shape, but nothing of what Uvarin had said helped him very much, he knew that the Powers could not see into the future, but perhaps Uvarin might have some idea. "Do you know what is going to come of all this, where my journey will end?"

"No. The Unfolding of the One is known only to the One, but I who helped to carve the First Promise believe it still holds true despite the faithless. We know only what we heard and what we saw at the beginning of time and we seek to do what is right, each in our own way, each according to our own truth." He looked around at the cave, with all its jars and scrolls. "We all accumulate knowledge, we gather thoughts and ideas together and we try to grind out wisdom, so that we may pass it on, but it is always only our wisdom, because the ingredients will never be the same, for we are all different. Only the One has true wisdom, knows the true path, the rest of us are just blind men fumbling in the wilderness, trying to point our children in the right direction and stumbling over each other in the dark." He then turned back to Michael once more. "You have done well, Michael that is also Mikael, but the journey will get tougher from now on. Keep faith with your companions, listen to your heart and remember your anger. Farewell."

"Wait, all of this is very well, but I need your help …" the cave began to drift into nothingness, but as the darkness closed in Michael heard Uvarin's voice as from a distance.

'And you shall always have it. Fear not the darkness, for now is the time for strength."

'Again, the same message,' Michael thought. *'What darkness do they mean?'* Uvarin's words rang around his head as his dream turned to the tapping of rain upon his face and Danil's hand upon his shoulder.

"Mikael, we must rise and move swiftly. There are riders not far off. Sorin thinks it is the Queen's men."

"How did they pick up our trail?"

"We know not, but Sorin is crafting a confusion of mist and noise which should allow us at least to put some distance between us and our pursuit. Come." He held out his hand and helped Michael up, between them they got the Piradi prepared, while Dak and Suani scattered spice and herbs to distract the riders' mounts.

Sorin stood holding Nuall's Staff above his head as he muttered to himself. At first, nothing appeared to be happening, but gradually from the ground around him mist rose winding, and coiling, and with it came the noise. Voices shouting, birds and beasts calling, wind, rain, and then the clamour of battle. The noise and mist rolled together over the sides of the hollow and spread out, weaving through the rocks, seeping into every crack and smothering all passages. As the volume of noise rose, they mounted, and rode as fast as the ground allowed out of the mist and into the morning rain. Michael looked behind him and he saw that the mist had formed a thick wall that stretched away on both sides of them, only the peaks of the rocky outcrops were visible and the ruckus that Sorin had created could still be heard.

"I think that will hold them for a while. There is no way that their Trell will ride through that, they will have to dismount and lead them."

"How long will it last?"

"I've no idea, Danil, I have never done that with the aid of the Staff. It was quite impressive, don't you think?"

"You are enjoying your new toy then?"

"Very much thank you, Danil, and now we must aim to reach the three bridges over the Rahk by midday."

★★★

10

Beneath the Mountains of the Nare

At first, they made steady progress, but soon they found that the ground began to rise, and the air became colder. The rain had stopped, but a wind now drove against them. Ahead, the mountains truly loomed over them, their scarred and weathered sides sported spines as sharp as broken glass and terrifying gashes deep into the mountain. Here and there, great lumps of rock had cracked away from the mountain and in falling they had become wedged, forming precarious shelves whose slopes shone white with snow. Michael knew that the Nare lived within the mountains, but to look at them it was strange to think of them as the homeland of an entire people.

Dak had seen him looking up at the peaks ahead. "Every peak a masterpiece, my friend, crafted by Ragarad as he dug a home for his children beneath them. They all have different names, and each has its own story. Amongst the more traditional families, children are often named after one of the peaks." He pointed out one of the tallest peaks away to their right. "Dakveen is there, third from the end, his tale is a long and sad one. Someday, Mikael, I will tell it to you, perhaps when all this over."

"I would like that, Dak, being named after a mountain sounds rather good. I was named after an Angel."

"An Angel? And that is?"

"Rather like the Valeen in a way, they have wings, you would see them as servants of the One."

"That sounds very special, Mikael, and therefore it suits you of course." He laughed, "Is it a common name?"

"Yes, very common."

"Oh, never mind, common is good too, I suppose."

The ground had now become quite steep and they had to search out the path that led to the bridges. Eventually they found it tracking backwards and forwards across the slope, the gradient was less sharp and the path itself was set with slabs to make a well-constructed road, so the going was easier. This meant that they reached the bridges well before midday.

The River Rahk flowed fiercely down a wide and rocky gully that marked the true border of the Nare lands, effectively cutting the mountains off from the rest of Taleth. The snows from the high peaks kept the river well sourced and its mighty waters roared at speed through the deep ravine that fell away before them. Access to the Nare's home was via three great bridges that had been carved from an enormous pillar of rock that thrust up out of the waters and spread like two great hands supporting the three spans.

"Behold Hruak, Grav and Treek, the three bridges, my friends, held aloft by the mighty hands of Ragarad himself." There was a note of pride in Dakveen's voice as he spoke. "Tradition has it that should an army seek to cross the bridge then Ragarad would withdraw his hands and send them to their doom."

Danil smiled wryly. "Yes, I had heard that tale, Dakveen, let us hope that the great Ragarad does not consider the five of us an army."

"Although we are all great warriors in our way, Danil, I suspect that even we do not quite constitute an army."

Sorin looked pensive. "What concerns me more is that there is no longer a guard set upon the bridges as there was in the past."

It was true; the bridges were empty and silent amidst the roar of the waters. At each end of the three bridges was a stone archway, upon each was carved a warning in Nare and in the language of the Cluath. Those facing out were clear in meaning.

'Friends of the Nare, welcome, cross with Ragarad's blessing.
Enemies beware his wrath, for death awaits you.'

Those on the inward facing read.

'Consider this traveller: Does duty and truth lie beyond the bridge?
If such is the case go in peace, if not return you home.'

Beyond the bridge there was a path leading around the towering faces of the mountains that climbed slowly towards the hidden tunnels that led to the caves within. The path was narrow, so they dismounted, and they led their mounts along the gently curving trail. After having walked for some time, Sorin called a halt.

"There is something not right here. We should have met some sign of the Nare. I cannot believe that the Elders would leave the pass completely unwatched. There is also the matter of the Piradi to consider. I think that we should group them to the rear if they don't object, then if we meet a problem …"

Dak interrupted. "What are we likely to meet other than the Nare, Master Sorin? What are you suggesting?"

Sorin frowned. "I will be honest with you, Dakveen, I have sensed danger for a while now, behind us and somehow above us. We are going to find defending ourselves difficult if we have the Piradi at our sides, and should danger come from the rear they will warn us. Also, it will give them a chance to escape back and across the bridge should trouble come from the front."

Danil agreed. "That is true, they will defend themselves better if we are attacked by returning to the open ground. If we are all cramped up together, we will hardly be able to fight."

Dak was angered by their supposition that there was trouble ahead. "I say again, what are we likely to meet other than the Nare? Unless you think that Corruption can stretch out and bring the mountain down upon us."

"Dakveen, I mean no insult, but where are the guards? Where are your kinsmen? The path is unprotected and so there may be anyone or anything ahead."

Despite Dak's protests the Piradi dutifully moved to the rear and Michael was glad that they now would have the chance to escape should the need arise. He knew that they could evade the Queen's men for speed, but there were worse things than the Cluath cavalry about. This rearrangement completed they moved on; the path began to level out which suggested they were approaching the tunnels. Dak still muttered behind Michael.

"I don't know what he thinks is up in the mountains, does he think the Tsarg can fly?"

As if in answer to Dak's question an explosion shook the mountainside some way above them. They all instantly pressed themselves against the rock face as a shower of shards and debris crashed past them. Another explosion came from a little way ahead, wordlessly Sorin ordered the Piradi to save themselves and to wait for them on safer ground, they did so as swiftly as they could, moving away down the path just as a third explosion shattered the mountainside directly above their heads.

"Someone is dropping blasting powder down at us, a group of Tsarg I think, it is hard to see how we will be able to repel them, since they are out of sight." Another explosion, this time just below them.

Suddenly Suani howled with anger, she had seen what the others had not. Just before the last detonation her keen eyes had caught, a thin neck, taut wings of dark red skin, and she had heard the terrified hiss. "They are using living creatures to carry the powder." A fifth explosion, their aim was getting better. "The monsters! Small flying lizards they look like, such cruelty, I will not stand by and watch."

She stepped forward and Michael went to pull her back, but Danil shook his head. Suani had started to whistle shrill and high, piercing notes that echoed around and up into the air. The notes were a call, a summons, Michael felt the hairs on the back of his neck twitch and tingle, moments later birds began to swoop down, they were hawks of many different sizes and breeds, they hovered for a second in front of her and then they flashed upwards. Snarls and shouts broke out and then a wooden crate crashed down the mountain side, spewing lizards as it fell. The creatures once free glided away on their thin leathery wings. More shouts erupted and then as Michael looked up, he saw the hawks darting away from the mountain, simultaneously he was thrown from his feet by a massive eruption. The Tsarg blasting powder must have been ignited by a stray spark and the result was catastrophic. The detonation cracked the mountainside and the ledge that the Tsarg had climbed up to in order to lay their trap tore away from the face and crashed downwards ripping a great gash as it fell. They had little time to scramble out of the way before it smashed though the walkway and caused it to collapse inwards. Dak, Sorin and Danil were thrown back along the path, but Michael and Suani dropped into the dark rent that had been cut by the rock fall and disappeared.

★★★

When Michael came to his senses, he found that he lay in utter darkness. He remembered nothing of the fall, but a swift check revealed no injury save for a nasty gash and bruising to his forehead. He ached, but he could move, he wondered if Suani had fared as luckily as he had. He raised himself up and he felt around himself, feeling only debris and shattered rock. He was going to call out when he heard sobbing coming from his left.

"Suani are you hurt?"

"Oh, Mikael, thank the Powers, you are alive." Her voice had none of its former confidence. "I thought that I was … down here on my own. I couldn't see anything, and I thought you were dead …" she broke into sobs again.

"Are you hurt?"

"I don't know, I don't think so."

"Stay there, I will come to you."

Michael moved carefully, feeling his way, towards the sound of her sobs. When he reached her, he put his hand on her shoulder and then he found her gripping him tightly to her in an embrace of utter relief. Her terrified tears poured down her cheeks and her sobs shook them both. Michael was taken aback by the sheer force of her emotion. Suani was a creature of air and light, of trees and grass, born with the scented breezes of the Antaldi forests around her. This oppressive darkness, not knowing how far they had fallen, how much rock hung above them, had turned her from the strong willed young woman, who had defied the Triad on Danil's behalf, into a scared and vulnerable little girl, lost and lonely, trapped far away from the sun.

"Oh, Mikael, what are we going to do?"

Michael realised that for the first time since his reawakening he was no longer the passive recipient of aid, no longer going to be guided and told what to do, for Suani he had now become the protector. He had been placed in charge. This beautiful and frightened woman was now entirely reliant on him. He felt a chill at the thought of what might happen should he switch while they were in this predicament and he said a silent prayer to anyone who was listening to let him stay for now at least.

"We need to start moving, Suani, Dak said that the tunnels and the mines run throughout the mountains, if we keep moving, we will find a way out." He almost added. *'eventually'*, but he thought better of it.

"I pray that you are right, Mikael, there is so little air down here."

"Take my hand and we will make a start." The words of Sylvan's message came back to him. *'Fear not the darkness for now is the time for strength'*. Uvarin had repeated the same words. Was this what they meant? "We must be strong, Suani."

"I will try, Mikael."

To start with, their progress was slow, and Michael had no idea if the direction that they headed in would lead anywhere, for the darkness was complete. They felt their way across the broken and scattered rocks, Michael was aware that they were in great danger because the rocks cracked from the mountain must have fallen behind them and filled the crack created by the explosion, there was no way of knowing how stable they were. Yet they could only move forward slowly, testing each surface, feeling for space to move into. Michael could feel Suani's mounting panic as they reached a point where they had to crawl on their hands and knees. He dreaded the moment when they would have to decide to turn back and try in another direction; he did not feel that she would cope with that.

Fortunately, just as the way ahead seemed entirely blocked, he saw a very faint glimmer of light, spilling around his right hand as he explored the surface in front of them. There appeared to be a way through, close to the base of the rubble that blocked their way, but they would have to slide through on their stomachs. He could not be certain how far it went or whether it would lead them anywhere, but he felt that he had to try, the light had given him hope.

"Suani, you are going to have to be brave now, we will have to slide through this gap. If I go first, you will be able to grasp my ankles as we move forward. It will be difficult, but there is light ahead, which has to be a good sign. Will you try?"

"Mikael, I will be honest with you, I am so frightened that I can hardly breathe. I want to scream and cry and be sick and if we now crawl into a tiny gap without knowing where it leads it will only make things worse. But I will take my strength from you and place my life in your hands. I can do nothing else. Yes, I will try."

"Good, I am going to lie down, take my ankles and you will feel me moving forward. Good. Can you see the light?"

"No, Mikael, for my eyes are shut."

Michael began to shuffle his body through the gap, if he had been as honest as Suani had he would have confessed to the same swirling feelings of panic. He tried desperately not to think of the amount of rock above them or that the gap was smaller than he had hoped, he just pulled himself forward as best he could a few inches at a time. He could not recall afterwards how long that dreadful sliding journey took, it seemed endless and then suddenly his groping hands reached a wider space and within a few moments he was pulling himself and then Suani into an abandoned mine working, along which air moved. The dim light, though very weak, had crawled down a crack in the roof of the tunnel from the mountainside above, it was not much, but they were as happy to see it as if it had been a golden sunrise. Suani was shaking, from the cold, the strain and the impact that this journey was having upon her. Michael knew that she needed to rest and so they sat with their backs against the tunnel wall, Suani nestled under his arm, with his cloak wrapped around them both. Michael knew that although they were both exhausted, sleep would be a bad idea. They were probably both in shock and they needed water, so he began to talk to Suani to keep them both awake.

"Tell me about your home, Suani, I have never been to the Antaldi lands."

"It seems so far away now, sitting here in this desolate tunnel, but it is beautiful even in winter when chill winds send the trees to sleep and strip some of their leaves. I love the time when the blossom bursts upon the boughs and the new leaves are vivid and bright. There are trees near my home whose leaves are long and thin, hanging down like tresses from the branches, they carry an oil of such sweet fragrance that to walk beneath the tree will make you dizzy, as a girl I would run through the branches to scent my hair after bathing. There are others that have blooms that soak up the sunlight during the daytime and then gently glow when the darkness falls; and there are some whose bark harbours a mould which glows of its own accord. We line our lintels with it, so we are never without light. I have rarely seen true darkness, Mikael, such as we have struggled through. Taleth has always provided me with a way to see and living as I do amongst the trees I would rather have the wind upon my face than hide away in a hole. I know to you I may seem weak and foolish to be frightened of the dark, but it is something I have never truly faced."

"You are neither weak nor foolish, Suani, we all have our own demons and you have faced yours well so far."

"I have done so only because you are here, Mikael. Without your strength I would have simply lain down and waited to perish." Suani took Michael's hand in the darkness. "I admire your courage and your determination, Mikael, it has given me hope when there seemed none."

"It is Taleth that has given me strength, Suani. Before I came here, I was a creature of anger and despair, devoid of love and warmth even for myself. I would have welcomed death but had not the courage to end my own life. Taleth and those within it have given me purpose, given me a path to follow and although I am still torn and troubled by doubt and confusion; I know that I must keep moving forward. I have become what you see, Suani, I was not a man to be admired before Taleth rebuilt me."

"From what my cousin has told me of your exploits it has done a good job."

"I suspect that much of that has been somewhat stretched in the telling, but I will not deny that I would not have believed the Mikael who Danil described could have ever existed, when I lay in Sorin's cave with my eyes bound with cloth."

"It must have been so strange for you, to find yourself in our world. I can barely imagine how you must have felt."

"To be honest it was a surprise to find that I was still alive. Everything …" Suani had put her hand to his lips to quiet him.

Her voice was a whisper. "What is that sound?"

"What?"

"Listen? That sound, can't you hear it?"

Michael strained his ears to hear what Suani was talking about. At first, he heard nothing and then he heard a creaking, groaning sound that from above. Although he had no experience of working underground a sixth sense told him that this was a sound that meant danger, a sound that required an immediate response. He leapt to his feet pulling Suani with him.

"Run! The roof!"

Suani did not argue and they both ran for their lives, just as the roof above them ripped apart and crashed down behind them. Michael had no idea where they were running, but the collapse had weakened the structure of the tunnel and the cave-in began to chase them snapping at their heels and throwing dust and debris into the air around them. He grabbed Suani's arm and he forced her in front of him, as they ran headlong with little chance to consider where it took them. Suddenly, they were no longer running on a rock floor. Their racing feet clattered on the wooden slats of a platform that led along the wall of the tunnel. Michael tried desperately to slow their progress, but he failed and with a terrible inevitability the old wood crumbled, and they fell, amidst the chaos of the collapsing platform.

Michael prepared himself for the impact, but when they struck water, he would have laughed had not the chill of the underground river torn the air from his lungs and left him spluttering and coughing. Suani surfaced beside him and gulped in air, her eyes wide with shock and cold. The current was not strong, but what little light there was had not revealed anywhere they could scramble out. The river curved a little way downstream, so Michael signalled to Suani that they should try to swim with the flow, he did not know how long they could remain in this freezing water, but there was little choice. As they rounded the bend, he was relieved to see that there was an old jetty and, another blessing, a tunnel that lead away from it. He struck out for the wooden poles of the jetty and clambered out, quickly reaching down to help Suani from the water. For a moment, they both stood there shivering in the gloom, then Suani began to laugh, a laugh filled with relief and release.

"Well, I have twice expected to die and survived. What next I wonder?"

Michael laughed with her, but he knew now that they needed to move if only to get warm, their best hope was to move along the tunnel that led from the jetty as quickly as they could and pray that they headed in the right direction.

"We must keep moving. That tunnel must lead somewhere. Are you ready?"

"No, but you are right and standing here serves no purpose."

They started along the tunnel which at least sloped upwards away from the river, but what light they had had further down now seemed to fade and they were soon back in darkness again. They had to move slowly for fear of stumbling into openings and the longer it went on the more Michael began to despair of ever finding a way out. Then at last there was light ahead, just around a sharp bend in the tunnel, but it was not natural light it was the red flickering glare of flames. What was worse it was accompanied by strange guttural shrieks that made their already chilled blood freeze.

Michael hissed to Suani to stay out of sight while he crawled forward to see what lay ahead, she shook her head and she followed him in the shadows of the wall. They edged forward along the wall until they were in position to see. What they saw horrified and angered both of them. A figure was under a terrible assault from a horde of reptilian creatures, larger and more vicious than lizards, being the size of small dogs, they swarmed over their prey biting and slashing with claws and teeth like jagged nails. Their red eyes burned as they tasted the blood that flowed from the numerous wounds they had inflicted, and their screeches echoed around the tunnel walls.

The flames came from two torches that their victim had dropped when the attack had begun. Michael had already drawn his axe as he ran forward, incensed by this brutal onslaught, and he stooped to grab a torch that he could swing with his other hand. He struck out at two of the lizards with his axe and sliced through their scaly hides scattering their innards across the floor. Suani picked up the other torch and swung it across the now prone figure to clear the attackers from his face while Michael continued his slicing and chopping. The beasts realised quickly that they were suffering heavy casualties and they vanished into the shadows. Michael harassed them as they ran and then spun around as he heard Suani scream. One of the creatures had leapt at her from behind and sunk its teeth into her shoulder, she had thrown it off and Michael slew it as it lay stunned, but Suani stumbled to the ground, her side covered in blood. Michael tore a strip from his tunic and pressed it against the wound and then turned to the figure stretched upon the ground.

He held up the torch and he saw it was a Tarr, a First One of Earth, and his wounds were severe.

His eyes were open but dim and clouded with blood. "My thanks to you friend, though poor they are, I am Ayx of the

Tarr." He paused, his breath was ragged, and it was an effort to speak. "The fangs of the Tskuson drip with a foul poison and my end will come soon. I beg you to honour a dying wish and allow me a peaceful end."

Michael bent down so that he was close to Ayx's head. "I am Mikael Dal Oaken, son of Halkgar, and if it is in my power, I will do what you ask."

"Ayx of the Tarr thanks you." He lifted his hand and held out a shard of crystal. "Take this. It is a memory crystal and it holds my thoughts and my words, which I would share with my people. I sought news of my brother Uxl in these mountains, and it is to him this must be given."

"I will do what I can to find him." Michael took the long crystal and he carefully tucked it into his belt.

"That is good. I will give you a gift that may assist you in this darkness, it is a fire rock, place it upon the ground and name it and it will give you light and warmth. This one's name is *Iolk-a-buan-a-katan* and it has served me well for many, many of your lifetimes."

"Thank you Ayx of the Tarr, warmth will be most welcome." Ayx then made him repeat the name several times to memorise it.

Finally, he was satisfied. "There then, that is good. Please put my body to the flame when I am gone, for I would deem it an honour to warm you. Now I die and return the life that was given me by the One, may you too find peace when it is time."

With these words, his eyes closed, and his chest stilled.

"Should we do as he asks and burn his body?"

"Yes, it will honour Ayx and keep off those vile lizards while I look at that wound for you."

They searched for a few scatterings of wood to start a blaze and found just enough, suggesting to Michael they were in an old mine working, then they set their torches to the meagre pyre. The flame leapt up and it was as if Ayx was keeping his promise to warm them for his body caught the flame swiftly and burned well. They were able to sit and draw in the heat knowing that the old Tarr's spirit would have been well pleased with the blaze.

When Suani allowed Michael to take a look at her shoulder he was shocked, the gash was jagged and evil, and it already showed signs of infection. He had no water to clean it properly, but he tore a fresh strip of cloth and he bound it tightly, he was well aware that a wound like this, that was undoubtedly from a poisonous bite, needed someone to deal with it properly, but he had neither the knowledge nor the skill. It struck him that if they did not find the way out soon, that Suani would be in severe danger. Neither of them had had drink or food for a good many hours and he was not sure how long they could go on without proper rest. But at least now they had some light. He decided that they must move on while Suani still had strength. She looked tired and pale, but she accepted his decision and taking a torch in her hand she followed along the tunnel which began to show more signs that it had once been part of the Nare's domain.

"If we ever get out of this Mikael, I will take you to my homeland and show you the blossoms and let you feel the scented breezes and we will go nowhere near any caves or tunnels or even burrows. Come on."

The tunnels wound on and on, with every indication that they had been mined out centuries before. They had initially been climbing gradually, but for the last hour, the ground had been level and any side openings they passed all seemed to lead down. Suani had at first matched his pace, but now she was tiring, and Michael could see in her face that her wound was worse than she was willing to admit. He was also aware that there were scurrying noises in some of the shadows behind them and he suspected that the Tskuson had tracked them waiting for a moment to attack. They had a distinct look of Tsarg about them and he wondered whether they were merely a predator who inhabited the tunnels or if they were controlled and sent with purpose. He was tired and beginning to lose hope that they would ever find a way out, when they reached a point where the tunnel came to a dead end.

For Suani it was the final straw, she sank to her knees and groaned. "I can go no further, Mikael, these tunnels have defeated me. I am finished."

Michael's eyes searched around desperately, the tunnel was as the others cut and crafted, why did it just end? Then the flame from his torch drew sharp shadows on the facing wall, there were foot holes, and looking up he realised that the tunnel continued above them, if they could climb the wall, they could continue.

"No, this isn't a dead end, Suani, it is just a break in the tunnel, maybe a defence against those lizards, if we can climb the wall the tunnel continues."

"Climb? How can I climb, Mikael? I have no strength and only one good arm, it is hopeless. Leave me here and go."

The words of the First Promise came back to him.

'Where there is Life – there is Love.
Where there is Love – there is Hope.
Where there is Hope – there is a Future.
Where there is a Future – there is Life.
Where there is Life – there is Love.'

He knelt down beside her and, taking the torch from her, he took her hand.

"Suani, it is never hopeless, not while we live, not while you have the scent of the trees to call you home, not while those we love and care for are out there, thinking of us. It is not finished until we allow it to be. I will carry you if I have to, but I will not leave you."

She looked up into his face and the tears that ran down her face sparkled in the flickering of the torches. "Mikael, I do not know from where you draw your strength, but I hope that someone somewhere is watching and will reward you for I fear that I will never be able to." She struggled to her feet. "I will once again try, for your sake."

Michael looked at the climb, it was perhaps twice his height. He took a torch and he threw it up into the darkness watching it cast its light as it fell back. The ledge at the top seemed clear and he risked throwing the torch again, it rolled away from the edge, but it stayed alight. He tried the second torch and succeeded on the third attempt. Now at least they climbed into light.

He helped Suani onto the wall and she moved carefully up while he stood close behind and supported her weight. The next few handholds required him to leave the floor and now it became tricky, he moved up to surround her and dug his fingers tightly into the cuts in the wall. He felt her weight against him as she threw her good arm up to find the next hold. She shook with the strain and he could hear that her breathing was forced; this was taking more from her than he had expected. She pulled herself up and then winced with pain as her shoulder swung in against the rock. He moved himself up behind her and he let her rest for a moment.

"Just two more, Suani and then we have reached the ledge and you can rest."

"I see it, Mikael, but … I am so tired."

He knew that she was close to collapse, but they had nearly made it. "I know, Suani, and we will rest at the top. I am certain we are near to more recent workings, just one last effort and we will be closer to aid."

He heard her sigh, but she began to move and once again he took her weight. She made the next hold and again he moved up. He expected her to rest again, but she wanted the climb to end and so she continued on to the next. He barely had time to move to support her and his grip loosened as she then reached for the ledge itself.

"I have the ledge, Mikael, help me over and I can then help you in turn."

Michael pushed against her and he grasped her left foot to help her scramble over onto the ledge, but in doing so he lost his own grip and there was nothing that he could do to stop himself from falling. He heard Suani's wail from above as he crashed to the ground, but he also heard the hiss and the scurry of the Tskuson as they raced across the floor of the tunnel to strike at their quarry. He was winded and dazed, but he managed to roll onto his front, and he pushed himself to his feet just as the first of the lizards reached him. He reached for his axe and smashed the butt into the face of his attacker, with the next swing he took its head, and then sliced downwards through the scaly skin of the next. Suani shouted to him from above and a flash of burning wood flew past him as he ducked and watched it burst amidst the Tskuson that filled the tunnel. Mikael took his chance and he jumped onto the wall. He climbed as swiftly as he could to the waiting arm of Suani which reached for him. Once over the ledge himself, he looked back. He had been right, the climb was a defence against these lizards for though they threw themselves against the wall they could not grip enough to climb, and the foot holes were spaced for longer arms and legs.

Michael lay for a while upon the ground beside Suani and took stock. He had not been bitten, but they were both now close to exhaustion. They would rest for a while and then try and move on. The tunnel at least moved upwards and appeared more recently used. He sat up and took the fire rock from his belt, Ayx had given him its name, it was strange to think of rocks having names, but he knew that the Tarr had sung the rocks and trees to shape them to their will. He set the rock before them on the ground and hoping that he had remembered it correctly spoke the rock's name.

"*Iolk-a-buan-a-katan.*"

The rock began to glow with the red light he had seen in the chamber of the First Promise and then again in the house of the Mualb. It was gradual at first, but it became stronger until they could both feel the warmth. It was not a fierce threatening heat, as fire could be, there was no danger in it, but it warmed them through and they both drew comfort from it. Suani laid her head in Michael's lap and he sensed that she would soon give in to sleep, and he did not have the heart to try and stop her. There was little hope now that they would find help for her, but when he had recovered his strength a little, he would carry her as he had promised. He knew that he must not sleep himself, but the temptation was growing, he shook himself and he tried to focus his eyes. Was there something moving in the shadows?

Had he fallen asleep, he thought that there were lights, no it was a shape. Suddenly he was wide awake, it was a wolf, a large white wolf of the Veyix. It moved slowly to him and touched his muzzle to his hand.

'I am Kyre of the Veyix that some call the Lost. You hold the memory shard of Ayx of the Tarr. I had come searching for him, but I felt him pass.'

'Kyre of the Veyix, you are most welcome. Ayx of the Tarr was overcome by the poison of the Tskuson, but we burned his body as he requested. We fell into these deep mines from the pass above when Tsarg attacked us and my companion is succumbing to the same poison that killed Ayx. I am Mikael Dal Oaken and ...'

'I know you, Michael that is also Mikael, and I have heard your tale. Your companion is in need of healing, but you also need sleep. Rest for an hour and I will guard you. Then we will seek aid together. The Veyix will always help the Uclan, for we have known your pain.'

'I will rest for I am tired, but please wake me soon, for her sake.'

'I will.'

Michael nodded and then he gave in to the pressure to close his eyes, he was asleep within seconds, but he was not surprised to find himself walking on a green hill, an azure sky above him and a gentle breeze in his face. What did surprise him was the figure walking down the hill towards him. Clad as a warrior of the plains he strode quickly with purpose, arm outstretched in greeting, it was Mikael.

"Well met at last, Michael Oakes, well met."

Michael took the outstretched arm and he tried to answer. "Indeed, Mikael. But how? Why?"

"I know not, perhaps whoever holds the reins feels that it is time we met properly, face to face, as it were. I think it would gain us little to try and fathom it. Let us just enjoy the chance to walk and talk, and for a moment forget the situation. There is much we can discuss, although I am privy to some of your memories I really know nothing of who you were before we became who we are."

"There is little of which I am proud, Mikael, I realise now that many of my relationships were broken ones, and I was angry at those who I should have loved most. I was angry at my brother for dying and at my mother for grieving for him. I saw no fault in myself. Nor did I see any when Mel left me, because I loved her so completely. I expected her to return that love, but what right did I have to expect that? And my anger meant that I did not grieve for her, I was simply filled with more anger. *'How dare she die and not give me a chance to hate her.'* Coming here has given me the chance to become something new, something more than I was. For that I am grateful."

Mikael walked for a while in silence and then he looked at Michael. "It is true when we look back, we see our faults more clearly. I resented my father's failings and they were none of his making, he failed to protect my mother, he failed to give me the love I demanded, he failed to return when he promised he would do so. And then, when I was given the love I had wanted, all I could think of was glory in battle and avenging the long dead. My mother would surely have pointed to Anith and scolded me for leaving it so long before we wed. I have anger now for those who betrayed me, but my anger at myself is greater, for my failure to see what I had. My father loved me in his way and although I begged him to let me ride with him, it would have been to my death. We are inevitably guilty of letting the days slip by unused and un-savoured, that may be so for many, but you have the chance now to change, a chance that I will never have."

"We cannot know how this may turn out, Mikael."

"Though that is true, I can see no way that ends with a future for me, my friend."

"We will see."

They walked on, and Michael saw the farmstead, and beyond, the tall white-stoned building with five sails like great fins, slowly circling, paddling through the sky. He could hear the splash of water pumping from the deep spring, taste the red water from the hidden pools, and hear the stamping and breathing of many animals, echoing from the stables. This was where Mikael had grown up, this was his home,

"You were lucky to grow to a man in this world, Mikael, it is beautiful."

Mikael laughed. 'In some ways, yes, Michael, in some ways. Would you have been different had you grown up here, rather than in your world with your strange noisesome boxes that carry you and the harsh unnatural lights and all the people?"

It was Michael's turn to laugh. "Oh, no doubt, I would have been different, Mikael, but I doubt if I would have been better. We were who we were, but now as you say we have become who we are, the Twice-Dead or the Twice-Born, take your pick. *'He that walks with another'*, *'the Ender of Days'*, I forget the rest."

"You missed out *'the Doom of Taleth'*, perhaps that is just as well, for it is our doom also."

"Perhaps." He looked at Mikael once more and then he took his hand. "Thank you, Mikael Dal Oaken, son of Halkgar."

"For what, Michael?"

"For giving me aid when it was needed. You could have sunk into yourself, into my mind, and stayed away. But you didn't."

"No, I didn't, and I am glad of it. And I will do it again, although the new Michael Oakes is less in need."

"Don't be so sure, stay close."

The dream began to fade, and Michael woke to the hot breath of a wolf on his face.

'Michael that is also Mikael, you must wake now. I sense that enemies are close, so we must move; they seek a way around this barrier. I know only some of these tunnels, but I have some sense of the direction we must take. Can your companion walk unaided?'

Michael laid his hand upon Suani's head to move her gently and he could feel the heat, she was burning up with fever, she moaned, but she did not wake.

'I think we will be lucky even to wake her, her sickness grows. But I will carry her as I promised.' He reached out his hand to the glowing rock and its glow faded, when he picked it up it was quite cool. He placed it in his belt as before and then he struggled to his feet, lifting Suani carefully into a position he could maintain.

"You will not be able to carry her for long, Michael that is also Mikael."

'Then we must hurry, Kyre of the Veyix, we must hurry.'

And so, they set off, Kyre scouting ahead and then returning to Michael to direct him along a side tunnel or merely to encourage him. He had to rely on Kyre entirely for he could not carry a torch and the tunnels were once again near to total darkness. Michael would not have thought it possible that he could have carried her as far as he did, but it became harder and harder to keep his legs moving forward. He had been running on sheer will power for some time when he stumbled to his knees and he found that he could not get up, however much he wished to. Kyre stood for a moment, considering the options.

"Michael that is also Mikael, I feel certain that there is help near and I must try to lead them to you. There is also danger close, but how close I cannot tell. I will be gone for as brief a time as possible. Now is the time for strength."

Darkness closed around him once again and he knew that he was now more vulnerable than at any time previously. He would barely have the strength to fight off an attack even if he could see the enemy, but he was determined that after all this, the end would not come here in the dark, he would find a way. The seconds slipped by and became minutes, although to Michael without any light, time was irrelevant, there was just the darkness. He strained to see something around him, but his tired eyes could not penetrate the gloom. Suani's breathing had become shallow and rasping, he could do nothing but hold her head and pray that help would come.

Then he heard sounds, some close by, scurrying, the scuttling of scratching feet, he reached for his axe, their eyes at least might give them away. There were other sounds too, thudding, pounding, what else was out there. He saw pairs of red dots in the dark and he prepared himself. He raised himself to his knees once more and knelt beside Suani.

"Come on then, I am ready, I have killed some of you already and I will kill more before the end. Come and feel the bite of my axe."

A chorus of hissing broke out and the eyes sprang forward, he swung back and forth, and he felt blood splashing across his arms, but there were too many, he could not move fast enough. Then flames and running feet and a great white snarling shape came across between him and the hissing and the red eyes. He tried to stand but could not and he fell forward over Suani's prone form, unconscious.

When he came to it took a while for his mind to grasp what had happened in the chaos of the assault and the rescue, and by the time he was able to focus his eyes, he saw Dak and another Nare bending over Suani and lifting her on to a makeshift stretcher, which they then lifted carefully. He heard Dak shout something to a third Nare who stood beside Michael, although his tired brain could not catch the words, and then he set off running away up the tunnel.

"We will follow, Mikael Dal Oaken, son of Halkgar, when you are ready, but our pace need not be as swift. It is a short walk only and I will guide you, for there is little light at first. My name is Ruakim Kemsik, viak Marak, viak Ukulik."

"Thank you, Ruakim Kemsik, son of Marak. I will lean on you if I may, for I am exhausted if truth be told and I think that I may have been bitten in that last attack." He had actually only just noticed that his arms stung and burned from several gashes and he could feel the warm dampness of fresh blood.

"Of course, come, you are in need of healing, and I am not skilled in the art. We will follow and then both you and your companion will be attended to."

They began to walk up the tunnel. Michael tried to walk as quickly as he could but he found every step to be more painful than the last. After a while he began to see the tunnel ahead and he realised it was getting lighter. The next corner they turned showed him the reason, they had reached, if not the surface, at least an area open to the sky. They came to a set of steps and the sight that met Michael's eyes took his breath away.

11

The Outcast's Return

The sun was high in the sky, which was cloudless and pale, below it stretched an expanse of rolling white that seemed to go on forever.

"Behold the Gorash Shakar, Mikael, the White Sea."

"Is that ice?"

"It is, Mikael, a frozen sea that is said to teem with fish who know not the full light of the sun, although I do not believe that anything lives beneath the ice. It is said that it will melt at the end of the world and the 'Wyrm of the Waters' will rise and devour the mountains. Another fanciful tale, I suspect. There may be strange creatures who live upon the surface of the frozen waters, but nothing that I have ever seen, or that comes close enough to catch."

"Where does it lead?"

"It leads to the utter north, where blood and air freeze and none can live but the ice demons of our legends."

"Has anyone tried to cross it?"

"Perhaps, but none has ever returned to tell what they found. Now you will see one of the cities of the Nare."

Michael had been so taken with the frozen wasteland that he had not looked to his left or right and the sight was equally worthy of the gasp that escaped his lips. Cut into the sides of the mountains was the homeland of the Nare, row upon row of dwellings, workshops, smithies and warehouses, separated by wide streets, curving archways leading to open spaces with fountains and waterfalls, towers with white stone roofs, they spread out before him. There were long strips of orchards, high upon shelves of stone, and what looked like fields winding in and out of irrigation towers, and windmills that turned lazily in the face of the chill breeze. Small groups of herd animals grazed in paddocks that sat amidst the grey stone. Michael had seen the dwellings of the Nare in the eyes of the Trillani, but he had never thought that they were such a spectacular sight. And yet as they started to make their way through the streets everywhere there was sign of the plague. Houses empty, work benches idle, women and children huddled together on the steps beside covered biers. They passed one walled field in which forty bodies lay bound in shrouds, waiting to be taken down into the mountain to be given back to the rock. Few moved around them as they passed, some stared from windows, but most were too busy, too broken or too ill to acknowledge or even notice their passing.

Ruakim, shook his head sadly. "This is the first city of the seven and the largest, Marl, my home, and I would not have had you see it for the first time as it is now. It was once thriving and busy, filled with the music of the hammer and the forge and the laughter of children. Here I grew to be a man and never once did the smile leave my face not even when the coldest winds blew, and the ice hung from the sails of the wind-catchers and the water froze in the pumps. But then the plague came and now no-one smiles as we all await death, and the only sound is the excavation of death pits."

They walked through the city towards an archway that lead back into the mountain. Here passages lined with tiles led to the council chamber of the Nare. Before they reached the chamber itself, Ruakim took Michael down a wide passageway that had many doors each with runic lettering upon them.

"These are the meeting rooms of the families. Each of the great houses has a room here where their representative can negotiate prices for trade or settle disputes or prepare pleas to go before the Mrauuk itself. At the end of the row is a meeting room for any who make representations to the Mrauuk who are not of the Nare. It will be here that your companion has been brought for it has been given over for the use of Master Sorin. Here we are."

He had stopped at a door that was unmarked and, when he knocked briskly upon it, it was opened by Danil.

"Mikael, well, you look better than I expected, which is something. Come in and sit down you must be fatigued beyond measure."

"I am tired and thirsty, but I am alive. How is Suani?"

He followed Danil into the room, which was large and relatively devoid of furniture. There were several benches around the wall and a long table and at one end a bed had been set for Suani, who lay pale and silent under a woven blanket. Sorin, who sat on the bed beside her, rose and came to him.

"Don't look quite so worried, Mikael, she will pull through, although I must admit it was touch and go, had you stopped any earlier and thus delayed my aid she would not have survived. Is it right that you carried her when she could no longer walk?"

"It was that or watch her die."

"She will I am sure tell us the whole story, when she recovers, but it would appear that you displayed tremendous courage and strength down there in the darkness, Mikael."

"I only did what had to be done, Sorin."

"Yes, Mikael, you did, but sometimes it is that that takes the greatest courage." Sorin noticed the blood soaking his sleeves "But you have been bitten too. Why was I not told? Come I have a wonderful paste that will help, it will sting more than a little, but for a great hero like you that is no problem." Sorin sat Michael down on a bench and ripped back his sleeves to expose the nasty gashes and cuts that the Tskuson had made in that final attack. He washed them carefully and then he applied the paste he had used before upon Dak. He was right it did sting, and Michael had to fight down a yell,

"What were those things? Are they a type of Tsarg?"

It was Ruakim who answered. "No, they have always inhabited the tunnels and the rivers below the mountains, but they have become more aggressive since the plague and, although it is a thing which has no sense in it, they seem to be organised and fight with a purpose, unlike before when their attacks were brutal but mindless."

Sorin looked up from binding Michael's wounds. "That is interesting, Ruakim Kemsik, because it suggests an intelligence that they do not naturally possess."

"That is what some of us have thought, but the Council will not allow such thinking, because it is against the accepted order of things, it breaks the Natural Law."

"Corruption's reach is long and beings like the Tskuson would be easy to bend to his will."

The door opened behind them and Dak entered with three Nare, all of them younger than Dak and one of them a female. The young males were very like Dak, though less care worn around the eyes and less sturdy of limb. The female was altogether taller and slimmer than the males, although by no means thin. Unlike the hairless males she had long dark brown hair which was drawn into a single thick plait high on the back of her head the rest of the scalp was shaved to leave a neat circle around the base of the plait. Her left ear was bedecked with earrings which appeared to be interlaced with a fine metal chain that supported many gemstones. The right ear was pierced once by a small silver rock hammer. Although her nose was not long; it was thinner than that which squatted on Dak's face and her deep brown eyes sparkled and shone. Michael had seen other female Nare on his walk into the city, but he had not been able to take in their appearance. He suspected that this young female was a beauty amongst her people, but her demeanour was modest, and she stood a few respectful paces behind Dak. Her clothing was leather as was that of her companions, but over the trousers she also wore a short, pleated leather skirt with intricate designs burnt into the leather and under her leather waistcoat she had a tunic of fine material edged with lace.

Dak looked at Michael. "You are a lucky man, Mikael Dal Oaken, there are few who would have had the strength and the courage to find their way out of the deep mines and fight off the Tskuson the way that you did. When you are recovered you can tell me the whole story, but for now it must wait."

Sorin had finished with Michael and he went back to sit beside Suani. "By the fact that you are alive, Dakveen, I assume that the Mrauuk have not killed you on the spot. What did they say?"

Dak laughed, which seemed to cause great discomfort to the two young males, but not the female, Michael noticed. "Oh, I am under sentence of death, that goes without saying, but they will see me and let me speak, which is a start at least. I am under guard as you can see, Shuok Nagesset, viak Huak and his brother Nameed are sticking to me like glue." He indicated the female. "Rotvee Bramkilik velak Nakeket, here has agreed to come and talk to us about what has been happening. She is not, like some, scared of being cursed by talking to foreigners, nor an outcast for that matter."

Rotvee bowed, and then she smiled broadly. "When the only excitement you have each day is the rise and fall of the hammers and the polishing of stones, a curse seems a fair price for meeting such noble guests, Dakveen Halak viak Thark, viak Varkind, viak Bakund."

Dak smiled. "You see, I told you that she was a brave girl, not afraid of naming a family line that has been stripped of all rights by the Mrauuk. She is of the house Bramkilik, the line that has given us our greatest craftsman in metal and stone."

Rotvee bowed again. "You honour me too much Dakveen, viak Thark, I just hit things with a hammer and hope that the stone is in a good mood."

Sorin came to greet the newcomers. "I am pleased to meet you Rotvee Bramkilik, daughter of Nakeket, the skill of your house is legendary, and I have no doubt that you are equal to the name. I am Sorin, I am here with Dakveen Halak to try and find a cure for the plague that ravages your people. We need to know what has been happening here in Marl and in the other cities of the Nare."

Rotvee nodded. "Your name is known to me, Sorin of the Majann, even though I have never travelled. I will tell you what I know, but first Ruakim Kemsik, viak Marak, you have been asked to attend the Mrauuk and report what you saw in the tunnels."

"Ah, yes, I will. I am sure that we will meet soon, Mikael, son of Halkgar, may your healing be swift." He bowed towards Michael.

"Thank you for your good wishes and your help, Ruakim, son of Marak."

When he had left the chamber, Rotvee continued. "You are a healer, Sorin, well, healing is what we need, for nothing has halted the spread of the disease. It began amongst the miners of Okk, some of their number had been sent to begin the reclaiming of an area of the older workings, in order to access the depths of the Iniki Caves beneath Dunark. The belief is that rich veins of ore and beds of gemstones lie as yet undiscovered and, after much debate as to who would have the rights to mine such fields, the families of Fruunik and Vuskar began to tunnel and explore to find the routes that they required. Those that returned told tales of strange mists and shadows that lay across the still waters that had filled the caves and how some of their number had succumbed instantly to the shadows and died within hours. They all were sick and weak, their breathing thin and shallow, none lived more than a few days and less than five days after there were others who fell to the illness. Nor did it stay within the city of Okk; it soon chose victims in Hevek and Rivik. Its spread could not be contained. Finally, the first victims in Marl became ill. It has taken less than two years and though we have done all that we can there is not a house or family in all of the seven cities that has not seen death save one."

She paused and looked around at Shuok and Nameed, who averted their eyes in embarrassment. "One house was not, is still not, affected, none have fallen ill in the house of Bramkilik. My own house has seen no deaths and no sickness. As you might expect this has caused great resentment amongst the other houses, but we can find no reason for it. We are no different other than in name and lineage, and we have not shut ourselves off from the world, we work to help the others find a cure, and yet none of my family is struck down. Although this is a good thing in a way it is also distressing to know that every day others die."

Michael noticed that as she expressed her sorrow for her people, she fingered what appeared to be a piece of broken green glass which hung from a chain around her neck. As she looked up her eyes caught Michael's gaze.

"Ah, you wonder at this broken thing, when we are so skilled. Why should I be wearing this? I admit it does look rather out of place, but it has sentimental value, it is all that remains of a crystal goblet that had been in my family for as long as anyone can remember. Tradition has it that it was a gift from a grateful traveller to one of our ancestors after he been rescued from a deep ravine, he had fallen into during a snowstorm. It was made from a green crystal that the traveller said was very rare, it could only be found in one place high in the mountains right at the western tip of the range. It was so beautiful that it was kept for very special celebrations, such as a marriage or the naming of a child, when it would be filled with Brak and passed around from person to person and all would take a drink. Sadly, over time it had become thinner and thinner until it finally broke. This piece is all that remains, and I asked if I could have it to wear as reminder of a once beautiful object."

Although Michael was tired and sore there was an alarm bell ringing in his head, there was something important here, but he had not quite managed to grasp it yet.

"I have never heard of Brak, what is it?"

Sorin sighed. "I am not surprised you have never heard of it, Mikael, for outside the Nare lands it is rarely found. It is a wine, made from the fruit of the Uttikbrak trees which grow only on the mountains of the Nare. The soil which they carried up from the lands below to create their fields and orchards has for thousands of years sat absorbing all the essence of the rock upon which it sits and so the fruits that grow have been shaped and flavoured by the mountains. They are dark and bitter and the wine they produce is thick and vinegary and not to the taste of any except the Nare themselves."

Dak was stung by this statement. "Sorin, you drink Tuoll which is far stronger and equally bitter to those who have not acquired the taste. Have you ever tried a good Brak?"

"I have tried Brak, Dak, but I would not know the good from the bad."

"Then you and Mikael shall try some before you dismiss it." He turned to Shuok. "I will not try to leave Shuok, viak Huak, and I am not going to do anything nasty to your brother so would you be so good as to find a flagon of the best Brak from somewhere for our guests."

Shuok looked at his brother, who shrugged silently and then he looked back at Dak. "I will do this for our guests, Dakveen Halak, but I hold you responsible for any repercussions."

"I assure you there will be none, Shuok, viak Huak, beyond a sore head or two."

Shuok turned and he stomped away, not happy at being sent on an errand by an outcast, but he was not willing to outface an older Nare, even a 'Hemmek'. Michael's fatigued brain whirred and clicked, and the alarms were becoming louder, but he could still not see what it was that had triggered them.

"When did you last drink Brak, Dakveen Halak, viak Thark?" Rotvee asked an obvious question. "Surely you would have had difficulty in finding it in the Wilderness."

"The outside world of Taleth does not deserve the title that the Nare gives it, Rotvee Bramkilik, velak Nakeket, but to answer your question, I last drank Brak when my brother and I drank in honour of our father after we had returned him to the rock. It was a bottle that my father had kept waiting for something to celebrate, something he never found."

Rotvee looked at Dak and Michael saw the change come over her, she had never really thought about what it was to be cast out, to be a wanderer, trying to hold on to some small token of the homeland that despite everything was home. She had never tasted the bitterness of exile and the finality, the cold hard certainty of the Law. For the Nare the Law was set in stone, in the very rock of the mountains and it was unbending and harsh. She had seen the sadness, the pain that her question had caused, and she stepped forward to Dak and bowed low to him and then, as Michael had found himself doing to honour the Trillani, she stretched out her left arm and she moved her hand palm upwards across from right to left.

"Kumil ta Ragarad, Dakveen Halak, viak Thark, tavish, ruuak na mikrilik fraraok, Rotvee Bramkilik, velak Nakeket, ka norlkimat vuaat. Hemmek nantak tavish, delk randat felkit."

Dak was surprised and quite obviously moved. Rotvee had apologised for causing him pain but she had gone further offering him a *'vuaat'*, literally a blood debt, to cleanse the way between them, it meant that he could call on her for her support or for her arms in battle. To Michael's great surprise she had also uttered the words that he had spoken amongst the ancient trees. *'Even the outcast is welcome when Doom is at hand'*.

Dak bowed low in return and then instead of making the same gesture he took her outstretched arm and he shook it warmly. "Kumil ta Ragarad, Rotvee Bramkilik, velak Nakeket, na krillkuur ta gaakota vikim ruuak vuaat. May it be a long time before I am in such need. But you warm my heart with your words."

There was a moment, just a moment, when Michael felt that what had just passed between Dak and Rotvee was of greater significance than anyone would have guessed and then Shuok returned bearing a tray with a wooden jug filled with Brak and goblets.

"Ah, now you will taste a true drink, Sorin. Come." He filled a goblet from the jug, and he handed it to Sorin, but Michael reached out and took it first.

"May I? There is something, I can't quite …" the smell was just as Sorin had described, rich and warm, like apples left too long in a box, or old vinegar bottles that still held the residue caught in the grooves of the glass. He sipped the liquid, its sharpness stung his throat, but the flavour was undeniable, filled with fruit ripened in a strong sun and the sharpness and the strength of the mountains. And then it hit him, rain dissolving the rock, filtering through the soil and rising through the veins of the trees to swell the fruit. It had all conspired to make an extremely acidic wine and if it was acidic even with his poor grasp of chemistry from school, he knew that acid would gouge away at even the hardest substance. That was why the crystal goblet had got thinner over time, the Brak had eaten away at the surface, the substance of the crystal becoming part of the liquid and that might mean …

"Rotvee, was the Brak your family drank on those special occasions, as strong as this?"

"Of course, we always used the finest Brak."

"I'm sure you did and gradually the goblet became thinner and thinner?"

"Yes, as I said until it cracked and some of it crumbled to dust. This is the only piece that survived."

"And all your family drank from the goblet? You didn't have guests or friends?"

"At weddings we had guests, but only the person joining the family drank from the goblet."

Sorin was becoming very interested in where Michael was going with his questioning. "What are you thinking, Mikael?"

"Well, I may be wrong, but I think it was the Brak that broke the goblet."

"What do you mean, Mikael?" Dak too was intrigued. "I know that it is strong, but how …"

"There are certain liquids which have the potential to eat away at other substances, gradually drawing that substance into themselves and eventually consuming the other substance completely. I know of one, that is made from fermented fruit, but it is weak, and I think Brak is another. It gradually consumed the goblet leaving it thinner and thinner, in just the way that the rain will wear away the face of a mountain over many years, consuming some of the rock and washing it into the soil."

"But where did the goblet go if the Brak was wearing it away?" Rotvee wasn't sure that she wanted to know the answer.

"It went into the Brak?"

The faces of the Nare were suddenly filled with horror, even Dak's, this was a sacrilegious notion. But what Michael said next was to shock them even more.

"And what's more I think that is what has left Rotvee and her family with an immunity to the Plague."

Rotvee became more and more discomforted by this line of thought. "I don't understand; what do you mean?"

Michael knew that what he had suggested was an anathema to the Nare, against all their ideas and their beliefs about the nature of their world, but he also knew that he was probably right. There was a way to prove it either way, but he didn't know if they would agree to it. He decided to bludgeon his way forward and ignore their sensibilities. "When one of these liquids works to eat away at another substance the liquid changes and gradually becomes something else …"

"This is outrageous!" Nameed was blocking his ears with his hands. "How dare you utter such blasphemy! How can something become something else?"

"You must not speak of such things." Shuok was equally appalled. "It is wrong to say them and worse to make us listen."

Michael looked at Dak, who after a moment, nodded as if to say continue. "The liquid changes becoming something else and that something else has protected Rotvee and her family from the plague. It is the only explanation."

"I didn't … we didn't know, we didn't mean to do anything wrong."

Sorin grinned with delight. "Mikael you are a genius, it is so simple. The crystal of the goblet combined with the Brak to make a powerful healing draught that has meant that the plague could not attack them. You are right, there is nothing else that matches the facts."

Nameed was determined to make them desist from talking in such a dangerous manner. "Stop this now! We will all suffer the wrath of the Mrauuk if you continue. You must cease this wicked nonsense immediately and we will report …"

"No, Nameed, son of Huak, you will not! You will not go running off to the Mrauuk." Dak's voice was quiet but determined. "We will explore this properly and then I will speak with the Council, for I see that this is the reason why I have returned." Nameed looked at him unconvinced. "Consider this, they already view me as a dangerous outcast, hence your guardianship, but if you report this matter they will see you as tainted by my influence, whereas if I present it to them then they will be forced to make up their minds, but you will remain blameless."

"But what he has said …"

"Is blasphemy, yes, Shuok has already made that point, but what if it is a cure that can save our people? Do you want to be the one who condemned your family to a slow death, because you were scared of a stranger's words?"

Nameed, looked at Shuok, who shrugged his shoulders. "Very well, as long as it is clear that we did nothing unlawful."

"That is understood." Dak turned to Rotvee, who still looked pale. "Rotvee, velak Nakeket, you have done nothing to be ashamed of, you and your family are also free from wrongdoing, but if Mikael is right then your family will be the saviours of our race, which is something for which your family will be remembered and honoured in years to come."

In response, Rotvee looked up at Dak and again there was something unspoken which passed between them before she nodded. "What do you want me to do?"

"Sorin? How may we prove this notion?"

"Well, I suppose if Mikael is right, then we should see if the shard of crystal reduces in the Brak and then test the liquid upon someone who has the disease. What do you say, Mikael?"

Michael was a little nervous that his memory of schoolboy science was being relied upon, but he had to agree that this would prove whether the Brak was the cure or not.

"Yes, I suppose so."

"Very well, but who will we find to test this on without alerting the Mrauuk before we can see if there is any change?"

Nameed looked as if he might speak and then he thought better of it, but Shuok had caught his movement. "Be quiet!"

"Yes, of course, it is nothing."

"Nameed, son of Huak, you were going to suggest someone?" Dak had seen it too.

"No, Dakveen, no … well, yes, but then I thought that it would be wrong, because I would become part of what you attempt, even though … no, I must not."

Sorin moved from Suani's side and he stood in front of Nameed. "You have someone in your family who is affected don't you?" He looked down but he didn't deny it, "And you are caught between a desire to save them, and the guilt that you would feel for breaking the Law?" Another nod. Sorin turned to Shuok. "Tell me who is affected in your family, Shuok, son of Huak, for this may save them."

"It is wrong, Sorin, we must not be seen to be part of this, we …" his brother interrupted, his heart spoke before his head.

"Muakir, it is Muakir Ulumik, velak Sheramkir, she is … not family, yet, but …"

"Ah, you hope that one day she will be, I understand. Well, then surely it is even more worthwhile attempting to save her."

"But her father would not let her drink the Brak, if he knew he would be furious. He sits on the Mrauuk, so …"

"But that is perfect."

"What do you mean?"

Sorin grinned. "Well, if we cure his daughter that at least should have some weight with him, when we tell him how we have done it."

Dak shook his head. "I am not sure that the Mrauuk even think like that Sorin, but despite the fact it is a little underhand, I have to admit that the idea has merit."

"Your skills as a diplomat are developing, Dak, and underhand is often the only way to proceed."

"Do you think she that might be persuaded to try the cure, Nameed?"

Nameed looked sheepishly at Rotvee. "She might, if Rotvee, velak Nakeket, were to ask her."

Rotvee looked, at first, as if she was about to refuse and then her face broke into a smile and she bent her head to remove the crystal shard from its chain. She stepped forward and she took the jug of Brak from the table and held it aloft. "This Brak I dedicate to you, Ragarad, father of our people, I alone among my family still hold to my prayers and I honour you, although some have mocked me for keeping faith. In your name I will put this to the test for you have given me life and kept my blood and my kin safe from harm. Watch over us your people." She dropped the shard into the jug and returned it to the table, her smile became a laugh. "Now, Dakveen Halak, viak Thark, viak Varkind, viak Bakund, if you are an outcast and a criminal, then so am I. And if your eyes speak from your heart then should we both survive this trial I will follow you either on your return to the wilderness or to a new home here in the mountains. And, yes, Nameed viak Huak, your feelings are reciprocated, Muakir wishes a union too, but you must first prove yourself to her father."

Rotvee's words had caused both Nameed and Dak to blush uncontrollably, which made her laugh even more. She looked at Sorin. "I will bring Muakir Ulumik, velak Sheramkir, to this chamber, wait for me, but do not let Dakveen Halak escape." With this she was gone, and an embarrassed silence reigned.

After a moment or two, Danil patted Dak upon the shoulder. "Congratulations, my friend, I did not hear your proposal, but the answer was clear enough."

"I am not sure I heard it either, Danil." Dak sounded somewhat shaken by the turn of events. "It just sort of happened and ..." his voice tailed away into his thoughts.

"Surely that is how it should be, Dakveen, though I am no expert."

Sorin found that Danil was looking at him. "Oh! And I am, Danil Lebreven, is that your insinuation?"

"Not at all, Sorin, but you have lived considerably longer than all of us and therefore should have had, how shall I put this, more experience."

The laugh that came was rueful. "I think not, truly I do. Despite my long years, I remember my vows." He turned to Mikael who had stepped closer to the table to look into the jug of Brak. "Is anything happening, Mikael? Or am I being impatient?"

"A little, Sorin." Michael looked closely at the surface of the liquor. "But there are a few bubbles appearing."

"And that means … what?"

"Well, I am hoping it means that the Brak is working on the crystal and is breaking it down, releasing a gas as a by-product of the reaction." He was met with blank stares. "Er … well, when the Brak eats into the crystal it only … swallows part of it and the rest … becomes the bubbles. Or something close to that. I know that bubbles are usually a sign that something is going on."

"I thought they meant that there was a fish somewhere under the water, but I hope there are no fish in the Brak."

"If your Brak is as strong as I think it is there is little chance a fish could live in it, Dak."

"How long will it take for the shard to disappear completely, Mikael?"

"I have no idea, Dak, I suspect that as the bubbles have increased in their number it may not be too long, but I cannot be sure."

Dak looked very thoughtful. "Rotvee Bramkilik was right to offer up a prayer, what we are doing could be momentous and we will I feel need all the support that we can get. She certainly has something about her, doesn't she?" He looked at Michael for confirmation.

"Dak, I am not an expert in the female of any species, but …" An image of Mel's face sprang into his mind fleetingly and then was replaced by that of Siraal with her sightless eyes, and then another face, Julia Sharpe. Here was a truth he could not deny, he was no expert. Mel had been the one, always, in a way even before they met, nothing was as real as what had been, and nothing had prepared him for when it was. What could he say? "But I know that when I loved, I loved with my whole being and,

for a while, I was repaid in kind. Rotvee seems to have an in-
dependent mind and a strength that would certainly make her a
fitting partner for such a well-travelled Nare as yourself. I think
she has made a good choice for you."

"That's what I was afraid of." He turned his attention back
to the jug of Brak upon the table. "Mikael, there are no more
bubbles coming to the surface, does that mean that the Brak has
consumed the entire shard?"

Michael looked into the jug and he saw that Dak was right,
the surface was now clear and still. "Is there another jug that we
could pour this into and then we could be certain?"

"I shall find one, unless Nameed, viak Huak, thinks I am
going to run away?"

"No, Dakveen, I do not think that you will run, but I will
come with you for that is my task as you well know."

"So be it. Come, we should not be long in searching, Mikael."

The two Nare left the room and Mikael turned to Sorin,
who had returned to tending Suani. He suddenly felt very tired
and he knew that their trials below ground were taking their
toll; in fact, he wondered how he had managed to stay awake
thus far. Sorin looked up and he appeared to notice the exhaustion in his face.

"Mikael, you should get some rest you must be completely spent."

Michael knew that he was right, but it suddenly came to him
why he was forcing himself to remain awake. "I am, Sorin, but
if I give in to sleep now, my fit may come upon me and I feel
that I am needed here."

Sorin nodded, Shuok was still with them and they could not
speak openly in front of him "That is an interesting point, but
here, take a drink from this flask, it will sustain you for a while
longer. We will have to face the Mrauuk soon and I would prefer to have you with me in spirit as well as body. It is a brew of
my own making that I keep to prolong my wakefulness for a
while should sleep be groping thickly at my mind." He handed Michael a small leather flask, there were words branded into

the leather, worn by time they were almost indecipherable, but he was sure that one of them was Calix. Sorin saw that he was attempting to read the inscription. "Yes, Mikael, it is a very old flask, but a special one. However, the liquid it contains is fresh, well fairly fresh, but it does last well … just take a sip and stop worrying for a moment."

Michael nodded and unstopped the flask. The liquid had a warm spicy flavour, that reminded him of cardamom, but it also seemed to quiver in his mouth and throat as if it had a life of its own. He had drunk energy drinks on occasion at home and he supposed that this was Sorin's equivalent, but he suspected that this one would have a touch more power. He was not wrong, after a moment or too he felt the quiver spread though him and the weariness, that had a moment before surfaced, was gone to be replaced by a tingling in his fingers and a buzzing in his ears.

Sorin chuckled quietly. "Yes, it does that to me too, but it is harmless, I assure you. I suppose if you took it continually it would probably kill you, for the release of sleep is necessary to sustain life. But I for one am not going to test the theory."

"No, Sorin, one sip will be enough I feel." He looked down at Suani, who at least seemed to have lost the grey pallor to her skin and was now sleeping peacefully. "How is she, truthfully?"

"As I said, she will recover, although she will bear the scars for a good while. The Antaldi, for all their dislike of war, have a great resilience and they heal swifter than most. A Cluath I suspect would have succumbed to the poison in her flesh before you escaped from the tunnels. She only survived through your determination to survive."

"I am just glad we made it in time, Sorin."

The door opened behind him and Dak entered carrying an identical wooden jug to the one which sat waiting upon the table. He was followed by Rotvee who supported another young female, Michael assumed this to be Muakir. She was dressed in a similar fashion to Rotvee, although her skirt was longer and of a very fine leather, drawn together with laces which gave it the appearance of webbing. She had fewer earrings, although she too had a chain which sported gemstones hanging from her left ear and through her right she had a silver scroll. She also had a woven blanket draped around her shoulders and her face was drawn and pale. Nameed followed them in and he closed the door. His face displayed his conflicting emotions and as he went to stand beside his brother, he kept his eyes to the floor, fearing they would betray him.

"This is Muakir Ulumik, velak Sheramkir, viak Nesskem, viak Muak. She has agreed to test our cure and she knows what it might mean."

Muakir looked up at them each in turn and then she spoke to Dak. "I greet you Dakveen Halak, viak Thark, viak Varkind, viak Bakund, and welcome your return, if it should mean an end to this curse. Rotvee has chosen well and I will stand with her when she calls for witness … should I survive." She bowed and was about to give the formal greeting when she stumbled.

Dak quickly moved to support her before she fell. "Come, Muakir Ulumik, forget formality, you are weak. Nameed a chair."

Nameed pushed his brother towards one of the benches along the wall and they moved it towards the centre of the room to allow Muakir to sit down. She nodded her thanks and then she looked up at Michael and the others. "Forgive my failure to greet you with more courtesy, I am weary of this illness and I know that soon it will take all my strength and it will leave me helpless awaiting death."

Sorin rose and bowed to her. "I speak for all of us, Muakir Ulumik, velak Sheramkir, when I say that we accept your greeting and we admire your courage, it is to be hoped that our assumptions are correct, and we can assist you in your need. We were about to assess whether the Brak we have prepared is ready. Were we not Dakveen?"

"Yes, we were." He handed the jug to Michael. "Mikael, would you mind?"

"Not at all, Dak, I am intrigued to be honest." He took the empty jug and he placed it beside its partner. He then lifted the jug containing the Brak and he began to carefully pour the liquor into the empty jug. The liquid glistened, and the rich bitterness filled his nostrils and stung his eyes. He was reminded of a friend of his mother's, who had made pickles and chutneys, her kitchen had smelt just this way whenever they had visited, the hot vinegar and spices, sweetness and sharpness combined into one cloud of sharp memory. When he had finished the jug was empty save for the smell. "Well, it is pleasant to be right for once. The crystal shard has become part of the Brak."

Both Nameed and Shuok made warding gestures, which drew a fierce laugh from Rotvee. "Well, let us see, Nameed, viak Huak, if this illicit brew can save that which you desire, despite your fears."

Michael poured a small amount of the converted Brak into a wooden beaker and Rotvee picked it up. "I have had a disturbing thought, Mikael, son of Halkgar, but I will share it with you when Muakir has drunk this." She turned to Muakir, who looked for a moment reluctant and then she took the cup. "Drink, Muakir, velak Sheramkir, and may Ragarad favour us all."

"Indeed, Rotvee, velak Nakeket, though I fear that he has forgotten us." She raised the cup and she drank the contents in one slow movement.

There was a silence, which Michael knew was to be expected, but he also took it as a sign of a lack of understanding and he felt that he needed to explain. "The effect is unlikely to be immediate, Muakir, I would hope though, that there is some indication that it has helped by morning."

She nodded and she went to rise, but this time it was Rotvee who took her arm. "Come Muakir, we will go just a little way to my family chamber, and you may lie down there."

"Thank you, and thank you, Mikael Dal Oaken, whatever the outcome, that an outsider is concerned for us most unusual, but most welcome nonetheless."

Rotvee helped her out through the door and the others were left in a limbo of silence that remained unbroken for what seemed an age until Suani broke it as she spluttered to wakefulness. "Oh, it is you Sorin, I had feared that I would be waking to the mists of the dead."

"Not at all, Suani, you are of a strong disposition and I am a stubborn healer. I was not going to lose you."

Michael joined Sorin by her bedside. Suani reached up and she took his hand in hers. "I owe you my life, Mikael, I would surely have died in that awful darkness, but for you. My life's blood is yours and I will repay my debt to you when my strength returns."

"Just rest and recover, Suani, forget about repaying debts, I did what any would have done in the circumstances."

"No, Mikael, you did much more than could have been expected of you and I thank the Powers that you did."

Sorin was anxious that she should continue to rest. "Suani, you need to talk less and rest more."

"Sorin, you remind me of my mother, with your fussing, although her beard was shorter, but I will sleep if you insist, I am still tired …" her eyes closed, and she was once again sleeping, but she had regained some colour and her breathing was steady and strong.

"Once again, old friend, you weave your spell and perform another miracle."

"No, Danil, this was just a healer's skill, miracles take a lot longer."

As if to dispute this statement the door was flung open and Muakir and Rotvee raced in excitedly. Muakir was flushed with colour and a smile danced upon her lips.

"Dakveen Halak, viak Thark, behold the return of hope to our people, Muakir had barely closed her eyes when she opened them again and was as you see her, free of the illness. It is a …"

"Miracle, Rotvee Bramkilik, velak Nakeket? Well, in one sense it may be, but it is also a result of Mikael's knowledge and understanding. Whether we had the help of Ragarad I know not, but I offer thanks to him and the rock and the soil that he gave us."

Sorin examined the excited Muakir. "Well, she certainly has the look of one who is free of disease, although I have only seen a few victims, and none close up for comparison. Any thoughts, Mikael, as to the speed with which it has appeared to work?"

"I would suspect it can only be because the concentration … the amount of crystal, to the amount of Brak. The liquor would have only rested in the goblet for a short time and thus only a tiny amount would have been consumed. We have made a strong draught because we have just one jug of Brak to a relatively sizeable piece of the crystal."

Rotvee suddenly remembered what she was going to say earlier. "Ah, yes, Mikael, I had meant to say this before, but I was looking after Muakir, we have but the one jug of the cure and it will not stretch to all the victims in the seven cities."

This was something that none of them had really considered although it was of course an obvious flaw in their plan. The jug of Brak even if they halved the dose that Muakir had taken would possibly go around maybe twenty victims and that was just the tiniest fraction of those that needed help.

"That is very true, Rotvee, and once we have faced the Mrauuk we will have to seek out more of the crystal." Sorin had finished his examination of Muakir. "You said that it came from a traveller, but where had the crystal come from?"

"As I told you, Sorin, the traveller said that it had come from the western most tip of the mountain range, a place high up, hard to find."

Michael, with growing awareness saw the way this chain was leading him. He felt he knew exactly where the green crystal could be found. "Did the traveller have a name, Rotvee? What race was he?"

"His name I know, but as to race, I was never told, though he was not of the Nare, his name was Uxl."

Sorin looked at Michael with a look that suggested caution and Michael nodded. He knew better than to reveal all of his thoughts he barely wanted to reveal them to himself. "Uxl of the Tarr is a name known to us, Rotvee, and that may be of some help in finding more of the crystal, although how we travel to the edge of the mountains is something that will need thought."

Muakir was surprised, but her excitement continued. "A Tarr, then the First Ones do still walk upon the face of Taleth as the legends say. Is it true they do not die?"

"They do not die of old age, Muakir, but they can be killed. Suani and I met one in the tunnels as we escaped from the depths."

Even Sorin was surprised by this. "We must hear more of this, Mikael, the full story of your journey obviously needs telling."

"I will tell it in full at some later time, Sorin, but suffice to say we came upon Ayx of the Tarr, brother to Uxl, who was close to death, overcome by the poison and the tearing jaws of the Tskuson. He had searched for news of Uxl throughout the mountains. We were with him when he died."

"The passing of such an ancient being is always a loss, Mikael, but we must speak of this, as you say, at some later time."

Dak now posed the next question and one that needed immediate consideration. "Well, when and how do we talk to the Mrauuk about this? The Council of the Nare are not the most approachable people as individuals, but together they are as of solid rock."

For a moment or two there was silence, then Sorin spoke with deliberation. "I think for many reasons," here he cast a look at Michael, which he knew meant that he expected him to switch at any moment, "it would be best to speak with them at once, not least because time is still against us and to delay will mean more needless deaths."

"I agree, Sorin, our priority must be to save my people and for that to happen we must face them. I will prepare the way; you must follow with Mikael and Rotvee Bramkilik, if you would accompany Muakir Ulumik. Danil, I must needs take Sorin from your cousin's side, would you watch over her while we confront the rock of the Law in all its dust and immovability?"

"Of course, Dak, there is little I could say to sway them, but should we need to make a swift departure I will be ready."

For the first time in a while Dak smiled. "I sincerely hope it will not come to that, but your caution is wise, and preparedness is never wasted, my friend." He turned to Nameed and Shuok. "Well then, lead on, your task is almost over, and fear not reprisal for if things go badly you cannot be blamed for the actions of a mad outcast and a few headstrong strangers."

Nameed smiled weakly but Shuok simply spun around and set off through the chamber door.

As Michael followed, Muakir suddenly said, "Shall I bring the Brak that cured me Dakveen Halak, viak Thark?"

Sorin's chuckle had returned to his old throat. "It is good that there are some wise young heads amongst us, Dak, presenting a cure without the cure would have been a clever trick."

"Yes, Sorin, a fair point. Muakir Ulumik, velak Sheramkir, you are a precious jewel among the maidens of the Nare, my thanks." Dak gave an exaggerated bow.

"Careful, Dakveen, last time you spoke to a young female you ended up betrothed."

Dak straightened as his face reddened and Muakir, burst into a very girlish giggle, which was followed by a conversation of whispers and laughter between her and Rotvee.

Dak tried not to show his embarrassment as he followed Nameed and his brother along the corridor. But Michael, although he was a few paces behind, could hear him as he muttered to himself. He was about to speak when Sorin's thoughts were in his mind.

'Michael, I tried in vain to find you and Suani with the staff, but something blocked my thoughts, maybe something in the mountain, maybe something worse, but I am relieved that you survived intact, much relieved, and grateful, as Danil is I am sure, that you saved Suani's life. You are much changed since first I helped you from the furs in my cave. You are stronger and more confident, more self-reliant than you were to begin with. I never asked you then, but I ask it now because I feel that you can answer. Did you believe what was happening to you? Did you acknowledge the reality of our world? Or did you think of us as a dream?'

Michael knew that he had changed, changed greatly during his time in Taleth and in his time at home since his revival. Was he more confident, stronger? He supposed he was. He was certainly a different man. As he walked along the long corridor of the families in the city of the Nare he tried to be as honest as he could.

'I think I did to start with; a wild series of imaginings fired by drugs and my comatose state. But they had ceased giving me drugs long before I began to see you and when the Tsarg turned up, it became at least clear that it was real, even if I could not explain or attempt to understand it.'

As they walked; here and there, they passed a Nare who stopped and began to whisper and point at Muakir, who moved now with energy and excitement, when they knew she had con-tracted the disease. What was this strange procession? Where was it going?

Sorin ignored it all and he carried on. *'You must tell me more of your meeting with the Tarr, but first I have had a thought as to what has gone on, Michael, and it may help you, it may not. We know that there is manipulation going on, we are all being driven to take a path that has been set out for us. Not just you, my friend, but Dak, Danil, Suani perhaps, and certainly myself. We have all started with our feet upon a stair that will take us to where someone wants us to go, or several 'someones', I cannot be sure. But before the trials that await us are attempted, before our choices our faced, before we shake the dice for one last time, we are being prepared. For me it was an awakening of a long dead name, a relighting of an ancient fire. For Danil it was facing the Triad and realising that he had blood and kin still in this world. For Dak it is now, it is this moment of truth before the Mrauuk that expelled his family to die in the wilderness alone.*

'For you it has been the whole journey, every step, every en-counter, every thrust and every new scar, every dream and every question that your heart has sought answers to and found none. Even your fall and your struggle in the mountain must have been part of this preparation. When you come to face your choice, as you undoubtedly will, someone decided that you had to be the man you have now become. For only then could you be the 'Decider', 'The Ender of Days', only then could you make the choice freely.'

'I am flattered that you think that I am ready, Sorin, but Uvarin hinted that if the Corruptor knew that I could no longer be manipulated and controlled that he may try to destroy me.'

'Did he now? Well, since he is now visiting you in your dreams openly that makes you practically a Majann. Come, my friend, Dakveen needs us, we will speak more of this if time allows.'

★★★

12

Before the Mrauuk

They had arrived at the Council chamber itself. The two sons of Huak had scuttled away, for fear of being tainted by the group. Rotvee had shaken her head sadly as they had left, but Dak had ignored it. They stood now before the two huge doors which were dark and solid, made from wood which grew on the plains, but were carved and inlaid with silver and gems. Intricate patterns each one a family, each one a heritage, each one a history, they spread out across the doors creating a circle of Nare aristocracy. The circle was surmounted on the right by an image of the mountains as seen from the northern side, with the seven cities portrayed in finest detail. To the left there was an image of Ragarad arms spread wide to shower gifts upon his chosen people. To Michael's eyes it didn't do him justice, but he wondered how many of the Nare had been privileged enough to have been granted an audience. As he continued to allow his eyes to drift over the silver patterns and the gemstones cunningly inlaid within the family emblems, he saw a patch that had been defiled, the pattern gouged out and the gems prised from the wood. It was obvious to whom that emblem had belonged, and Michael could only imagine the pain that it must be causing Dak as he stood before the doors and waited.

After a few moments, a voice spoke from within, amplified somehow within the walls, it boomed out above them from hidden openings.

"Hovaash! Ka frual na ruulkrim, meenash takk ta koav Mrauuk tikelmkit Nare." Although Michael understood the warning, *'Beware! Go no further wilderness-dwellers, name yourselves in honesty to the council of the Nare',* he kept silent to allow Dak to 'prepare the way' as he had asked.

"Kumil ta Ragarad, ilk meenash Dakveen Halak, viak Thark, viak Varkind, viak Bakund. Uoth kerakim Rotvee Bramkilik, velak Nakeket, viak Hriok, viak Thulim, ut Muakir Ulumik, velak Sheramkir, viak Nesskem, viak Muak. Tashem kerakim Majann Sorin ut Mikael Dal Oaken, viak Halkgar. Tavish ta koav Mrauuk ut nelketh rak hesham."

There was a pause and then the voice spoke again. "Nelketh rak hesham ta koav Mrauuk, Dakveen Halak, Hemmek, ut kerakim." Michael watched Dak and he made no sign that he had registered the deliberate slur, the lineage replaced with one word *'Outcast'*. He held his head high as the doors opened and he strode forward defiantly into the Mrauuk, the centre of Nare Law. As they followed him in, Michael saw that the grandness of the doors was but a precursor to the splendour that lay within. They walked between two pairs of pillars of shimmering and polished stone; these were part of two circles that ran round the chamber. In the centre thirteen chairs of similar stone were arranged in a wide arc, the chairs were plain, but the floor was a stunning mosaic of tiles, which appeared to display the history of the Nare from the awakening beneath the mountains to the founding of the seven cities. Overhead, the natural rock of the mountain had been shaped around the rich blue veins of ore that ran within it to create an amazing image of the skies of Taleth as the sun set, to reveal stars and darkness beyond. Around the walls were more carved and painted images of figures of the past, heroes of the Nare throughout history.

Not all the stone chairs were occupied; the outer seat of each arm of the arc was vacant, as was the central chair. The rest held the members of the Mrauuk, the Council of the Nare. Most of them were older than Dak by a good many years, a few were younger. All wore a deep red sash and a black cloak with a high collar, symbols of their status as members of the Council.

Dak stopped at the centre of the arc and he bowed. "Kumil ta Ragarad, ta koav Mrauuk."

None of the Council rose to bow in response, but the Nare who sat to the right of the empty chair, spoke. "Dakveen Halak, Hemmek, brueem lakir ta Nare?"

Dak straightened up and he looked around at each of the faces of the Mrauuk. "I will speak in the Cluath tongue, if I may, Sheramkir Ulumik, viak Nesskem, viak Muak, because we have guests who do not understand the language of the Nare, although I dare say that they would be more courteous than my own people appear to have become. Although you have little time for ruulkrim, 'wilderness-dwellers', these are my friends to whom I owe my life."

Another council member to Dak's left spat out a comment. "Hemmek gruath na taketek carukkit!" *'An outcast's life is hardly worth saving!'* Michael began to realise how difficult this was going to be. However, Dak carried on, ignoring the insult.

"I have come before you, with my companions, to tell you that we have discovered a way to beat this vile curse that is destroying the families of the Nare."

The Council members now began to speak all at once, but Sheramkir raised a hand for silence, his accent was thick and solid as the mountains, he spoke the Cluath as one who had learned it reluctantly and used it rarely. "That is a bold claim, Dakveen Halak, a bold claim for an outcast."

"An outcast, Sheramkir Ulumik, viak Nesskem, who has risked all to bring this to the attention of the Mrauuk."

"Be that as it may, Dakveen Halak, but can you substantiate your claim? Can we see proof?" Sheramkir's face betrayed little, age and care had creased his forehead, but there was little way of knowing his thoughts.

"You can, Sheramkir Ulumik, viak Nesskem, your daughter Muakir had shown signs of the disease had she not?"

"That is true, but what …"

Dak turned and he gestured for Muakir to come forward. "Here is your proof, here is your daughter and she is free from the illness."

Muakir stepped forward and she bowed to her father and the rest of the Mrauuk, her father rose, but he did not approach her. "Is this true, daughter, are you now free of the illness?"

"It would appear so, my father, my lungs are clear, and I can breathe freely again." She paused for him to respond, when he did not, she continued, her tone betrayed a note of disappointment. "Are you not pleased?"

Sheramkir looked for a moment like a small boy caught with his hand in the sweet jar. "I am most pleased, my daughter." He then turned to look at Dak with confusion in his eyes. "And was it Dakveen Halak who effected this recovery?"

"It was, my father, Dakveen Halak, accomplished this with the help of his companions and with the assistance of Rotvee Bramkilik, velak Nakeket."

Sheramkir seemed to be searching for the words that he needed. To Michael he appeared to be rolling back the pain of acceptance without showing emotion in front of his compatriots. He was overcome with relief, an unexpected miracle; he was realising that Muakir was not going to die. The chamber became silent around him as he came to a decision. "It would appear Dakveen Halak, viak Thark, viak Varkind," The tension in the air grew palpable as several of the members of the Mrauuk sat forward in their stone chairs with an audible hiss as Dak was addressed for the first time in the proper formal manner, but Sheramkir continued. "It would appear that thanks are in order." He stood and bowed formally. "You have my thanks and that of my house. Muakir is to me a treasure above all that lies within the heart of the mountains, and … although perhaps I do not show it always, I am most proud of her."

Muakir's face broke into a smile and she now bowed to her father. But then one of the council got to his feet. Michael saw that it was the one who had spat out his insult at Dak earlier. His face was twisted in disgust, and he spoke the Cluath words as if they burned his mouth. "But how was this jagdikit, this trick performed, Dakveen Halak, Hemmek?" There was no naming of ancestors, no forgiveness. "Explain yourself, I am not persuaded so easily for I have no daughters."

Dak stepped towards him, Michael knew that here would be the testing of it, and he feared that the chances of success looked slim. "I will explain myself Bruak Shiveer, viak Vikalik, viak

Nassik, and not forget my manners, perhaps if you had daughters they would remind you occasionally of yours."

The two Nare stared at each other, one eyes blazing, the other staying calm but resolute. Bruak broke first and he muttered an oath under his breath before he sat back down. "Begin, Hemmek!"

Dakveen sighed and then he turned to Sheramkir and the others. "What I am about to tell you is strange, and what is more was discovered by chance. It is thanks to my friend Mikael Dal Oaken, son of Halkgar, that we may begin to understand it and see the possibilities which could lead to saving our race, my friends, saving thousands from a lingering death, that too many have suffered already and are suffering at this very moment. Which one of you has not been touched by the plague? Which one of you has not known loss? Which one of you has not felt in their heart the threat of death's hand closing around you?"

Bruak leapt to his feet again, pointing an accusatory finger along the line of seats at the furthest member of the Mrauuk. "He has not! Raise your hand and acknowledge your house, Gariok Bramkilik, viak Hriok, and while you are at it tell us how your family and yours alone are spared this curse?"

Gariok, rose slowly, shaking his head. "Bruak Shiveer, viak Vikalik, you are a bitter old fool if you think that I have in some deliberate manner avoided the disease. I am as saddened as any by so many deaths. I consider the whole of the Nare my kin and weep for their plight. As you all know I have no notion why it is that my family survive, and others suffer, if I had had such a notion, I would have revealed it long ago."

"Don't play the sanctimonious fool, Gariok Bramkilik, viak Hriok, your kin were always close with their secrets, dark secrets too I wouldn't wonder. Your family has always won more than its fair share of commissions, we all know that. What have your family got that the rest of us haven't?"

Rotvee was bursting at this attack upon her family honour and finally she could not contain herself. "Your jealousy and hatred for my house is well known, Bruak Shiveer, but if you are accusing my kin of sharp practice, then …"

"Hold your tongue, girl!" Bruak was beside himself with rage. "How dare you speak without permission or status within this chamber! Mrak karlak muat grashult!"

This insult, one of the worst that he could have uttered, was both ancient and well known. *'Your words are but the bubbling of sewer filth!'* There was shock amongst all of the council members, but it was Dak who spoke first as Rotvee stood, visibly shaking by this outburst. "Know this Bruak Shiveer, viak Vikalik, viak Nassik, that you have insulted Rotvee Bramkilik, velak Nakeket, my betrothed, in front of witnesses, and when this session of the Mrauuk is completed I will require your apology or you will be brought to account and face my axe in combat."

Michael could not tell whether Bruak was more taken aback by Dakveen's challenge to combat or his declaration that Rotvee was his betrothed, but his eyes betrayed confusion and his anger faded as he realised that none of the others appeared to be rushing to his defence. Gariok, who had cast a quick questioning glance at Rotvee, during Dak's speech, as if to say, *'And your father is aware of this, is he?'* sought to calm the situation.

"Dakveen Halak, viak Thark, there is no need for combat, Bruak Shiveer, viak Vikalik, will apologise I am sure, when he has had a chance to calm himself a little. When the blood rises then words flow that cooler heads contain, as they say; and niece pray be silent, I am here to defend our House and its interests and I will not fail in my appointed task. If I require your assistance, I will be certain to ask."

Rotvee nodded. "Yes, my uncle, I ask forgiveness of the Mrauuk. I should not have spoken without introduction."

Sheramkir acknowledged her apology. "Thank you, Rotvee Bramkilik, velak Nakeket, but we have strayed from the matter in hand. Bruak Shiveer, viak Vikalik, please return to your place and allow Dakveen Halak, son of Thark, to complete his explanation."

Grudgingly Bruak did so, but his face remained thunderous, and Michael could not see this as improving their chances of being favourably received.

Dak continued. "My explanation will absolve the House Bramkilik of any suspicions that you or any others may have, Bruak Shiveer, viak Vikalik, viak Nassik, but it must be said that it was the fact that none of that house had died, which led us to our discovery. There was in their possession a family heirloom, passed down from father to son along the line of Bramkilik. It was a goblet, made from a rare and beautiful dark green crystal, a gift from Uxl of the Tarr, given many centuries ago to one of that House, who had been of great service to him. It was so exquisite that it was considered too fine for common use and it was kept for special occasions, such as weddings and namings, when all would drink strong Brak from it."

Sheramkir nodded. "Of this goblet I have heard, Dakveen Halak, son of Thark, but I thought that it was not now a thing of memory, broken through age and use."

"That it was, Sheramkir Ulumik, viak Nesskem, long use had thinned the crystal to the point that it broke and much of it became dust. One single shard remained which was presented to Rotvee, velat Nakeket, as a memento, she wore it from a girl to this very day, upon a chain around her neck. But is this not a strange occurrence? How many of you can recall a crystal, solid enough to be cut and shaped, being anything other than unyielding, beautiful, yes, but hard as the day it was mined. That is the nature of crystal, and although they can shatter, or be broken, they do not in normal circumstances fade away." He paused to let this sink into the assembly. He was calmness itself, unlike Michael who knew that every step took him closer to the edge of the precipice that was the Law. It was like watching a very slow fuse fizzing its way towards an explosive charge, as the moment of inevitable detonation approached time seemed to have slowed to a crawl.

"Why then had this goblet, which was crystal made, become over the years thinner and thinner? What had happened to the fabric of the goblet? And if it was disappearing where had it gone?" The fuse fizzed on; the chamber still hung on Dak's every word. "If our race had not been attacked by this cursed disease, we would have never even asked that question. For as you have pointed out, Bruak Shiveer, viak Vikalik, so succinctly, only those of House Bramkilik are spared. If that was true, then it was also true that only those who had drunk from the crystal goblet were free from taint of the plague."

A figure along to Dak's left nodded, his age and sadness echoed in his voice. "You are quite correct, Dakveen Halak, viak Thark, my nephew, Hashett Ikklemit, viak Ukliket, is alive though his brother Uttmesh is dead, and he is wed to a Bramkilik."

"Quite so, Yagash Ikklemit, viak Karlint. Here we have the very crux of our discovery; somehow drinking from the goblet of green crystal had protected them. But what was it that they had been drinking? Surely it was merely a fine old Brak similar to that which all of us have drunk many times in our lives. No, it was not just Brak. Somehow the goblet had changed the liquor into a cure for this plague, and in doing so it weakened its very fabric." The fuse fizzed and sparked as it drew near to its destination. "The Brak had in some way consumed the crystal, changing itself in the process." Michael could hear the unease that was spreading among the members of the Mrauuk, like frost emanating from Dak's feet, their stone seats had chilled and they were feeling the discomfort. "Could this really be the case? Could such a simple thing save our race? Yes, it could. For we placed the single remaining shard into a jug of fine old Brak and within minutes it had been consumed and from that jug Muakir has received the changed Brak that has cured her of the disease." Detonation, the fuse had done its work.

Although Michael had suspected that the elders of the Nare would be shocked when they were told what had been done, he was stunned at the anger, the outrage and the sheer explosion of vitriol that burst from the mouths of the majority of the Mrauuk. That they did not physically attack Dak and the others was because that would have violated their own code, but they shouted their abuse and their disgust in a cacophony of words and phrases, that made Michael wish that he had not been gifted with the ability to speak and understand the tongue of the Nare. The few who remained seated, which included the member who had one surviving nephew, shook their heads, but kept silent.

As the wave of rage flowed over him, Dak stood impassive waiting for their ire to cool sufficiently for them to take stock. But when amidst the insults and the cursing the word 'death' became more and more frequent, he raised his hands and although those who had risen did not reseat themselves, they did become still.

"Members of the Mrauuk, now that you have purged yourself of your spleen, can we return to language more suited to this ancient chamber? Whatever your opinion is of what we have done there is no escaping the fact that this jug contains a cure for the plague."

Sheramkir took a step forward, his eyes dark and fierce. "Even though that is true, Hemmek, it will be cast upon the fire upon which your body shall burn. Ka arak ta fruarl Dakveen, Hemmek, ka arak ta garek limak Vrulat!" Those Nare who stood started to clap slowly and steadily, looking towards the few that still sat with stern aggressive stares until one by one they stood and reluctantly joined the rhythmic smack of hand upon hand. Michael knew what they meant before Sorin's words sprang into his head, but he knew also that he was not going to abide by the warning. *'They have sentenced him, and therefore, by association, us, to death and then burning, condemning even his spirit after death. Do not interfere I will speak to them when they cease this confounded clapping.'*

Dakveen had not moved, but he was pale, and his face drawn. Rotvee, although her eyes were angry and resentful, was visibly trembling; she had placed a hand around Muakir's shoulders, to comfort her for she looked close to tears. Sorin was pensive; as he made ready to speak, but it was Michael who stepped forward and silenced the terrible death knell. After Dakveen had reached the end of his speech, once the initial shock at their reaction had passed, Michael had felt an anger building, an anger that for once he was going to unleash. Unleash against this bigotry, this defiant ignorance, this vile stupidity, this brutish obsession with the Law. He let his fury build as the bullying drove all to their feet; he let it build as Sorin warned him to remain silent. And then he stepped forward and he opened the flood gates.

"Hovaash Mrauuk! Hovaash! Ruuak na krillkuur randat onak Nare Vrulat. Mrak limak ta fruarl, ta garek, krill Nare." He spoke in as strong and as confident a manner as he could muster, he wanted to gain the maximum impact. None of the council knew that he spoke the Nare tongue and he chose his words carefully. *'Beware Mrauuk! Beware! Know this, there can be no doubt the Doom of the Nare is pronounced. Your words sentence to death, to oblivion, the whole Nare race.'*

The effect was immediate, all hands were stilled, all throats silenced and all eyes wide. Here was a ruulkrim berating them in their own tongue, the shock mounted as Michael threw wide his hands wide, palms upwards and played what he hoped would be his trump card.

"Kemek Ragarad, Kemea gruash. Jaom irak carukkit vil Nare fralkim ryuagathak. Jaom na randat threlsh Nare muat viakett vik ruuak. Kemek Ragarad ut meenash takk rulbruam." *'Hear me Ragarad, hear my prayer. Let these words be the saving of the Nare in spite of themselves. Let not doom fall on the Nare for they are only children in understanding. Hear me Ragarad and show us your wisdom'*

It was a bold stroke, but a gamble which could have consequences way beyond what Michael had hoped for. He knew that there was a strong possibility that nothing would happen, but he also knew that Ragarad had sent him there, and he had asked him personally to deliver Dak to the home of his ancestors and so he would be watching. His words hung in the air and nothing sought to disturb them. Seconds passed, and all remained still as the rock beneath their feet. Muscles strained, hearts beat, and breath strained for release. Still nothing. Michael began to think that his faith had been misplaced, and Sheramkir Ulumik had decided that this ruulkrim had played his hand and lost. He opened his mouth to speak and then he fell to his knees as the ground erupted beneath him.

The brightly painted tiles showered upwards in a fountain of colour, scattering in the air to smash upon the stone chairs and rain down upon the heads of the Mrauuk. Their own history had exploded upwards and had flung itself in accusation into their faces. Rising through this whirlwind of rock and ceramic came the figure of Ragarad himself, many times larger than he had been when he had spoken to Michael. His burning red eyes flashed as he surveyed the prone figures of the Mrauuk, his marble grey body pulsed with the turquoise and silvery black veins that Michael had seen before. He was even more magnificent and rugged than he remembered. When he spoke, his voice shook the mountains from peak to root,

"Viakett! Viakett! Kemek! Ragarad lakir ta Nare. Kemea rulbruam ut arakilam!" *'Children! Children! Hear me! Ragarad speaks to the Nare. Hear my words of wisdom and tremble!'*

He had risen now to the height of the chamber roof and his towering frame was a terrifying sight for the assembled Mrauuk. Here was the very god that they had named in their ceremonies, but few had really believed existed. Here was the Power that had created them, and that they had forgotten or discarded. Those that stood gawping, joined those who had already thrown themselves to the floor at his terrible words.

Michael had hoped that Ragarad would manifest himself in some way, in a voice or in a message, that he would appear in person in this apocalyptic manner had not occurred to him. Nor could he have predicted what Ragarad did next.

"I will speak in the tongue of the ruulkrim, since you have defiled the language that I gave you. You would condemn the Nare to a lingering death, rather than accept knowledge given as a gift. This I cannot allow. Your days are over; the Mrauuk shall no longer rule with such blindness and ignorance. You are dismissed, all except those that stand for the houses of Ikklemit and Bramkilik. Until new members are chosen, they it will be that shall dispense justice and law with Dakveen Halak, viak

Thark, viak Varkind, viak Bakund, who I name as member to represent his house, fully restored to status throughout the seven cities. Furthermore, I name Muakir Ulumik, velak Sheramkir, as Seer to the Council and she it will be who hears my words for you, and when she speaks all will listen.

"Long have you kept the custom of the empty chair, which waits for me to take my place at your head, but how many have ever thought I would? Well, she will sit there when she speaks for me and none will oppose her. It is time for the Nare to live again and move forward, taking their feet out of the past and step-ping towards the future. To this end remember the ruulkim that prayed and called me forth, Mikael Dal Oaken, son of Halkgar, I name him as my emissary, and he shall have all the rights and privileges of one true mountain born.

"And so, you disbelievers do not think this a jagdikit, I will burn my will upon you, you shall bear a mark of shame until a time when I feel that you truly believe and only then. Hovaash Nare! Hemmek tavishik viliakim! Faith must be reborn to wipe away your shame!"

As his massive frame began to return below the ground the former members of the Mrauuk began to scream in pain and terror, clutching their right hands to themselves in futile at-tempts to stave off the will of Ragarad. Each hand was burn-ing, the smell of flame-seared meat rose around the chamber, their screams continued as the floor recovered its shape and the mosaic returned to cover it. When the floor was still, the cham-ber doors flew open and armed guards raced to protect their leaders from a threat that appeared now to be prominent only in its absence. Bruak Shiveer was one of the first to stumble to his feet and clutching his damaged hand he faced Dak who had not moved, nor had Ragarad's dramatic entrance and exit wor-ried him. He was a believer. He knew that Ragarad knew his deeds to be honourable and his intentions pure. He could face his god without fear.

"Are you happy now, Dakveen Halak? Was this the plan all along, return to the mountains and take your revenge, depose the Mrauuk and take control? Tell me how did you manage that performance, was it the work of your pet Cluath Majann, did he …" But Bruak's words died in his throat as suddenly his forehead smoked and bubbled as Ragarad's mark began to appear just above his eyes. He threw himself to the ground and he tried desperately to put out the fire that seared his skin, but he could not and giving in to the pain, he staggered to his feet and fled the chamber.

As his terrified screams echoed still, Sheramkir, with a pale face and eyes cast down got to his feet and then he knelt before Dak.

"Dakveen Halak, viak Thark, viak Varkind, viak Bakund, I humbly ask your forgiveness, I have been too proud, too vain, too worldly to listen to the words of Ragarad, and I willingly bear this mark of shame as a punishment." He raised his hand and Michael saw for the first time what Ragarad had done, he had branded them with the word *'Kemek'* which meant *'hear me'*. "I will do whatever is needed to help restore the Nare to health, even if it would appear to be against the traditions that we have always lived by."

Now at last, Dak moved. He bent forward, took Sheramkir by the arm and helped him to his feet. "Sheramkir Ulumik, viak Nesskem, viak Muak, I am sure that in most things you have done your duty within the Mrauuk, and when Ragarad sees fit I am sure that you will be restored to represent your house."

"No, Dakveen, my time is over, I will look to my children and …" here he smiled towards his daughter, "grandchildren to restore honour to my family." Muakir blushed but she returned her father's smile. He then addressed the guards who had been variously helping those afflicted by the brand and who now stood in a confused group by the doors of the chamber. When he spoke, it was with great dignity, but his voice was now tinged with humility.

"Hear me; Nare of all Houses, Ragarad has spoken. This is my last pronouncement in this chamber. From this day until great Ragarad shows us we have deserved his love, the Mrauuk will consist of only three members, Dakveen of the House Halak." There were a few gasps of surprise at this. "Gariok of the House Bramkilik and Yagash of the House Ikklemit. My daughter, Muakir Ulumik, shall have free entrance, unimpeded by any, to this chamber and sit as the chosen Seer of mighty Ragarad. Also, Mikael Dal Oaken, son of Halkgar, although Cluath born is granted the status of a member of the House Halak, and he and his heirs shall be treated for all the days until the mountains pass, as a true mountain born. These are the words of Ragarad himself. Spread them to all the seven cities, along with the news that a cure has been discovered and that hope has returned to the mountains." He turned back to Dak. "Thus is my task complete, and I wish you well in your new role Dakveen with all my heart."

He held out both hands to shake Dak's and then he stopped in surprise, for the brand had vanished from his skin, he turned his hands over and back as if searching for where it had gone.

Dak laughed quietly. "It would appear that just as Ragarad's justice is harsh, his mercy is swift."

"As you say, Dakveen, son of Thark, I am thankful, but I had not looked for such quick redemption. I ask you to give me a task that will allow me to earn this redemption."

Dak thought for a moment. "Well, we still have the problem that so far the jug that your daughter carries is all the cure we have, and that we must seek the crystal in the far peaks, but it would ease my worries if you were the one to select those most at risk from the illness, those children that are close to death in each of the Houses and administer some of the cure to them. Muakir can assist you. It is a strong brew I think and hopefully it will stretch a long way. Save as many as you can, and I will concentrate my efforts on finding more of the green crystal."

Sheramkir nodded his assent. "This the House Ulumik will undertake and those that we cannot cure we will seek to make as comfortable as possible until you return."

Muakir moved closer to her father and she whispered quietly into his ear, he laughed. "Alright, my jewel, it will be so." He looked round for Nameed. "Nameed Nagesset, viak Huak, viak Daleem, is it true you have an understanding with my daughter?"

Nameed snapped out of the trance that he appeared to have been in since Ragarad had appeared. "Er … yes, that is correct Sheramkir Ulumik, viak …"

"Oh, no time for all that, Nameed, if she wants to marry you, then that is settled, we have too much to do to worry about long courtships and formal betrothal. You will marry when our task is complete, and the seven cities are free from the plague. Agreed?"

"Absolutely, Sheramkir Ulumik, viak … absolutely."

"Good. Come on then, both of you, we have work to do."

With these words, he nodded to Dak, Michael and Sorin in turn and then he bustled the happy couple away. The astonished guards helped the other stricken members of the Mrauuk out of the chamber, some mumbled and complained, some just shook their heads and held their hands hidden against their chests. Within a few minutes the room contained only Dak, Rotvee, Sorin, Michael, Gariok Bramkilik and Yagash Ikklemit.

Yagash had taken his seat and it was he who broke the silence that had fallen after the others had left. "Well, Dakveen Halak, mighty son of Thark, that was quite some meeting of the Mrauuk and I have attended many, some of which sent me very quickly to sleep, I can tell you. I for one am glad to see that your House has been restored, although I cannot say that you will have an easy time being accepted. It is one thing being appointed by Ragarad himself when he is here and eminently visible, it is quite another to persuade those who have not seen him of the validity of your restoration."

Dak walked towards a chair that had been empty for a very long time at the far end of the row. "I am well aware of that, Yagash Ikklemit, viak Karlint, but it is good to be able to take this seat and feel that my House is restored, although that was not why I returned. I returned because these good friends of mine persuaded me that it was the will of Ragarad, and it would appear on reflection they might have been right."

Sorin began to laugh, in fact he laughed until he began to cough, and Michael thumped him on the back. "Dakveen Halak, son of Thark and so forth, you have a talent not only for blunt diplomacy but also for understatement. 'We might have been right?' I think you would agree that Ragarad needed you to return, although Mikael here seems to be the one who has communion with the mighty ones."

"All I did was voice a prayer, Sorin, anyone could have done that."

"No, Mikael, none but you would have had that effect I suspect, which is probably why someone made sure that you would be here. I must admit that the faces of the Mrauuk were a delight when you began to speak their tongue with such fluency."

"Yes, Mikael Dal Oaken, son of Halkgar, that was a surprise to us all." It was Gariok who now also took his accustomed place. "How is it that a Cluath warrior speaks our language as well as those of us who are native to it?"

"It is a rather complicated tale I am afraid, Gariok Bramkilik, son of Hriok, and should we return intact from the search for the source of the crystal, I will gladly sit beside you with a jug of Brak and tell you the whole tale."

This time it was Dak who laughed. "Ah, my friend, not only do you speak our language like a mountain born, you overflow with our culture. That promise I will hold you to, an evening of long stories and strong drink is a prospect no Nare would ever be able to resist."

"I accept, but note my words Dak, *'should we return intact'*, we first have to find more of the crystal and that means a trek further into the mountains."

"It does, Mikael, but we can shorten the time it might take by calling our steeds back from the plain and riding the wide road at the base of the range. We can travel along the river until we reach Rivik and then begin the climb into the mountains. Do you agree Sorin?"

"Yes, that seems the best way. How long will it take to reach the place where we must start searching?"

It was Rotvee who spoke, but she was uncertain as to how to start. "I would speak, but am I given permission, Dakveen Halak, son of Thark? I am a mere girl."

Dakveen shook his head. "Now, do not start pretending a deference that is not in your nature, Rotvee Bramkilik, velak Nakeket, you are as entitled to speak here as any and I am sure that your uncle would agree that your council and your advice will be well received."

"Of course, Dakveen, but she is, as she says, a female, will she know when to be quiet again?" The twinkle in his eye betrayed his jest and Rotvee dutifully nodded.

"I will attempt to always be brief, uncle Gariok." He smiled warmly at her. "As for our journey …"

Dak interrupted her. "Our journey?"

"Yes, Dakveen, our journey, and I will brook no argument in this regard; I will accompany you and make sure that you return. Our journey will take possibly two days before we leave the road. After that a day's climb, maybe two, and we should be in the region that we assume Uxl referred to in his tale."

Dak pondered this for a while. "Very well, then our party should include representatives of at least two of the Houses that have been shorn of representation on the council, so that they may see we act for all the Nare."

Yagash nodded. "A good thought and if they set off with haste, while you prepare your mounts, they can make some headway on the road before you overtake them. Thus, your journey will be more swiftly completed."

Sorin clapped his hands and grinned. "I think, Dakveen, that this new Mrauuk of three will do well. Now I think we all could do with some rest, particularly Mikael and I will relieve Danil of his position at his cousin's side, while he sets off to find the Piradi, who I suspect will be waiting for him."

Dak rose from his new position. "I agree with all of that, Sorin, and I will walk with Yagash and Gariok and select those members of the other Houses that will be sent ahead of us." Before he moved further, he bowed formally to the empty chair in the centre of the arc, "Kumil ta Ragarad." His actions were copied by first Yagash and then Gariok. Then all three turned to face Michael and bowed. Dak spoke for all three.

"The thanks of the Nare are due to you, Mikael Dal Oaken, son of Halkgar, and your name will be honoured in all the seven cities."

Michael bowed back but he was not in the mood for a long speech. "Yes, thank you, Dak, now as Sorin said I need to sleep, probably for a week."

Dak smiled broadly and he nodded in agreement, so together, they moved out of the chamber. As they passed the door Michael noticed that where there had been the hideous gash in the stone there was now all the marks, sigils and names of the House Halak. Ragarad had truly restored Dakveen to his home, he was about to point this out when it began to peel away like scales before his eyes and he felt darkness take him. He fell forward but felt no thud upon cold floor instead his head rested upon a pillow and his ears heard voices from outside the door of his room.

★★★

Sylvan sat and waited patient and still at the edge of the rise that led to the bridges. The rush of the Rahk below, crashing endlessly along the ravine, echoed in the darkness and sang of an age of hurt. There was no way to tell from her features the sorrow that burned in her heart; nor the anger that boiled within her breast. She had searched long and hard for the spirits of the dead, walked the paths of the pack and called from the peaks to the weeping moon. Death was not an ending for the Wolves of Taleth, for they were Avali. They were born of the mind of the One amongst the winds that blew before time, singing their song of ecstatic joy in the unending realm, weaving the long night into a bright rich darkness that warmed the breath of eternity and fired the unfathomable mind, as Taleth was drawn from the sweet scent of the heavens.

For love of the One, they chose their paths, gifted their own fragment of imagination and the chance of creation, some tasked with steering the still rudderless world and leading the Taleth born from the shadows into the fresh new light. In the heart of each and every wolf, which beats to the rhythm of the rock and river, tree and towering cliff, pulsing with the soul of Taleth itself, there lay a shadow blown with the memory of a wind. None forget their birthing, none forget their true form, none forget their bond with the One, but neither do they forget that returning is beyond their choosing; the end of time itself will call them home to sing once more in the dancing darkness.

She named them in her heart as she did every day, at every moment's pause. The dead, the torn, the violated, the lost: Karlynn; Bryelle; Friesse; Nilus; Tiriel; Uvan; Balior; Huinshi. Brothers and sisters, kin and blood, driven screaming from their physical form into a purgatory of wandering. And yet she must move on, Sorin still had need of her, the Majann were her charge, and now more than ever, the pack needed to be certain and clear of purpose, fealty assured and strong in duty. Those seven of the Nemett who now walked the paths of the Dri had proved useful here in the north and, though the gathering of the armies of the Cluath threatened the stability of the lands on both sides of the Heran, much of Taleth now slept in an uneasy peace, shifting in her sleep as the tension mounted, but moving from day to day as before. She had listened as Sorin had told her what had befallen them in the mountain pass, and she had quietly nodded her approval of the way that Michael had coped. He had become strong and was starting to grow in wisdom, something that could only inspire confidence and be all to the good. She had listened as Sorin told her of the Mrauuk and the manifestation of Ragarad, perhaps the guidance of the Trillani would no longer fall on deaf ears. She had listened as Sorin had explained their plan to gain the high mountains and she whispered quietly to herself the prayer of the Ancient ones.

'Steps are carved in stone, but feet must climb.
Trees stand in the earth but reach for the sky.
Let my truth be stone and my path be earth,
Let my song be pure as clouds that glide
Above the chamber where secrets lie.'

Kyre could assist them in their quest, but will he see that as his path, for clouded are the ways of the Lost, clouded and scattered is their truth. She knew that Kyre was on his way, but it was not him for whom she waited, as unmoving and unmoved as the hands of Ragarad beside her, she sensed that there were others moving also, three were approaching the bridge from the mountain side. These were the ones for whom she stayed her journey. Three Trillani were moving slowly in the shadows of the mountain, their pace steady their heads held erect for they were in their own domain, the paths of their pack ran through and over these great monuments, these ancient stones. Here they were wisdom and truth, guide and protector. Here their duty sang its song for those who would hear.

The three wolves separated, and each moved across one of the three bridges stopping at the centre of the span to sit and await Sylvan's greeting. She paused briefly, closing her eyes, drawing back the bitter taste, storing away the pain, and then she sent her thoughts.

'Greetings to my Brother and Sisters of the Trillani. Sylvan of the Dri has need of passage through the lands of the Nare, that she may aid Sorin of the Majann in his quest. Long may the mountains stand, and all your paths run true.'

'Greetings, Sylvan of the Dri, Jaahkir of the Trillani, bids you welcome, and we give you free crossing into the Lands of the Nare. May you find what you seek and that your path be that of truth. We know of your loss and we share your pain. Reckoning will come and there will be a time for righteous vengeance. He that with vile intent and corrupt thought twists and tears the threads and the very fabric of Taleth, shall at the last know the force of our justice and be brought to account.'

Sylvan listened to the song of the river and the whispers of the shadowy depths and she knew that Taleth heard all and saw all. *'It may be that the accounting will not be for us to know, Jaahkir, but, yes, justice will fall in time, may it please the One. For now, we will continue to follow the paths of our packs in truth and duty and remember those that wander and know no longer the commune of their kin.'*

'Your words are wise, Sylvan of the Dri, and yet there is a small part of me that watches the Cluath give way to the fire in their blood as they seek revenge for themselves and does not disapprove.'

'That is the Cluath way, Jaahkir, but violence is wasteful and soaking the soil of Taleth with blood is not the answer it may appear to be.'

Jaahkir nodded in the dark. *'No, Sylvan, it is not, and we have seen too much death already here in the seven cities. But the Hemmek has returned and we have hope again.'*

'He is Hemmek no longer, Jaahkir. Sits he not now upon the Mrauuk?'

'You are well informed, Sylvan, for that is indeed true and there may yet be further outcomes to the dismissal of the Mrauuk by mighty Ragarad.'

'Surely there are none who would question the authority of one appointed by Ragarad himself?'

'I am afraid the reputation that the Nare have for stubbornness is based in fact, Sylvan, there are those who mutter in the dark or whisper behind their hands. We will see what comes of such petty envies and ignorance, but Dakveen Halak and the other members may need more than a cure for the plague to establish their position in security.'

'That is sad news, Jaahkir, but I trust the Trillani will give guidance if any will listen.'

'We will, Sylvan, and indeed we have a new Nare Seer who may listen better than most.' Here Jaahkir paused. *'Although since Seer Muakir Ulumik has become, does it now fall to you to guide her?'*

Sylvan knew this to be mere politeness on his part, for he knew the answer before she sent it. *'No, Jaahkir, she has been chosen by Ragarad for this task and is not born to it, for her the normal rules will not apply, so she remains within your care.'*

'That is well and ...' Jaahkir paused again, this time because something approached. It was another wolf. *'Stay your feet and name yourself!'*

The shape that approached through the darkness was a large white shape, a wolf of the Veyix, strong, tall and defiant. It was Kyre and he strode to Sylvan's side before answering the challenge.

'I am Kyre of the Veyix, that some name the Lost, and I know you Jaahkir of the Trillani, I have walked the paths and passes, crags and tunnels of these mountains many times as you are well aware. But I will ask for traditions sake, if that is what you require. I ask the Trillani for permission once again to travel the paths of the Nare for I seek Uxl of the Tarr and that I may also aid the quest of Sylvan, while following my own truth wherever it will take me. I also offer greeting to Sylvan of the Dri and ask her permission to tread the paths of the mountains with her, should she see some benefit in my companionship.'

'You are welcome, Kyre of the Lost, we give you free passage across into the Lands of the Nare, may you find him that you seek. Any aid that you may give to Sylvan, and thus to Sorin, will serve to help the Nare and for that we would be grateful.'

Sylvan stood and she turned her head to greet Kyre. *'Kyre of the Veyix, you are most welcome, and I gladly accept your offer of aid and companionship. It is the time of the Uclan, the Hemmek, and those that are lost are no longer alone in the wilderness.'* She then began the chant of her pack, words that had given comfort in their moments of strife and loss; the other wolves joined her and completed the chant with their own words.

'In honour of the One we become the Pack.
In honour of the One we walk upon the earth.
In love of life we will serve.
In love of life we will ward.
In love of life we will guide.
In soul we are the Avali, in name we are the Dri.'

'In soul we are the Avali, in name we are the Trillani"
'In soul we are the Avali, in name we are the Veyix."

And then together, they sang the ancient songs, to the Cluath and to the Nare merely wolf howls on the night wind, to the packs a timeless remembrance of their unique place in the Unfolding of the One.

★★★

13

Balthazar Earthroot

It was initially difficult for Michael to focus his senses and to re-attune to the world of wallpaper, bed sheets and double glazing. His heart was still listening to the slow beat of time within the mountains and the words that he heard seemed strange and flat compared to the craggy syllables of the Nare tongue. But after a while he realised that there was a voice that he did not recognise, David and Netti were talking with a woman, friendly yet firm in her tone and extremely clear in her diction, precise to the point of sounding mannered.

"I would not suggest anything that was superfluous or unnecessary, Miss Spinetti, I assure you."

"Yes, I accept that, Doctor Cavendish, but I suspect that he will resist any further investigation. He has had, as I am sure you will appreciate, rather a lot of that sort of thing to contend with."

"Oh, I am sure that is the case, but if it has not yet got to the bottom of these continued lapses then much of it could be considered a waste of time. Doctor Fellows is a leading expert in the field of recovered or recovering coma patients and his studies are becoming widely accepted."

Michael was fully conscious now and his mind tried to match his pulse for speed. *Why had David and Netti felt the need to call a doctor? And why was this particular one so intent on calling in an expert?* They should have known that doctors were the last thing Michael needed attention from. Sooner or later, one of them was going to suggest drug therapy and he would be of no use to anyone in either world. He decided attack was the best form of defence and that they should all know that he was awake.

"Netti? Is that you out there making all that noise? Can't a guy get a decent sleep around here?" The reaction was all that he had hoped for, the door opened, and David stepped quickly through, followed by a bustling Netti, whose mouth opened to speak, but was interrupted by Doctor Cavendish who was close on her tail.

"Ah, the mystery patient has awoken and has a voice. Now at least I can directly ask some of the questions the answers to which I have, so far had to guess."

Michael looked hard at David, who mouthed. *'I will explain when she's gone'* and he had the decency to look embarrassed. Whereas Netti was going for the *'grasp the bull by the horns'* approach, and her eyes said loudly, *'listen very carefully Michael, this is important.'*

"This is Doctor Cavendish, Peter; she very kindly came to take a look at you yesterday, because we were so worried about you. You had been unconscious for three whole days by then and you had gone so cold, that we could hardly find a pulse. It was almost as bad as that time, just before we flew back from Australia, although you probably don't remember very well, I was at my wits end and that very dishy young doctor from Malaysia helped us out. Not that I can remember his name, I wish I could. I'd look him up on Facebook if I knew it. Anyway, she thought that she should pop back in to check on you, which was really good of her wasn't it. Now she wants to ask you a few questions, if that's alright and while she does that I'm going to fix you something to eat, I bet you're famished aren't you?"

Michael was slightly wrong footed by her calling him Peter, but as she went on, in her usual style, without taking a breath, he realised just how clever she was being. She was fussing in such a way as to give him the back story that he needed and prevent Doctor Cavendish from beginning to question him. The scenario had obviously been designed to make it hard to quickly request any medical history, hence Australia and a non-existent Malaysian doctor. She hadn't mentioned who David was supposed to be or what their relationship was, but it was enough to go on for the moment. She had said that his temperature had dropped. That must have been when he and Suani had been shivering in the subterranean river. He had to admit three days was a long time for him to have been gone. He would have probably been just as worried if the roles were reversed. *'Oh, well, can't be helped now, work with it and see where it leads.'*

Michael eased himself up in the bed so that he was sitting. Doctor Cavendish was a small thin woman, with a smile that was intended to put him at his ease, but completely failed to do so. Her auburn hair was neat and business like; swept back as it was into a tight bun, it reminded him of a ballet dancer, and the smart navy suit that she wore seemed incongruous. Her face was tight, and her eyes driven, the sharp nose surmounted by expensive designer spectacles with frames that matched her suit. She had moved with the same confidence that pervaded her speech. When Michael spoke, she had looked at him with all the intensity of a hawk.

"Yes, Doctor … Cavendish, I am awake. You said you have some questions for me."

"Indeed, I do, Mr. Spinetti, your sister has filled me in on some of the circumstances surrounding your accident and she has explained that you remember nothing at all until you awoke to find yourself in a hospital bed. That is all very normal in these cases, but what is not as usual is the relapses that you seem to have been having, particularly when your body appears to go through such severe physical changes, that your sister thought that on this occasion that you were actually dying. Can you tell me whether you have any sensation of time passing or of the world around you when you become effectively residually comatose?"

Inwardly Michael explained. *'Yes, I do, but it not this world, nor anything that you would recognise and as for time passing, well, how shall I put it, it is different.'* Outwardly he said. "None at all Doctor, I may dream, I suppose, but I don't remember anything. I don't feel tired when I wake up, if that means anything."

Doctor Cavendish pursed her lips and then she nodded. "It is commonly thought that if we do not dream then we are not fully rested when we awake, whether or not we realise that we have dreamt. But that is not conclusive to my mind. Unless you have become subject to a form of seizure that is akin to sleep, or once it has occurred allows you to recover through sleep. But that would not explain the sudden drop in temperature; you should not have lost that body heat so quickly, Mr. Spinetti, that is the point. It was almost as if your body had been plunged into freezing water, which as you know can kill within minutes."

'Yes, it was cold, but we came through it, I had Suani to worry about.' "Well, as far as I know that wasn't happening, was it Netti?"

"No, of course not Peter, I just noticed how terribly cold you were when I was straightening the bed. It was quite a shock, I can tell you, and when …"

Doctor Cavendish interrupted Netti before she began another long speech. "That is why I definitely think Doctor Fellows should have a look at you. He may be able to shed some light on your continuing condition, Mr Spinetti."

'There is nothing that some high-powered researcher can tell me, Doctor, unless he can help me cure the Nare without recourse to the source of the green crystal, that would be useful, then I would not have to choose.' "I don't really want to spend my life being poked and prodded by researchers, Doctor Cavendish."

"No, of course you don't, but it is important to get to the bottom of this before we suddenly find that your condition has become life threatening."

'My condition may threaten the life of a whole world. Can you do something about that?' "I suppose that is true, Doctor Cavendish, if you really insist that I see him, I will have to. When is that likely to be?"

"Oh, not for several months, I suspect. He is an extremely busy man, but at least now that I have your consent, I can discuss a consultation with him. I suspect that he will be intrigued by your case."

"I don't think I am that interesting, Doctor Cavendish, or important." *'At least not here.'*

"Oh, but you are, Mr Spinetti, very interesting indeed." She turned to Netti and fixed her with her fierce eyes. "I will be in touch, Miss Spinetti and if there is any change in your brother's condition, another relapse for example, I want you to call me at once."

"Yes, of course, Doctor Cavendish, I will. Let me show you out. It was good of you to call, I do appreciate it, really I do, not all GP's would be this thorough these days." Netti led the doctor out of the room and David and Michael could hear the conversation continuing as they made their way down the stairs. "I have friends in other towns, who can't even get an appointment for a fortnight."

"Ah, well, I think that myself and Mr. Perkins run an efficient practice and …"

Michael's heart stopped and then it began to race, he was about to leap from the bed, but David frantically signalled to him to wait. Netti too had been caught unawares and had fumbled with the door, but she recovered quickly. "Mr. Perkins? Is he one of the Doctors?"

"No, no, he is my Practice Manager, I took him on six months ago and he has been such a find. I'm not sure what I would do without him now."

The door was open and Netti shook the Doctor's hand as warmly as she could manage. "Thank you again, Doctor Cavendish, and I will let you know if there are any further problems."

"Yes, yes do. You can call me any time or get in touch through the surgery."

"Goodbye." The door clicked shut and Netti raced up the stairs, the words out of her as she came. "I'm sorry, Michael, really I am, but it may just be a coincidence, there must be a lot of people with that name all over the country and …" She saw the expression on Michael's face and for once even Netti was lost for words.

Michael did not speak immediately; he tried to regain the confidence and the control that had helped him in the darkness below the mountains, there was little to be gained and possibly much to be lost through panic. He knew that he would be close to journey's end when he returned to Taleth and then they would have to face the result of his choice in both worlds. If Mr. Perkins sought to intervene in this world, then he would have to rely on David and Netti to protect him. It was clear that Mr. Perkins was significant, but how and why was still so far from clear that any pre-emptive response was futile. He would take every day as it came and face each challenge as a bend in a dark tunnel, slowly, but with the knowledge that even the bleakest dark does not mean the end of all things. There is always hope.

'Where there is Hope there is a Future.
Where there is Future there is Life.'

When he finally spoke, both Netti and David were surprised by his control. "It can't be helped and there is little to be gained from worrying about what Mr. Perkins might or might not do. I would rather have avoided further medical attention, but I am sure that you did what you thought best, which is all I can hope for and I am grateful. We will face Mr. Perkins and ultimately Doctor Fellows when we have to. As for the present, I think you mentioned some food, sister dear."

Netti had been all ready with further apologies and explanations, but instead she laughed with relief "Well, Michael, I am glad to see that someone is being calm about the whole business, and yes, food, that is a good idea, I have some fresh bread, and there is pesto and Dolcelate in the fridge, so I will put some pasta on. Is a vaguely Italian lunch okay with you two?"

"Sounds delightful, Netti. David can you sort me out some clothes while I have a brief shower."

"Certainly, Peter, old man!"

★★★

Once he was washed and dressed and sitting down to Netti's *'vaguely Italian'* lunch, which was very good, he had to admit, David filled him in as to the sequence of events in this world.

"You switched when we were on the Tor. I thought that you had wandered off in the fog, but I found you standing very still staring out into the mist. We walked you home and then put you to bed. We didn't worry the first day, but after two days, we tried to get you to drink a little, unsuccessfully, by the third day we were beginning to worry, you had never been this inactive before. You know we had always been able to move you around, and sometimes you would even take water or food without much trouble. But this inactivity was starting to get to us. Then when Netti was just straightening the bed around you, she realised how cold you had become and when we couldn't find a pulse, we decided that we had to ring a doctor."

Netti took up the story. "I'm already registered with that surgery, so we decided that we should make you my brother, who had just returned from Australia where you had suffered an accident that had left you in a coma for six months. That way at least for a time, she won't find out that we gave her a false name. I picked Peter out of the air, I'm sorry, I didn't realise it was your brother's name, David told me."

"It doesn't matter, Julia's mother called me Peter too."

David suddenly snapped his fingers. "That's what I had forgotten; she rang up, twice in fact."

"Who? Julia?"

"Yes, the first time to speak to you, the second to ask how you were. She left a message too, I wrote it down in the hall, but I didn't understand it. She also asked me if you had a friend you went to Cornwall with, which made no sense at all to me. Any thoughts?"

"Not really, I think it's a family joke that she hasn't fully explained to me yet. Perhaps she will at some point. Can I borrow your phone after dinner?

"Of course, but first you must tell us what has been happening in Taleth and why you did go suddenly so cold."

"That was freezing water, just as the Doctor suspected, but I will start from the beginning …" David and Netti hung on his every word as he took them through his meetings with Uvarin, the Sha–ellev and then deep into the heart of the mountains. He found telling them much easier than in the past, maybe because he knew more of what was going on, or maybe it was that he had taken control of his own story. Once he had told them of the discovery they had made in Marl and how the Nare had reacted, the cheese had been finished and they were sipping coffee in the kitchen while David assisted with the dishes.

David was the first to question him directly. "So you think that the only way to get more of the green crystal is by smashing the casket that holds the Chiatt grain?"

"Something like that, yes."

"But won't that cause the world to end?"

"On that, opinions are divided."

"And you are the one who has to choose."

"Yes, for what it's worth."

David paused in the act of drying a plate. "Have you decided what you are going to do?"

Michael tried to be honest with his old friend, perhaps more honest than he had been with himself. "Sometimes I think I have and then I realise that I haven't yet. We are not currently at that moment and I will face the decision when I ultimately have to." He finished his coffee. "Can I make that call now, David?"

"Yes, my phone is on the table in the hall."

"Thanks."

Michael went into the hall and picked up the phone, he found that he was actually quite nervous, and he tried to convince himself that he wasn't. He found the number in the call log and he rang it, praying that he did not get Mr. Chambers again; he wasn't in the mood for that.

"Hello, Michael?"

"Hi, Julia, how did you know it was me?"

"Because I logged David's number under your name."

"But it could have been David ringing up."

"Why would he be ringing me?"

"I don't know."

"Are you sure you're not still comatose, Michael?"

Michael relaxed a little. "No, I'm not, just being slow. How are you, anyway?"

"I am fine; I was worried about you though. David said that they had to call a Doctor."

"Yes, apparently my body temperature dropped dramatically very suddenly and so they called the local surgery."

"And someone came out? They must think you're related to royalty; a home visit is unheard of unless you're the Queen's cousin and even then, you must be a least half dead." An interesting detail that Michael decided to consider later.

"Yes, she fussed about and she wants me to see some high-powered friend of hers, Doctor Fellows, so that he can prod me and poke me and add me to his list of research data no doubt."

"Fellows? I think I did some work on a piece by him, a lot of nonsense about sleep and dreams, and coma patients."

"That sounds like him. By the way please explain about Cornwall. You had David very confused the other day, and I need enlightening about it too."

Julia laughed, and Michael felt a thrill that he had forgotten ripple through him. "I'm sorry, Michael, it was a family joke that got started because of Dorothy; remember her, running off to Cornwall with her men friends. Well since she implied to my mother that whenever she felt like a bit of male company in her bed, she would go for a weekend in Cornwall with Harold, or someone else if he wasn't available. So, in our family going to Cornwall became synonymous with sex, and conversely if someone was gay then they didn't like Cornwall. Very silly really, but a habit I have found hard to break."

It all made sense and Michael felt very stupid for not picking up on it. *'That was why she had asked me if I liked Cornwall, she was making sure that I wasn't gay'*, which implied several things that pleased Michael to no end.

"I think I follow now, Julia, I was being terribly dull-witted about it all, wasn't I?"

"Not at all, you probably thought that I was completely crazy. But no harm done, and you do like going to Cornwall. Not that there is anything wrong with being gay or celibate for that matter, it's just that I rather hoped that you weren't."

285

"No, I'm not and Cornwall is lovely, but I meant it when I said I haven't been for a good while."

She laughed again. "No, nor I, in fact I would be hard pushed to remember the last time I went. Anyway, since you didn't ring up just to talk holiday destinations at me, tell me how you are."

Michael paused for a moment, he suddenly wanted to tell her everything, all his fears and his worries all his lost desires all the pain and the darkness that he had shared with no-one in either world, but he knew that he couldn't, not yet, that made him remember his anger and he felt Uvarin's eyes upon him. So, what did he say?

"I'm really not sure, Julia, I suppose at the moment I feel fine, I've just had a very pleasant meal and now I'm calling you, which all makes me feel pretty good, but I know inside somewhere there is still something that is wrong, even if it can't easily be seen." *'Surprisingly honest as far it goes,'* he thought.

"Perhaps you just need to find the reset button, Michael, which may be hidden deep and will cause some trauma when it's pushed, but ultimately it might be worth it. Surely you'll gain more than you'll lose."

Michael was suddenly caught up inside her words, she was right and more right than she should have been, could have been, without knowing what he was thinking. He tried to cover a growing excitement that proclaimed loudly that he had been meant to meet her, hear what she had to say. "You may very well be right, Julia, but do I look that broken?"

"No, not at all, but you don't want to be trapped forever in some half-life where you cannot do anything for fear of shutting down at a vital moment, that would drive you crazy. I couldn't cope with that at all, I'd much rather be either on or off, not switching randomly between them." Michael tried to put her penetratingly perceptive comments down to a natural ability to assess what needed to be said, but it was difficult. He wondered how she would act if she knew the full story.

"But if there genuinely was a chance to push a reset button and there was no knowing what would happen, quite possibly it could all go disastrously and very finally wrong. Would you push it then?"

Julia paused, as she contemplated what he was actually asking. "Do you mean a kill or cure scenario?"

"Yes, I suppose I do."

"Is that a real possibility then?" Her tone, earlier convivial almost flippant, was now suddenly emotional.

"I don't know, but what if it was. Would you risk everything for a chance to be renewed?"

There was a definite silence now, which almost lasted too long. When she spoke there no doubting the emotion now. "I don't know, Michael, if you are trying to tell me that you are more ill than you initially said, or that you are genuinely asking me what I would do. I am going to assume that you have been truthful, as I don't want to deal with the other possibility, and I will answer on that basis and be honest with you as far as I can. I would push the button, Michael, even if it risked everything, because I am selfish. I like you, Michael. I found your company refreshing, something that I desperately needed, and I realise that this is rather sudden and reckless, but I really want to get to know you more and spend time with you. I want that more than I had thought possible, maybe because I need a break from Mother, maybe just because I thought that all that had passed me by, but for whatever reason I would rather have a consistently working version of you, or none at all.

"Oh, I know that sounds harsh, but when I rang and David said that you were still unconscious, I was upset and angry. Where had you gone? I wanted you back from wherever it was. You have become a chance of escape, Michael, and I suppose that I want a real hope or no hope at all." She stopped, and Michael battled to control himself, there was so much in her words, so much that needed a response, he had not been ready for the emotion that had swept over Julia as she spoke. "I'm sorry, that was a little more full-on than I meant it to be. It's just that sometimes …" Her voice faded as she waited for Michael to speak.

"Don't apologise, sometimes it is best to let our heart speak as it feels, restraint just drives you down into yourself and you end up cold and unfeeling, I have found that to my cost." He was suddenly reminded of how hard he had found it reacting to Ayan's outpouring of emotion, he hoped that he had moved on since then. "What you say should sometimes be who you are, and you have helped me realise a few things, remember a few others and bless the stars for some light in the dark. If I am to be your escape, then perhaps you are to be my guide back to a life that I thought had gone forever. I know that you are right, Julia, and I hope that I can be what you are looking for. I am no more ill than I have told you; I have told you what I know myself. I can't match you for words, I'm afraid, but if the option of a reset arises, I will push it and hope that luck is with us."

There was a silence. It was as if they had arrived at a junction in the road and there were consequences whichever direction they took. Whatever was said now would be significant, Michael knew that, but he also knew that he was unsure what should be said. This was a woman he hardly knew, nor did she really know anything about him and yet they were both stating a need that had remained undeclared. It was as if they had both been waiting for an opportunity to open up to someone, someone whom they hoped would understand. There was a risk involved, but now the die was cast, and both waited with some anxiety for the result. It was Julia who spoke first.

"Do you dream, Michael, well, I know we all dream, but do you remember yours?"

It was not what he had expected, but it was at least a turning that he could follow. "Yes, I do, I have very vivid dreams actually. Why do you ask?"

"Because I do too, very vivid, very real, often about my childhood, or places I have visited. But also …" she hesitated. "This is going to sound very strange and I have never told this to anyone else, I have dreams about places that I have never been, people I have never met. Is that odd do you think?"

Michael thought of some of the 'dreams' that he had since waking up in the hospital, he wondered what sort of dreams she referred to. He knew full well that his were memories, manipulations and visitations, none were normal, if there was such a thing. "No, I don't think it is odd, Julia, there are lots of reasons why we dream of places that we don't recognise as real, or people we feel we do not know, mostly its imagination, but sometimes I think they are constructs of our own making, initiated by something we have read or heard. I think lots of people have dreams like that."

"I'm not crazy, then?"

"I don't think so. Why, are you disappointed?"

"No, not really. It's just that some of them are so real, you know and there are characters that keep appearing, but if it's not so unusual …"

Michael was tempted to tell her about some of his dreams, but he knew that this was not the time. "I think it's a good sign, Julia, it shows that you are sensitive and imaginative."

"Thank you, Michael, that's a good point and I will remember that, I did wonder if it was just me trying to escape even when I am asleep. I was tempted to talk to my doctor about it, but she seemed quite a severe woman so in the end I didn't bother. She's been good with mother though, so I can't complain. Right then, when are you taking me out for tea and cake, as you promised?"

Michael was almost thrown by this tight curve, but he managed to stay in control. "Well, why not this afternoon, if you can get away that is?"

"Perfect, Mother is going to tea with a group of ladies, some charity thing that my neighbour organises; I can drop her and meet you. I will have to collect her again, but it will give us a good hour or two … if you are sure that you are up to it, that is?"

"Yes, of course, where shall I meet you?"

"How about outside the church of John the Baptist, then we can take a stroll down the High Street and decide where to have our cakes? It's nearly two now, so how about meeting at three, is that okay?"

"Absolutely fine, that will give me time to shave and change."

"Good, I'll see you later then and Michael … I am glad Mother found you for me, it sort of makes up for a lot of other things."

"So am I, Julia, see you later."

"Bye."

As he re-joined the others Michael's mind was full of nagging little doubts, mainly about not living up to Julia's expectations of him. He hardly realised that Netti had spoken to him.

"… I know it's out of the blue, but I can't really say no, can I so, I hope you don't mind, Michael …"

"Sorry, what was that, I missed the first part?"

"Oh, well, I was saying that some of my women friends get together regularly and have a dinner party, nothing grand, but Marjorie, who's turn it was to host has had to go to London for family reasons and the others have asked me to act as a stand in, since it would have been my turn next anyway and I know that it's out of the blue, but I can't really let them down, so you two don't mind a group of ladies descending upon you tonight, do you."

David had obviously been pre-warned that this might be on the cards. "How many is a group, Netti?"

"Oh, six, usually, but if Marjorie isn't coming then five, so eight of us all together with you two."

"And they allow males at these gatherings, do they?"

"It has been known, David, and they will just have to put up with it, won't they. Michael are you okay with that?"

Michael desperately wanted to say no, but Netti had been such an invaluable companion since they had met her that he felt that he owed her this. "Yes, I suppose so. If your friends don't mind."

"No, of course not, they will be intrigued that I have two men living with me. They will be a little inquisitive, do we go with real names or …"

Michael made a snap decision. "Yes, we do, I think at some point soon we will have to face up to some of the people who might be looking for us, so we might as well start getting used to being ourselves again. That doctor is a different matter, but

I will handle her and anyone else she has in mind to introduce me too. The one thing that you must promise me is that you will not let anyone fill me with drugs, whatever the reason behind it, my mind must be clear at all times, wherever I am."

Netti was a little taken aback with the earnestness of his answer, but she agreed with him immediately. "Of course not, you have our word on that, but I agree about the names, Michael, it will be a relief for all of us if we feel that we are not running anymore."

David nodded. "I'm with you on that too, Michael. We give ourselves the chance then to prepare properly for how we approach answering any real enquiries and I think with the contacts I have that we should be able to come out of it reasonably unscathed and then perhaps begin to live a little more normally again."

"Oh, I can't guarantee that, David, at least not for me, but we might be able to establish a status quo that will work."

He turned to Netti, who was mentally creating a menu, shopping list and a cooking schedule. "What time are they going to descend upon us, Netti?"

"Drinks at six, to eat at seven-thirty, is the usual."

"Good, I am going out for a while, but I will be back in good time. If something happens, then Julia will bring me back here."

"Oh, good, are you going to see her then?"

"Yes, Netti, I am, and I will tell you all about it when I get back, I assure you."

Netti beamed. "Excellent! I hope that you have a lovely afternoon; David is going to help me shop for tonight, and then he will be acting as my sous chef."

"Am I? Wonderful! And I had such a full afternoon already planned."

"Nonsense, you would have sat down with a book and a glass of wine and done nothing, if you had had the chance."

"If the wine and the book were both of quality than that is a fine way to spend one's time, but it seems that my hopes have been dashed."

"Oh, poor you, now I want you working on the wine list, I will run through the menu as we drive, and you can decide what we need. Can we drop you anywhere, Michael?"

"No, no thanks, I can walk into town."

"Right, David, grab your wallet, we are on a mission."

Michael had to smile as he watched David being bustled out of the house under guard with Netti beginning to describe the first course to him; not that David didn't seem to be enjoying it, for him it was all new and whether or not their relationship had developed any further while he had been 'away', it was obvious that they were quite content indulging in domesticity together.

When they had driven away Michael went back up to his room and he sorted out a smarter shirt, a pale blue one that he had noticed among those which David had procured for him, and then he went into the bathroom and shaved carefully. He had only shaved once since his re-awakening and he realised that since he had not developed a beard then firstly the nurses and then he assumed that David or Netti had done the honours. The electric razor was David's spare and as such an expensive one, it made swift work of the stubble although he avoided running over the scar tissue, where possible. He knew that there was no hair there and also that the razor would skim harmlessly across the dark red marks, but he was reluctant to put it to the test.

As he looked at his reflection his mind filled with images of those who he had met in Taleth, faces flickered across the mirror, Sorin, Danil, Ayan, Suani, Dak, and many more, one flashed past that he knew he recognised but he couldn't remember who she was; an oddly familiar face, but out of place in the line of people he had just recalled. He shook off the uncertainty and he completed his shave, splashing some of David's aftershave across his face he ran a comb through his straggling hair and then went to finish changing. The afternoon was not cold, so he wore his lighter jacket and he set off feeling as smart and presentable as he could make himself.

The short walk from the house to the High Street took little time and he decided to sit on one of the benches outside the church to wait for Julia. He had checked the time before he left so he knew that he wasn't ridiculously early. The High Street was moderately busy, and all the passers-by walked with an unhurried gait, suggesting there was no need for stress or discomfort on this particular afternoon. Michael watched an old van trundle past, the green of the previous paint job easily visible through the scratches in the current pale yellow. It was emblazoned with the name of a local plumber and sanitation engineer, Les Haynes, and the stunningly brilliant slogan, **"Trouble with Drains? Then it's time for Haynes!"** This was followed by the inevitable mobile number and the web address. *'What did we do before the ability to contact the entire population via the web?'* he mused. A voice broke into his thoughts.

"Those are some shoes, man, although I suspect that someone slew a friendly bovine for them."

He looked around and he saw that he had been joined on the bench by a man small in stature, but long in hair. Dark brown and twisted into dreadlocks it was held back by a rainbow coloured band knotted to one side. His clothing was equally colourful, striped knitted jumper and baggy trousers of the patchwork variety. His feet were bare save for an ankle bracelet of beads and bells. He was smiling and he appeared harmless, although Michael took nothing for granted; his experiences had at least taught him that.

"Sorry, what did you say?"

"Your shoes, man, they are a fine pair of shoes, but leather, so they will smell of death."

"Oh, I see, I find that they tend to smell of polish, but I take your point. You are vegetarian then?"

"Vegan, my friend, vegan! Let our animal brothers walk the earth free. That's what I say, no chattels, no pens, no slavery."

"Well, you are entitled to your opinion, I suppose."

"I am entitled indeed, and I have a title now, a true name that my sisters and brothers call me, not the name I had of old, that stank of the shame of imperialism, and capitalism, and all the other 'isms' that they invent to cover their sins. We have names that we can be proud of and we can use with gentleness, as we learn the path of wisdom. It is a name that I will take with me when I transmigrate to another form upon my passing. Do you have a name that you can be proud of, my friend?"

This strange and rather earnest young man had penetrating eyes for all his bizarre exterior.

"My name is Michael Oakes, and I have got used to it, so I am unlikely to change it."

"Not a bad name, man, an Angel of the trees, not bad at all, that wouldn't sound out of place at all. I am called Balthazar Earthroot, because I was the third of the males to join and I was nearest to the ground. But despite your death smelling shoes you seem a good man, Angel of the trees, so I will name you friend, and should we meet again I will allow you to call me such in return."

With this he stood up and taking a hand-rolled cigarette from somewhere in his hair he wandered away, lost in his own version of the world. Michael followed him with his eyes when he heard his name being called by a voice he recognised. Turning round, he saw Julia a little way off down the High Street and so he rose from the bench and he moved towards her, nerves once more rising in his chest as she approached, he didn't want, things to be awkward, after the emotion of earlier. Julia dispelled all his fears by throwing her arms round his neck and kissing him with all the joy and wonder of a long-lost love reclaimed.

"Oh, Michael, I am so pleased, I more than half expected to see David waiting for me ready to explain that you had gone travelling again. But who were you talking to, I saw someone leave as I crossed the road?"

"Ah, that is a new friend of mine, well, so he tells me, called Balthazar Earthroot. He liked my shoes but suspected that they smelled of death."

"What a wonderful name, this town is full of the strangest people, but most of them are harmless, at least I hope they are. Did he want money or something?"

"No, just to tell me that my shoes smelt I think."

"Well, I can't smell anything, except a rather expensive aftershave if I am not mistaken. What's it called?"

"I have absolutely no idea, its David's; most of the stuff I have either belongs to him or has been bought by him. Don't you like it?"

"Yes, I do, I just wondered what it was. It does smell rather like something that a woman might get for a man, though, are you sure it is his."

Her eyes told him she that she was teasing. "Maybe Netti bought it for him, I really don't know. I haven't shopped for myself since the accident. In fact, the day I met you was my first real sojourn out on my own."

"Goodness and look how it ended up."

They had begun to walk down the hill and had reached 'The Goddess and the Green Man' a green-fronted shop that sold Pagan literature and every sort of accessory that the modern-day pagan might require. Incense drifted out into the street and corn dolls hung in the window.

"What do you make of all this, Michael?"

"What this particular shop or the revival of Paganism in general?"

"Either or both, whichever you like."

Michael looked at the images of the Goddess and although they meant well none of them came close to representing what he had beheld in Cerlinith's glade, the true power of a nature goddess unleashed, there was something worth worshipping.

"I think it is completely understandable. If you were brought up listening to the stale stammerings of a vicar with little imagination and no charisma, surrounded by dull hymns and dusty cold churches, then someone comes along and says, *'in the old days we worshipped a beautiful woman whose very body gave us life, whose wild singing drew the flowers from the ground and the buds from the trees and whose rain was sweeter than wine,'* I think I know which way I would turn."

A young woman who had been standing in the doorway of the shop, stepped forward and grasped Michael's arm. "That was really beautiful, truly, you spoke almost as if you had met her yourself. Are you a writer?"

Julia laughed. "Michael, you seem to have missed your vocation, you really should be a Pagan preacher."

The young woman, who seemed by her accent to be American, started to apologise. "Oh, I'm sorry, ma'am, I didn't mean to be rude, it was just that what your husband said was so moving and …"

Michael was going to correct her, but Julia got in first. "Yes, he can be like that sometimes. You should here him when he really gets going, he writes about art mainly, but he does have a way with words, doesn't he?"

"He surely does, ma'am, perhaps he should be writing about the rise of the Goddess."

Julia tugged at Michael's arm. "That's not a bad idea, you know, we could take rooms here and I could help you with the research. We must talk it over, nice to have met you, Miss."

"You too, sir, ma'am." As they turned away Michael heard the young woman repeating his words to the owner of the shop.

"I think you have just become a legend in your own lunchtime, Michael."

"And you are a terrible tease. Why did you let her think that we were married?"

She looked up at him. "Why not? I'm escaping remember and this is a part of my disguise. Anyway, I thought that it was rather nice that she assumed we were. We must make a reasonable couple at least to the casual observer. You don't mind, do you?"

"No, I don't mind at all, Julia, I am extremely flattered, both that she liked what I said and that she thought I was a reasonable match for you."

She squeezed his arm again. "Now, now, dear, not too much gushing praise, we're married, not dating, remember."

Michael had to laugh at that, although she was probably right.

"And while I'm at it, where did all that stuff about worshipping the Goddess come from, it was rather more heartfelt than I expected. Are you a secret tree-hugger then?"

"No, not really, I just feel that if you are going to believe in something that you might as well make it someone with some charisma and obvious power, that's all. It's hard to see the hand of God in things these days, his name has been associated with too much hatred and killing, but Nature, now there is a force that you can see. A tiny seed growing to a tall tree, a field of corn rising, fruit ripening on the branches, and when she is angry floods and devastation. It's all a bit more exciting than *'we shall now sing Hymn number 460 'In days of old on Sinai''*"

His impersonation of a Church of England Minister caused Julia to burst out laughing again and as they moved further down the high street, ignoring the stares, Michael felt the bond between them grow. They decided to stop at the Blue Note Café for tea and they were soon deep in discussion about childhood reminiscences of being scrubbed and brushed and marched to church on Sunday morning. Michael could not remember a time, in this world at least when he had felt so at ease, he knew it was a fleeting moment and circumstances were likely to provide plenty of barriers to the contentment he felt with Julia, but for the moment he could pretend, and he could tell from her eyes that Julia indulged in a similar fantasy. No other world, no mother, no responsibilities, easy things to say, but he knew that they were both slaves to their respective fates.

For some reason, the word *'slave'* rang a discordant bell in his mind. Julia was in the middle of a story about the visits that their Vicar had made to her home, when she was a child, her eyes sparkled and her whole face beamed with the memories and the chance to talk freely to someone. "… And he was the sort of person who thought that he was good with children, only he really wasn't. He would bring a bag of sweets and open them, displaying the contents, and then make you beg for one, just asking nicely wasn't enough, you had to plead." She scrunched up her face in imitation of her childhood self. "*'Please, I beg you, please can I have one.'* After all that they usually weren't very … Michael are you alright?"

Her childish pleading had finally clicked into place a nagging thought that had scrabbled around at the back of his mind, he

297

finally knew who she had reminded him of on their first meeting and her words had made the connection. *'Help us! Please, I beg you, the Queen means to sell us,'* hers was the face of the woman being taken to be sold. For a fleeting moment, he had seen the blood and the tears flowing down Julia's face. The resemblance was striking. He shook himself back from wild thoughts and sudden doubts, he stumbled an explanation.

"I'm fine, sorry, just something you said about Vicars must have triggered a memory, and you suddenly reminded me of someone I met once."

"Someone wild and exotic I hope."

"I didn't know her well; just met her once and I can't even really remember where."

"So, my face is not memorable then?" He knew that she was only pretending to be upset, but he countered anyway.

"No, quite the reverse, very memorable, that's why I remembered her, but since she didn't have your vibrant personality there is nothing else to remember except her face." His answer pleased her, and they settled back to reminiscences, but Michael had been unnerved by the similarity and one track of his mind was considering whether it was not just a superficial coincidence.

Julia looked at her watch. "Oh, God, look at the time, I need to pick Mother up, I'm sorry, Michael, I will have to dash."

"I'll walk you back to the car."

"No, don't worry. It's been lovely, more than that really, but I can't think of the right word. I just feel so free when I am with you, is that silly?"

"No. Not at all, I feel like that too. When can we meet up again?"

Julia stood up and Michael got up to face her. "I'm not sure, let me have a look at what Mother is up to. Work's pretty slack at the moment, which is rather nice in a way. I will ring you and …" She hesitated and then she kissed him almost fiercely. "Please, when I ring, try and be there."

He reached up and held her shoulders and then he kissed her in his turn. "I will do my best, I promise."

Her smile filled him with warmth and pleasure and as his hands left her shoulders, she took them and held them for a moment. "I know that we have not been acquainted long, Mr. Oakes, but I feel that deep down we have known each other for an age." Then her bubbling humour returned. "But don't tell anyone around here that or they'll have us straight on the regression couch and tell us we were Lancelot and Guinevere, or Abelard and Eloise or some such, I'm quite happy being Michael and Julia, just embarking on an adventure together."

"Absolutely, so am I."

"Goodbye, then, see you soon." She kissed him again, quickly this time and was away through the door. Michael stood for a moment and then he sat back down. He decided that he would have another drink before venturing back. The prospect of a bunch of inquisitive ladies all resembling Netti was one for which he needed to prepare.

★★★

14

The World Beyond Ours

When he got back, preparations for the dinner party were well under way and Netti was guiding David through his first experience of making a nut roast while she muttered out loud her worries about the setting of the cheesecake.

"Ah, Michael, I hope that you had a good afternoon, I'm sure that you did, now there is plenty to do, so get your jacket off and roll up your sleeves."

"Don't argue, Michael, just say, *'yes, Chef'* and do as she says, it will be less painful that way." Michael could tell by his tone that David was actually having a whale of time; he had always been quite a good cook, although he rarely cooked when he was in town and his mother would never have allowed him near her kitchen at home, but he suspected that this would be his first hard-core vegetarian feast.

"Fine, just let me scrub up then."

Within minutes, he was busy peeling and dicing a large swede, with Netti's voice rattling on in the background, one moment issuing instructions, the next offering background on the guest list, it was like a high-speed train that every now and then jumped from one track to another, without apparently losing speed.

"Marcia Fielding is probably my oldest friend down here, she moved down way before me and it was she who helped me sort out the premises, which reminds me – Michael you haven't seen them yet have you, she used to teach singing and piano in Wells, but she's semi-retired now, which means that she only takes on the pupils that she wants. I think her father left her a tidy sum, so she is quite comfortable. Michael, can you wash those raspberries for me, thanks. She is lovely, though she does tend to get rather loud when she has had a few glasses of wine. Oh, that reminds me, Michael those glasses that are out on the table will need a polish, I think.

"Then there's Pippa Downley-Martin and Ursula Rushton, they live together on a converted farm on the way out towards Butleigh, they're not partners or anything. Ursula moved in after Pippa's husband died, well, killed himself actually, but we're not supposed to know that. It was some financial irregularities that were being investigated, but it was all covered up and his colleagues gave him a nice funeral, so it's all been forgotten. Do you think there is going to be enough cheese, David, or should I send the boy, here, out for some more?"

"There's plenty, Chef, honestly, stop panicking."

"I am not panicking, just asking. Oh, Michael, I've scribbled down the menu on that pad, you couldn't type it up and print it off for me could you, we've got into the habit of keeping a record you see so that we don't repeat ourselves too often. There's a menu template in documents, in a folder labelled Menus funnily enough. You can do it when you've finished with those parsnips. Now, who haven't I mentioned, oh, yes, Daphne and Joan, now they are partners, have been for a long time and I have never known their surnames, they've always just been Daphne and Joan. They have a gift shop in Wells but they live in Glastonbury; been here since King Arthur's time by the look of them. I have no idea how old they are, it could be anything from sixty-five to a thousand, but they are an absolute hoot the pair of them. They seem to have met so many people and done so much, and some of the stories are so outrageous it is hard to tell if they are making the whole lot up. Their cooking is dreadful, but they have the best wine cellar I have ever seen. When it's their turn we cheat and bring the food with us while they supply us with wine that none of the rest of us could afford without a mortgage. Most of it apparently gifts from friends abroad."

Michael had finished his latest task and so, signalling to the still talking Netti, he picked up the list and went into the study where a laptop sat on the desk attached to a small printer, which he saw was already loaded with some bordered card. It actually felt very odd to be sitting down at a computer. It was the first time since his accident and it felt strange and incongruous to be using this device, when in Taleth he was used to the 'magic' of thought and the directness of speech.

The computer was hibernating, so it only took a few moments to open the relevant folder and find the template, which Netti had already dated and set. He looked down at the paper in his hand. Martha Spinetti's handwriting was absolutely in character, fast flowing and spidery, with more loops than was entirely necessary and very few straight lines. Still it was readable, and Michael successfully typed the menu, which read,

Autumn Salad with Fruit Compote

Nut Roast
Accompanied by roasted cherry tomatoes, mashed swede and Caramelised onion gravy

Lemon Cheesecake
With Raspberry coulis

Cheese Board

He printed off eight copies and was reasonably pleased with the result. He then took them through to the dining room and began polishing the wine glasses on the sideboard. It was good to be involved in a simple task under someone else's direction. It was like the second interval in a three-act opera, where everything is building nicely to a climax, but then there is a pause, a chance to take a stroll and prepare for the catharsis of the final act. He did not know where they would have reached on his return to Taleth, but they were on their way to the heights of the peaks at the coldest and bleakest end of the chain of mountains. They would have ridden as far as they could, but he suspected that at some point, they would have to resort to progress on foot. He was certain that he knew the final destination, he had seen it, but how far or how high he had no idea and certainly he had no way of knowing how long it would take to reach it. He also knew that in the far north, winter would be in full swing and that meant snow and bitter cold.

He wondered for a moment how Suani was, Sorin had seemed certain that she would recover fully, but Michael had seen the poison burning beneath her flesh, indeed he had felt it himself, although mildly. Even with Sorin's help she would surely not to be in a fit state to accompany the others on their journey. That led him to think about who would be with him when he awoke to Taleth. Sorin had hinted that he might be needed elsewhere; Danil may feel that he should join the Frinakim if they finally join forces with the King's army. Would he be stripped of all his friends as he finally came to the choice he was apparently destined to make? Tuggid and Gath were far away facing Faradon and his renegades, Ayan and Greer too rode towards battle. If the others also felt they had to leave then he might find the mountains a very lonely place.

He had finished the glasses and apparently from the sounds coming from the kitchen the final act of the drama in there was beginning. He was sorely tempted to polish them again and delay further instructions, but he thought better of it. David would be in need of moral support, at the very least.

When he reached the kitchen in fact most things appeared to under control and Netti was just about to go and change.

"Ah, Michael, just help David keep an eye on things while I change and then we can sort out setting the table properly. Most things are done, you could slice a few lemons for drinks, that would be useful. Oh, and you could do a couple of bowls of olives, they're in the fridge. Back in a minute." She swept out and for a second or two there was only the sound of bubbling, sizzling and the fan of the oven. Then David looked at Michael and he shrugged in such a pathetic way that Michael had to laugh.

"If the rest of your Chambers could see you now, David, I think they might have to revise their opinion of you."

"Oh, don't be so sure, I was once shown a picture, taken secretly on someone's phone of the Honourable Mr. Justice Bleeming QC wearing a pink apron, sleeves rolled, up to his elbows in pastry and he is one of the Judges that if you're defending you don't place any bets on yourself. What's more I know of two Lady Judges who regularly win competitions for their sponge cakes."

"I'm not surprised at all, David, if I was judging a cake contest and I knew one of the entrants could send me to prison, should she ever have the chance, I think I would let her win too."

Now David laughed. "Are you hinting at corruption in the East Kent Women's Institute Broad Oak Branch? I must inform the press; they love a good story of corruption and dishonesty in the judiciary."

"I'm not sure that it would sell many papers, David, or many cakes for that matter. Still I must say you seem to be enjoying this touch of domesticity."

Serious for a moment David looked at Michael earnestly. "You know I am. I didn't think I would, but I am, and it wasn't something I had ever thought would give me any pleasure at all. I suppose at some point I have to make the decision to go back to the real world, but all this is becoming more and more tempting. Is that crazy?"

"No, David, not at all crazy. You've done a good few years in the service of the Law and a break seems to be doing you good. Mind you, going back probably won't be easy if you find this too comfortable."

"I'm sure you're right, but I'll face that when it comes to it. Perhaps I'll stop practising and lecture or teach."

"My God, now I know that you really are doomed, if you are thinking like that. You know that you earn five times what lecturers do."

David snorted. "Well, possibly, but it isn't all about money, you know."

"I'm only teasing, David, you do what you want, we can always sell those awful paintings of mine if we have to …"

"Oh, that reminds me, when you were away, I did a bit of digging and I looked up what your paintings are going for and although they have fluctuated a little in the confusion over whether you are actually dead or not, they all seem to agree that you won't be painting for a while, so they have been rising rapidly in value."

"I hope you got hold of my agent and told him to sell some of them. They're all hideous and I don't want them."

"Well, I sort of assumed that, so I managed to get hold of him eventually. He was reluctant at first, I think he still thinks that you are going to wind up dead and he wants to hang on to them and sell them himself, but I told him, as your legal representative, that all of the ones salvaged from the gallery should be sold and that if he could sort it out quickly that you were happy to double his commission."

"Oh, I bet he loved that."

"Yes, he realised that double his money now might be his best bet, but I think he may buy a few himself, just in case you do confirm his suspicions and show up dead, as it were."

"So, he's selling them off then."

"Yes, he's going to organise an auction and transfer any money into your account. Now if that causes Mr. Delgado or whatever he is really called to be interested again, then we will just have to come as clean as we can with the police and try and work out a story that they will accept."

"That suits me, David. I can't see myself painting again, not for a long, long time, but if we get a bit of capital out of it then it will all help in the long run."

Netti's voice drifted down from the landing. "I hope you are keeping an eye on everything, boys. I'd hate to have to get new kitchen staff, good people are so hard to find these days."

"No Chef, it's all in hand." David made a hopeful expression which had Michael laughing again and then he looked at the time and he suggested that it was time for them to make themselves presentable for the evening.

For Michael, the evening passed quite quickly, the ladies doing most of the talking. The food was excellent, the starter in particular, a collection of vegetables, baby carrots, parsnips, new potatoes, green beans and courgettes; each prepared in a different way, with a light fruit sauce, was wonderful and it reminded him of the simple but tasty food he had become used to in Taleth. He was also spared too much questioning and he realised that, probably due to Netti's skilful and enthusiastic preparation that they were much more interested in David.

The guests were very much as she had suggested. Marcia, who was over fifty, but wouldn't have liked you to say so, was loud and flamboyant. Her garish spectacles sat defiantly on her nose and she wore her hair long and her clothes bright. She was pleasant enough; her voice suggested a singer and she had a way of saying everything as if it should have been obvious from the start. Pippa held herself tightly in check and was for the most part happy to listen rather than talk. She had a long sad elegant face, lined by age and care, but still attractive, although Michael felt her eyes were slightly too small and her nose a little too long for the balance to be a totally successful one. Ursula was a different sort entirely, round of face and body, but bullishly happy about it. Her large brown eyes, which were framed with gilt framed glasses, had an honest, open look, as they roamed around focusing on each person in turn whether they were speaking or not. She wore her black hair in a short ponytail, and she could give Netti a run for her money when it came to sentences with a sight too many clauses for comfort.

"But you see, Martha, as I said to Pippa only the other day, when we were over at the Waitrose, you know the new one, you must try their pastries, they are wonderful, as good as any you can get in Paris, well almost, and their veg counter is excellent too, there really isn't any substitute for home produced honey, not if you want a proper flavour, I mean so many of them have all sorts of stuff that the bees have been after, and the flavours all come through, well, I think they do, ours are so lucky that they can feed on the lavender plants most of the time, it makes all the difference."

"I couldn't agree more, Ursula, …"

And Daphne and Joan were everything that Martha had promised, made to be a couple, of indeterminate age, both dressed in smart, but comfortable suits and extremely, almost severely, sensible shoes. Daphne was slightly taller and wider than Joan, while Joan was darker of hair and keener of eye than Daphne. Their speech had become over the years habitually combined into an intricate dance, some of the nuances of which only they were privilege to. Michael found them oddly fascinating.

"Do you remember the Bishop of Saskatoon and his honey, Joan?"

"Oh, I do, Daphne, I certainly do, best honey in the whole of Saskatchewan, but such a stammer, his sermons on a Sunday could go on for hours."

"If someone didn't remind Gareth the organist to interrupt him with a hymn before it got too long."

"He was a fine young man, Gareth, took a great shine to you, Daphne, he had a proper thing for you, didn't he?"

"He did, and I quite liked him, until I caught him giving you private lessons on his organ, Joan dear."

"Oh, that was nothing, and I never could get the hang of it, just too many knobs, Daphne, I never was any good with them."

"It would have come to nothing anyway, not after he applied for that post in Kampala."

"Didn't you get all chummy with the Consul in Kampala, dear."

"No, Joan, that was Kabala, different country."

"Henry Fanshaw, that was his name, tried it on with all the girls, engaged or otherwise."

"No, dear, you are thinking of William, his brother, he was the one who put his hand on my leg when I was playing Schubert at Lady Caroline's birthday party."

"Oh, that's right and you didn't flinch until you had finished and then you broke three of his fingers."

"Don't exaggerate, Joan, I only broke two of them, the other was just bruised. Daddy was furious with me; it meant that he was without a spinner for most of the season."

Michael noticed that this could continue and flow seamlessly in and out of the conversation that sailed around it almost without interruption. He learned of their visit to Vienna and an encounter with a one-legged violinist who claimed to be related to Mendelssohn, while at the same time half listening to Marcia declaring that she had recently taken on a pair of twins who had sat for their Prep-test after just two months of lessons. And yet for all their lively discourse and colourful pasts, he still found that they all paled beside the women of Taleth, Ayan, Suani, and Siraal, so full of life and energy, so rich, so vibrant of speech, even Neemar Dal Ganard, with her peaceful acceptance of life's harshness and blessings in equal measure. Only Julia matched them, or at least she did to him, even if his eyes were as biased as any in such a situation. How would Mel have compared, he wondered? Something he no longer needed to think about, which was a good sign, surely. He was so absorbed in his role as observer, musing upon those around him, that when he was asked a direct question, he was slow to react.

"So, Michael, now that you have made such a stunning recovery, will you be returning to your writing?" It was Ursula. "I never read much about art. I tended to rely on other people filling me in on the details, you know, if you stand by a painting in a gallery long enough someone will either tell you about it or tell their friend about it loudly, so that you can hear, isn't that true, Pippa."

"Oh, don't ask me, if it's paintings I like then I'm not listening, if it's paintings I don't like then I don't need to listen do I."

"But you know what I mean, Pippa, there is always someone willing to impart their opinion whether you want to hear it or not. You must have seen that in your experience of galleries, Michael, surely."

Michael wanted to say, *'Actually the last gallery I was in was blown up'* but he didn't. He saw Netti trying to catch Ursula's eyes, but they were wandering around the table, he decided to be pleasant, it was still the interval between acts and the curtain had not risen. "I have found in the past that art galleries and exhibitions are invariably filled with a large number of art critics, both professional and amateur; and most of them, and I include myself obviously, talk a lot of rubbish most of the time. That's why I liked to write about art and painters from a historical point of view; they're not around to argue, so you can say what you like."

David laughed, but Ursula had decided to push this questioning further. "But you studied your subject and so you are qualified to speak about it. I mean otherwise what is the point of studying at all."

"Oh, I studied at college, although David would probably point out, only when I had too, and by some miracle I succeeded in getting a good degree, but just because I can tell you that Canaletto was born on 28th October 1697 in Venice, doesn't necessarily give me the right to tell you what you see in a painting or what you should see in a painting. Art speaks to the individual don't you think?"

"He said that his painting was a Canaletto, Daphne, do you remember?"

"Who, dear?"

"That man we met in Cairo, when your cousin got stung by a hornet."

"No, he had some Constables, Joan, and they were rather boring I recall, all trees and rivers, rustic never appealed to me."

Ursula was not giving up, now that she had finally drawn Michael into the conversation. "Yes, I grant you we all see things differently, but there must be something that makes a great painting. Is it technique, natural talent, vision, I mean can you teach someone to be a great artist, like you can a singer?"

Marcia broke in. "Oh, great singers are born not taught, Ursula. You can train a voice, but you have to have something to start from, the talent must be there."

"Alright, that may be true, but how does that work in painting, Michael, surely, technique is paramount."

Michael was trying hard not to find this irritating. "If someone has good technique and training, they can produce a good picture, an imitation of life, like a camera does. But an artist doesn't do that, an artist produces what he sees, what he feels, what he breathes, what his heart sings to him, about the world around him. He doesn't just paint a picture, he draws the world into himself and he pours it forth onto the canvas in such a way that the onlooker for a moment, just for a moment has the chance to see the world as he sees it, whether it is the horrors of his nightmare or the raptures of his soul."

"So, anyone can produce great Art then?"

He was losing his battle, she was deliberately misunderstanding, and he was out of practice at this sort of gathering. "No, not just anyone. Anyone can paint a picture, they can learn to use paint, study form and perspective and composition, but no one can teach you to see the world with your own personal vision, it is either there or it isn't. I could get Marcia here to teach me to play the piano and even if I was good, displayed aptitude, became technically brilliant at playing it doesn't mean I could write a Chopin Etude or an aria like Puccini. Think of it as if there are two different worlds and one is our normal one, fine for every day, but sometimes flat and lifeless, and then there is another, vibrant, dynamic, alive, exciting to every sense, in the truest meaning of the word 'sensational'. That is what a true artist must feel and, occasionally, he is able to let others take a peek through his eyes and see it for themselves."

He stopped and realised that for once everybody had been listening to just the one piece of conversation. He also saw by their faces that he had spoken with more passion than he had meant, but he could not escape it now and that was how it felt, he had tried to tell David and Netti before. He could see that Ursula to continue and was contemplating telling her that the greatest works of art he had seen recently were the magnificent carvings in the Chamber of the Mrauuk in the mountains of the Nare, when Joan broke the silence.

"I can never remember, Daphne, was it your mother or my mother who met Puccini?"

"I can't remember either, Joan, but it may have been my great aunt Clarissa."

"No, Clarissa was my great aunt. I think your great aunt was called Edith or was it Ethel?"

"Are you sure? Wasn't your cousin Edith the one who shot some Germans who broke into her farmhouse."

"Did she? I don't know, dear. Anyway, Puccini was Italian not German."

"Elgar, Joan, your mother met Elgar."

"Elgar wasn't German, Daphne, any schoolchild could tell you that."

"Not some of the ones I teach, Joan, old thing, one of them played so badly during one lesson that I had to clean my glasses to make sure he wasn't playing with his arse." The laughter at this remark broke the momentary tension and it allowed Michael to calm himself a little Netti helped by asking him to help her take out some plates and then return with the coffee.

Michael felt he should apologise, but when he began, Netti shushed him. "Oh, don't worry about it, Ursula was just playing her little games and they are all very intrigued about you of course. You just caught them off guard when you were so passionate about it all, I suppose most of the time they hear people sounding off without any real feeling behind what they are saying, and it must have been a shock to find someone prepared to speak from the heart. It all made sense to me and now we'd better rescue David."

Just as they were going back into the dining room, they met Daphne and Joan, presumably on a trip to the bathroom, Netti let them pass as she carried the coffee pot in. When Michael went to follow, Joan touched him lightly on the arm.

"You are quite right, you know, when you see it, the world beyond ours, it makes your heart beat like a wild thing, doesn't it, Daphne."

"Oh, certainly, everything trembling with life, so real you could almost touch it, so exciting that your skin burns and tingles, Joan, tingles and burns."

"Just the once though, one single peek and then it fills your dreams, and nothing is ever quite the same again, is it, Daphne."

"Never quite the same, Joan, never quite the same." And then they turned away to accompany each other to the toilet as they had been doing most of their lives.

Michael didn't know what to think. These were not the ramblings he had heard earlier; they had heard his words and had felt the need to tell him that they had seen … well, what had they seen? The world through the eyes of an artist? They seemed to have met the whole world in their time so that was entirely possible. But Joan had specifically said, *'the world beyond ours'*. He was perplexed, but he decided not to worry about it for now, there were more pressing matters to attend to, the coffee cups for one.

Michael's words had either been forgotten or they had each chosen to let it drop and the rest of the evening passed without further incident. Daphne and Joan made no further reference to what he had said and they began a long and complicated tussle between themselves as to who had really lost the Contessa's necklace and whether if it had fallen into the Isis during the garden party, whether it would still be there or whether it would have drifted down stream, although at one point Joan's suggestion that a fish had swallowed it and then ended up on the college dinner table was dismissed as a dream. Marcia continued to get louder as Netti had predicted she would, and she entered into a heated discussion with Ursula about the relative merits of various operatic tenors. Pippa described a recent trip to Salzburg to David and Netti, who seemed quite keen on the idea of a trip into the mountains, while Michael finished his coffee and wondered how far into the mountains he had already travelled.

When it was all over and the guests departed, and they had tidied away and filled the dishwasher and rinsed everything else, ready to go in the second load in the morning, David suggested a brandy in the living room as a night-cap and neither of the others disagreed.

"Well, Martha Spinetti, how do you feel it all went?"

Netti took a sip of the brandy and sat back in her chair. "I think … I think that some of my friends are as mad as a box of frogs, and sometimes during the evening service we weren't even in the same church, let alone singing from the same hymn sheet, but given all that, I think it went really well."

"I agree, and your friends are no crazier than the rest of the world, Netti, they are all extremely interesting in their own way. What do you think, Michael?"

"Oh, it was definitely a spectacular success, Netti, the food was really good, all of it, full of flavour and the wine, though I missed you explaining what they all were David, because I wasn't listening, was good too. Even Daphne and Joan were impressed by that dessert wine you flourished, that didn't look like it came from Waitrose. What was it?"

"Oh, the Sauterne, it was a Chateau Raymond Lafon that was in Netti's cupboard, although she can't remember who gave it to her. I looked it up, it retails at seventy-five pounds a bottle."

Netti laughed. "If it was that expensive it probably came from Daphne and Joan in the first place, I don't know anyone else who buys wine at that price."

"I can see why you drink it out of small glasses."

"It was good though."

Michael was laughing too now. "Bloody well ought to be for seventy-five pounds."

The brandy had warmed them all, ready for sleep. "Now, we'll have none of that language from you kitchen boys, I can't abide swearing amongst the staff, I want you both up early in the morning scrubbing the floors."

"I think, Madam Chef, that may be out of the question, scrubbing I can manage, but scrubbing early in the morning I feel, after that meal and such excellent and expensive wine, may well be completely beyond me."

"Oh, in that case, I shall just have to beat you out of bed myself."

Michael noticed David's covert smile at this remark. "Which will entail you getting up even earlier than us, which would appear to be a flaw in your evil scheme."

"True enough, I feel in that case that we will celebrate the Feast of St Anselm a bit early and take the morning off."

"Is that St Anselm or St Anselm of Lucca?"

Netti responded to Michael's teasing with a grin. "I don't know, I didn't know there was more than one. Anyway, I was the one brought up Catholic not you."

"Ah, a degree in Art History is useful in such matters, St Anselm of Lucca was painted by somebody and became the patron Saint of Mantua, for some reason; he probably died there."

David finished his brandy. "Wasn't it Mantua where Romeo went when he was exiled from Verona for killing Tybalt? Or was that Padua?"

Netti had begun to giggle. "It was Mantua and we are beginning to sound like Daphne and Joan, the three of us, which I think is a sure sign that we should all be in bed."

Michael nodded and he drained his glass. "I agree, but this brandy is not a patch on the Tuoll that Sorin and the others delight in. Still it does the job. Well done, Netti, a good night's entertaining."

She smiled and drained her own glass. "Thank you, and after all the alcohol I have consumed tonight it may well be me who doesn't wake up for three days. Come on."

★★★

Michael more than half expected the dream that had begun almost as soon as sleep took him, but it was not a place he recognised at all. A harsh orange light beat down and the ground upon which he walked was hard and cracked. Here and there, it flashed and sparkled as if a multitude of tiny jewels had been scattered. What vegetation there was seemed thin and weak, thrusting up though the gashes in the baked earth. There were no trees and the flat expanse around him appeared to stretch away forever. He walked on in this seemingly barren landscape for a long while and then he realised that there was a line of hills ahead. They must have been hidden by a heat haze for they were dark and clear now upon the horizon. At one end, they rose steeply to high peaks. At the other, the incline was steadier, but there they were ridged and jagged. Beyond the hills he could hear a distant rumbling of thunder. A shadow fell across his path and a harsh voice that he recognised immediately made him look up. Her crimson hair hung loosely, but there was no wind to disturb it.

"Is this what you want, outling? The devastation that you see will spread if you continue on the path you have chosen. Although sleeping they lie for now, you would wake them to ravage the land once more and if you look for protection from my kin then you are a fool."

Michel tried to speak, but the dry air caught in his lungs and his voice failed him.

"There is not one of them who truly cares for those who walk upon this earth, not one who serves her children as I do. And how would you serve? You would destroy all for those rock crawlers who prefer to rot in ignorance rather than seek their own salvation. Is this what you truly want?"

Again, Michael found that he could not reply, and this made Takden even angrier. "Very well then if fire and destruction is what you crave so be it." The ground around him shook and he was suddenly surrounded by gouts of flame bursting up from the splitting earth, he threw his hands up across his face and then he felt the fierce heat become not flame but sea spray and lowering his hands he saw a rolling crashing ocean spread out before him. He was alone upon a thin promontory that jutted out into the foaming waves, but Takden's voice still hung in his ears.

"The ocean will rise and hurl its force upon the land, sweeping in a wave of death across your beloved plains. Would you drown all the world in your blind folly?"

As if in answer to her question, the water below him balled itself into a frothing white fist and rearing up above his head it smashed itself down upon him, knocking him from his perch and sending him tumbling towards the churning water below. The impact drove him under the surface, but as he fought to reach the air, he realised that the water had become still and that it felt warm upon his skin. As he broke through into the daylight once more, he found that he swam not in a wild ocean, but in a calm blue lake, surrounded by tall trees that leant low over the water brushing their trailing branches gently against the liquid sapphire below. In amongst the vegetation that overflowed the banks were a throng of flowers of stunning vividness and variety. The colour, and the richness of the scene danced before his eyes, enticing him. He swam closer and was caught in a rush of scents and smells, each fighting the other to seduce his nostrils and ravish his senses. Then, suddenly, his feet were grabbed from beneath the waters and held in a vice like grip, he was caught off guard, he was dragged down viciously into the azure dark, and the voice began again.

"All that beauty, all that life, ecstatically bursting from the fertile land, untouched, unseen, and one man has the power to turn it to a pile of dust. How can that be right? How can that be fair? How can that be allowed? It cannot! It must not! It will not!"

His lungs began to burn, his head began to pound, his heart thump wildly and then he fell forward on to lush grass. Takden's words echoed in his head as he gasped for breath. Around him, a gentle rain fell which caressed him gently and ran warm across his face. He got to his feet and as he did so, he saw that he wore a green robe patterned with oak leaves, bound at the waist with a belt of plaited silk. He had worn it before, he remembered it well, although it seemed an age past now. When Cerlinith spoke to him he was not surprised, and he turned to face her.

"Welcome, man of oak, Michael that is also Mikael, Ender of Days, Bringer of Doom, Twice-Born, Twice-Dead, and any other title that you have acquired in your travels." Her voice betrayed no irony or judgement, but her green eyes sparkled with a fiery humour.

Michael bowed. "Greetings, great one, and I assume thanks are required."

"They are unnecessary, Michael that is also Mikael, our sister has grown cruel and foolish in her isolation and although I spared you the pain of her anger and torment, she could not have killed you, for you are not actually here." She paused for a moment. "At least I do not think she could, although she perhaps could persuade you to die."

"Do you mean that she could have made me believe that I was dying to such an extent that I would kill myself through my own belief?"

"I am not certain. Even though I have many powers and I can do wondrous things in this world of ours, Michael that is also Mikael, I know so little about you. I have watched you since I first found your spirits wandering in the darkness at the rim of our world and I knew deep within my being that I must be the one to give you strength and healing, but I knew not why. Now that my brother Uvarin has helped us to understand that your way is to be your own, that your choice a free one, I have wondered at the purpose for which you were brought here. I do not see the ending that some may feel is coming, I sense a future in you though what it is I cannot tell. I will accept whatever Taleth is or becomes upon your choosing."

"May I ask a question, great one?"

"You may, I will answer if I can."

"Why is Takden so set against me?"

"Ah, well, as I said she has grown cruel and she stands apart from those she should call kindred. Uvarin believes she has become misguided by her love for her creations, her Shaellev, but I do not know her mind or her purpose. She has certainly made them powerful and … different to the other races. I find them strange and unlovely creatures, but I will not judge her for she is my sister and her will is free. She sees you as a threat to her children, perhaps. But if you are, then Carun and I, Hantor and Minead, Yvelle and Palleon, and Ragarad should feel equally threatened, but we do not.

Does that answer your question? I fear that it doesn't, but it is all that I can tell you."

Michael bowed again politely. "It is good of you to grant me the benefit of your wisdom, great one."

Cerlinith laughed, a sound that rang with the rippling of streams and the cascading of waterfalls, it echoed with the rustling of grass and the bursting of buds as the blossom explodes upon the trees. "Oh, Michael that is also Mikael, you are a man to charm the wildest heart, I suspect the women of your world must find you irresistible."

"I am afraid not, great one, although there is one who appears to find me pleasurable to be with."

Cerlinith smiled and she stretched out her arms. "Then I give her my blessing, Man of Oak, and wish you both well. Farewell and fear not the darkness, for now is the time of strength."

The dream faded and as it did, so Michael realised that the words that Cerlinith had used were subtly different in meaning. Did she mean that she felt that he was now strong enough? Whereas the others had implied that there was still a way to go to find the strength that he needed. With this thought and the feel of the gentle rain upon his skin, he awoke.

★★★

15

'And so, by the First Light of Dawn ...'

He was still in his bed in the house in Glastonbury, which surprised him a little. He knew that he would switch to Taleth soon and the waiting was beginning to aggravate him, what else needed to happen before he was ready. He lay back and he looked at the ceiling dappled with the moonlight. He had obviously not pulled the curtains fully across, but the moon looked strong and bright, so getting out of bed he crossed to the window and opened them fully.

His room was at the back of the house and it overlooked the large garden, which was lined with small trees and sturdy shrubs such as laurels and rhododendrons. There was also a bougainvillea next to the first of the two Japanese cherries. The moon was full, and it lit the garden with an eerie pallid light, causing everything to appear different, even familiar things. The shadows too were given a hint of extra depth, as if a step too far into the dark would lead you into places forbidden to those who dwelt in daylight. There was no wind to speak of and everything seemed still until a movement caught his eye.

At the far end of the garden there was a small shed in front of the back fence, a figure was appearing around the shed, thin and wiry, and he was looking up at the house. Michael instinctively backed away into the shadow of the curtain. The intruder stayed by the shed for a few moments and then moved further forward and clung to the trunk of the larger of the two apple trees. He was still visible from the house and his manner began to make Michael think that this was no ordinary burglar. His face was uncovered, but still too far away for Michael to see his features, and he carried no bag or tools of the trade, not that Michael was sure what they would have looked like if he had seen them. There was also the fact that there was no easy access to the fence he had obviously climbed, to get to the back fence of this house. He surmised that you would have to cross the back gardens of at least five other properties. Why go to such lengths to get to this one?

The figure started to move again. He certainly didn't move as though he was used to creeping around gardens in the moonlight. As he got closer Michael leaned forward to try and catch a glimpse of his face, something about the angular way that he moved reminded him of … Mr. Perkins! He had turned his face to look at the house as he stepped out of a shadow and the glare of the moon had revealed the thin pinched features. *'Mr. Perkins! What was he doing here and this time on his own, no thugs or acolytes this time to assist him?'* Doctor Cavendish must have discussed Michael with him already and so he would now know the address. But why were there no Tsarg with him? Come to think of it he had never seen Mr. Perkins with Tsarg, had he? At the hospital he had only heard him and at the lake the men who chased him had disappeared, but he had never actually seen their faces. He had always assumed that Perkins was part of the twisted schemes of the Corruptor. What if he wasn't? What if he was linked to Taleth in some way, but not to Khargahar, to someone else? Wild thoughts ran through Michael's mind as he reached behind him for his trousers. *'Mr. Perkins must be fairly close to the house by now,'* he thought. *'I must try and see.'*

He moved as close as he could to the window, and he saw that Mr. Perkins had reached the last section of lawn and was apparently contemplating how he might gain access to the house. Michael hoped that this would take him some time, since he was presuming it wasn't one of Mr. Perkins' regular activities. He was about to make a dash for the door and get downstairs before he did any damage when something burst from the shade of the trees on the left of the garden. A large animal bounded across the grass and leapt into the space between Mr. Perkins and the house. Michael could not see the creature from his vantage point, and it had moved with such speed that he was unsure what it was. He reasoned that it was too large for a fox, so it had to be one of the neighbours' dogs, although a dog that size would have been inside or secured in some way. He turned his attention to Mr. Perkins. He stood frozen with terror, his eyes wide and his mouth open. He looked like a man who for the first time in his life believed that he was face to face with death. Michael waited for the snarl, the snapping teeth, but it never came. Something made Mr. Perkins expression change to confusion and shock, and then he turned in an instant and he fled the way he had come, the sound of him scrambling up and over the fence and crashing down on the other side could be heard distinctly echoing across the still garden.

The animal had not moved, Michael was sure of that, and so he ran as silently as he could out of the room and down the stairs. The beast should have been standing in front of the French windows that opened off the dining room, but the garden was empty. There was no sign that anyone or anything had been there. He walked slowly back up the stairs to his room and he decided that as he was fully awake now, he might as well get dressed and go for a walk. With a cursory trip to the bathroom, he soon stood in the hall ready to leave the house when two things stopped him. One was a thought that he might as well check the garden as he was now dressed; the other was that he should really leave David and Netti a note to say where he had gone. He knew that they would probably consider him extremely irresponsible, but he needed to get out into the air. He would take whatever consequences arose. He wrote the note first, just explaining that he couldn't sleep, and he had gone for a brief walk, then he carefully unlocked the back door and braved the moonlit garden.

The moon had moved further on in its arc and so the angle of light had changed and hence the shape and the placement of the shadows. He saw nothing close to the house to suggest that anything had been there, so he stepped carefully across the grass and he cast his eyes around the shrubs and the plants that bordered the lawns. Nothing. He walked all the way to the shed and even there he could see little sign that a man had climbed the fence and squeezed his way around the back of the shed, of course Michael had not explored this far in daylight, so he had no real way of knowing what, if anything, had been disturbed. He gave up and he walked back to the house. He wondered if he had perhaps dreamed or imagined it all. Then he saw something in the soft grass to his right, something that must have been hidden minutes before, but the moon continued to move and the shifting shadows changing their shape. It appeared to be a darker patch of grass, but in fact was a depression, a print, but not of a foot, of a paw. Michael's heart pounded as he looked more closely, it was large, very large if it was a dog, but to him there was no doubt that it was the paw of a large wolf.

He knew that that was unlikely, impossible even, but it seemed to make sense out there in the strange light of the passing moon, a wolf had foiled Mr. Perkins and had allowed him to leave, possibly spoken to him, hence his moment of confusion and shock. Had someone sent at the very least the image of a wolf to protect him? Could an image leave such a print behind in the grass? He had no way of knowing, but it gave him plenty to think about as he closed the back door and went back into the hall. He checked that his note was visible on table by the phone and then, picking up his walking stick, he left the house, locking the door quietly behind him.

The moon was almost setting, and the light was now that cold dark that settles in for a couple of hours before dawn begins. There was no-one around as his wandering led him down into the town where the streetlamps shone brightly along the High Street and the occasional car that passed seemed intent on its own business. He let his feet take him where they would as he struggled to grasp what had happened. When he had been attacked previously; when the assailants had been Tsarg forced through into this world, there had never been any assistance sent, never any aid offered. Perhaps because, until now it was clear that there was little real danger, the purpose was to cause fear and distraction.

It was clear that he was being driven to seek the crystal casket, but who had unleashed the plague upon the Nare, surely that must have been the Corruptor's doing. So many had already died, so he must be certain that breaking the crystal and exposing the Chiatt Grain will lead to a release from his imprisonment. If so, why had he put barriers in his way, why not just take him there where he needed to be? Or is it that he is not as powerful as he appears to be? Uvarin had hinted that Michael could not be controlled because he was angry and therefore less receptive to the Corruptor's direction. Perhaps that was so, but if the destruction of the crystal meant certain escape for Khargahar, then why were the others willing to help him? Except of course Takden, who had made it perfectly clear that choosing to save the Nare was the wrong path; hers was obviously a completely different agenda. It had all seemed straightforward for a while, but now he came close, his doubts rose again.

What right did he have to make the choice in any case? He was an outsider, an Uclan, Hemmek, whatever they wanted to call him. What was there to be gained for him after making this choice, he really could see no future that led to a normal life. If he truly was the Doom of Taleth and he released a destructive force that would destroy their world for ever, what was going to happen to him? Even Oppenheimer had had the sense to stand well back. Was he too about to become *'Death, the destroyer of Worlds'*? But that had to be his choice, didn't it? He could not leave an entire race to die, knowing that he had the power to put an end to their suffering.

What was it that Takden had been trying to show him? The burned desert, the wild ocean and the verdant jungle, were they areas of Taleth that so far, he had not visited? He had never really asked about the geography of the world as he had moved through it, save for some conversations with Havianik about the Cluath lands and the politics of the Heran River. He had seen a few maps on the walls in Tath Garnir but taken little notice of them. Of course, he did not want to bring destruction upon the whole of Taleth, but why was she so against the possibility of a positive outcome for all of them; that Khargahar was deceived by thoughts of freedom and that release from his prison beneath Fellas could also mean that he could ultimately be defeated. The other Powers appeared to be ready to take the risk, they had not hindered his journey and although some had helped more openly than others, none that he had encountered so far, except Takden, had been openly hostile. No, he knew what he must do, and the consequences would just have to sort themselves out.

Michael looked around him and he saw that his steps had now brought him back to the junction of Magdalene Street and Fisher's Hill. He carried on up the slope, knowing that he now headed for the Tor. It seemed a logical place to go; he could watch the sunrise just as thousands of others had done throughout Glastonbury's long history. The air had grown chill now and he knew that dawn was not far off. He could have turned off and returned home when he reached Chilkwell Street, but he didn't. He turned right, and headed for the turning into Wellhouse Lane. He had expected to see more people about, but no-one else seemed intent on greeting the new day from the damp summit of the hill. He walked up the lane and into the field feeling suddenly nervous, as if he had stepped out onto a stage and was being watched by a hidden audience.

The grass felt cold and damp even through his *'death smelling'* shoes and he quickened his pace so as to sooner reach the path. The feeling of exposure continued to grow as he made his way up to the ridge and along towards the tower. He was really cold now and he wished that he had at least returned to the house to get a heavier coat, but it was too late now, he was here, and he turned himself towards the east to await the sun. His mind wandered into thoughts of how ancient man had viewed the rising of the great fire in the sky but he contented himself with the knowledge that at least the Celts, who had lived here, did not fear every day that it would not rise unless their God-Emperor said so, as the Egyptians had believed. He was just about to walk around a little more to warm himself up when he saw figures in the field below. Figures that were running towards the hill, he turned, and he looked to the town-ward side and he saw similar hunched shapes making their way across the grass. Looking around he realised to his horror that they were coming from all directions. At this distance, he could not make out what they were and so he had no idea who he was about to face. Had Mr. Perkins rounded up a group of thugs to assault him or would these shambling outlines turn out to be Tsarg, and would they still be as easy to dispel? He gripped his walking stick and he prepared himself to face the onslaught. In the east, he saw the darkness beginning to fail and the edges of a new day readying itself below the horizon.

And so, by the first light of dawn he stood, upon the summit of the hill, his wolf's head stick poised to swing, his body tensed. As he waited his mind returned to the battles into which he had been drawn; Mikael began to chant a song of the Cluath that rose with the sun to strengthen his resolve and to give power to his arms.

'Hear me now you that name yourselves our foe!
Cluath steel bars your way ahead.
Hear me now you that seek to bring us low!
The path you seek is littered with the dead.
We do not flinch from duties' call,
We do not shirk when horns are blown.
The way of the warrior is all
The life the Cluath has ever known.
Turn back now or meet your end,
For our weapons we have drawn,
It is too late to make pretence as friend
Blood must be shed, or we shall be forsworn.'

As the first Tsarg, for such they were, crested the hill, Michael roared his defiance.

"Death to Corruption! By all the Powers you shall have none of me!" and he hurled himself at the snarling faces.

He fought with a strength that surprised them and many of the Tsarg were driven back, some even tumbled down the hill. But they did not vanish, there was no snap, no disappearance. Whether this was because Khargahar's will was strong in them, he did not know, and he did not have time to think. He knew that he would tire soon and then they would overwhelm him, he tried to move from the top of the hill and allow some chance of escape, but it was near to impossible. The snarls and the yells of the Tsarg betrayed both their fear and their panic, as if they knew that time was short. Just as they were redoubling their efforts, help arrived in the unlikely form of a bedraggled, but colourful procession. They had broached the summit of the hill oblivious to the clamour of the battle due to their own enthusiastic but somewhat chaotic beating of drums and playing of whistles. Michael didn't see them arrive, but he heard above the combined commotion a voice he recognised, Balthazar Earthroot was leading the line.

"Hey, what's going on with all the fighting, this is a sacred place, people, you can't bring down a friend of mine with no repost, we must help the Angel of the Trees, guys." And with complete disregard for personal safety and accompanied by shouts of "Follow the Earthroot!" and "That's so uncool, come on people, save the Angel!" Balthazar led his peculiar brethren into battle with roars and whoops. Michael wondered what they saw as they rushed to his aid, but to his relief, as they began to swing their drums and their tambourines at the Tsarg, there was the sound of the familiar snap as they vanished back to the depths of Corruptions prison.

With the help of his new-found friends the attack was soon repelled, and the Tor was free of Tsarg. Michael expected to be immediately faced with questions about his attackers and how and why they had just vanished, but there were none. The group simply took it all in their stride. The attackers had been here, but now they had gone, problem solved. They simply got on with their original plan and sat down upon the damp grass to drum in the dawn.

Balthazar, who was obviously the self-appointed spokesperson of the group, sat Michael down and he pointed to the rising sun. "We do this on a regular basis, friend Angel, but we have never had to fight for a pitch before, still it's all good Karma man, helping a brother in trouble, even one wearing such nice, but dead, shoes." He took a pouch from a hidden pocket and he began to set about rolling a large joint. He did it with practiced skill and Michael was suitably impressed, although he politely refused once it started to make its way around the circle of friends. Their mood was infectious though and when one of them proposed dancing a victory dance to the accompaniment of the drums, he didn't resist the hands that pulled him to his feet. It began quite slowly, circling around the five drummers but it soon began to pick up pace. Michael's head was already spinning when he felt a familiar tug and saw the dawn light cracking around him, he realised he was about to switch to Taleth. He managed to stagger a few paces away and then sit down upon the grass as the wild dance continued and he was then torn away by the cold winds of a snow-covered mountain side.

He found himself sitting on the snow and staring deep into him was a pair of eyes, the eyes of a wolf. It was Kyre of the Veyix.

'Ah, you have returned, Michael that is also Mikael, welcome. The snow lies heavy upon the mountains and our progress has been slow, but we approach our goal. Master Sorin is in conversation with Master Vitta of the Antaldi for I think news has come from King Leenal. It may be that he requires the old man after all. Also, Sylvan has been communing with the packs, for we must make a choice regarding our part in all of this. It will not be an easy one, for once made, it cannot be undone. But then perhaps we are at a moment of choice for the whole of Taleth, are we not?'

Michael got to his feet. "It is good to see you again, Kyre of the Veyix, I have much to thank you for."

'I do my duty as best I can and follow my truth wherever I perceive it to lie, Michael that is also Mikael. There are some who will only aid those for which they have been given care, but

to me that is short sighted, care given to one is care given to all and thus all will benefit.'

Michael nodded his agreement and then he looked around him. They were high up in the mountains here, and the air was thin and piercingly cold, frost hung around his face clinging to his breath as it seeped from his mouth. There was a layer of cloud some way below where they stood, but the slope here was not steep. They appeared to be heading towards the nearest of a set of three peaks, that rose like cathedral spires high above him, and he could see that they followed a trail that now led between sharp flanges of rock, natural buttresses that reached up to support the towering spikes. A little further on, he saw Sorin standing in a state of deep concentration with the staff of Nuall held out before him. To his right stood Danil, Dak, Rotvee and two other Nare he did not recognise. Beyond them slightly higher up sat the great grey wolf Sylvan, calmly watching the proceedings, but as Kyre had hinted also in commune with members of the other packs. It appeared that their journey was on hold until Sorin had finished this conference with his fellow Majann.

Michael looked once more downwards and he saw that as the cloud shifted in the wind, glimpses of the land below became visible. The slopes of the mountain spread out below them like a torn and crumpled sheet, twisted from a night of disturbed sleep. Snow lay in the folds and if there was vegetation it was out of the compass of his vision. What wasn't, was a line of figures that he spotted, not that much further down the slope, quite obviously tracking their trail.

Kyre had noticed his look of surprise. *'Yes, they are extremely persistent are they not. They have been tracking us for many days. Danil believes them to be the men sent by the Queen to recapture you and to capture Sorin, although that would be an unwise move. But it is strange that they should be quite so diligent in their task. Any normal soldier would have made camp by the three bridges and waited for us to return, for there is no other way off the mountains of the Nare. Jaakhir of the Trillani is shadowing them, but they are a large group, twenty in all and they may still be a problem to us. Jaakhir has also sensed others on the mountain but he cannot yet say who they are, which I find strange.'*

"It would seem either the mountains or ourselves are extremely popular at the moment, Kyre of the Veyix."

At that moment Danil called to him. "Mikael, since you are now once more worth talking to, would you care to join us?"

It appeared that Sorin had completed his discussions and he needed to impart the news to them all. He moved to join the group, Kyre stayed where he and stared down into the clouds below.

Sorin looked pensive, but he gave Michael a brief smile as he approached. "Ah, you have returned, that is well timed, for matters move on at a swifter pace than I had anticipated. The traitor Faradon has now gathered all his force and he seeks to drive Leenal and his armies back towards the lowlands. His army is strong and outnumbers Leenal maybe four to one or more. Some of the Lords of the Cluath seeking to protect their homelands have reneged upon their oaths and sent fewer men than they should or in one case none at all. I fear that they will rue that decision should Leenal prevail. Leenal has crossed the great river to face the enemy, with as much support as has available. The battle that approaches may be the conclusive one, or it may not, it is hard to tell, but Leenal has had second thoughts about reliance solely upon Piat Kahord and he has sent word in secret via Master Vitta that he requires my aid. I cannot refuse him even though he deserves a curt response, the lives of many may depend upon my presence." He looked up at Michael half expecting him to plead with him to stay, but Michael had long suspected that he would be alone with his thoughts when the choice must be made and so he set Sorin's mind at rest.

"You must do what is needed, Sorin, as you always have."

Sorin was pleasantly surprised and he showed it in his eyes, although he said nothing directly. "Very true, Mikael. To this end, Vitta has dispatched our two friendly Valeen to transport Danil and I to the field of battle. It would seem that the Antaldi have taken stock of their situation, or they have been prevailed

upon by higher powers, and have sent bowmen to Leenal's aid."
Sorin paused for a moment as if to enhance the final part of his
message. "The Triad have even requested that Danil lead them."

Danil laughed out loud. "Have the old Triad died and been replaced, that they should so quickly be swayed from loathing to trust?"

"No, Danil, but I think that Blessed Yvelle has taken a shine
to you after Suani's efforts and you are at least now in favour. Do
your best to keep it that way."

Danil bowed low. "Of course, Master Sorin, I shall be most
careful."

Michael was pleased for his friend but knew now that he was
being robbed of all support save for Dak. His mind turned for
a moment to Ayan and Greer. "What of the Frinakim, Sorin,
are they now riding with the King?"

Sorin shook his head. "Not yet, though Teldak has them
guarding the armies' flanks regardless of any direct orders and
the groups of riders harry the enemy where they can, ensuring
that there can be no move made that is hidden or secret. The
Frinakim will play their part despite Grald's long held grudge."

"When will the flyers reach us?"

"Within the hour I suspect. Vitta, had already sent them as
close he could without appearing to overreach the authority of
the Triad."

A thought struck Michael. "What if that group of Queen's
men reach us before we have found what we are looking for?
Kyre said that there are twenty of them."

Here Rotvee spoke up. "Only twenty? Then they will be of
little consequence since we have you and Dak with us, Mikael
Dal Oaken. I have heard all about your exploits in battle."

"Maybe you have Rotvee Bramkilik, but I fear that Dakveen
has a tendency to exaggerate. And my point is still valid Sorin."

"It is, Mikael, and I had not forgotten them, which is why
we should be moving. There is little of the journey left if Kyre's
information is correct. The source of the green crystal lies in a
chamber not half a day's climb further on. As for our pursuers,
I am putting my mind to the problem as we speak."

Behind Sorin Sylvan suddenly leaped into a standing position and let forth a long low howl. Everyone turned to look where she was facing, but there was no sign of any intruder. The great wolf then faced them all and she bowed her strong and noble head. Michael heard her words inside his mind, which surprised him.

'Sorin still holds the Staff of Nuall, Michael that is also Mikael, so I can speak through him to you. The time is upon you, Michael, Ender of Days. The Packs have chosen and the Dri will lead the other packs to the aid of the free races of Taleth. We have chosen, Twice-Born, Twice-Dead, and although some may meet an end that they did not look to have, we will no longer stand by and let Corruption drain the life blood from Taleth. Fear not the darkness for now is the time for strength.'

And then as she raced away through the snow, he heard the chanting begin, it was as if he heard a multitude of voices through her, the old song had new lines.

'In honour of the One we become the Pack.
In honour of the One we walk upon the earth.
In love of life we will serve.
In love of life we will ward.
In love of life we will guide.
In love of life we will fight.
In love of life we will prevail.
In soul we are the Avali, in name we are the Dri.
In soul we are the Avali, in name we are the Aurian.
In soul we are the Avali, in name we are the Raell.
In soul we are the Avali, in name we are the Trillani.
In soul we are the Avali, in name we are the Linath.
In soul we are the Avali, in name we are the Nemett.
In soul we are the Avali, in name we are the Veyix.
In soul we are the Avali, in commune we shall be The Pack.'

Michael turned to Sorin, who looked almost triumphant. "They have decided to enter the fight?"

"So, it would appear, and the Cluath and the Antaldi who face Faradon will be glad of them. I never held with their vows of peaceful non-interference anyway, but when the Corruptor moved to attack the Dri it was such a desecration of the ancient laws that they have cast aside all vows, save those to the One and their duty to protect. About time I might add. Now we must be moving."

As he turned away Dak came forward and he slapped Michael hard on the shoulder. "I thought that you were never going to return my friend, three days you have been gone. I have still to properly show my thanks for what you did in the chamber of the Mrauuk. Let me introduce these two before we proceed further, this is Hakard Shiveer, son of Krall, son of Vikalik, nephew to Bruak and this is Kodeet Fraleket, son of Hashett, son of Vargat. They were chosen to represent the other Houses on this search." The young Nare each bowed in turn. "Now we apparently are nearing the end of our search and that is good for we have been too long about it, and we have yet to return, although we may be able to move more swiftly on our way down the mountain."

"Not too swiftly, Dak, we are very high up."

"Indeed, we are my friend, indeed we are." He laughed as he led the others away to follow Sorin and Danil.

Their journey through the snow was not as difficult as Michael would have thought because the snow was quite solid under foot and the incline was gentle, for they had crested the main rise and approached the cathedral spires that lay ahead. They had been walking for maybe an hour and a half when shadows passed across the snow in front of them and the two Valeen swept down to land on the crisp snow. Laniaal stepped forward to hail them.

"Greetings Master Sorin, well met again. And you Mikael Dal Oaken, Fah Devin sends her good wishes, she is recovering well and bids you remember your promise to visit her. Danil that is called Lebreven you are much spoken of these days among the Antaldi, it is good to see you again. How fares your cousin, we were told she was badly wounded."

"Greetings, Laniaal and you Thinvere. She is recovering her strength, but she would have died underground but for the courage of master Dal Oaken here, it was he who carried her out of the deep tunnels."

"Ah, that is a story we must hear, when time is free for tales and these days of struggle are done. Are we to set off immediately Master Sorin?"

"That is up to you, Laniaal, you are the one doing the flying. Are you not tired?"

"Yes, a little, my friend, but perhaps you do not understand the nuances of flight enough to realise that rising to this height was largely a matter of using the rising currents of air as you may have seen the birds do. And as for going down, from this height we could glide half the way to Tath Garnir on a single wing beat. So, we can leave at once, if that is your wish."

Sorin was about to answer and then he stopped as if listening. His brow furrowed and his face grew grim and dark. "Yes, I am afraid it must be, Sylvan has sent word, brief but to the point. Piat Kahord has vanished and Faradon has begun his march to the river, with many more Tsarg at his command than we could possibly have suspected. Battle now is inevitable."

"Then come, treachery must be responded to with defiance and courage." He handed Sorin the harness that they had used before. Thinvere gave a similar one to Danil and as they prepared Sorin spoke rapidly and with little of his usual humour.

"Mikael take this stone key and find the door that it opens, your destiny lies behind that door and perhaps that of all of Taleth. Do not let the fact that you are robbed of your friends at this moment influence you; you will never be alone for we are with you in spirit, just as we know, that you would ride with us into battle if you had the chance. Find the source of the crystal and save the Nare if you can, that is your task. There may still be dangers ahead, but you have grown strong and now is a time for strength. Remember, the First Promise.

'Where there is Life – there is Love.
Where there is Love – there is Hope.
Where there is Hope – there is a Future.'

Michael completed it for him.

'Where there is a Future – there is Life.
Where there is Life – there is Love.'

"I remember, Sorin, do not worry. You go, you are needed." He turned to Danil. "May your arrows fly true, my friend, I would have fought with you again, but you must strike for us both."

Danil shook his arm warmly and then he spoke quietly so that only Michael could hear. "Take care, Michael, for all that you had no choice in being drawn into our battles you are a man I am proud to call friend." Michael felt the emotion in his words, and he knew that they came from his heart. "I will give our fair captain your regards, should we meet this side of death." This required no answer Michael could give in words and he simply nodded.

Danil then turned to Dak. "Dakveen Halak, son of Thark, son of Varkind, son of Bakund, I wish you a long life and all that you desire from this world. Though our friendship has been short I believe you to be as true a soul as any I have met." Dak responded with a bow. "Now come, Valeen of the Antaldi, and grasp well, for I think should you drop us we will still be falling when the sun rises tomorrow."

Dak raised his arm in salute and farewell as Laniaal and Thinvere took to the air with their burdens, rising only a little way before plunging out of sight in a long gliding dive. Rotvee turned to Dak and Michael.

"Well, it is up to us to complete this quest, then."

Michael agreed. "It is, and we must move before the Queen's men reach us for we are now a much-depleted force."

"True enough, Mikael, but Sorin felt that we were close to our goal. He seemed to think that you know where we are heading, is that true."

Michael felt that he could not reveal all that he knew of their destination. "I have dreamed of this place Dak, but that dream may have been sent to misguide us, so we must be on our guard."

Kyre chose that moment to stroll back from further up the slope. *'I think we have reached the path to the door, Michael that is also Mikael. There are steps under the snow, and they lead into the mountain.'*

Michael answered out loud so that the others could hear. "Excellent, Kyre! We have reached a path into the mountain; my friends it appears we are here at last."

For the first time Hakard Shiveer spoke. "What exactly are we expecting to find at the end of this path?"

Michael looked at Hakard, there was something about the way he asked this question that made him uneasy. "I will try and explain as we walk." They started to follow the white wolf of the Veyix who paced slowly a little way ahead. "It is my belief that within the mountain we will find a secret known only to the First Ones, the resting place of many remnants and artefacts of the ancient days when Taleth was young. The First Ones have guarded them throughout the years that have passed and it if from this place that the goblet of green crystal came. It is also my belief that we will find more of that green crystal inside."

"Then we only have to find it and take it back with us?" Again, his tone set Michael on edge.

"I do not think it will be that simple, Hakard Shiveer, son of Krark, for there may be First Ones who still guard the entrance or the chamber within."

"What of them, our need is clear, should they seek to delay us we will take what we need." His words displayed arrogance and ignorance in equal measure, but Michael was spared from answering by Kodeet who turned to his fellow Nare with a look of disgust etched clearly upon his face.

"Would you take what is not freely given, Hakard Shiveer, viak Krark, and lower yourself to the level of thief and brigand? That would be a poor way to save our people."

335

Hakard snapped back, barely hiding his contempt. "I would do what must be done, Kodeet Fraleket, viak Hashett. Our task is to secure the safety of the Nare, release them from this curse, I will do whatever is needful to attain that end."

"Then you are indeed a fool, Hakard Shiveer, viak Krark, for, when life is done, and we are judged, it is by our deeds that we shall be known, and an unworthy deed is a stain that we would surely never wash from our hearts."

Hakard sneered at him, much as Bruak had done in the Mrauuk. "You are like most of your House Kodeet Fraleket, a sanctimonious idealist, who deserves to be wiped out by the plague."

Kodeet kept calm in the face of his insults. "And you, like most of your House, are ignorant and rude, Hakard Shiveer."

"I am a realist, Kodeet Fraleket, and I place duty and survival above sentimentality and dubious morality."

Dak had kept quiet during this exchange, but now he turned to Hakard and his face was as stony as the rocks which rose beside them. "You will guided by me in your actions, Hakard Shiveer, viak Krark, and should we meet anyone within these mountains, whatsoever their race you will show them all respect and courtesy. You are here because I requested it; do not make me regret that decision."

There was a tense few moments as Hakard glared at Dak, but eventually he dropped his eyes and he accepted Dak's declaration. "Very well, Dakveen Halak, son of Thark, son of Varkind. I will be guided by you."

They had reached a point in the path where the snow thinned, the overhanging rocks offering some shelter from the elements. Here the steps were visible to all. It was not quite a cave, because some snow had breached the rocks, nor was it dark, for enough light penetrated from above to allow them to see. They moved forward more slowly now, feeling that they were approaching the conclusion of their journey.

Michael knew that there were First Ones inside the chamber, for he had seen them in his dream. What he did not expect was their way to be blocked before they reached it. It was blocked. By Uxl of the Tarr.

***

Sylvan ran through the rocks and the crags at the base of the mountains, deftly avoiding shale and crevices, calling constantly ahead to draw the packs together. Once she had made the crossing of the bridges, she would join with those of the Trillani who had been chosen to race to the battle. They would make for the gap in the mountains which poured the Heran out on to the plains, there it was possible for a strong wolf to leap from boulder to boulder across the crashing water as it churned and tumbled over the falls. From there they could race down the edge of the range that rose to the mighty peak of Fellas and seek to join the forces of the Frinakim that fought to keep the northern flank of the army safe. It was a journey that might take men on even the swiftest Piradi three days; they hoped to reach them around noon of the following day. For they would not ease their pace, nor stop for rest; they would draw strength from the eternity that was their spirit. They had chosen to fight, despite voices that counselled still for the ways of observance, but Sylvan knew that they had made the right choice. For she was certain that in her heart she would have known, even now as it pounded to keep this wolf body racing through the shadows, if she had chosen the wrong path.

She sang as she ran, an eerie sound for any that had ears to hear, raising wolf song to the sky and hearing echoing calls around her. The Trillani were waiting and she did not slow her pace as they parted to allow her to cross the bridge, bounding after her with howls that echoed high amongst the jagged peaks and rang in the chambers of the seven cities of the Nare. The wolves of Taleth were racing to war against all history and tradition; they would make Corruption pay for the rending of the Dri and the sundering of the Veyix.

Sylvan sang again the names of the dead. *'Karlynn; Bryelle; Friesse; Nilus; Tiriel; Uvan; Balior; Huinshi.'* And she added those others who had died at Corruptions hand, *'Tharive; Lonett; Brothers and Sisters, kin and blood!'* The names were

337

drummed into the soil of Taleth as she ran, her paws pounding the earth. Shadows appeared to her left as the members of the Nemett, who had shadowed Michael and the others, returned from the mountains edge, but their pace did not slacken, their purpose did not waver.

A group of foresters felt the pounding through their thick boots and looking up through the trees they saw the racing wave of wolves sweeping towards them. They fled in terror before this onslaught and hurried to bar doors and windows spreading tales of thousands of giant wolves attacking the Cluath lands and killing all who stood in their way. It mattered little for none would have dared stand in the face of this assault and the wolves heeded them not. Hearing the rushing waters of the Heran they redoubled their speed and sought the crossing of the falls. Taleth had never seen the like of this army nor heard the anger and the sadness in the song that followed its passage.

★★★

16

Upon the Mountain Top

Michael bowed in greeting to the ancient being. "Greetings Uxl of the Tarr, it is good to see you once more, although it is a meeting I did not expect."

Uxl bowed in turn. "Greetings, Mikael, I found my path returned me to this place, for it would appear that all truths lead us back to our beginnings." He then bowed respectfully to Kyre. "Greetings, Kyre of the Veyix, it is good to see one of your kind here in this ancient place." He then turned to the four Nare, and he greeted them in their own tongue. "Tavish, viakirirm onak Nare, Kumil ta Ragarad."

Rotvee and the two younger Nare were astounded to hear this being that had been drawn in their childhood tales as a simple slow creature, speaking their own language with such ease; Dak's mind held little of their prejudice and ignorance. "Kumil ta Ragarad, Uxl of the Tarr, I am Dakveen Halak, viak Thark, viak Varkind, these others are Rotvee Bramkilik, velak Nakeket, viak Hriok, Kodeet Fraleket, viak Hashett, viak Vargat and Hakard Shiveer, viak Krark, viak Vikalik. Mikael has spoken of you and told us something of your long journey."

"Indeed, it has been long, Master Nare, maybe even longer than the lines of your Houses, that you love to recount." There was no judgement only gentle humour in his voice. "I have no line, before or after me, I am just Uxl and Uxl is what I am. My truth has taken me from the first days to here and here I am, guardian of the door that lies behind me. A door that is opened by a key, a key that I gave to Sorin of the Cave. What has become of it, Mikael? Does he still have it?"

"No, Uxl, he gave it to my keeping before he was carried away to answer the summons of the High King." Michael reached into his belt and he took out the stone key. As he did so he remembered the crystal memory shard that Ayx gave him.

"Ah, so Sorin has gone? And now you would enter the Ruok Vuall, the Place of the First Ones, in his stead?"

"That is our wish, Uxl of the Tarr. Is that something that your truth will not allow?"

Uxl was silent for a while, then he looked around at the group. "Kyre, as a wolf of the Veyix, may come and go as he pleases, but for others to enter I must have knowledge of what it truly is that they seek. For it is an ancient sacred place, holding many secrets and many truths that were given into our trust at the beginning; should I open this to any who make the journey to this place? I do not think so, although I am only a Tarr and not one of the newer races, and I am old, as old as the steps that you have climbed, I have considered much in my solitude and I know that hasty decisions are often the cause of much regret."

Michael saw that Kodeet was about to make some comment and he suspected that it would be less than useful, so he replied to Uxl's philosophising. "Uxl of the Tarr, you have journeyed long and seen many things from the wonders of the early days to the strife of the first war against Corruption. You helped sing the trees to grow and the waters to flow, you have walked paths that none of us have seen or can hope to see and we respect your wisdom and your truth but enter we must. For within is surely the culmination of my journey and my truth has led me to this door. I would ask you to trust me and to allow me entrance, not just in my name, but in the name of Ayx of the Tarr, your brother, who dying gave into my hands this memory shard that he wished me to deliver to you should we meet." Michael held out the crystal shard and he saw a change in the face of the Tarr.

He reached out to take it with steady hand, but his voice held more emotion than they had yet heard. "It is as I feared, Ayx is dead. I could no longer hear his song in my head, and I heard only pain and sadness." As his fingers closed upon the shard of crystal it began to glow and the voice of Ayx rang out against the rocky walls.

'From the beginning, I am Ayx of the Tarr, I have walked amongst the newly grown mountains and watched the rivers spring forth for the first time. I have sat beneath the first trees and sung with them of leaf and blossoms yet to come. I have caressed the rocks and breathed the smell of the soil. I saw the five races step from the hands of the Powers and receive life from the One, I heard the new songs that gave them language and gave them names. I felt the ground rumble with the anger of Khargahar in his prison and I heard his treacherous lies as he sent Corruption out to poison all life. I have heard the agony of the First Ones of Fire, trapped still in his cavern underground, where he draws out their eternity of pain and twists them into forms of life that mock even their own existence, longing for death, but knowing no such release; endless punishment, endless agony, as the children he spawns from them are slaughtered and their blood stains the soul of Taleth forever.'

Michael was stunned by these words, breathlessly uttered by the disembodied voice. He knew that the First Ones of Fire had been drawn into Corruption's schemes and had somehow become the Tsarg that he had seen and fought, but he had never before considered the truth of their becoming. That there still existed some of the very first beings, like Uxl and Ayx, imprisoned by Khargahar beneath Fellas, and that somehow, he had spawned from them in some awful mockery of birth, the entire Tsarg race, spawned them simply to die upon the swords and spears of the Cluath or the axes of the Nare. He had seen the terror in the eyes of the Tsarg as he had faced them in battle, but now he realised that their whole existence was filled with an agony grown from the warped and twisted manner of their beginning. He wondered if they might somehow be rescued from their torment, although he suspected that would mean ending their suffering forever.

'I have travelled the deserts and explored the dark places beneath the mountains; I have paced the ice fields and stood upon the shores of the ocean. In the marshes and swamps I have watched the growth of giant plants and the scurrying of tiny insects. I have seen so much of Taleth and yet I know that there is so much more to see. Poison has ended my days, poison born in Corruption, poison has filled my body with a fire

that drains my strength. These words I bind within this crystal for my brother, my kin, Uxl, should he still walk the paths of truth. I give it to Mikael Dal Oaken, for he has eased my ending and he will honour my bones with fire at the end. He is a man of truth and honour and I urge you give him your trust, my brother, for although I know not his truth, I sense that it is of import for us all. He has that about him that is Taleth, whole and entire, but he is also not Taleth in any way. But this should not be feared for also I sense the Powers in him, he speaks as one whom the Powers have named friend and we are all but servants of the Powers when all that is true is ended. Give him your trust, my brother, and remember me in song when a time comes again for singing.'

The echoes of Ayx's voice rang around them and none sought to break the silence that settled after they had finally drifted away. Michael watched Uxl as he held the crystal and he turned it over in his fingers, there was no change in his expression, but he was obviously moved by the dying words of Ayx and was pondering what had been said very carefully. Eventually he spoke.

"I had not thought to be using this key save with Sorin at my side, and it was to this end that I gave him the key, in case my bones would not carry me to this place once more. But now he is not here, and we must make decisions without his wise words. You have come to this place, Mikael Dal Oaken, driven by circumstance and purposes that have not been entirely your own, that much I can tell, but for some reason I can see nothing beyond that will give me aid and so I will heed my brother's wish and trust you and the Powers' faith in you. We will use the key to give you entrance. Come."

Michael was relieved, for he knew that they would have been left sitting on the doorstep with no thought of what to do had he refused. "I thank you, Uxl of the Tarr, and I will try to honour your trust in all that I do." He handed the stone key to Uxl, but as he did so he heard voices behind him, and he spun round to see that their pursuers had finally caught up with them.

There were twenty of them, all clad in the livery of the King's guard, but it was not this that sent a shock wave through Michael that left him momentarily stunned. The man at the front of the party, the obvious leader of the group was Mr. Perkins, or some trick had produced his twin. He looked oddly misplaced in the armour of a warrior, but his screeching voice could not be mistaken,

"Stand traitors! Submit to the justice of the King. Your lives are forfeit for crimes against his person, surrender or you will not leave this mountain alive. I am Jarrad Ranell, cousin to the Queen, and I speak with her full authority as regent in the King's absence."

Dak had already drawn his axe, along with the Kodeet and Rotvee, Hakard held a short sword and a curved dagger. "I care not who you are, nor to whom you are related, you shall not hinder us Cluath. You are far from Tath Garnir and in the lands of the Nare and I say with the full authority of the Mrauuk that should you take one step further your lives are forfeit to me and I shall cast you down the mountain to smash your worthless bones upon the rocks below."

Michael shook himself from his stupor and he drew his own weapon. "The Queen must really have taken a shine to me, Jarrad Ranell, that you come all this way to retrieve one poor prisoner. Or is your purpose other than you have stated and you seek to prevent me from completing my journey?"

Jarrad Ranell, or Mr. Perkins, was not to be cowed by words. "The Queen would have slain you in an instant, and cast you from the walls of the city, but the King ordered that your life be spared. Merely a stay of execution, plainsman, not a pardon, your death is certain, as will be that of your companions if you will not submit."

Dak laughed at this. "Tell me, Cluath, how do you then intend to leave this mountain? You can only leave the mountains of the Nare via the three bridges and do you think they will be unguarded?"

Jarrad sneered. "We are here, Nare, and there were none to stop us on the bridges when we crossed."

Michael knew that Dak was bluffing, but he suspected that the Trillani might become involved if necessity required. "Ah, crossing this way is easy, Cluath, but leaving without permission is something completely different."

Jarrad's voice reached an even higher pitch. "Enough of this. Where is Sorin of the Cave? We must take him too."

'Ah,' thought Michael, *'now we see the plan. Sorin was to be captured and taken back, preventing Leenal from receiving assistance. Is this then some plot of the Queen to take power herself?'* Openly he spoke only of Sorin, but he knew that there was more to this than simple pursuit. "Sorin is not here, Jarrad Ranell."

Now Jarrad looked discomfited, he had been sent to secure both Mikael and the Majann and things were going wrong. "How? We came behind along the only trail, he has not passed us. What trickery is this?"

It was Rotvee who answered. "Know you not, Cluath, that we of the Nare are partial to the taste of flesh? It comes from our long isolation in the mountains. We see no point in keeping prisoners and so Cluath miscreants who stray into our lands are roasted, it saves feeding them. And if we are really hungry even an old Majann will seem tasty."

Despite the obvious nonsense of this reply, it was clear that prejudice and the mistrust of the Nare went deep in the Cluath psyche for every man of the party took a small step back at these words. But Jarrad Ranell was beside himself with rage. "Your jesting will amuse you less when you lie bleeding in the snow, Nare. Where is Sorin? Tell me, now!"

Michael knew that eventually this would come to a fight and he tried to assess the situation. He was not sure that Uxl would even defend himself, although he was clearly strong enough to deal with several of the guardsmen should he chose to do so. He knew that he and Dak were experienced fighters but did not know whether the other Nare had ever faced real combat, he suspected not. He realised that Kyre was nowhere to be seen but he hoped that he was aware of what was going on.

"Sorin has gone, Jarrad Ranell, taken to the battle that you wish to keep him from by an Antaldi Valeen, who as you know can fly and thus evade your pursuit with consummate ease."

The effect this had on Jarrad was peculiar, he was clearly seething with rage, but he also showed signs of fear, this was a mission that was not supposed to fail. His agitation spread to the men under his command. They had expected an easy capture perhaps, but now it looked as if they were going to have to fight and then find a way of escaping the wrath of the flesh-eating Nare. They had spread out into an arc and one of them on Michael's left was getting very twitchy.

"What are we waiting for, Captain? There are twenty of us, let us kill them quickly and get off this cursed rock."

Dak turned to face the speaker. "Come on then, friend, if you seek death, I can help you find him."

"It is your filthy Nare blood that shall be spilled. Your kind are good for nothing more than mending carts and stoking fires."

"And yours are good for nothing at all, Cluath, for they fight like rutting skarl and rut like durg!"

This insult was too much for the guardsman and he rushed at Dak, who met his charge with a blow that toppled his assailant to the floor splitting his armour and spilling blood across the rocks at their feet. Two others chose to follow their comrade, but Rotvee leaped across their path and a severed head went spinning into the snow beyond the rocks, the other met much the same fate as the first, but as he fell something happened that caused all to stand frozen where they stood.

While Dak had been positioning himself to take his swing at the second guardsman Hakard had stepped behind him and as the slain Cluath fell to the floor he drove a dagger deep into Dak's back. Dak staggered forward and fell into the arms of Rotvee whose face had drained of blood. Hakard stepped back and he spat out a phrase that Michael had heard before.

"Hemmek gruath na taketek carukkit!" *'An outcast's life is hardly worth saving!'* "Die, traitor, none insult the House of Shiveer and go unpunished."

Before Michael could react from the shock of this treachery, Kodeet had turned and swung his axe towards Hakard's neck, but the other Nare was too quick and he ducked beneath the blow, kicking Kodeet back towards Michael. "Come on then, Fraleket, if you think you can take me. I doubt it, for your House are not known for their skill at arms, or at anything else for that matter."

"Ka arak ta garek, Hakard. Your crime is beyond all comprehension, your name shall be struck from the lists as shall your House."

The group of guardsmen stared in fascination at the scene that unfolded before them. None of them were going to interfere for Rotvee still held her axe that dripped with Cluath blood, although her attention was focussed on Dak who lay silent in her arms. The two Nare circled each other thrusting and feinting seeking a moment to draw a move from their opponent that would give them an opening. Michael stood undecided, he wanted to sink his axe into Hakard's treacherous heart, but he feared that if he missed a decisive blow then Kodeet would be in danger. He need not have worried, Kodeet for all his lack of real combat had been trained and he knew that his axe was the superior weapon; he was also lighter and quicker than Hakard. He had begun to force Hakard back towards the bodies of the three Cluath soldiers and when Hakard missed his footing in the blood that streamed from the fallen guardsmen, he struck slicing through Hakard's neck in a clean blow. The body sank to the floor, adding to the red that stained the rocks.

"So, die all traitors!"

He was about to turn to Dak and Rotvee when Jarrad Ranell awoke from the trance that had taken them all. "You are the traitors, Nare, and now that you have completed half our task, we will finish the job. Take them!"

The guardsmen did not get a chance to respond for then it was that Kyre reappeared. He had sprung from the shadows of the rock and he stood poised in front of Jarrad Ranell, his face now looking exactly as Mr. Perkins had looked in the garden in Glastonbury under the moon.

Michael heard the terror in his voice as he urged the men on. "What are you waiting for? Kill the beast!"

But none were brave enough to approach the huge wolf and Jarrad's state went from terror to frenzy. "Kill it! Kill them! We must not fail in this!" Still no-one moved, each seeking to protect his own skin, none wishing to become part of the pile of bodies. As the standoff continued, the air around them began to glow and shimmer and then beside Jarrad a figure began to appear, the figure of a woman with crimson hair. It was Takden.

"Why have you not completed your task, Jarrad? You swore to me that this time you would not fail."

Jarrad squirmed where he stood. "He is protected, Mistress, see, the wolf shields him as it has done before."

Michael's mind, still shook from the dagger thrust that had felled Dak, but he was making connections and answering questions. Mr. Perkins was a servant of Takden, not Khargahar, it was she who had been scheming all along, to prevent his arrival on this mountain top.

"Fool and weakling! The wolf will not stand in your way, they are sworn to assist and advise, not fight their wars for them."

Michael found his voice at last. "That is where you are mistaken, lady, the packs are at this moment racing to battle. I feel that Kyre may well take the same attitude towards your slave Ranell here."

"Silence! You should be dead already; I will deal with you myself if I have to." She raised her hand as if to strike Michael with it, but another voice rang out around them.

"You shall not interfere here in my mountains, Sister. I forbid you. You have your secret children, go back to them." It was the booming voice of Ragarad.

"No! Ragarad, I shall strike this abomination down and end this farce. You shall not stop me." She raised her hand again, but the blow did not fall, for Ragarad spoke again and there was no restraint this time his voice shook the rocks.

"I shall stop you, Takden. You have not grown as powerful as you think that you can outface me here in my domain. Go, before I become angry."

There was a crack and Takden vanished, along with Jarrad Ranell. This left the guardsmen leaderless, but they were no cowards, they did not run, and the stand-off remained. There was no sound save for a rasping of breath that came from the stricken Dak. Michael was not sure what the men had seen or heard of the discourse between Takden and Ragarad, as they seemed focused on the jaws of Kyre and Kodeet's axe. Michael decided to try diplomacy.

"Men of Tath Garnir, this is a hopeless situation, for you, but not for me and my companions. If you leave now, I will try and prevail upon the Nare to let you return across the bridges unscathed. If you seek to fight us, you will all die, for even should you defeat us, the revenge of the Nare will be swift. Surely you can see that flight is the only option."

There was a moment when this was considered, but it was dispelled when a burly figure in the centre of the arc, who had obviously assumed command, replied with defiance.

"You are wrong, traitor. We are men of Tath Garnir, and we will kill you in revenge for our fallen comrades and then we will return across the bridges casting any Nare who oppose us into the gorge below. You cannot frighten us with a pet wolf and trick voices in the air; we are Cluath, the sternest and most loyal of all the races and we will not falter." There were murmurs of agreement from the others.

A voice behind them made them all fall silent. "They are certainly the most conceited of all the races, but no more will die here today." As the voice spoke a mist rose around the feet of the guardsmen and one by one, they fell to the ground in a deep sleep. The voice belonged to a hooded figure who now stepped into the open. It was Siraal and she was not alone, a woman was with her also hooded, but her clothes were patched and torn, apart from the cloak that was identical to the one which Siraal wore.

Michael had to shake himself from the shock of seeing her here, but he first stooped to Rotvee's side, Dak lay in her arms, there was little sound of breathing now and his eyes were closed.

Instinctively Michael took his hand and Dak's eyes opened, his voice was faint, and it was obvious that the end was near.

"Mikael, this is a sorry end, to climb so high and fall at the last step. I would have liked to stand beside you in battle once more, but it is not to be." For a moment his eyes closed, but then they re-opened. "Save my people, Mikael Dal Oaken, son of Halkgar, friend of the Nare and honoured member of my House. Save my people."

"I shall, Dakveen, do not worry, we shall not fail."

"Good, because I would hate to have to come back and haunt you all until you did." He turned his eyes to Rotvee. "Rotvee Bramkilik, velak Nakeket, viak Hriok, I name you to the Mrauuk in my place, I would have stood as your husband before all the Nare and blessed the day, but now you must be strong and lead our people out of ignorance. Do not mourn me, but do not forget me."

Rotvee's voice shook with emotion as she replied, and the tears fell across Dak's face. "Dakveen Halak, viak Thark, viak Varkind, I would have stood as your wife before all the Nare and blessed every day of my life, but I will lead our people if they will let me. And I will mourn you in my soul every second of every day and I will rejoice that I knew you for even this short time."

A smile broke on Dak's lips. "Good, that is good." Then his eyes closed, and his heart stopped. And there was silence on the mountain.

After what seemed an age of sadness, Kyre let forth a howling cry.

'The Trillani will know of this treachery and the Mrauuk will be told, Michael that is also Mikael, as will Sorin should the opportunity arise. But now we must move on for night approaches and with it the cold. The bodies of these men can be left to the carrion birds to remove, but what of the traitor Hakard Shiveer?'

Michael knew that there should be more time for grief, but he felt the urgency of the chill in the air and he stood and addressed Rotvee and Kodeet. "The body of Dakveen we will bear with us in honour into the mountain and set his soul beneath stone as is the tradition, but what do we do with Hakard Shiveer?"

Rotvee looked up, her face still wet with tears. "Cast his remains from the mountain, if Ragarad decrees he will find his place in the rocks, if not then he will be washed away in the river and his treacherous soul will be condemned to wander forever."

Kodeet agreed. "A fitting solution, Rotvee Bramkilik, ve-lak Nakeket. And I think that the Cluath should join him let the birds feast away from us at least."

So it was that the bodies were thrown out from the path to disappear out of sight below them, save for the head that Rotvee had severed which could not be found. It was then that Siraal, who had hung back while they had spoken with the dying Dakveen came forward,

"Let your companion be wrapped in one of my cloaks, my friends, it is of good cloth and worthy as a shroud for one of status."

Rotvee had not taken note of Siraal until now and she was surprised by her offer. "Thank you, but I do not know you, lady."

Siraal removed her hood, Michael saw once again her beautiful features and her strange blind eyes. "I am the Hooded Seer of Tath Garnir and I have followed these men who sought you since they were tasked by the Queen with your capture, but I did not know of Takden's involvement until now, although I have had much advice from other quarters, they chose to conceal that information, if indeed they knew it."

"Welcome, Seer, it is a sad sight that greets you, although I should thank you for your aid."

"It is but a simple trick and they will awake before they freeze, but had I known of the treacherous intent that lurked within the mind of your companion I would have acted sooner."

"It is a thing which cannot be undone, and my heart is sore, but had I known I would have split his skull to spill his thoughts long ago. The offer of the shroud is welcome, but will your companion not be cold?"

"I have another in my pack, not as good quality, but thick and warm. Nurelle give me the cloak and let us dress this fallen warrior."

On a day of shocks Michael might have supposed that he was now ready for anything, but what followed left him breathless and shaking. The woman who removed the hood and cloak was Julia, or rather the face was Julia. The woman was the slave who had pleaded for his help back in Tath Garnir. Now that she stood before him, he could not believe that it was not Julia Sharpe, she was identical, and the poverty of her clothing did nothing to detract from the attraction that Michael had felt in the tea rooms so recently. Nurelle looked at Michael strangely.

"I feel that we have met, master, but I know we have not. Tell me if you know me, for I remember little of what has happened to me."

"I'm sorry, we don't really know each other, but I saw you briefly in Tath Garnir. You asked for my help."

"I'm afraid I don't remember much until the Seer rescued me, master."

Siraal drew Michael aside as the others arranged Dak's body in the cloak. "I found her wandering naked and bleeding in the woods near Tath Garnir her mind almost gone, she had escaped the slavers, but had been captured, beaten and abused by a band of thieves who lurk in those parts to ambush traders' caravans, I'm afraid that I was rather glad when I found their bodies heaped in a pile and burning. I think these guardsmen here were responsible, which is partly why I ended the battle before it began. They are not bad men they are just obeying orders." She drew closer to him and she raised a hand to touch his face. "It is good to feel you close to me again, Mikael, although I know that it is wrong of me, I cannot resist my desires."

Michael felt her body press close against him. "I am glad that you are here too, Siraal, for I am fast running out of companions."

Siraal smiled. "I will be your companion for as long as you wish, Mikael, whether my calling forbids it or no."

Michael let his mind rest for a moment upon the sweet breath of Siraal, before he allowed reality to return. "Come we must enter the mountain, before the night closes in."

"Very well, but I will be close by, Mikael, remember that." With that she replaced her hood.

Together Michael, Kodeet, Rotvee and Nurelle lifted the body of Dakveen Halak upon their shoulders and they turned towards Uxl of the Tarr. He had remained impassive throughout as if these events did not concern him, but now he bowed low.

"So, passes Dakveen Halak, son of Thark, son of Varkind, son of Bakund, Nare of the mountains. Kyre has spoken to me of his life and he was worthy of entrance into the place of the First Ones. Come we will find rock to mark his grave." With a nod to Siraal he added. "A Seer is also worthy if they are true to their path." She bowed in thanks, which brought a smile from the Tarr.

Uxl turned and he led them along a tunnel which sloped gently downwards inside the mountain summit. Its roof was high and the sides smooth, the floor was paved with great slabs of dark rock which sparkled with lines of ore and fragments of gemstones. After a short walk, they reached a pair of doors which looked to be of similar rock to the tunnel floor. They were plain save for a round indentation high in the right-hand door. Uxl reached up and he pressed the stone key into this keyhole and the doors began to swing open, smoothly and silently.

"This is the first of the five doors; it is plain for it faces the outside world and thus has a stone key. There are four more doors one for each of the First races and each with its own key, none could enter here without aid from a First One. That was our way of sealing this place from all who might enter, it seemed appropriate even in those innocent days to have a refuge from the whirling wildness of the new races, for whom our ways seemed slow and strange. This next door is the Earth door. It is behind this that we will lay your friend to rest, for he is of the earth and rock."

They passed through the first doors and they found themselves in another tunnel similar to the first, but this one was lit by light from glowing rocks set into the walls and floor. Michael assumed that they were sung into use by the First Ones as the fire rocks were. The tunnel began to curve around and downwards, Michael guessed that the chamber they sought would be beneath them, deeper into the mountain. After a brief walk, they reached the Earth door, which was made of a beautiful grey stone veined like granite. It was decorated with carvings of mountains, smooth rolling hills, and stony deserts, each in turn so detailed as to make you feel that you walked amongst them. There was no discernible keyhole or mechanism, but Uxl reached into the pouch that hung from his belt and he drew from it a handful of earth, this he tossed high upon the face of the door. The earth did not fall, it became part of the door, appearing to fall as a cloud of dust upon the mountains. The door obediently split into two and swung open with equal grace to the first door.

The tunnel inside was again lit by rock light but was wider here and decorated with wonderful carvings, some of the mountains outside and above them. There were images too of the Tarr singing amidst the trees and the rivers of the newly born world, they moved from place to place stroking the rocks to life and weaving the land into an intricate tapestry. Rotvee stood and stared around her.

"This is truly a wondrous chamber, Uxl of the Tarr, and fitting for the tomb of a mighty soul such as Dakveen Halak."

"It is a pleasant place, Rotvee Bramkilik, and it will give his spirit comfort I am sure. Come there are rocks aplenty at the side of the tunnel, they are rocks that we can sing to life should we need them, they will serve us well."

Dak's body was laid upon the tunnel floor near to one wall, and they arranged rocks to form a covering, Uxl then bent low over the rocks and he sang long low notes into the neat pile. When he stopped the others saw that the rocks had fused themselves together into a single stone sarcophagus, upon which were runes, the ancient writing of the early Nare, they read, *'Here lies Dakveen Halak, son of Thark, son of Varkind, son of Bakund, the Outcast who returned to save his people.'*

Rotvee smiled. "My thanks, ancient one; it is a resting place that will give him comfort." She then raised her head and stretching her arms before her she recited the ancestry of Dakveen Halak, as best as she could from what he had told her on their journey. Then laying her hand upon the stone she bade him farewell. "Sleep now, Dakveen, your trials are done, ours I feel are just beginning."

With that they turned to walk to the next door, which again was further along the curving tunnel. These next doors were the Water door. Here the stone was a blue grey and decorated with carvings of springs, fountains, waterfalls, rivers and the mighty ocean. As before, the carving was so subtle and beautiful that the eye followed the curves and twists of the water, flowing, rising in spray and cascading down from the heights. They stood quietly as Uxl stroked the doors with his fingers.

"They are beautiful, are they not? When these were made, we used no tools to cut or scar the rock, the songs that we sang told the stone what water was, and it became as you see. Such was our way in the early days, and yet the Cluath called us names for our patience and calm. The fire that burns in a hasty heart is not always pure, they say."

He opened these doors with a sprinkling of water from a small bottle that he carried in the same pouch. The water was absorbed by the stone, to fall as gentle rain upon the rivers and streams that flowed below. As they entered it was as if they stepped into a secret pool. The rock glowed blue and the walls appeared as rolling waves and flowing rivers. Michael found later that it was hard to recall the feeling within that section of the tunnel for it seemed so magical. Above them the seas and the oceans crashed, around them deep waters lay, shadowy figures swam riding the currents and plunging deep to the ocean floor. They walked in silence through the curving waters to the Fire door.

This door was of glowing dark stone, scarlet in colour, and the designs were of rising flames, so intense were the markings in the stone that it was difficult to persuade yourself that you were not looking into the heart of a roaring blaze. Uxl took a small rock from his pouch and he whispered to it, it began to glow along one side and this glowing edge Uxl drew gently down the centre of the door, which acquiesced to his touch and swung open. They entered this next section expecting to be walking through flames similar to those on the door, but they were surprised to find that, although the rock light was indeed red, across the walls were images of creatures similar to Uxl, though smaller, who stood beside flowing pools of lava, or breathed fire upon rock to reveal liquid metals.

They knelt with their hands deep in the rock, guiding its molten flow, giving it power to shape itself and rise into the mountains. They held aloft smooth stones that blazed with heat and warmth. They danced in the flickering flames of fiery pits, joyously revelling in the flames that licked about them. They were images that sang of life and fierce energy, excitement and expectation, they sang no long slow songs, they sang with the twist of the flames, with the leaping of the fire. *'This is what the First Ones of fire had been like in the beginning,'* Michael thought. *'How sad and terrible that they have become the weapons of such a cruel master.'*

Uxl had paused here before the images of the First Ones of Fire and sadly shook his head. "They sought not the path of slow steady thought, their desire was for the vigour of the fire, the heat of the flame. At first Khargahar helped them, encouraged them to explore the deep roots of the One's new world, but he trapped them when their desire became a need, a lust for the surging thrill of using force, of releasing power. Our brothers were drawn down into his prison and they could not escape. There is not one of us who has not felt their pain, for it is unending."

They continued along the tunnel to the fifth door. Michael recognised the enormity of Uxl's revelation. The First Ones were all linked, Earth, Water, Fire and Air, each could feel and experience the joys and the successes of the others, but they could also feel their pain. A pain that continued, that became ever crueller and more extreme as Corruption drew his perverted children from their beings. He realised with a jolt that the death of every Tsarg who had died under the swords of the Cluath or the arrows of the Antaldi could be felt by the First Ones. His mind reeled when he remembered the painting of the ancient battle, where thousands upon thousands of Tsarg were slaughtered. He wondered if Sorin knew or had Uvarin and the others conveniently avoided this terrifying fact.

The Air door when they reached it, was made of stone as bright and blue as the summer sky, but there was no decoration upon it save a small cloud floating in the centre level with Uxl's head. He pointed to the cloud,

"Only the breath of the First Ones will work upon this lock, for it remembers the old days. But first before we enter you must rest and refresh yourselves. Our walk down into the heart of the mountain will have seemed to you a short one, but that is not the whole truth. Two days have passed since you passed through the first of these doors." Michael was stunned. *'Two days?'* He looked at Uxl, who nodded and continued his explanation. "Yes, Mikael, two days, or nearly so. The path is an old one, very old, and it is so filled with memories that time itself is heavy and slow, for you wade through time itself. Your return will take little time at all, in terms of the outside world. I know it is strange, but this is such an ancient place it must be allowed to make its own rules I think."

It was a strange silent meal, eaten as it was surrounded by the rock as blue as the bluest sky. No-one spoke, for words seemed out of place here. Uxl stood waiting patiently at the door, lost in his own thoughts, humming quietly to himself. When they had finished, he pointed again to the door.

"The memories of rocks are long and clear, they forget nothing. In the breath of the First Ones there is an echo, a memory, a sweet reminder of the breath that the One breathed upon us to give us life in the days of becoming." He leaned close to the door and he breathed upon the cloud. Once more in complete silence, the door swung open, but behind was no longer a tunnel, they had reached the chamber at the heart of the mountain's peak, Ruok Vuall, the Place of the First Ones.

***

Sylvan raced on now, joined by many more of the Dri and a good number of the Raell. They were across the river and now in the forest heading down towards the agreed place of meeting. Their number was growing, and they would be a mighty force, although not the total of any pack, save the Dri who had all chosen to join the battle. She knew their names and their scents well and she had held commune with all as she ran. When they were all met then they would rest and eat, for their bodies were in need of such normal things, even if their immortal spirits needed nothing more than purpose. She was closer to Sorin now and she heard his voice seeking her.

'Well met. Sorin, may your path be blessed within the Unfolding of the One.'

'Sylvan, well met indeed. Strength and honour to the Pack. May the chase run true and the hunting be good.'

'I hope it is, old friend, for we are hungry now as we have not been in a long time.'

'Well, the Cluath herds can spare some meat I am sure. What news from the mountain?'

'It is not good, Sorin, they have been betrayed and Dakveen Halak slain by one of his own.'

Sorin's thoughts registered his shock and his grief.

'This is evil news indeed. But what of Michael and the others.'

'They will enter the mountain, for they have met with Uxl of the Tarr.'

'As Michael feared, he is alone at the moment of choice.'

'He is almost alone, Sorin, for the Hooded Seer has aided them against the Queen's men and is with them still it would seem.'

'Ah, that is intriguing, for she seems guided by more than one of the Powers and her allegiance hidden from all. Still that is good, although the loss of Dakveen is a heavy one to bear.'

'There will be many more deaths today, Sorin, and none can say who will stand when all is done.'

'That is true, Sylvan, the battle will be a bloody one and I feel that it will be upon us soon, darkness will not deter them. Fare you well, old friend, you have chosen well, and you shall avenge the fallen.'

'Strike hard and strong, Sorin who is and Calix who was, now is the time for strength.'

Sorin was gone and Sylvan ran on. She sensed death in the air, and she could smell the fear and the anger that meant Tsarg. They would meet their enemy very soon. But had their enemy looked to be facing the Pack? This she doubted, the Corruptor was very sure of himself, but his planning could not have included a decision that they themselves never thought to make. This gave them a chance to make a difference, and make their efforts tell. She prayed to the One that it would be enough. The hunt had begun, and it was going well, they would eat sparsely and be ready. The voices of the Pack were joining as they reached their goal.

'In honour of the One we become the Pack.
In honour of the One we walk upon the earth.
In love of life we will serve.
In love of life we will ward.
In love of life we will guide.
In love of life we will fight.
In love of life we will prevail.
In soul we are the Avali, in name we are the Dri.
In soul we are the Avali, in name we are the Aurian.
In soul we are the Avali, in name we are the Raell.
In soul we are the Avali, in name we are the Trillani.
In soul we are the Avali, in name we are the Linath.
In soul we are the Avali, in name we are the Nemett.
In soul we are the Avali, in name we are the Veyix.
In soul we are the Avali, in commune we shall be The Pack.'

★★★

17

The Chiatt Crystal

The chamber that stood before them was wide and its curving ceiling reached high above them, it was decorated to resemble the sky above the mountain tops, and it gave them the impression that they stood in the open air. Around the walls were tables and shelves which held objects and scrolls, caskets and jars, each obviously of some special worth or value, for they each had their place, each separated by a respectful distance from the others. But it was towards the centre of the room that their eyes were drawn for this is where a great casket stood. It was higher than a man and double that in length and it was, as Michael knew it would be, made of the dark green crystal that they sought, and just as Michael had dreamed, across it lay the body of a great white wolf. It had not decayed in any way; something in the air of the place had preserved it in an almost mummified state. Around the casket stood four of the Auwinn, the First Ones of Air, and they were exactly as in his dream, shaped like Uxl, but with bodies that appeared as fluid, drifting, it was as if you looked at solid clouds, or clouds at least that had a solid skin to them. They sang in voices that were like ghosts upon the wind, a wordless song that filled the chamber with a vibration more sensation than sound itself. Michael stepped into the chamber and the song stopped. The Auwinn turned to face him with their eyes of swirling cloud.

At first, they ignored Michael, Siraal, Nurelle and the two Nare, as they faced Uxl and bowed slowly to him. They spoke together as if their long vigil together had left them of one mind. "Greetings, Uxl of the Tarr, long have we awaited your return to this place. You have travelled far and seen much since you left us. A thousand lives of the new races do not extend to the time that we have waited, but maybe our song nears its end."

Uxl bowed in reply and there was sadness in his voice when he spoke. "It may be so, my friends, in truth. I give you greetings, Ai, Iol, El and you Olix, last of your kind you are for certain, for none have I sensed in all my journeying. The Shiell, First of Water, I could not find, although I have sensed that they live yet. For the Tarr there are now but three for Ayx has relinquished his spirit. We are few and the old ways are now not remembered save by us and those we sang to, the rocks and the rivers, the trees and the clouds, they remember us, and they call to us, but now we can no longer answer for we fade."

The four nodded. "We felt the passing of Ayx, and we sensed the poison in his veins, but his ending was good and his Truth he passed to you. For the others, we too have sensed the Shiell, but we cannot hear them. Perhaps they are hidden, we can no longer tell. Then our song truly is ending, if we are the last, but still we keep our vigil and our ward."

They then turned to Kyre who had paced silently along behind the others deep in his own thoughts. Now he walked forward and bowed his great head.

"Greetings, Kyre of the Veyix, your kin lies before you, but her spirit has long since fled, she vowed to keep our vigil with us, but no cub came to accept her spirit and her frail body was meant to live only a brief time."

Michael heard Kyre's reply and he felt his sadness. *'Greetings, ancient ones, sadly death amongst the Veyix is not uncommon, for our Pack was broken long ago and commune was no longer possible. Those of us that live are still ready to serve as we have always been. Hayleth would have seen it as her duty to honour your watch, her passing was felt, and her spirit is honoured wherever it wanders. The Lost will never forget their own.'*

The stillness in the air gathered around them like a cloak as the Auwinn contemplated the fate of the lost. Michael felt that even the act of breathing was disrespectful here and he tried to still the sounds of his heart. Eventually the First Ones of Air turned towards him and they addressed him directly.

"And now who has come to this place that we do not know? Two Nare of the mountains, bearing a heavy sadness, a deep hurt, and three Cluath, each different each unusual it would seem. This is a sacred place, an ancient place, it was constructed in the earliest of days, it has listened to songs of many thousands of years and it holds all within its walls, all within its rock and stone. The First Ones, those who still live, could call this home should they have need, for only a First One may gain entrance. Uxl has brought you here and now you must speak and explain why you have come."

Michael felt those strange eyes boring into his soul as he prepared to speak, he knew that he must be politic and slow in his approach for what he was about to do was a momentous and possibly a sacrilegious act. As he drew in his breath to speak, he felt Siraal move to his side and take his hand in hers. She whispered, close and quiet.

"Just begin by introducing us all."

Michael felt her love through his fingers, and he decided to follow her lead.

"Greetings, ancient ones, it is an honour to behold such as yourselves, who have breathed the first air, felt the first sweet breeze. I am Mikael Dal Oaken, son of Halkgar, born upon the plains, raised amidst the green fields and the rolling downs. This woman of Tath Garnir is known to all as the Hooded Seer, interpreter of visions and dreams, advisor to the Queen and a servant to her people. Her companion is a poor woman who has suffered abuse at the hands of brigands, but she remembers little of her past, Nurelle she is called. The Nare you have asked of are Rotvee Bramkilik, daughter of Nakeket, son of Hriok, a member of the Council of the Nare, the Mrauuk and with her is Kodeet Fraleket, son of Hashett, son of Vargat, a worthy Nare indeed and from an illustrious House. The sadness they bear is the death of our companion, Dakveen Halak, slain by a treacherous hand upon the mountain top."

There was a pause as this information was assimilated. "The House of Bramkilik we know, for they have always been renowned craftsmen and artificers, the House Fraleket we do not know, but we will accept your word as to their status. The Hooded Seer of Tath Garnir is a name we have heard for the whispers in the wind have named her. You are welcome child of Uvarin, and may your sight always be clear and true."

The ghostly reverberations paused and then when they resumed there was an odd tone to their voices. "And now for you Mikael Dal Oaken, son of Halkgar, we have heard your name, we have felt the sound of it echoing through the rocks and the mountains, pulsing in the air that swirls with the four winds and races through the tree tops. But you have many names it would seem, for we have heard the echoes of these also. Twice-Dead, Twice-Born, Ender of Days, the Decider, the Doom of Taleth, Uclan, Outsider, you have been called all of these. It is hard for us to understand and even harder for us to grasp your Truth, your purpose."

Michael felt Siraal stiffen at his side and he saw her step forward and raise her arms to the Auwinn, her voice rang with a deep timbre that resonated through the chamber, she spoke with the Sight upon her and she spoke with power.

"Hear me!
You that breath the ancient air,
Hear my words and heed them well,
For the voices in the wind have spoken truly.
He that comes as Uclan, Outsider,
Sent to death by his own kin,
Born again to walk upon the face of Taleth,
He shall be reviled by blood and Lord alike,
But friendship and love he will find,
Despite their hatred.
From beyond he comes to choose for all,
The Decider, the Doom of Taleth,
This he is, has always been,
But he fears not the darkness,
Nor the waters,

Strength and honour are his,
Let all be forsworn, he will stand true.
He comes in hope
To bring life to the afflicted,
End suffering and torment for those that burn.
He will begin the Ending,
Make clear the path for the Stars that shall fall.
His touch will break chains, unlock secrets,
Wake the waters and restore the forgotten.
Doom he is, Doom he has ever been,
But Doom is not evil if souls are pure.
All that lives shall see their reflection,
Find their other, reclaim their balance.
Now is the time of choice,
Now let the drums of Doom begin to beat,
The Ender of Days is come."

She slumped forward as the sight left her and Michael moved to catch her. Her white sightless eyes stared blankly for a moment and then she blinked and was back in herself, she gripped his arms and tears burst forth as her sight receded.

"Oh, Mikael, sometimes it is pain beyond bearing, to live this life."

For a moment, all he wanted to do was hold her and kiss joy back into her face, caress away the agony of duty and submission, but he knew that his task was not yet completed. He turned to Nurelle who helped Siraal to her feet and stood close to support her. Michael turned back to see what effect the words of the Seer had had upon the Auwinn.

They had turned to look at each other and were obviously contemplating what had been said. Michael waited and he allowed Siraal's words to settle into his thoughts. Some of it was clear enough and spoke of what had already happened, but the rest puzzled him. *'He will begin the Ending.'* Does that mean that this is only the start? And the mention of *'Stars that shall fall.'* Enevien had spoken of stars, but what did it mean? And the reference to reflection and reclaiming their balance, seemed out of place here. The choice still seemed simple, but the outcome was apparently going to be more complex than he had imagined. He knew now that although he had known for a good while what he would have to do, he had no idea at what would happen when he did it.

The Auwinn turned once more to face him, their faces betrayed no emotion, nor was he able to guess their mind from their eyes. They spoke slowly and with great deliberation.

"We have listened to the words of the Seer and cast our minds out into the mountains to learn what might be learned. The plight of the Nare we abhor, and we sense the long arm of Corruption in all this suffering and death. We have seen the gifting of the crystal in Uxl's memory and we realise that this is the same crystal as stands before us here in this chamber. We cannot sanction your destruction of the casket in order to save the Nare, but nor can we ignore their plight. Therefore, we cannot advise you and although we fear what you may do we will not stand in your way. You will make your choice and act as you see fit, our place is not to stop you or aid you save in reverence to the dead. We will remove the body of the wolf Hayleth from the casket and lay her bones to rest with honour. When that is done you shall be free to do what you will."

Michael nodded, but he did not speak for they had moved to lift the body from the casket. As they did so Kyre sang an ancient song that Hayleth would have known, a wordless howl it seemed to Michael's ears, but he knew that it had meaning for the Packs. His thoughts turned in that sound to the gathering of the wolves who by now must have reached the forces that were set in bloody opposition to each other. The fighting might have already begun, he tried to picture his friends in the midst of battle, but the images would not come, he saw them instead as they had seemed when filled with joy. Their faces swam before his eyes, Ayan and Greer, Danil and Suani, Tuggid, Gath and Palvir, and finally Sorin chuckling into a flask of liquor as he and Gath shared a joke. This was how his heart told him to see them, the battle would come, but that was not what they struggled for. They fought for joy and life, they fought to live free and unstained, and they fought for a future beyond the darkness. For the darkness was not to be feared, for now was a time of strength.

Hayleth had now been laid in a far alcove of the chamber and the Auwinn had returned, but they did not stand at each corner of the casket as they had previously done. They stood now on the other side to where Michael and the others stood. The casket was now between them and Michael was free to approach. The others did not move as he took the six steps that were needed to close the distance between himself and the crystal casket. He paused before it and he saw that the surface of the crystal was acting as a mirror, casting his reflection in a strange unearthly green world. It was as if he now stood within the casket, but as he stared at his reflection it became not him, but Mikael gazing back at him,

'Well, my friend, here we are poised, wondering if this is why we have been made who and what we are. I know that you are afraid, just as I am, afraid that we do the will of the Corruptor, but what choice do we really have? Condemn a race to near extinction? We have known for a long time that this is not an option. Then what are we to do. Within this crystal casket lies the Chiatt Grain, can we achieve our goal without releasing it into the air, we do not know. Can we open the casket without breaking it? No, it is old beyond reckoning and it will crack when we touch it. Can we retrieve the crystal that holds the Grain without damaging it, while the casket breaks around it? Again, we do not know. Do we take the chance and risk the consequences?'

Michael thought about what had been said to him by the Powers, by Cerlinith and in particular by Uvarin, but he also thought about what Julia had said about a reset button, perhaps that was truly what this was all about and only an outsider could do it. If he was an agent of Corruption then this was no reset it was escape and power and revenge, but it felt like none of these. It felt still like a mercy mission, that the Nare needed

365

him to save them and the prophetic words that Siraal had uttered in this very chamber spoke of a future beyond this moment, a future where balance was restored.

'Mikael, you and I are reflections, in a mirror that has been distorted, and it is still distorting both us and our surroundings. Perhaps balance must be restored to all by a creature like us that is 'balanced' one by the other, or at least partly so.'

Mikael smiled in the strange floating world within the crystal. *'You do what you feel is right, my friend, the future will not affect me whatever it is, if there is one at all, which I seriously doubt. I only hope that whoever has planned this big joke is having a good laugh at our expensive, otherwise it will have meant nothing at all.'*

Michael hoped that he was right that the Corruptor was not controlling him, that he was acting freely, for then even if he did what the Corruptor wanted, it would have been done with the love of life and Taleth and its people so it could not, must not, lead to evil. He remembered Sorin's words to him, he had said to trust his heart and Uvarin had told him to trust Sorin. He reached up and he touched the casket.

★★★

A howl went up from Sylvan's left and the sound of drumming began, the Tsarg were attempting to begin an advance that would out flank Leenal's forces, but none of the scouts had returned so they approached blindly. Sylvan looked across through the trees to where Ayan sat sternly upon her Piradi mount, behind her stretched long lines of Free Cluath riders. Grald Dal Hammett had not summoned them, had not asked for their council, but he knew that they were there and within his heart he had thanked the Powers for them, for the Tsarg number could not be counted and Faradon had Cluath cavalry under his command who wore the mark of the serpent. The Frinakim sat impassive awaiting the call to charge and Sylvan turned her head to view the Pack that sat in similar silence, ready at a sign from her to leap into the fight.

The drums continued, snarling voices could be heard, the snap of the whip as they were marched forward. Sylvan knew that the darkness would shroud their number, but their number was not important for they would all die, she had sworn it. Khargahar would pay for her Sisters, her Brothers, her kin, her blood. And although these Tsarg were only his instruments they must be removed before the Avali could taste the flesh of the Corruptor himself.

Red eyes glowed in the dark, which was momentarily broken as the clouds that had covered the moon shifted throwing the pale, yellow light upon the hideous faces that stamped through towards the forests edge. A movement caught her eye and she saw Captain Dal Stordik raise her fist. Sylvan rose where she stood, and she felt the Pack rise behind her. The fist slammed down, and two sounds resounded through the trees a thousand Cluath voices shouting as one, *'Death to Corruption'* and the howl of two hundred wolf throats hurling defiance in the face of the enemy. Sylvan leapt forward and she drove down upon the line of snarling Tsarg. Battle was joined.

★★★

The green crystal began to crack and to crumble as his fingers brushed against it. It cascaded down upon the floor around him, shards and fragments aplenty for the cure that was required. As his hand passed further into the casket his fingers lighted upon a crystal of a different nature, it was warm to the touch and it did not break. As he drew it forth the casket continued to collapse around him. The crystal in his hand was fashioned into the shape of an eye it glowed from within and it became hotter as it sat within his hand, soon it would melt or burst into flame. He knew that if that happened the Chiatt Grain would fall to the floor with the broken crystal and touch Taleth. In an instant, he saw a way through, hold the Grain, prevent it from falling. Knowing that he could not be certain what would happen he said a silent prayer to all the Powers that he was making the right choice and then he held aloft the crystal and he squeezed his fingers around it. It shattered with a thunderous crack and his fingers found the Chiatt Grain within and he closed his hand around it. He suddenly knew why it was him who was here for this. The Grain was free, unleashed, but as he had hoped it did not fall and touch Taleth, it touched him that was of Taleth and yet was not. It was free and yet still not loosed upon the world. He felt it burning his skin, as it burrowed into the flesh of his hand and the pain drove him to his knees.

In his head he could hear laughter, but the laughter of more than one voice. Khargahar laughed it was true, he could feel his chains beginning to loosen, but they did not break, they did not shatter and disappear and someone else was laughing too, there was something that Khargahar had forgotten, something very important. The pain in Michael's hand was excruciating he heard his own voice cry out as darkness took him and he fell to the floor of the chamber amidst the shards and the fragments of green crystal. But he did not awaken immediately to damp grass. He found that he was floating, and he opened his eyes. He was drifting in the clouds above Taleth, the laughing voice was showing him the whole of Taleth spread out in the moonlight like a rumpled tablecloth. He saw the battle raging, white mage fire bristling like lightning amidst the forces of Corruption. He saw the Queen plotting in Tath Garnir with the Lords who had failed to answer sworn oaths to Leenal. He saw the capital of the Nare where Muakir and her father moved from house to house administering tiny drops of the precious cure to keep their people alive until their return. He saw the deep chasms below Fellas and a shadow stirring midst the dark and ugly flames. But he also saw that out at sea that there was something that stirred there, something that had power and it was now released from the deepest of sleep.

The laughter turned to words in a voice that was all voices, a sound that was all sounds, understanding came as much through feeling as through comprehension.

'Michael Oakes, you have done well, and you too Mikael Dal Oaken, son of Halkgar, but this is not the end, this is merely the beginning. Remember this, new despair brings new hope, new foes will bring new alliances. This is a time of strength and you have been strong. But strong you must continue to be, your true task will become clear as your journey continues, but for now the first part has been successfully completed. Fear not the darkness.'

The darkness and the damp in the air swept around like a cloud and he felt the cold beneath him, but it was now the cold of the grass. Dawn had broken over Glastonbury and he now wished that he had worn his thicker coat. He struggled to his feet and he felt the damp seeping up through his socks. Someone had stolen his shoes and he suspected that he knew who it might have been. He looked at the light that crept across the country-side with his mind full of thoughts of a battle raging far away and a swirling ocean. He began to make his way down the hill. Some questions had been answered but there were new ones bursting into life within his mind. However, the voice had been right, this first part of the journey was over, and he felt a certain warmth in the fact that he was headed for a place that he now looked on as home.

★★★

END OF BOOK TWO

Michael's Journey will continue in
'Dreams of Fire'
Book Three of 'The Journeys of Michael Oakes'

The World of Taleth
Including the Ancestral Lines of the Nare
[Names in bold appear within the book, others are referenced, or appeared in Book One]

The Powers
Cerlinith *(f) Associated with Nature and growth*
Carun *(m) Guardian of animals*
Hantor *(m) Guardian of the Cluath*
Minead *(m) Guardian of the Cluath*
Yvelle *(f) Guardian of the Antaldi*
Palleon *(m) Guardian of the Antaldi*
Ragarad *(m) Guardian of the Nare*
Takden *(m) Guardian of the Sha-ellev*
Shintani *(m) Guardian of the Sylian*
Uvarin *(m) Guide to the Majann and the Seers*

Khargahar *(m) The Corruptor*

The Wolves
(Spirits of the Avali)

The Aurian *Guides of the Antaldi*
Dravion *(m)*
Massil *(m)*
Mishrel *(f)*
Tharive *(f)*
Grinier *(f)*

The Dri *Guides of the Majann and the Seers*
Balior (m)
Bryelle *(f)*
Friesse (f)
Huinshi (m)
Karlynn *(f)*
Nilus (m)
Sylvan *(f) Companion to Sorin, the Majann*
Tiriel (m)
Tulok *(f)*
Uvan *(f)*
Vinar *(m)*

The Linath *Guides of the Sylian*
Feaz *(f)*

The Nemett *Guides of the Sha-ellev*
Kuvarish *(m)*
Ushkoriv *(m)*

The Raell *Guides of the Cluath*
Hishak *(m)*

The Trillani *Guides of the Nare*
Grevial *(m)*
Jaahkir *(f)*

The Veyix *Guides of the First Ones* **(The Lost)**
Hayleth (f) *[Deceased]Her spirit appears to Michael*
Kyre *(m) Present at the breaking of the Chiatt Grain*
Lonett *(f) [Deceased] Companion to Uxl of the Tarr*
Zedak *(m)*

The Races

The Auwinn
Ai
Iol
El
Olix

The Tarr The First Ones of Earth
Uxl *The 'First of the First'*
Ayx

The Antaldi
Danil Lebreven *(m) Antaldi/Cluath, Archer of the Frinakim*
Enevien *(f) [Deceased] Seer to the Antaldi*
Fah Devin *(f) Of the Valeen*
Fah Nalisse *(f) Member of the Ruling Triad*
Fah Risall *(f) [Deceased] Former member of the Ruling Triad*
Laniall *(m) Of the Valeen*
Mirell *(m) Nephew of **Vitta***
Nuall *(m) [Deceased] Majann of the Antaldi*
Reveen *(f) [Deceased] childhood friend of Fah Devine*
Sentielle *(m) Of the Valeen, tasked with carrying Vitta*
Suani *(f) Cousin to **Danil Lebreven***
Tarien *(m) Member of the Ruling Triad*
Tendiste *(m) [Deceased] Of the Valeen*
Thinvere *(m) Of the Valeen*
Tuali *(f) [Deceased] Mother of Danil Lebreven*
Ulin Ruan *(m) Messenger*
Vitta *(m) Majann to the Antaldi*
Vuar *(f) Member of the Ruling Triad*

The Cluath
Anith Dal Stordik *(f) [Deceased] Sister of Ayan*
Ayan Dal Stordik *(f) Captain in the Frinakim*
Brakis *(m) [Deceased] Sorin's father*
Buack Dal Ganard *(m) [Deceased] Grandfather of Danil Lebreven*
Calix (m) *Legendary Majann of the Cluath*

Cassiell *(f) Daughter of* **Leenal** *and* **Finah**

Cathal *(m) Thug for Hire*

Dinar *(m) [Deceased] High King before Kintell*

Duvan *(m) Petty thief*

Fahb *(m) Hired hand in Tath Garnir*

Faleck *(f) Rider of the Frinakim*

Lord Faradon *(m) Leader of the rebellion against Leenal*

Faras Hal *(m) [Deceased] Ancestor Faradon who gave his name to the city*

Filain *(m) Son of Lord Faradon*

Filius *(m) Bard to* **High King Leenal**

Finah *(f)* **Leenal's** *Queen*

Frappo *(m) Thief and murderer*

Frella *(f) Head of the attendants at the King's Court*

Galeanid *(m) Seer to the Queen*

Galmin *(m) Rider of the Frinakim*

Garull *(m) [Deceased] Ancient Majann of the Cluath*

Gath Dal Hurik *(m) Soldier of the High King*

Gillad *(m) Orphan boy, servant to Ayan*

Grald Dal Hammett *(m) General of the Cluath army*

Greer Dal Stordik *(m) Rider of the Frinakim, cousin of Ayan*

Grineth *(f) Piradimuatt, Piradi master for the Frinakim*

Halkgar dal Oaken *(m) [Deceased] Father of* **Mikael Dal Oaken**

Hanallin *(m) Son of* **Leenal** *and* **Finah**

Hargarth *(m) [Deceased] A famous Cluath Cavalry Captain*

Havianik *(m) Rider of the Frinakim*

Hooded Seer *(f) (See* **Siraal***)*

Jael *(m) Legendary Cluath warrior*

Jarrad Ranell *(m) Soldier in the pay of Queen Finah*

Kintell *(m) [Deceased] High King in the time of the first Great War*

Krakis *(m) Petty thief*

High King Leenal *(m) Ruler of the Cluath*

Magellin Lucastor *(f) [Deceased] Famous Bard of the Cluath*

Maltir Dal Stordik *(m) Father of Greer*

Manal *(m) Attendant to the King's Court*

Mettak *(m) Rider of the Frinakim*

Meneld *(m) [Deceased] First High King of the Cluath*

Mikael Dal Oaken *(m) Ender of Days (see also **Michael Oakes**)*
Muat Lise *(f) Seer of the Cluath*
Nargus *(m) Hired hand in Tath Garnir*
Neemar Dal Ganard *(f) Grandmother of Danil Lebreven*
Palvir Dal Tharl *(m) Soldier, son of **Tuggid Dal Tharl***
Piat Kahord *(m) Majann to **High King Leenal***
Raldor *(m) Soldier in the service of Lord Faradon*
Rikat *(m) Servant to **Galeanid** the Seer*
Sarath Dal Ganard *(m) [Deceased] Father of **Danil Lebreven***
Sepho *(m) Attendant to the King's Court*
Shalkim Dal Oaken *(m) Mikael's uncle*
Sianal *(f) [Deceased] Kintell's Queen*
Siraal *(f) **The Hooded Seer** of Tath Garnir*
Sorin *(m) Majann and Healer*
Starak *(m) Soldier in the service of Lord Faradon*
Teldak Dal Hammett *(m) Leader of the Frinakim, Grald's brother*
Terann Dal Farak *(m) [Deceased] Orphan servant to Calix*
Tiok *(m) Sorin's childhood name*
Tuggid Dal Tharl *(m) Soldier of the High King*
Utho Treek *(m) Rider of the Frinakim*
Varell *(f) [Deceased] Sorin's mother*
Vinat Dal Stordik *(m) Cousin of Ayan*
Yathis *(m) Guardsman of Tath Garnir*

<u>The Nare</u>
Barak Duralk *(m) [Deceased] Nare stone worker*
Bakund Halak *(m) [Deceased] **Dakveen's** ancestor*
Bruak Shiveer *(m) Member of the Mrauuk*
Churak Ulumik *(m) [Deceased] Legendary metalworker*
Dakveen Halak *(m) Exiled Nare*
Dunark Halak *(m) [Deceased] Brother of **Dakveen***
Gariok Bramkilik *(m) Member of the Mrauuk*
Hakard Shiveer *(m) Nephew of Bruak*
Hashett Ikklemit *(m) nephew of Yagash*
Kodeet Fraleket *(m)*
Malak Bramkilik *(m) [Deceased] Nare stone worker*

Muakir Ulumik *(f) Daughter of **Sheramkir***
Nameed Nagesset *(m) Brother of **Shuok***
Rotvee Bramkilik *(f) Niece of **Gariok***
Ruakim Kemsik *(m)*
Sheramkir Ulumik *(m) Member of the Mrauuk*
Shuok Nagesset *(m) Brother of **Nameed***
Ukliket Ikklemit *(m) Brother of **Yagash***
Uttmesh Ikklemit *(m) [Deceased] Nephew of **Yagash***
Yagash Ikklemit *(m) Member of the Mrauuk*

<u>The Sha-ellev</u>
Uphik-Mresh-Ludim *(m)*

<u>The Sylian</u>
Ukthor *(f) Lost Majann of the Sylian*

<u>The Piradi</u>
Furaam *(m)*
Korinne *(f)*
Luac *(m) Bonded with Faleck*
Metta *(f)*
Sakia *(f) Bonded with **Danil Lebreven***
Turic *(f) Bonds with **Michael***

Ancestral Lines of the Houses of the Nare

(Showing only those Houses and members referenced in Books One and Two. For complete family trees please see The Kakal Nuurk in the archive of the Mruaak).

Halak		**Bramkilik**	
Rulakin		Krakim	
(founder)		*(founder)*	
*		*	
Yarirk		Malak	
Bakund		*	
Varkind		Thulim	
Thark		Hriok	
Dakveen Dunark		Nakeket Gariok	
		Rotvee *(f)*	

Ulumik		**Shiveer**	
Shesslit		Trelkem	
(founder)		*(founder)*	
*		*	
Shuktet		Dilarik	
Muak		Nassik	
Nesskem		Vikalik	
Sheramkir		Krall Bruak	
Muakir *(f)*		Hakard	

Ikklemit		**Kemsik**	
Hvograk		Jurdak	
(founder)		*(founder)*	
*		*	
Bveluk		Iakat	
Karlint		Ukulik	
Yagash Ukliket		Marak	
Uttmesh Hashett		Ruakim	

Nagesset		**Fraleket**	
Kualk		Varshek	
(founder)		*(founder)*	
*		*	
Kriak		Thuak	
Daleem		Vargat	
Huak		Hashett	
Nameed Shuok		Kodeet	

Fruunik		**Vuskar**	
Ikkurin		Grikog	
(founder)		*(founder)*	

FOR AUTOREN A HEART FOR AUTHORS À L'ÉCOUTE DES AUTEURS MIA KARAIA ΓΙΑ SYΓ
OR FÖRFATTARE UN CORAZÓN POR LOS AUTORES YAZARI ARIYORUZ CONOL VEREL IM SZ
AUTORI ET HJERTE FOR FORFATTERE EEN HART VOOR SCHRIJVERS TEKQS QS AUT
SERQE DLA AUTORÓW EIN HERZ FOR AUTOREN A HEART FOR AUTHORS À L'ÉCOI
CAXO BCEÑ DYUIOÑ K ABTOPAM ET HJARTA FÖR FORFATTARE À LA ESCUCHA DE LOS AUTO
A DA SYTGAPHT UI CUORE PER AUTORI ET HJERTE FOR FORFATTERE EEN
ZOINKERT SERCE DLA AUTORÓW EIN HERZ FI
CAO BCEÑ DYUIOÑ K ABTOPAM ET HJARTA F

The author

M.R. Reynolds was born in the 1950's and raised in the heart of England. He proceeded to endure the rigours of the Catholic education system. Inspired by his parents and two influential teachers, he developed a love of literature, drama and music. M.R. studied the piano, the clarinet and wallowed in Shakespeare, Dylan Thomas, and Tolkien. He began to compose songs, write poetry and plays; something that he has not quite managed to give up. The author went to University in Manchester and trained as a teacher teaching Music, English and Drama. Forty years later, he retired. M.R. has written many plays and musicals for young people to perform, as yet unpublished. He began to write seriously in the latter years of his teaching and this now takes over most of his time. He still finds time to watch live music from a wide range of genres, from Classical to Goth and Metal, he also enjoys visiting his family, the theatre, and the cinema.

novum 🔺 PUBLISHER FOR NEW AUTHORS

M.R. Reynolds

Awakening

ISBN 978-3-99064-977-0
498 pages

Michael Oakes is reborn living two lives. Journeying between his earthly life and a wild and dangerous world of brave warriors, hideous monsters, and highly mysterious wolves, he encounters helpers as well as fearsome enemies. What are the wolves not telling him?